BLACK ICE

BLACK ICE

A THRILLER

Brad Thor

EMILY BESTLER BOOKS

ATRIA

New York   London   Toronto   Sydney   New Delhi

EMILY
BESTLER
BOOKS
——————
ATRIA

An Imprint of Simon & Schuster, Inc.
1230 Avenue of the Americas
New York, NY 10020

This Emily Bestler Books/Atria Paperback Canadian export edition July 2021

EMILY BESTLER BOOKS/ATRIA BOOKS and colophon
are trademarks of Simon & Schuster, Inc.

For information about special discounts for bulk purchases,
please contact Simon & Schuster Special Sales at
1-866-506-1949 or business@simonandschuster.com.

The Simon & Schuster Speakers Bureau can bring authors to your live event. For
more information, or to book an event, contact the Simon & Schuster Speakers
Bureau at 1-866-248-3049 or visit our website at www.simonspeakers.com.

Manufactured in the United States of America

1 3 5 7 9 10 8 6 4 2

Library of Congress Cataloging-in-Publication Data has been applied for.

ISBN 978-1-9821-8014-0
ISBN 978-1-9821-0414-6 (ebook)

"Kill with a borrowed knife."

—GENERAL TAN DAOJI

For Carolyn Reidy—
Of Manhattan, Southampton, and Paris.
My friend and publisher.
You lived life really, really well.
Thank you for everything.

*"In the decades ahead, rapidly melting sea ice and increasingly navigable Arctic waters—a Blue Arctic—*will create new challenges and opportunities off our northern shores. Without sustained American naval presence and partnerships in the Arctic Region, peace and prosperity will be increasingly challenged by Russia and China, whose interests and values differ dramatically from ours."

—Department of the Navy, *A Blue Arctic: A Strategic Blueprint for the Arctic*

PROLOGUE

78°55'30"N 11°55'20"E
Arctic Ocean
Svalbard Archipelago

Helicopters, it was said, didn't fly—they merely beat the air into submission. But halfway between continental Norway and the North Pole, it felt as if the air were winning.

As sleet slammed against the exterior, another sixty-plus-mile-per-hour gust rocked the airframe. The rotors groaned in protest. There was only so much the helo could handle. They were pushing it beyond its limits.

Scot Harvath didn't need to see the water to know the slate-gray ocean was roiling with whitecaps. This far above the Arctic Circle, where moisture from the south collided with icy polar winds, massive depressions formed, unleashing nightmare weather.

If anything went wrong, there would be no rescue. No one back at the U.S. Embassy in Oslo, much less anyone at the White House, would acknowledge him, or the mission he was on.

He glanced at the cracked face of his watch, blood crusted atop its bezel. *Just a little farther,* he thought to himself. *We're almost there.*

Ignoring the pain in his ribs, he reached for his pack and opened it. Everything was still in place. *Take care of your gear and your gear will take care of you.* It was a mantra that had saved his life again and again.

Under his mountaineering jacket, he felt the cold press of metal against his skin. No one knew if the odd-shaped key, hanging from a piece of paracord, would even work—not after all this time.

If it didn't, all of the danger, all of the risk, would be for nothing, and the consequences would be deadly. Failure, however, wasn't an option.

That was the world he lived in. He wasn't interested in easy tasks. In fact, he had always chosen the most difficult, the most perilous assignments.

It was how he was wired. No matter how bleak the scenario, he would never give up. Success was the only outcome he would entertain.

But as yet another gale-force blast of frigid air convulsed the helicopter, causing it to swing violently from side to side, he began to have his doubts.

Moments later, an alarm began shrieking from the cockpit, and Harvath knew they were in trouble.

The pilots, though, were able to regain control. The bird was still swaying, but nowhere near as badly as before. It looked like everything was going to be okay.

Then there was an earsplitting crack. It sounded as if the helo had been hit by lightning. It was followed by the tail rotor completely shearing off. And as it did, the helicopter began to spiral.

They were going down.

CHAPTER 1

There was only one problem with summer in Norway—it was too short.

Sitting at his favorite outdoor café, Harvath raised his face to the sun. The warmth felt good. *He* felt good. Better than he had in a long time. The last two months had been exactly what he had needed.

He and Sølvi had bounced between her apartment in the city and the cottage he had rented out on the fjord. It depended on her schedule. As one of the newest Deputy Directors at the Norwegian Intelligence Service, or NIS for short, she had been pretty busy.

Because the commute was easier from the apartment, they usually stayed in Oslo during the week and headed for the fjord on Fridays. That was fine by Harvath. He had enjoyed getting to know the city. There were plenty of museums and cultural sights, not to mention great bars, restaurants, and cafés.

Most mornings, if Sølvi didn't have to leave too early, they would go for a run. The lush Akerselva River Trail was a favorite, as was the Ekeberg Sculpture Park. For safety, they always mixed things up, never frequenting the same location two days in a row.

In addition to running, Harvath had joined a neighborhood gym. When they were at the cottage, he would swim—a lot.

The physical activity had been restorative. After losing his wife, he had stopped taking care of himself. But now, the weight he had shed was back. He had returned to his full level of fitness. And while he still consumed alcohol, it wasn't like before. A half-empty bottle of wine could sit in the fridge for days before they finished it off.

In a word, he was happy. *Really* happy. Sølvi was an amazing woman. She was not only beautiful, but smart and talented as hell. To be honest, she was probably smarter and more talented than he was. The only realm in which he was confident that he had her beat was experience. But even then, it was only because she was several years younger.

Despite the age difference, however, they shared something very powerful, something that went beyond their physical attraction to each other. Her past was as dark and troubled as his own. They had both been shattered but, in coming together, had found a way to glue their pieces into something better, stronger.

Ultimately, what he loved most about her was her sense of humor. It was a sign of how intelligent she was.

It was also a coping mechanism. The espionage business could be exceptionally brutal—a fact he knew all too well.

Devoid of meaningful relationships, spies often became disillusioned, cynical. Many checked out via booze or other vices—another fact he knew all too well. He had resolved not to allow that to happen to either of them again.

He wanted to make Sølvi happy—as happy as she made him. Second chances were rare in life. He was determined not to screw this up. Which was why mapping out their next step was proving to be difficult.

It was one of the best summers he'd ever had. They had squeezed every drop out of it. The cottage had come with a boat, and they had gotten out on the water as often as they could. A few mornings, he had even used it to drive Sølvi to work, dropping her at the dock adjacent to The Thief hotel, where she'd catch a ride to the office.

There had been barbecues and beach parties. A rotating mix of friends from NIS and the CIA's Oslo Station had drifted in and out of their lives—both in the city and out on the fjord. It was rare to see a weekend where they weren't hosting some sort of get-together, or attending someone else's. It had been wall-to-wall fun, and it was no surprise that no one wanted it to end. But at some point, it had to.

He had burned through all of his sick leave, as well as his vacation days. To say the office was "eager" for him to return was an understatement. In fact, his boss had told him in no uncertain terms that if he wasn't back the following week, he would be "cashiered."

It was a dramatic term to have used. Not *fired*. Not the more genteel *let go*. But *cashiered*—the public humiliation of having one's military insignia ripped away and sword snapped in front of one's comrades.

It was an old-school term. *Really* old-school. Yet it was perfectly in keeping with the Cold War–era warrior he reported to.

He couldn't blame the man for wanting him back. Had their situations been reversed, he would have felt the same. In fact, he was surprised that he had been allowed to stay away as long as he had. That's where his next step with Sølvi got tricky.

There was no telling where he would be sent, much less for how long. On the whole, his were quick in-and-out jobs. What they weren't was predictable.

In an attempt to give their relationship some structure, something for the two of them to look forward to, he had printed out a calendar.

The idea was to ink specific dates they felt certain they could be together. The additional hope was that, in between his assignments, he could swing through Oslo to see her. With her promotion, she was wedded to headquarters. Any hope of tagging up with him on an assignment in a hotel room in some far-flung, exotic locale was out of the question. Their best chance of seeing each other was in Norway.

It would be tough, but not impossible. He was committed to making it work. And when he set his mind to something, he made it happen.

With the clock ticking down, he wanted their remaining time together to be special. They had been eating a ton of takeout lately, so tonight he decided he'd cook a real American dinner. Something for just the two of them. It would be a night he could freeze in his memory and replay until he returned and they were together again.

He finished the last sip of his kokekaffe—a popular Norwegian afternoon coffee served black and slightly cooled. Standing up, he put on his sunglasses and strolled across the cobbles of Christiania Square, toward his favorite butcher shop.

Though it was a bit of a walk to the food hall in Mathallen, it was worth it. Annis Pølsemakeri had the best meats in town.

Out at the cottage, there was an old smoker that he had made his mission to get up and running again. Once he had, he decided to throw a Texas-style barbecue. When he asked friends where he could get the absolute best brisket, ribs, and pork butt, everyone had said "Annis."

The staff had been so friendly that he had gone back again and again—even just to pick up ground beef for burgers. They were an amusing bunch and tried to upsell him into horsemeat or beef tongue, seeing good-naturedly if they could gross out their American customer. They had no idea that over the course of his career, he had eaten much, much worse.

After buying a couple of T-bones at Annis, he would hit Vulkan Frukt og Grønt AS for fresh vegetables. He figured it was a safe bet that they'd have potatoes and salad fixings. Hopefully, they'd have fresh ears of corn as well.

Once those items were taken care of, all he would need was a nice bottle of wine and dessert.

Not far from the food hall was a Vinmonopolet. He'd probably have to pay through the nose for a good California red, but if they had one, he planned on ignoring the price tag. He wanted their dinner to be as American as possible.

All that was left was to figure out dessert. Apple pie felt a bit too on the nose. What's more, while he could grill or smoke up a storm, he was no baker.

Since Sølvi was a big fan of dark chocolate, he decided that's where he would focus. There was a stall in the food hall called SebastienBruno that sold chocolates, but what she really liked were Belgian chocolates. He made a mental note to keep his eyes peeled for any along the way.

After dinner, if there was time, they could stream a movie. Her passion for classic Hollywood films was bottomless. So far, they had watched *Casablanca*, *Lawrence of Arabia*, *Psycho*, *The Godfather*, *On the Waterfront*, *North by Northwest*, and *Citizen Kane* together. Tonight, he wanted to introduce her to *The Night of the Hunter*, from 1955. It was unsettling, but a classic nonetheless.

A few blocks from the food hall, he spotted a small boutique that looked promising for quality chocolate. But when he was fifty yards away, a taxi pulled up and disgorged a ghost.

The sight of the man stopped Harvath dead in his tracks. His eyes had to have been playing tricks on him. The man he was looking at was dead.

Harvath had killed him himself.

CHAPTER 2

Not only had he killed him, but he had hung around just long enough to make absolutely certain the man was dead.

How the hell was he now seeing him alive? And what was the man doing in Norway?

There was only one way to find out. Giving up on his errands, he fell in a safe distance behind and followed.

The man walked at a moderate, confident pace. Had Harvath not been trained, he might not have noticed the moments at which the man checked to see if he had a tail.

Thankfully, Harvath not only noticed but had anticipated them and made sure he wasn't seen.

He tracked him for two blocks until they came to a large, busy boulevard. Taking advantage of a changing traffic light, the man rushed across at the last minute, just as vehicles were beginning to accelerate. Harvath had no choice but to wait. Had he run after him, he would have exposed himself and blown everything.

While he waited, he watched a tram arrive and kept his eyes glued to it. As far as he could tell, the man hadn't boarded.

Once the light changed, Harvath recommenced his chase. But by the time he arrived on the other side of the boulevard, the man was gone.

There were all manner of shops, bars, restaurants, and apartment buildings he could have disappeared into. Something told Harvath that he hadn't opted for any of them. He was still on the move. The question was: Where?

Up ahead, two smaller streets split off from the boulevard, like spokes from a hub. If he was correct, and the man had continued in this direction, he had a fifty-fifty chance of picking the right direction.

The street closest to him was narrower and offered more opportunities for a person to ascertain if they were being followed. It was the one Harvath would have chosen.

Half a block down, he realized he had made a mistake. There was no sign of the man. He must have taken the other street. Turning around, Harvath quickened his pace and headed back for the boulevard.

Once there, he hurried to the next intersection and then, slowing down, casually turned the corner.

This street was a bust as well. Harvath walked all the way down, but no luck. His quarry had vanished.

More than a little ticked off, he prepared to turn around and head back, when something caught his eye.

It wasn't the man he was looking for. It wasn't even someone he knew. But he couldn't turn away.

Oslo was a safe city, but, like anywhere else, it wasn't immune from trouble. And what he was looking at was definitely trouble. He could feel it in the marrow of his bones.

An older, well-dressed woman was being steered toward an ATM by two not-so-well-dressed men in their mid-twenties. The young men each had her by an arm and kept looking over their shoulders.

The look in her eyes told Harvath everything he needed to know. These weren't a couple of Boy Scouts helping an old lady cross the road. She was being mugged and she was terrified.

It looked like an "express kidnapping," something he'd first heard about out of Mexico. Criminal gangs would grab a person, take them to the nearest ATM, and force them to withdraw as much money as possible.

Today wasn't going to be their lucky day.

He stayed far enough back so as not to arouse suspicion and waited until they had reached the ATM before making his move. There, he knew the men would have their attention divided. One would be pressuring the woman to hurry up and withdraw her cash while the other kept an eye open for any sign of trouble.

Harvath was quite skilled at *not* looking like trouble. It was only when he was right on top of his target—if they even saw him—that they realized how much trouble *they* were in. And so it was at the ATM.

Pulling out his wallet, he removed his bank card and approached the machine. The young man functioning as the lookout held his hand up and said something in heavily accented Norwegian. Whoever this guy was, he hadn't grown up in Norway.

"Sorry," Harvath replied. "I only speak English."

"Machine broken," said the man. "Find different."

His English sounded like it was just as bad as his Norwegian.

"They get sticky." Harvath smiled, moving toward the ATM. "Sometimes they just need a little tap."

As he moved, so too did the lookout. The young man stepped right in front of him and put his palm into Harvath's chest to stop him.

Contact. *Game on.*

Since the man had offered Harvath his hand, he figured it would be rude not to accept it.

Grabbing the lookout's wrist in a joint lock, Harvath tucked in his head in case he threw a punch with his opposite hand, and pressed down. Instantly, the man's knees buckled.

As he fell toward the sidewalk, Harvath thrust his right knee up into the man's chin, knocking him out cold. It was then that his partner made a fatal mistake.

Instead of spinning the old woman and using her as a shield, he let her go and pulled a knife. It was obvious why these two were pulling robberies and not running IBM.

To the attacker's credit, he was skilled with a blade. He not only knew how to hold it but also how to come at his opponent. This wasn't his first knife fight.

But Harvath had been in his share of knife fights as well. In fact, he had a recent scar on his chest that he had spent all summer covering with sunscreen. He had no intention of getting cut again.

On the man's first slash, Harvath failed to trap the blade and control it. The tip of the knife had come within a whisper of his abdomen.

When the attacker lunged at him again, he was ready, but the mugger was fast *and* slippery. Harvath barely got control of the man's wrist.

As he did, the man drew the knife back behind him. Harvath went with it.

When the man tried to drive the knife forward again, Harvath rotated his wrist and helped him cut deep into the back of his own knee.

Dropping the blade, the attacker cried out, but Harvath wasn't finished. Before the knife had even hit the ground, he surged upward with a palm strike into the man's jaw, knocking him backward into the ATM.

The mugger's head must have hit the keypad and completed the interrupted transaction, because moments later the machine spat out a bank card and a stack of cash.

Harvath removed both and handed them to the old woman, who was standing, frozen in fear, only a few feet away.

"Thank you," she whispered. "Thank you for everything."

"You're welcome," he replied.

As he turned to leave, police cars—with klaxons blaring—came racing up from both ends of the street. It was the last thing he needed.

He didn't want to interact with law enforcement. He had spent the whole summer off the grid—not on anyone's radar. All he wanted right now was to simply fade into the background and disappear.

Disappearing, however, wasn't in the cards. A small crowd had gathered and the police had him well in their sights.

Watching the patrol cars approach, he attempted to reassure himself that at least things couldn't get any worse.

But if he had learned nothing else in his life, it was that things could *always* get worse.

CHAPTER 3

By the time he returned to the apartment, Sølvi was already there. As he had lost interest in grocery shopping, he had opted for takeout from their favorite dim sum spot—a restaurant called The Golden Chimp, not far from Oslo's central train station.

Setting the bag on the kitchen counter, he kissed her hello.

"Let me see you," she said, turning him around. She had been bugging him to get a haircut and he had finally given in.

She had asked if she could pick the spot and he had agreed, as long as it was a proper barbershop and not some fancy hair salon. He wasn't a salon kind of guy. Somehow, she had found a way to split the difference.

Technically it was a "barbershop," but one geared toward hipsters. If the bike rack outside hadn't been enough of a red flag, the cooler full of green juice and mineral water inside should have been.

By the time Harvath figured out he'd been tricked, it was too late to turn around. The receptionist had taken one look at him, figured out who he was, and welcomed him in English.

Sølvi must have given the woman a description of him when she had called and made the appointment. Soon enough, he was beginning to suspect that wasn't all she had given them.

After being escorted back to a chair and introduced to his barber, he sat down and explained to the tattooed man what he wanted. Nothing crazy. Just a little off the top and sides.

Oiling his clippers, the barber replied, "No problem."

Twenty minutes later, when the man held up a mirror so that he could see his haircut from all angles, he was convinced that Sølvi had been behind it.

Not that it was bad. It was just different. A lot of things this summer had been different. But different, he had been learning, could be good.

"I like it," she said, nodding approvingly. "Stylish. Takes ten years off of you. Five more and we could almost pass for the same age."

Normally, that was the kind of joke he'd laugh at. He wasn't in the mood and she noticed. "What's going on?"

When they discussed work, they did everything in their power to steer clear of classified issues. Their countries were allies and fellow NATO members but separate, sovereign nations.

Holding out his hand, he gestured for her phone. Once she had given it to him, he took it, along with his own, and tucked them away in the other room.

"I need a favor," he said, walking back into the kitchen.

"What kind of favor?"

"I saw somebody get out of a taxi today. If it has a passenger-facing dash cam, I need the footage. I also need to know where the passenger was picked up, how they paid, and anything else the driver may have seen or overheard. Do you think you can get that for me?"

She thought for a moment. "I know somebody I can ask. I assume you have a license plate or taxi number?"

"I can give you both."

"Plus the address where the driver dropped the passenger off."

Harvath nodded. "As well as a physical description."

"As long as it isn't for an attractive female, eighteen to twenty-two, I don't see a problem."

He blew by that joke as well. "And I'd like any CCTV footage near the pickup and drop-off locations."

"That's going to be more difficult, but I'll see what I can do. Are you going to tell me what this is all about?"

He was asking her for a lot. The Norwegians had strict data privacy laws. It was time for him to offer something in return.

"Several years ago, I was sent to China on an assignment."

"This isn't when you got caught in a hurricane on Macau, is it?"

"No. This was much more recent."

"What kind of assignment was it?"

"The Chinese were planning a terrorist attack on the United States. We disrupted it. When our President confronted their Premier, the Chinese denied it. Once we had presented them with the evidence, they claimed it was a rogue operation by one of their intelligence chiefs."

"And you were sent to confront the chief."

He shook his head. "No. I was sent to kill him."

She was no stranger to killing, though she was certain her scorecard was nowhere close to his. That said, she was also certain that, like her, he found no pleasure in taking another human life.

It was a sad fact of their business that sometimes there was no other recourse and it simply needed to be done. For some, the only language they understood was violence.

As the old saying went: People sleep peacefully in their beds only because rough men—*and women*, she was known to add—stand ready to do violence on their behalf. The two skills most necessary for a nation state to survive were its ability to keep secrets and covertly project force. Lose either ability and your country was doomed.

"So, this man you were sent to kill. I assume you were successful?"

"I never stop until I am."

"And that's who you saw get out of the taxi?"

He nodded.

"Any chance you were mistaken? It has, after all, been several years. Maybe he just really looked like him?"

Opening the refrigerator, he pulled out a bottle of beer. "You don't forget those faces. It doesn't matter how many years it has been."

He had a point. Like a branding iron seared into her subconscious, she could recall the face of every person she had ever been tasked with dispatching. The one consolation of having to carry those mental pictures was that they all deserved what she had meted out to them. She felt no pity. No remorse. The people of Norway slept peacefully in their beds at night because she was ready, willing, and able to do violence on their behalf. End of story.

"Whatever information I can dig up for you, if I can dig up any at all, it didn't come from me. Deal?"

"Deal," he replied, popping the cap off of his beer and changing the subject. "There's a bottle of white in the fridge. Do you want a glass with dinner?"

Moving to him, she placed her hand against his chest. "I can't. I have to go back to the office tonight."

He understood. It was a cruel twist. As his time with her was winding down, her work was spinning up. He appreciated that she had snuck out to eat with him—even if it meant she'd have to turn around and go right back.

"How long do we have?"

"Enough time for dinner."

"Dinner and . . . ?" he asked, his voice trailing off as he smiled at her.

She smiled in return and kissed him. "Just dinner, I'm afraid. The good news is that I'll be able to make those calls for you as soon as I get back to my desk."

It was yet another thing they had in common. She was as driven as he was. She cared too much about Norway to give up her career and follow him back to D.C. He cared too much about the United States to give up his career and stay in Oslo. The silver lining was that they were both committed to making it work—no matter how many frequent flyer miles it cost them.

"Plates? Or straight out of the containers?"

"I've got enough time for plates. In fact, we can even sit down at the dining room table like adults," she said before looking down and asking, "What happened to your hand?"

He hadn't even noticed. "What about it?"

"The inside of your right hand. You've got a bruise. Where'd that come from?"

"This?" he asked, turning his palm over. "It's nothing. Don't worry about it."

"Something's up. What are you not telling me?"

"It's nothing," he repeated. "I probably just bumped it at the gym."

"Now you're lying."

She was right. He was. Lying was part of his job and he was quite good at it—when he wanted to be. He didn't want to lie to her, though.

"I got in a little shoving match this afternoon."

"A *shoving* match?"

"You might call it a scuffle."

She looked at him. "What happened?"

"A couple of street thugs tried to rob a little old lady at an ATM. I helped them realize it was a bad idea."

"That was *you*?" she asked, her eyes widening.

"What are you talking about?"

"It popped up on my news app. Let me go get my phone."

Harvath watched as she headed to the bedroom. He was allergic to publicity and avoided the spotlight like the plague. Media attention was like kryptonite for spies. He had survived a bad brush with the press in the past, but it had been difficult.

When she returned, she opened the app, pulled up the article, and handed him her phone.

"You know this is written in Norwegian, right?"

She rolled her eyes. "*Americans.* You've been here most of the summer and have made zero progress."

"That's not true," he protested. "*Du har vakre øyne.*"

"Pickup lines telling me I have beautiful eyes don't count."

"*Faen.*"

"Nor do curse words. Give me my phone back."

He gave it to her and she translated the story into English. It was short and mercifully devoid of details. No names were given. It stated that a Western tourist had foiled the mugging of a Norwegian senior citizen. Both of the perpetrators had been injured during the altercation and had been transported to a nearby hospital for observation. Once they were cleared by medical staff, they would be transported by officers to the Central Police Station, where they would be booked and await their arraignment.

He smiled when she finished. "Like I said. It was nothing."

"You saved a Norwegian citizen from being robbed and sent her attackers to the hospital. That's hardly nothing."

"You're right. I also brought home takeout."

"Yes, you did. Thank you. Let's eat before it gets cold."

· · ·

After they had finished dinner, Harvath offered to take care of the dishes so that she could get going back to the office.

Brewing a coffee to go, she gave him a kiss goodbye and headed out the door. He was sorry that she had to return to work, but he was hopeful she'd be able to track down footage of his ghost.

Once everything was cleaned and put away, he decided to watch a movie by himself. While he'd had his heart set on *The Night of the Hunter*, he figured it best to save it for when Sølvi could watch it with him. Instead, he planned to watch his all-time favorite, *The Magnificent Seven*.

He retrieved his phone, grabbed another beer, and headed into the living room, where he made himself comfortable on the couch. Booting up the film, he settled back and tried to lose himself, to not think about anything that had happened this afternoon. If there was one movie that could make him forget everything, this was the one.

It had been his father's favorite as well. Once a year, the vintage theater in San Diego would bring it back and, if his father was in town, they would cross the bridge and see it together. And not just once but over and over again. Like his dad, he could recite every line by heart. Some kids went to baseball games with their fathers; he went to the movies.

Not until he was an adult did he realize why this film spoke to his father. It was a story about courage, about professionalism, about doing the right thing and protecting the weak. All of which were hallmarks of his upbringing.

He had made it all the way to the closing credits, when his phone chimed. It was an encrypted message from Sølvi. The taxi in question did have a passenger-facing dash cam and she had been able to secure a copy of the footage. Taking a deep breath, he clicked on the attachment she had sent.

As the video began to play and he saw the passenger enter the cab, he had only one thing to say.

"Gotcha."

CHAPTER 4

D ennis Wo had never been subtle—about anything. He was a slick, flashy, wildly successful, young con man. Part Bernie Madoff and part Frank Abagnale Jr., he had pulled off the biggest scam in Singapore's history.

On the eve of his twenty-sixth birthday, he was about to be charged with embezzling four and a half billion dollars from the nation's largest sovereign wealth fund.

After receiving a tip, he had fled for China, leaving his cars, penthouse, and several very pissed-off girlfriends behind.

They weren't the only ones, though, who were angry. The Singaporean government was out for blood.

For a country that prided itself on law and order, what had transpired was an outrageous scandal. All of the corrupt politicians who had assisted in the plot had been rounded up and thrown in prison.

It was a good start, but Singapore wouldn't rest until Wo had been apprehended. The government planned to put him on trial and make a very public example of him. To that end, an Interpol Red Notice had been issued for his arrest.

When the warrant landed at the Hong Kong Department of Justice, it was purged from the system. The powers that be in Beijing had made it clear that Wo was a guest of the Chinese Communist Party and nothing was to happen to him.

The CCP liked that, even in exile, the young con man was a thorn in Singapore's side. He backed opposition candidates, pushed anti-government propaganda, and was seen as something of a Robin Hood who was eager to fund populist causes.

As long as he continued to be useful, the CCP would continue to give him sanctuary. And as long as he kept running, Singapore would pursue him.

In addition to the Red Notice, the government scoured the globe for bank accounts and assets which they could claw back.

While Wo had managed to put a fortune beyond their reach, there were some items he couldn't keep hidden.

His two-hundred-foot yacht had been impounded in Tahiti. Paintings he had given to a beautiful European actress had been repossessed and put up for auction. Properties from Bombay to Brussels—even those buried in sophisticated blind trusts—were being seized.

But the worst of it, the most painful of his losses, were happening to him in the United States.

America had been his playground, his childhood dream. He had purchased a massive home in Bel Air and hobnobbed with the Hollywood elite.

He threw incredible parties. He gave lavish, expensive gifts. He called famous actors, musicians, and media personalities his friends. Whoever said money couldn't buy happiness hadn't had billions of it to throw around. Wo was having the time of his life—until, suddenly, it had all come crashing down.

Through its Ambassador in Washington, the Singaporean government had lobbied the U.S. Department of Justice to open an investigation and help recapture as much of the stolen money as possible. Because Wo had invested so heavily in American real estate and business ventures, there was plenty to get.

But the most embarrassing part of the process was the FBI accosting his friends and threatening them with criminal prosecution and jail time if they didn't surrender the gifts Wo had given them. The Rolex watches, the European sports cars, the diamond jewelry—all of it had to be handed over.

Soon enough, none of his "friends" would take his calls or answer his texts. One by one, they began to unfollow him on social media. It had felt to him like his life was unraveling. He needed to stop the bleeding. So, he had turned to the one thing he understood best—people.

It was all about influence. Influence the right people and any problem could be remedied. Right now, what he faced was a political problem. Therefore, he needed political influence. And the fastest way to political influence was via money—lots of it.

In America, the only thing that mattered was the party in power. They controlled the levers of government. Get to the right person and the investigation could be made to disappear. It was the way of the world. He who holds the gold gets to make the rules. Or at least he who holds the gold can get access to one who makes the rules.

The problem with America, he realized, were its laws—especially when it came to political donations. There were so many regulations, all of them nearly impossible to navigate. What he needed was a guide, a *fixer*. He found one, and then some, in Spencer Baldwin.

An accomplished businessman and longtime political fundraiser, Baldwin was a true Washington insider. He went to all the best events, knew all the right people, and could access almost anyone within the government.

Politically agnostic, he didn't care what party a politician belonged to, as long as that politician could further his ends, or the ends of one of his clients. He was exactly the man Wo needed.

Ever cautious that Singapore might send a snatch squad after him, Wo kept a low profile and was constantly on the move. He arranged for Baldwin to meet him in Shanghai and covered all of his expenses.

In an opulent suite of The Peninsula Shanghai, Wo made his American guest an eye-popping offer. He would wire ten million dollars into an account of Baldwin's choosing and work would commence immediately.

If Baldwin was successful in getting the American government to drop its case against him, Wo would then transfer a completion fee in the amount of one hundred million dollars.

He didn't care how Baldwin got rid of the investigation. Only that it went away ASAP.

For Baldwin, who had been having financial troubles, it was like manna from heaven. He didn't need to think twice. He agreed to the deal right there in the suite and flew back to the U.S. the next day to get to work.

Wo had left the meeting feeling upbeat about his prospects. It had taken him a while to find Baldwin, but the man definitely appeared to be the answer to his problems in the United States. Once the investigation was dropped, he could work on getting citizenship. He didn't want to remain in China any longer than he had to.

Which brought him to the safe house he was approaching and the meeting he was about to have. He loathed the terms of his confinement. More than that, he loathed the person he was required to report to.

While the Chinese referred to their policy as "safe harbor," it felt a lot more like house arrest. And the woman he was about to interact with, Xing Fen, was his sadistic jailer.

The joke was that Xing, short and unattractive, had become a member of the Politburo and one of the People's Republic of China's four Vice Premiers the old-fashioned way—by sleeping her way to the top. It couldn't have had anything to do with being first cousin of the General Secretary and one of his closest confidants. The Chinese Communist Party expressly forbade all forms of nepotism.

Wo had been told to meet her at a safe house not far from Beijing's Jianshan Park. Much like Xing herself, the structure was bland, with zero adornment.

After a pat-down by her security detail, Wo was shown into the living room. The Vice Premier sat on a worn leather couch. On the low table in front of her, someone had prepared tea.

Wo hated tea—always had. But what he hated even more were the "delicacies" Xing brought with her to these meetings. She specialized in finding the nastiest street food available.

Tonight she had picked up fried scorpions on a stick, grilled centipede, and pan-seared grasshopper. Capping it all off was a plate of horribly pungent Hunan tofu—the scent of which was triggering his gag reflex. He was positive that she did it only to remind him who was in charge.

She had been a colonel in the People's Liberation Army and had served her time in Military Intelligence. She understood the dynamics of power.

Though Wo was half her age and grew up in another country, he knew it would have been disrespectful to turn down her hospitality. She was his host, after all. But more important, she held his fate in her hands.

They exchanged greetings and he sat down. When she offered him tea, he politely accepted. When she offered him food, he also politely accepted, though inside he was ready to throw up.

"Dennis," she said, addressing him by his given name the way one does in the West. "I understand you have requested permission to travel to Hong Kong."

"Yes, Vice Premier."

"Is there something wrong with Beijing?"

"No, Vice Premier."

"Then what is it?" she asked.

"Hong Kong reminds me of home."

"The arts and culture? Or do you mean the nightclubs and gambling in Macau?"

There was no use in lying to her. She was well aware of his interests. "Yes, Vice Premier. The clubs as well as the casinos in Macau."

She looked at him for a long time as if she were trying to gauge how much of a security risk the trip would be.

For his part, Wo didn't allow himself to get his hopes up. It would have been great to get out of Beijing for a few days, but the rug had been yanked out from under his plans so many times that he had learned not to count his chickens before they hatched.

Xing seemed to delight in granting approval for his sojourns, only to rescind permission at the very last minute. The excuse was always the same: "security concerns."

Frankly, it was laughable. She always sent state security officers with him when he traveled, and he was certain that his communications were being monitored. They had even made him download a tracking app on his phone and required that he keep it with him at all times. Canceling his travel at the last minute seemed more like a subtle form of torment than a legitimate concern over his safety.

"Maybe we can come to an arrangement," she suggested.

Wo took a sip of his tea and waited for her to go on.

"The gentleman you are using in Washington, Mr. Baldwin. We would like you to make contact and offer him an additional piece of work."

"An additional piece of work?" he asked, hesitant to allow anything that could distract from his own case. "What are we talking about?"

Smiling, Xing picked up one of the skewers and removed a fried scorpion with her teeth. As she began to chew, she said, "There's an impediment we need removed."

•   •   •

They talked for twenty minutes. More specifically, Xing talked and Dennis Wo listened. She wanted to make sure he understood exactly what she expected and how the Americans were to be handled.

Once she was confident that he understood the bigger picture and his precise role in it, she bid him good night and had him escorted away from the safe house.

"Do you trust him?" her second-in-command asked. He had been standing out of sight, listening to the conversation.

"No. I do not. If he can double-cross us, he will."

"So why give him such an important task?"

"Because he has connections."

"So do we."

She shook her head. "He has *American* connections. They will be far less suspicious of him and much more open to cooperation. Diplomacy is a subtle art form."

"I prefer the darker arts."

"I know you do, which is why you work for me. Speaking of which, let's talk about Norway. Has our asset arrived?"

The man nodded. "He landed in Oslo this morning."

"Excellent. I want you to reiterate to him that we will accept nothing less than his complete and total success. No matter what, he must accomplish his mission."

"I understand. I will make certain of it."

CHAPTER 5

As soon as Sølvi had sent him the footage, Harvath had put together a report and had uploaded it via a secure link back to D.C. He hadn't been crazy and his eyes hadn't been playing tricks on him. It was exactly who he thought it was.

All that had been left to do was to await instructions. There was no telling when they would come. There was also no telling when Sølvi would be back from the office, so he had decided to turn in.

She slid quietly into bed a few hours later, trying not to wake him. Wrapping his arms around her, he pulled her close. He loved how her naked skin felt against his.

In the half-light pouring through the window, he could just make out the tattooed line of thin blue script running down her spine. It was a quote from Sartre: *Il est impossible d'apprécier correctement la lumière sans connaître les ténèbres. (It is impossible to properly appreciate the light without knowing the darkness.)* A perfect metaphor for them both.

They eventually fell asleep, tightly held in each other's arms. Four hours later, the landline phone on the nightstand screeched its double chirp, signaling that someone was calling up from the lobby. It had to be some sort of mistake.

The phone was on Sølvi's side of the bed. Harvath listened as a quick back-and-forth took place and then she buzzed the person in.

"Who is it?" he asked, checking the time.

"It's the police."

"What do they want at this hour?"

"I don't know. They say it's important."

"Are you sure it's really the cops?"

"I'm sure," she said, turning on the light and getting out of bed. "Martin is a deputy head at Kripos, the National Criminal Investigation Service. I've worked with him before. He wouldn't be here if it wasn't serious."

"You didn't get the taxi dash cam video from someone in his department, did you?"

"No, I used another source."

"But it was someone inside the Norwegian Police, right?"

She nodded and, as she did, Harvath's heart sank. If he had gotten her into hot water, he'd never forgive himself. This kind of thing, especially in privacy-focused Norway, could be a career ender.

They had barely gotten dressed before there was a knock on the apartment door. Sølvi went to answer it.

Hanging on a peg in the hall was a heavy canvas jacket. Stashed in one of the pockets was a subcompact .45 caliber Glock G30. It was more than enough firepower to blast through the door and cut down any threat that might have been standing out in the hallway.

Risking a glance through the peephole, she saw that it was indeed Martin and opened the door.

He was wearing his customary business suit and was accompanied by two uniformed officers. He asked if he could come in and she stood back, opening the door the rest of the way and allowing them to enter.

They walked down to the kitchen, where Harvath had just started a pot of coffee. When Martin addressed him in English, he had a feeling they weren't here to talk to Sølvi.

"May I please see your passport?" the officer asked. "In order to confirm your identity."

"Stop," Sølvi commanded. "What's this all about?"

"It's okay," said Harvath. "It's in the bedroom."

Martin nodded at his two patrol officers to accompany Harvath to retrieve it.

"Are you going to tell me what's going on, or not?" Sølvi asked as the men walked to the back of the apartment. "C'mon, Martin. Do you even have a warrant?"

The police investigator removed a folded piece of paper from his jacket pocket and handed it to her.

She scanned it and said, "Nope. There's not going to be a search of my apartment. I'll call my boss and we'll quash this immediately on grounds of national security. So don't even think it's going to happen."

"I don't need to search your apartment. The warrant is pro forma."

"Then why are you doing this?"

"You know about what happened yesterday? At the ATM?" he asked her.

"Of course. Scot prevented a woman from being robbed."

"He did. Every member of the Oslo Police Service thinks he's a hero. As do I."

"Then what's the problem?"

"There was a physical confrontation."

"Of course there was. The criminals pulled knives on him."

"*One* of them," Martin clarified, "pulled a knife."

"Officers found a knife on the other when they arrested him."

"We just want to ask some questions."

"I assume you took a full statement from him at the scene. Why now? And why with a warrant?"

Martin looked up to make sure his men were not in earshot and, out of a modicum of caution, lowered his voice. "It has become politicized."

"What has? Saving someone from being the victim of a crime? How the hell does that get politicized?"

Martin double-checked again to make sure his men were not near and then made his eyes go cross and pantomimed someone getting their bangs cut with a pair of imaginary scissors.

Sølvi drew a sharp breath. "You have got to be kidding me. Astrid? Astrid Jensen?"

Jensen was a minor political figure with an outsized voice. It was outsized in comparison to her position in the Norwegian Parliament, not to mention her tiny party's influence in Norway. She was known for having a crossed left eye and hair that looked like she cut it herself. Why she would care about a foiled robbery was beyond Sølvi.

"What does this have to do with her?" she asked. "Why would something like this even be on her radar?"

"I'll give you one guess about the background of the perpetrators."

One guess was all she needed. If Jensen was involved, it could only mean one thing. "Asylum seekers?" she asked.

Martin nodded.

"*Faen,*" came her one-word response.

Jensen was more activist than politician. She and her party were champions of immigrants' rights, which was a noble endeavor. Where they got sideways with most Norwegians was when they took the side of immigrants and asylum seekers regardless of the evidence. No matter how heinous the crime—rape, assault, murder—Jensen and her party always blamed Norway and its "system."

Just as annoying, she and her party always stood in the way of meaningful reforms meant to better integrate those same immigrants and asylum seekers. As far as Jensen and her comrades were concerned, attempts to assimilate newcomers—no matter how much it would improve their lives—was a human rights violation of the highest order.

The headaches that caused to Norwegian Police were incalculable. Time after time, Jensen and her party had put forth fabricated versions of criminal events that were simply not true. It had a false, unfair, and corrosive effect on the image of the police, particularly in Norway's immigrant communities.

In short, good cops—the majority of the nation's force—found it increasingly difficult to do their job and keep *everyone* in the country safe.

Harvath, trailed by the two patrol officers, came back into the kitchen and handed over his passport.

"Thank you," said Martin as he scanned it. Everything matched up. *Scot Thomas Harvath. American. Five-foot-ten. One hundred and seventy-five pounds. Brown hair. Blue eyes.* Closing the passport, he slipped it into his pocket.

"Am I going to get that back?" Harvath asked.

"Eventually."

"You're keeping his passport?" challenged Sølvi. "Seriously?"

"Listen," replied Martin. "I'm going to save us all a lot of time. I don't like having to do this, but I'm going to do everything by the book."

"Because Jensen is all over this."

"*Because,*" he emphasized, "we're professionals. If Mr. Harvath wants, he may have an attorney present. Per Norwegian law, the state will pay for it."

"I don't need an attorney," said Harvath. "I told the officers everything when I gave my initial report. If you take me in, the only thing you're going to get is practice."

Sølvi looked at him. "You've got nothing to lose. Let them provide you an attorney."

"Don't worry. I'll be fine."

"Scot—" she began.

But before she could continue he turned to Martin and said, "Let's get this over with."

CHAPTER 6

Kripos Headquarters was located in a mixed industrial and residential part of Oslo known as Bryn. The long, five-story, orange-brick building was framed with gray windows. There were so many flagpoles in front that it could have been a stand-in for a United Nations structure.

They parked in the underground garage and took the elevator up to the third floor. There, Harvath was shown into a rather luxurious interrogation room. If it wasn't for the one-way glass running down the opposite wall, he would have thought he was in some chic Scandinavian boardroom.

The walls were covered in gray fabric, the floor carpeted, and instead of the cheap metal chairs and tables he was used to seeing in police interrogation rooms back in the States, here the furniture was all crafted from walnut.

"Does Kripos rent this space out for photo shoots when it's not being used for questioning?" he asked.

Martin smiled. "This is one of our nicer ones. Consider it a professional courtesy."

"I will. Thank you."

"Would you like some coffee or a bottled water before we get started?"

Harvath was tempted to go for the water, just to see if he'd be offered a choice between still or sparkling, but opted for the caffeine instead. "Coffee, please. Black."

Gesturing for Harvath to take a seat, Martin disappeared and returned a few minutes later with two mugs—something Harvath never would have offered anyone he was interrogating. If he offered coffee at all, it would have been served as a reward for cooperation, tepid, in a Styrofoam cup. Piping hot liquid in a ceramic mug was handing him two things he could use as weapons. Either Martin was careless, or he was convinced that Harvath wasn't a threat. Seeing as how the Norwegian was a deputy head of Norway's lead law enforcement investigatory branch, he figured it was the latter.

Setting down the folder tucked under his arm, Martin turned on a digital recorder and stated his name, rank, time, and date, as well as the nature of the interrogation. He then asked Harvath to state and spell his full name. Once more, he made Harvath aware of his right to have an attorney present at Norway's expense, which Harvath once again declined.

"Okay, then," said Martin. "Let's get to it. Shall we?"

They spent a good hour, going back and forth through what had happened—both leading up to and at the ATM. Harvath answered the man's questions as honestly as he felt was reasonable.

He explained that he had been at Kafé Celsius on Christiania Square before heading north toward the Mathallen Food Hall to shop for dinner. He left out the part about the taxi and the man who had gotten out of it.

A couple of times, Martin professed to be confused about Harvath's route. There were quicker, more direct ways to get to Mathallen.

Still, Harvath's response remained the same. He was on vacation and in no hurry. He had been to Mathallen multiple times and always selected a different route so he could see more of Oslo.

Unless they had him on CCTV, which he hoped they didn't, there was no reason for Martin to doubt him. Hell, even if they did have him on CCTV, it had nothing to do with what had happened at the ATM.

Eventually, Martin dropped it and switched to a new line of questioning.

"You have said you are on vacation. From what?"

"From America."

The Norwegian smiled. "Not from *where*, Mr. Harvath. I know from where. I have your passport, after all. Let me be more specific. What is your occupation?"

Harvath chose his words carefully. "I'm a consultant."

"*Consulting.* That's a very broad industry. Specifically, what kind of consultant are you?"

"Security."

"As in cameras and burglar alarms?"

"Sure."

"Would you care to elaborate?"

"Not really," Harvath said.

Martin opened his file folder and began perusing the contents. Without looking up, he asked, "What kind of background qualifies one for employment as a security consultant?"

Harvath's finely tuned BS detector was starting to kick in. "I suppose it varies from company to company."

"How about *your* company?" the Norwegian asked, looking up. "What qualified you?"

"Besides charm and good looks?"

"Besides that."

"They sought me out," said Harvath.

"Was that because of," Martin asked, returning to the file, "your tenure as a United States Navy SEAL, or the additional work you did with the United States Secret Service detailed to the White House?"

"Those sound like very interesting careers."

"I'm guessing there's lots more after that, but despite my best efforts, it's a black hole. I couldn't find a thing. I have my suspicions that your employment became even more interesting."

Harvath had no idea how the man had been able to unearth that much about his background. They had drifted far beyond what he felt comfortable with. He needed to either get control of this interrogation or find a way to pull the plug.

"If you're looking to leave Kripos and pursue a career in security consulting, I'd be happy to give you some pointers, but over breakfast at an Oslo restaurant. I'm starting to get hungry. Why don't we wrap this up?"

Martin smiled. "We wrap up when I say we wrap up. Is that clear?"

Harvath looked up at the one-way glass, certain he was being observed, and smiled back. "Of course."

"Back to my previous question: Are you now or have you ever been a

United States Navy SEAL and/or a member of the United States Secret Service?"

"I don't want to sidetrack us, but do you normally treat people who protect your fellow Norwegians and stop criminals like this?"

There was a pause as Martin looked up at the glass, almost reluctant to proceed, before he hardened his visage and returned to his questioning with a renewed determination.

"Mr. Harvath, are you familiar with something called the continuum of force?"

Harvath knew exactly what it was, but he wasn't going to give the Kripos officer the satisfaction. "Can you explain it to me, please?"

"It is the theory that law enforcement officers have numerous tools at their disposal to deal with threats. It starts with things as simple as one's authority and the words they use, transitions through things like pepper spray, baton, or Taser, and goes all the way to use of lethal force. In other words, the remedy employed must be proportional to the threat."

"As perceived by the law enforcement officer."

"Yes," Martin agreed. "As perceived by the law enforcement officer."

"In other words, if a subject is a block away holding a knife, you can't shoot him. But if that same subject is ten feet away and charges you with the knife, and you believe your life is in danger, you are allowed to go right to lethal force."

"Exactly," said Martin, who then realized what Harvath had done and tried to correct the record. "That's a hypothetical, of course."

"Remind me again why I'm here."

The Norwegian looked up at the glass once again before reengaging. "Under Norwegian law, self-defense is permissible, but only proportional to the threat."

Harvath looked at him. "I have no idea what we're talking about. Do you have a problem with how I handled things at the ATM? If so, let me hear it. Because none of this makes any sense."

"In Norway, we hold members of law enforcement and the military to a higher standard when it comes to how they handle themselves in cases of self-defense. They have superior training and that training needs to be viewed on a scale of proportionality."

"Are you saying, in the face of being confronted by two attackers—one of whom pulled a knife—that I applied *too much* force? That somehow *I* responded disproportionately?"

"That is now the crux of our investigation," Martin stated. "How do you reply?"

Knowing his answer might end up entered as evidence in court, he organized his words with precision. "Fearing for *my* life," he said calmly, "as well as for the life of the woman at the ATM, I did what I felt was necessary to stop the threat. And I did so without employing lethal force."

"That last part may end up being debatable."

Harvath was confused. "How can that be up for debate? Both of the attackers are still alive. What aren't you telling me?"

"The second offender," said Martin. "The one who pulled the knife. The doctors think that when his head struck the ATM, he developed an aneurysm. Shortly after arriving at the hospital, he had a stroke. He's in a coma."

CHAPTER 7

Harvath was stunned. It was a huge piece of information and the police had taken their sweet time in giving it to him.

Nevertheless, it didn't change anything. He had done the right thing and would do it again in a heartbeat.

"Dirty pool, Martin," he said to the Kripos officer. "You and I are done speaking. Either charge me with a crime or call me a cab."

The man was about to respond, when there was a knock at the interrogation room door. Another officer stuck his head in, said something in Norwegian, and then left.

"Apparently, your lawyer is here," Martin revealed as he turned off the recorder.

"What lawyer?"

"Sølvi must have been busy. A representative from your embassy has also arrived. I'll leave you alone to talk."

Standing, he picked up the file folder and left the room.

Moments later, Holidae H. Hayes, the CIA's tall, redheaded Oslo Station Chief, entered.

"Don't say anything," she instructed. "We're going to have you out of here in a few minutes."

"Who told you I had been brought in?"

"No talking."

He did as she asked and closed his mouth.

Five minutes later, a distinguished-looking man in a well-tailored suit and carrying a Ghurka briefcase joined them.

"Mr. Harvath," he said, handing over the passport that the police officer had taken from him, "you are free to go."

"Thank you, Johannes," replied Hayes. "I appreciate your help."

"It is not a problem. I have informed the special prosecutor that, short of charges being filed, Mr. Harvath will not be doing any further interviews."

The attorney handed Harvath his business card. On the back, he had written his mobile number. Then the three of them left the interrogation room and headed to the elevator.

As they rode down, Johannes and Hayes made small talk about a high-profile divorce case that was getting a lot of attention in the local papers.

When the elevator doors opened, the first thing Harvath noticed was Martin. He was standing across the lobby, speaking with an odd-looking woman. When she saw him, she shot him an icy glare.

"Who's that?" he asked as Hayes steered him toward the exit.

"Astrid Jensen. Member of Parliament and all-around pain in the ass. She's the reason the police brought you back in for more questioning."

"Was she behind the glass during the interrogation?"

"Probably."

"What's her beef with me?"

"She's looking for headlines and is hoping you'll provide them."

"That's definitely not going to happen."

"I agree," said Hayes. "And Johannes made that crystal clear to the police prosecutor's office. That doesn't mean she can't still make trouble."

"What kind of trouble?"

"She's not just a politician; she's also an attorney. She knows her way around the law. It was her idea to have you brought back in and questioned on the use-of-force issue. Like I said, she's looking for headlines. 'U.S. Navy SEAL Beats Up Immigrants, Puts One in a Coma' would be a nice starting place for her."

"Those weren't a couple of altar boys," he muttered, preparing to shoot her a glare of his own.

"Eyes front," Hayes advised as they neared the glass doors. "For what it's worth, the police didn't want to bring you in. They bowed to political pressure. The hope is that this will go away."

"What does your gut tell you?"

"It tells me we have bigger problems on our hands right now."

He held open the door for her and they stepped outside. "What kind of problems?"

"Your ghost sighting has set off a lot of alarm bells back at Langley."

"What do they want done about it?"

"Not here," she said as they arrived at her vehicle. "I think it's safer if we talk back at the embassy."

CHAPTER 8

The United States Embassy to the Kingdom of Norway was located in a bucolic neighborhood called Makrellbekken, about three and a half miles from the city center.

Set among tall trees and rolling hills, the modern multistory compound had been constructed from gray stone. Its sleek rooftops, as well as its polished windows, were a pale green that amplified the pastoral setting.

Hayes waited while Harvath was screened and then led him to her section. At a heavy security door, they placed their phones in a cubby and she swiped her ID through a card reader. There was a hiss of air as the locks released. Hayes pointed at a conference room, told him to help himself to coffee, and that she'd be there in a moment.

He had been in a lot of embassies around the world and one thing was for certain: the decorating budgets all worked from the outside in. The deeper down you drilled, the cheaper the furnishings became. It was no different here in Oslo. The only saving grace was that, while inexpensive, everything at least had a degree of Scandinavian chic to it.

Helping himself to a cup of coffee, he grabbed a seat at the conference table and waited for Hayes. No doubt, she had as many questions for him as he did for her. What he would have to settle on was how much he was willing to tell her.

When she walked in, she came carrying her laptop and a stack of files. Dropping everything on the table, she poured herself a cup of coffee and then took the seat next to him.

"Hell of a start to the day," she remarked.

"I've had worse."

"Knowing you, I don't doubt it. Nice haircut, by the way."

"Okay if I ask some questions now?" he inquired, ignoring the compliment.

She leaned back in her chair and took a sip of her coffee. "Go ahead."

"I assume Sølvi told you I had been brought in for questioning?"

Hayes nodded. "She did."

"Did she also tell you that I didn't want a lawyer?"

"Yes."

"So?"

"So Astrid Jensen is like dog shit: Once you've stepped in it, it's important to get rid of it as quickly as possible. If you don't, the stink will follow you everywhere."

"But you said yourself that the police don't want to bring this case. Not only do we have a witness, whom I saved, but the attackers probably have rap sheets as long as my arm. I'm also going to assume that the ATM has a camera, and if it doesn't, this is Oslo, which means there's gotta be one close by. Even if we don't have perfect footage of what went down, I'd say we've got a near airtight case."

"What you need to understand is that this isn't about being airtight. I already told you. This is about headlines—for *her*. She doesn't care that you doled out an ass-kicking to a couple of small-time hoods. All she cares about is that Norwegians at large *think* she cares. It's about building up her political capital. Nothing more."

"She's a typical politician, then. How about I apply for asylum? Then the story becomes immigrant-on-immigrant violence. It'll be like magic. *Poof!* She'll instantly lose interest."

"Very funny," said Hayes.

"You're too worried about this. What's the worst that could happen? If the cops don't want to bring the case, the police prosecutor isn't going to bring it."

The CIA chief leaned forward and set her coffee on the table. "For starters, how about if she gets you banned from Norway? She doesn't have to make this a criminal case. She can, and likely would, turn it into a human rights issue. She could make so much noise that the Norwegian government tosses you out just to get her to shut up."

He didn't like that prospect. Not a single bit. If he couldn't legally get into Norway, it would make seeing Sølvi extremely difficult.

"How do we make my Astrid Jensen problem go away?"

"I'm already working on it," she replied.

"Thank you. And thanks for showing up with the lawyer. Even if the police are not inclined to come after me, it's good for them—and for Astrid Jensen—to see we're serious."

Hayes smiled. "They know we're serious all right. Johannes is one of the top lawyers in the country. You could hear the collective butt cheeks of the entire Norwegian Police Service tightening when we walked in the door."

Harvath was as pro–law enforcement as they came, and took no delight in things being made difficult for good cops, but the remark made him grin. Changing gears, he asked his next question as broadly as possible. "How do you, and more importantly, Langley, know about my ghost?"

He could have asked if Sølvi had told her, but he didn't want to implicate Sølvi in getting him the dash cam footage. Better to play it a little uninformed and see how Hayes responded.

"Pretty simple," she said. "Your boss called my boss."

"He couldn't have called your boss. Not without—"

"Calling the President first. Yeah, he did that. Then the President told them both to work together and share everything they had."

"And because the target was spotted here, your boss called you."

"Immediately," Hayes replied.

It made sense. Harvath worked for a private intelligence agency whose number one job was to help handle the most sensitive national security operations while the CIA was undergoing massive reforms.

In essence, The Carlton Group was the "condo" where the CIA's most pressing matters were living in while the Agency as a whole was going through a down-to-the-studs, full-scale gut renovation.

Harvath took a sip of his coffee. "Were you able to uncover anything?"

"Yes and no, technically speaking."

"I don't get it."

"As far as the United States government and the Central Intelligence Agency are concerned," she explained, "what you saw, you *didn't* see. And even if you did see it, we're not getting involved."

"Define *we*."

"*We* would be the United States Embassy, Oslo, and all personnel therein."

"Right. Because that makes *total* sense."

She held up her hand to stop him. "You, on the other hand, do not represent the United States government or the CIA and can, for all intents and purposes, do whatever you want."

One of the biggest reasons Harvath's company had been established was to be able move quickly, without the burden of Congressional oversight and bureaucratic red tape. It also afforded the upside of imbuing the American President with plausible deniability.

What he didn't understand was why play that card now. This was red meat for the CIA. They should have been all over this, setting up surveillance operations on the Chinese Embassy and working every single contact they had.

He looked at her, his BS detector fully switched on. "Why the pass?"

"Because the current U.S. Ambassador to Norway is, as my British friends would say, a wanker."

"Excuse me?"

"You know how this stuff works. The CIA operates out of each U.S. Embassy because it grants us diplomatic cover. The deal, which I think is insane, is that the Ambassador gets read in on all operations and gets final say. It subordinates the Central Intelligence Agency to the State Department.

"And don't get me started on how ambassadorships are nothing more than popularity contests, awarded by POTUS based on how much cash a candidate raised or how effective a spokesperson they were during the campaign.

"Way too often, these people are playing pretend diplomat. They have next to zero grasp of geopolitics, the workings of the Intelligence Community, or the intricacies of achieving our objectives abroad. They get drunk, throw dinner parties, and the American taxpayer foots the bill."

While there were some exceptional Ambassadors, Harvath didn't disagree with her. He did, though, find her take interesting. "Aren't you angling for an Ambassadorship in the next administration?"

"We'll see what happens. There's a lot of road between now and then."

"But if your candidate does win?"

"If, and that's a big if, I were to be offered the privilege of serving, I think I'd do a damn good job."

Short. Sweet. And to the point. He had to give Hayes credit. Brevity, after all, was the soul of wit.

"Back to your feelings about the current Ambassador: What's the problem with him?"

The CIA Station Chief tried to decide where to begin. "First off, he's impossible to brief. He has the attention span of a gnat. He's also incredibly arrogant. Thinks he knows more than anyone else. Maybe that's from making millions in Silicon Valley, or maybe he's just wired that way. The outcome is the same.

"When it comes to handling him, though, the Norwegians are smart. I think they had his number before he even arrived. Whenever they want to get his attention, regardless of the issue, they don't invite him for a sit-down with the Prime Minister or send their Minister for Foreign Affairs but rather they use their very young, very attractive climate minister.

"I don't like it, but I have to give them credit. We assigned a priapic moron to this post and they're doing everything within their power to take advantage of it."

"You're not a fan of the Ambo. I get it," he said. "But what does he have to do with you sitting this one out?"

There was no reason to hold anything else back, so she didn't. "Because the Norwegians are using him to put the CIA on ice."

CHAPTER 9

It was a shocking assertion. "You told the Ambassador about our ghost and *he* revealed that information to the Norwegians?"

Hayes shook her head. "He's stupid, but he's not *that* stupid. Operational security has actually been one of the few areas in which he has done a halfway decent job."

"Then how are the Norwegians exerting influence? They're a NATO ally, after all. They should have no problem with us running this to ground."

"Earlier in the year, the Ambassador was told in no uncertain terms that we were to lay off the Chinese. No surveillance. No recruitment. Nothing."

"That's insane."

"I said the same thing, but the Norwegians were adamant."

"Why? What could possibly justify that position?"

"Ten years of crippling economic and diplomatic sanctions out of Beijing."

"Over what?" he asked.

"Do you remember back in 2010 when the Nobel Peace Prize was awarded to a Chinese dissident? At the time, it was a huge deal. His name was Liu Xiaobo."

"I don't remember the exact details, but I remember it happening."

"Well, Beijing was not happy. In fact, the Chinese Communist Party was pissed. *Really* pissed. It was also vindictive. At the State Department, they like to say the Chinese have as many types of statecraft as the Eskimos have words for snow. To get back at the Norwegians, the CCP launched a campaign of 'coercive' diplomacy.

"In addition to freezing diplomatic relations with Norway, they used multiple tools in their toolkit to damage their economy. They blocked Norwegian salmon imports, restricted business investments, moth-balled trade deals, refused to issue visas to Norwegian citizens, and for-bade their own people from tourism to Norway. It was brutal. Norway was bleeding red ink, but they didn't cave. They held fast and refused to rescind the award. Eventually, China blinked.

"There has been a thaw—both figuratively and literally. Relations are slowly warming. They learned a painful lesson and don't want to rock the boat again."

"Norway took an admirable stance," Harvath said. "That takes guts. But the Chinese don't do anything unless there's something in it for them. What changed?"

"That's the literal thaw in all of this. The ice in the Arctic is melting. As it does, there's a race on to secure massive deposits of precious min-erals, natural gas, and oil. Sea-lanes, previously frozen, are opening up, which offer new and faster shipping routes.

"The Chinese," Hayes continued, "want to get their fingers into as many of these pies as possible. Therefore, they're playing nice—not only with the Norwegians, but with the other Arctic member states as well. Canada, Denmark, Iceland, Finland, Sweden, and Russia. The only Arc-tic state to have told them to go pound snow is the United States."

"Because we're an Arctic state via Alaska."

"Correct."

"What happened?"

"A couple of years ago, China released its first policy paper on the Arctic. In it, China declared itself a 'near' Arctic state."

Harvath laughed. "What does that even mean?"

"Absolutely nothing. It's a made-up term. When asked about it at a press conference, our Secretary of State laughed out loud too. China's northernmost settlement is over nine hundred miles away from the Arc-tic Circle. It's nonsense—to everyone—except the Chinese. To them, this is deadly serious. The Russians are serious too.

"Back in 2007, the Russian navy sent a camera-laden mini-sub fourteen thousand feet beneath the North Pole. There, via a robotic claw, it planted their flag on the seafloor. Ever since, they've been signaling that almost 500,000 square miles of the Arctic is an extension of Russia's continental shelf and should belong to them."

"Is there any truth to that?" Harvath asked. "Do they have a legit territorial claim?"

"None at all," she replied. "They don't have a shred of evidence. Just like the Chinese, they're making it up. But when you repeat a lie often enough, even the liar starts to believe it, and this is where it gets dangerous.

"In the last twenty years, Russia's military spending has increased one hundred and seventy-five percent. We spend ten times more than they do, yet it's not how much they're spending that's the problem but *where*. They've fully prioritized the Arctic."

"And we haven't."

"Unfortunately, that's correct. In particular, Russia has focused on beefing up its Northern Fleet. They've been adding more submarines capable of launching nuclear-tipped ballistic missiles, reopening old Soviet naval bases, refurbishing old airstrips, and building brand-new military installations throughout the region. As one of our esteemed United States senators recently said, 'The Russians are playing chess in the Arctic and our administration still seems to think it's tic-tac-toe.'

"He wasn't wrong. It took something pretty chilling, if you'll pardon the pun, for the administration to sit up and take notice. Last August, a Russian sub surfaced near the North Pole and fired a Sineva-type intercontinental ballistic missile."

Harvath was familiar with the weapon. "Those can carry nukes," he said.

Hayes nodded. "That same day, another Russian sub in the Arctic, while remaining submerged, launched a Bulava-type intercontinental ballistic missile."

"Which can also carry a nuclear warhead."

"Correct. One of the missiles landed in an unpopulated location on Russia's Pacific coast. The other hit their Kanin Peninsula. With these two acts, the Russians have made it clear that *if* they ever officially declare that chunk of the Arctic—and all of its resources—is theirs, they have the means to defend it. Suffice it to say that the Arctic quickly received the administration's attention.

"The Pentagon updated its national defense strategy, clearly delineating that Russia and China had bumped terrorism out of the top spot as the greatest potential threat to American national security. Whether we stumbled into a conflict in the Arctic that escalated, or whether the Arctic was used as a staging ground for an attack on the homeland, we couldn't half-ass our policy there any longer.

"So, while the Russians have made substantial investments in the Arctic both militarily and commercially, they have begun partnering up with the Chinese on projects, which we find troubling—to say the least."

He couldn't blame her for feeling that way. Alone, the Russians and the Chinese each were bad actors. Put them together and nothing good would come of it. U.S. Intelligence was very much against any such cooperation and sought to thwart it wherever possible.

"China declares itself a 'near Arctic state' and gets laughed at," he said. "So what are they hoping to get from a country like Norway?"

"A foothold. Hell, even a toehold. Anything that can give them access and a modicum of respectability in the Arctic. It's the old chestnut about the camel's nose in the tent, except there are no camels in the Arctic. But there are polar bears. And like the Chinese—"

"They can be extremely dangerous," he said, finishing her sentence for her.

"Precisely."

Harvath was well aware that the United States saw China as its single most important security challenge. The last U.S. defense bill included more than two billion dollars aimed at countering China. Their military satellites, artificial intelligence, and cyberwarfare capabilities—not to mention how they had been closing the gap with U.S. firepower via hypervelocity missiles, robotics, and unmanned systems—had turned them into what the Pentagon now referred to as a "near-peer" rival.

"How do they begin to get access in the Arctic?" he asked.

"Through something called the Belt and Road Initiative. It's the focus, the crown jewel, of the CCP's foreign policy agenda. They're in pursuit of two major goals: to have the world's strongest economy and one of its strongest militaries. To make that happen, they're going to need food, fuel, and raw materials. They simply cannot create enough, on their own, inside China. So they have to look outside."

"To countries like Norway."

"And about seventy others," she explained. "Along with a string of international organizations. The Chinese call it strategic investing. Critics call it the development of a global, China-centric trade network. Essentially, what they're doing is purchasing influence—seats at very important, very exclusive tables. All in an effort to diversify and lock in the commodities they need to fuel their growth over the next one hundred–plus years."

"What, specifically, are they trying to do with the Norwegians?"

"They've made a couple attempts, through a cutout—a wealthy Chinese hotel developer—to buy massive tracts of land up above the Arctic Circle. The developer claimed he wanted to build an 'eco-resort.' The government in Oslo saw through the ruse and purchased the land itself, shutting the sale to China down. This, by the way, was similar to a play the Chinese launched to buy a Canadian mining company that operates in Canada's Arctic. That attempt was shut down by the Canadian government.

"Recently, Beijing has been involved in something else. The mayor of Kirkenes, a small, economically depressed Norwegian coastal town above the Arctic Circle, has been openly soliciting Chinese investment. Per Norwegian law, he's not doing anything illegal. It's a loophole of sorts and the CCP loves it."

"What does Kirkenes have that the Chinese would want to invest in?" he asked.

Hayes took another sip of her coffee. "A port. With infrastructure. And a lot of room to grow. That's where the Russians and all of the melting ice comes in.

"As the largest trading partner for about two-thirds of the world's countries, most of the items China imports and exports move via cargo ships. Due to the nature of the earth's geography, those ships are forced to transit some very tense choke points.

"The Chinese have always been very sensitive to the Strait of Malacca, which is heavily patrolled by the United States Navy, and the Strait of Hormuz, which is subject to tumultuous geopolitics.

"If, at any point, one or both of these get locked down, the Chinese are screwed. Their economy begins withering almost instantly. Because of that, they've long been searching for an alternative. But none existed—until now.

"The Northern Sea Route stretches along Russia's Arctic coast, from Siberia all the way to the Barents Sea. With temperatures in the Arctic rising twice as fast as the world average, the ice has been turning to slush for longer and longer periods each year.

"By using the Northern Sea Route, which they refer to as the Polar Silk Route, the Chinese would shorten the journey to Europe by forty percent. Instead of China to Rotterdam taking forty-eight days, for instance, it would only take twenty-eight. That's a huge savings of time and money, not to mention avoiding the U.S. Navy and the all-too-unstable Middle East."

"Plus," Harvath added, "avoiding black swan events like that container ship the length of the Empire State Building that wedged itself sideways in the Suez and completely shut it down."

"Exactly," Hayes agreed.

"But what's the appeal of Kirkenes?"

"It's the first ice-free European port after exiting the Northern Sea Route. The mayor's pitch to the Chinese is to have them help fund the improvements and make it their Arctic shipping hub. The cargo could be off-loaded in Kirkenes and transported via an "Arctic corridor," which would include an as-yet-to-be-built high-speed rail system and an undersea tunnel to move the goods deeper into Europe."

"Sounds like they would make a fortune," said Harvath. "Not to mention the amount of jobs and tax revenue something like that could create."

"The downside is that it would give Beijing the toehold they want, which, in our estimation, would eventually turn into a stranglehold. The State Department has lobbied hard against it. The Norwegians don't like us poking our noses into it, but they're a vital, strategic partner. We store a lot of U.S. military hardware in northern Norway in case of war. We can't allow the Chinese to exert any undue influence over them."

"But if they're telling the Ambassador not to run intel operations," he said, "haven't the Chinese already won?"

"Not yet. There's just one little problem with the proposed Arctic corridor."

"What's that?"

"Are you familiar with who the Sámi people are?"

He was more than familiar with who the Sámi were. They inhabited the northern regions of Norway, Sweden, and Finland, as well as the Kola Peninsula, where several of them had helped save his life when he was being pursued by Russian mercenaries. They were brave, tough, good people. He nodded.

"The corridor," she went on, "would run straight through their reindeer grazing lands. Those lands are protected in perpetuity. They cannot be violated without their consent.

"Beijing, of course, reverted to what it always does when it can't use force: It tried to buy the Sámi off."

"Which I'm positive didn't work," he said.

"No, it didn't. In fact, the Sámi were deeply offended, in particular because it came on the heels of a pretty bad rumor."

"What rumor?"

"That the Chinese had been attempting to develop a highly pathogenic form of chronic wasting disease aimed at the Sámi reindeer. When they were unsuccessful, they decided to offer bribes."

"That sounds like something the Chinese might try—especially if they thought they could get away with it. Is there any truth to it?" he asked.

"Nothing that we've picked up."

"It's a good piece of disinformation, though. Whoever started it should get a medal."

"For the moment, what matters is that the deal is in limbo. The players are searching for a work-around, but it doesn't look promising," she replied. "Which means we can focus full-time on your ghost."

"I thought the Ambassador pulled the plug on all things China."

"He only said CIA couldn't *run* ops. He never said anything about supporting someone else's."

"Meaning *me*."

"Meaning The Carlton Group. They've been given the green light on this. From what I hear, you've been given an ultimatum. It sounds like your time card back home has accumulated a bit of dust."

"I've been captivated by Norway's scenic beauty," he responded.

She chuckled. "I'm well aware of what Norwegian beauty has you captivated."

Hayes was part of their circle. She had been out to the cottage for cookouts, as well as multiple dinner parties at Sølvi's apartment. He was counting on her to make sure he didn't get banned from the country. "Are you sure you can take care of Astrid Jensen for me?"

"Absolutely."

"Then I'm in."

"Good," she said. Waking her laptop, she adjusted the screen so he could see it. "Now let me take you through what we uncovered on our ghost."

CHAPTER 10

D ennis Wo had made it clear that money wasn't an object. He wanted his fixer in Southern California ASAP and had told Spencer Baldwin to charter the first private jet he could find.

Wanting to be true to the "spirit" of the agreement, Baldwin had hopped onto the website of a charter company he had used in the past and then clicked on the tab for its most luxurious aircraft. From there, he had selected a Bombardier Global 7500. With its fourteen-passenger capacity and over sixteen hours of flight time before refueling, it had been more than up to the task of getting him from D.C. to the West Coast.

At such a high price point, catering was included, and he had opted for two dozen fresh oysters and a gigantic Maine lobster, along with two spectacular bottles of ice-cold Chablis. His wife, who hated flying, had given up telling him that he drank his red wines too warm and his white wines too cold.

It was a weird thing to criticize your spouse over. What did she care how he liked his wines? Complaining that he spent far too much on wines would have been more legitimate, but that's where they were at this point. No matter what he did, she wasn't happy with it. The fact that they had recently been on the verge of filing for bankruptcy had only made things worse.

Yet the fact that he had landed such a whale of a client in Dennis Wo, and had turned their financial situation completely around, hadn't made things any better. Somewhere a line had been crossed and she wasn't willing to come back over it.

To be honest, he didn't care anymore. Overweight, with hypertension, and pushing sixty, he only had so many good years left. He might as well make the most of them. And flying like royalty was a hell of a way to do it.

After dinner and drinks in the main cabin, he retired to the entertainment suite to watch some cable news before lying down for an hour in the master bedroom.

As they touched down in Southern California, he felt better rested and more energized than when they had left D.C. Funny, he mused, how luxury travel could do that. This was definitely the good life and he wanted more of it. Much more.

Waiting for him on the tarmac was a chauffeur and a glossy black Mercedes sedan. Rush hour was over and at this time of evening the ride wouldn't take long.

He relaxed in back, checking emails and scrolling through the texts on his phone. Twenty minutes later, they arrived at their destination.

The hotel was the pinnacle of elegance. Every space, from the splendidly planted grounds to the sumptuously decorated rooms, was a feast for the eyes. Baldwin had stayed at the hotel years ago for a series of meetings with wealthy Southern California donors. It was one of the most memorable weekends of his life. He was glad to be back—even if he wasn't staying long.

Opening the app on his phone, he texted his contact to let her know he had arrived and asked if she wanted to meet in the bar. Seconds later, she texted back a room number.

He had reached out to some SoCal political operatives he knew to get a little background on the woman. Lindsey Chang had worked on a couple of local and state-level campaigns but was best known for being able to coordinate donations from the Chinese-American communities in LA and San Diego. One contact said he thought she had been a political science student at UCLA, while another said she had studied public policy at USC. Her background was somewhat difficult to pin down.

For his part, all Dennis Wo had said was that the meeting was about an important piece of business, to keep it on the down low, and that the woman would explain everything.

It was a little cloak-and-dagger, but Baldwin had always fancied himself the James Bond type. In fact, had his life been different, maybe he would have pursued a career with the CIA. The idea of glamorous international locales, beautiful cars, and even more beautiful women had always held a certain appeal to him.

He took the elevator to the top floor and padded down the carpeted hallway to her room, where he knocked on the door.

It took her a moment to answer, but when she did, she took Baldwin's breath away. She had long, dark hair, high cheekbones, and the fullest lips he'd ever seen. She was impossibly thin and beautifully bronzed and looked like she could have been an actress or a model. He was instantly smitten by her.

Standing back so he could enter, she offered her hand, which he took. As he did, he couldn't help but stare at her white blouse, its first four buttons open, and how it clung to her body.

Her stylish black trousers looked like they were part of a suit ensemble, the jacket undoubtedly hung somewhere in her dimly lit suite. She wore heels that made her almost as tall as he was. They looked expensive. *Everything* about her looked expensive.

"Thank you for meeting me," she said, flashing him a smile of perfectly white teeth.

He felt flushed. It had been a long time since a woman had made him feel this way. "It is absolutely my pleasure," he replied, almost too enthusiastically.

Chang smiled again and led him into the living room, where she gestured for him to take a seat. There was a fire in the fireplace and the sliding glass doors to the veranda were open. From outside, he could smell the salty sea breeze and hear the crash of the ocean.

"Something to drink?" she asked as she walked over to the bar. "Don't tell me: You're a bourbon man, correct?"

He was ready to be whatever she wanted him to be, but it just so happened that he *loved* bourbon. Next to a great bottle of wine, or two, there was nothing like an exceptional bottle of bourbon. And from where he was sitting, he could make out one of the rarest and most sought-after in the world: Pappy Van Winkle's Family Reserve 23 Year.

The legend was that it was so exclusive and so cherished that a priest from Kentucky had given a bottle of it to the Pope and wound up short-listed for cardinal.

Baldwin didn't know if that part was true or not, but he did know that if James Bond was going to sip bourbon with a gorgeous woman, this was what he'd be drinking.

"I'll have a Pappy's, please. Neat."

Chang poured one for him, one for herself, and then joined him on the couch in front of the fire.

"Cheers," she said as they clinked glasses.

"Cheers," Baldwin replied.

Closing his eyes, he swirled the bourbon, put his nose into the glass, and inhaled. It was one of the most exquisite things he had ever smelled. Though he couldn't help but wonder if the nape of Lindsey Chang's neck would give it a run for its money.

Opening his eyes, he looked at her and took a sip, letting the delicious brown liquid roll around in his mouth before swallowing. If at this moment God decided to take him, he was quite certain he could die a happy man.

"Good stuff?" she asked.

"Exceptional."

"I'm glad to hear it."

"So, Ms. Chang, what can I do for you?"

"First, it's Lindsey. And second, how are things looking for Dennis?"

Baldwin was usually circumspect when it came to his clients, but in this case he was willing to make an exception. "It's always hard to tell with the DOJ. I just had lunch with someone from the Office of Legal Policy. I think we're making headway."

"By all accounts you are a smart, very well-connected man who figures out how to make things happen."

She was flattering him. He liked it and he smiled. "It's all about who you know and what they need."

"I'm hoping you can help me with something I need."

"I would love to. Just tell me what it is."

Chang flashed her smile at him again. "China is the world's second largest liquified natural gas importer—second only to Japan. Alaska, while known for its oil and gas reserves, never sufficiently developed its LNG export capabilities.

"Despite an explosion in worldwide demand, Alaska is missing the boat. Its annual GDP is fifty billion dollars and has been dropping every year for the last nine years. Depending on its oil wealth to keep itself afloat is a losing proposition. If it's going to survive, it must quickly begin exploiting its LNG potential."

"And China wants to be part of that exploitation," Baldwin noted.

"Don't think of it as China. Think of it as a consortium of investors, along with an experienced Chinese oil and gas corporation."

"To do what, exactly?"

"A third of the world's undiscovered natural gas reserves are estimated to be up in the Arctic, at least half of them in Alaska. A plan known as the Alaskan Liquified Natural Gas Project recently received Department of Energy and EPA approval. It envisions mining along the North Slope and building a pipeline and liquefaction plant. The price tag is projected to be around forty billion dollars. Though it will create anywhere from twelve thousand to nineteen thousand jobs, Alaska doesn't have the money. My consortium does.

"Not only can they help finance the project; they can help with all of the construction and secure Chinese contracts for as much of the LNG as the project is willing to sell."

"Sounds like a slam dunk," he replied. "How can I help?"

"Some roadblocks have popped up in D.C. We need you to clear them and to make sure that both of Alaska's senators are on board."

"And if I do?"

"If you do," said Chang, leaning forward so he could look down her blouse and see the tops of her breasts, "you'll be able to name your price."

CHAPTER 11

The man Harvath had killed, the man he thought he had seen getting out of a cab the day before, was Colonel Jiang Shi of the People's Liberation Army.

Jiang had worked in the PLA's intelligence division known as "Second Department" and had been in charge of China's unrestricted warfare program.

It was Jiang who had set into motion a crippling attack meant to plunge the United States into the dark ages. The attack had failed, though, because of one reason: Harvath.

To make sure Jiang would never threaten America again, Harvath had been tasked with traveling to China and ending the colonel's life, which he did in quite a graphic manner.

The killing was meant to serve as a warning to anyone and everyone intent on harming America, her people, or her allies: *There is no place you will ever be safe from her reach.*

Seeing Jiang getting out of the cab and then seeing his visage on the dash cam video had been startling, to say the least. The report he had sent back to D.C. had set off alarm bells throughout his organization, which was why his boss had reached out to the Director of Central Intelligence.

The only thing that made any sense was that Jiang had to have had a body double. After the whole plot had unraveled, the Chinese claimed that he had been operating alone and that they had no knowledge of his attack until after the fact. No one in Washington believed them.

In hopes of distancing themselves from culpability, the Chinese had willingly given him up. They had Jiang moved to a retreat for influential CCP members, had allowed Harvath into the country to carry out the deed, and had even driven him to and from the airport in a limousine. A double cross would have brought down on them the ultimate consequence. There had to be another answer, and it hadn't taken the CIA long to find it.

Jiang had a cousin who bore a remarkable resemblance to him. It was a misidentification anyone could have made—even Harvath at seventy-five feet away on the street. Just looking at the dash cam footage, it was near-impossible to say it wasn't Shi—except for one thing: his age.

Shi's face had been frozen in Harvath's mind years ago. The cousin was now the age Jiang had been when Harvath had killed him. Had the CIA not had a source inside the Second Department, they might never have solved the mystery.

But as it was, the mystery wasn't completely solved—not yet. In fact, identifying the cousin only raised more questions, particularly in light of what Han Guang did for a living. It seemed that espionage ran in the family.

Han was currently billeted to the Ministry of State Security, or MSS, in Beijing. It was considered one of the most secretive intelligence organizations in the world. His posting there was less than a year old.

He had spent two decades as a Special Forces operative, rising to the rank of captain in the PLA's naval Sea Dragon unit responsible for anti-piracy and hostage rescue near water. He cross-trained with the Snow Leopard and Mountain Eagle commando units, honing skills in anti-hijacking, bomb disposal, riot control, and counterterrorism.

For the next ten years, he had been attached to something called the People's Liberation Army Strategic Support Force. Its mission was to provide Chinese forces with the edge in space, cyber, and electronic warfare. It wasn't clear to the CIA's source what he did there, nor why he had recently made the move to MSS. All he knew was that both postings were heavily focused on "disruptive" espionage.

According to the CIA's source, Han was half spy, half highly skilled saboteur. His arrival in Oslo had put a lot of folks in D.C. on edge. One plot to destroy the caves containing America's military hardware had already been foiled. If Han had come to do something similar, or for some other nefarious purpose against the United States or Norway, they wanted to know about it. They also wanted it stopped—no matter what.

After fully briefing him and laying everything out, Holidae Hayes opened a secure video call back to D.C. On it were their bosses: Gary Lawlor, Director of The Carlton Group, and Bob McGee, Director of the Central Intelligence Agency.

Harvath was told that he would have support from Hayes, but only to the extent that she was able to give it. McGee didn't want her getting sideways with the Ambassador if it could be avoided.

Lawlor announced that he had placed Harvath's team on standby. If they were needed, they could be wheels-up immediately.

"Any questions?" McGee asked when they were done.

Harvath had one. "Can CIA officers from the Oslo station do surveillance on the Chinese Embassy?"

The DCI didn't hesitate. "No. None of them can be seen taking an active role. That includes Hayes."

"Then I'm going to need my team."

"Roger that," Lawlor replied. "We'll get them in the air."

"Anything else?" asked McGee.

Harvath wanted to know how far he could fill Sølvi in. He knew better, however, than to ask that question.

This entire thing had *diplomatic time bomb* written all over it. They hadn't inquired as to how he had secured the dash cam footage, but both McGee and Lawlor knew he was dating a Deputy Director from the Norwegian Intelligence Service. They had to suspect that she might have been his source and was therefore somewhat read in on the situation. He'd have to play things by ear.

"No," he replied. "Nothing else."

With an admonition to maintain a low profile and stay off the Norwegians' radar, his boss ended the call.

He went over a few details with Hayes, and once he had left the secure area and had retrieved his phone, he texted Sølvi again.

They had already traded texts while he was en route to the embassy.

She had been relieved to know that Martin had cut him loose and he was no longer at Kripos.

Now that his business with Hayes was wrapped up, Sølvi suggested they meet for an early lunch. She wanted to debrief with him. She also mentioned that she had something to give him. They agreed to meet in an hour.

That gave Harvath just enough time to head back to the apartment, shower, shave, and change clothes.

He hadn't noticed it last night—probably because he had been so obsessed with thinking he'd seen Colonel Shi—but as he stepped inside the apartment, it felt different.

Everything up to last night had been part vacation, part fantasy. He and Sølvi had been playing house, both of them knowing it couldn't last. Now his work life had intruded and had pierced the bubble.

He always knew he'd be leaving Oslo and returning home. It didn't matter how much he cared for Sølvi. In the back of his mind, his job had been beckoning him—quietly at first, but slowly getting louder.

It was more than a paycheck to him; it was a calling. He didn't need the money. He had more money secreted away than he could ever spend in retirement.

To her credit, Sølvi had known as well. While she didn't come right out and say it, she had understood that he was restless, that he felt he needed to get back. That it was important to him.

Just as he had appreciated her coming home for dinner last night, he appreciated her breaking away for lunch today. She was making the most of the little time they had left. As was typical of both their personalities, they would squeeze as much out of the remaining days as possible.

Sølvi had made a reservation at one of their favorite spots, hos Thea. It was a tiny, intimate restaurant in what used to be a butcher shop in the upscale Frogner area.

The chairs and tables were covered in white linen. The gray walls were adorned with oil paintings. The open kitchen functioned as a stage where the chef, who was also the restaurant's colorful owner, performed.

The menu featured extraordinary Mediterranean cuisine and was complemented by a wine list that was pitch-perfect.

As he entered, he saw Sølvi at their favorite table near the back. Even in her business attire, she looked stunning. Looking up from her phone, she smiled and gave him a wave. He smiled in return and walked back to join her.

When he arrived at their table, he bent down to give her a kiss. She placed her hand gently on the back of his neck and held him, making sure she got a nice long one.

Once she finally broke off their kiss and released him, he gave her one more quick peck before sitting down.

"You look pretty good for someone who began the morning in police custody," she said.

"I'm eating lunch with the most beautiful woman in Norway," he replied. "How could I be anything but good?"

"I bet you say that to all the Norwegian girls you have lunch with."

"But with you I mean it."

Sølvi laughed and reaching into her briefcase, removed one of her personal stationery envelopes, and handed it to him. "Happy Halloween."

"It's a little early for Halloween, isn't it?"

"Open it."

He did and saw it contained a high-capacity SD card.

"CCTV footage of your ghost."

"I love you," he said. "You know that, right?"

"I bet you say that to all the Norwegian girls who bend data privacy laws for you."

"Only the hot ones."

She pressed her hand to her chest, feigning pride, before saying, "There's a couple of things on the footage we need to talk about."

"Such as?"

"You need to work a bit harder not getting caught on camera."

He laughed. "The only way not to get caught on camera in Oslo is to live in Bergen."

"We never did make it to Bergen," she lamented with a smile. "Such a beautiful city."

"I'll bet you our lunch bill that my face doesn't show up anywhere on this footage."

"Neither does your ghost's. You both did an admirable job of not looking at any of the cameras. If I hadn't seen what you were wearing yesterday, I wouldn't have been able to tell it was you. Same with him. If a camera hadn't picked him up getting out of the taxi, it would have been impossible to track him."

"How about facial recognition?" he asked. "You've got his face from the dash cam video. Any chance you could run it against Norwegian customs and immigration?"

"Already done. It's on the disc. Along with a scan of the passport he used. He's traveling under the name Zhang Wei."

"Well done. Thank you. Lunch is on me."

"You're damn right it is. Plus, I'm going to pick the best bottle of wine they have, we're each going to enjoy one glass, and then you're going to take the remainder of the bottle home to my place and put it in the fridge for later."

"Done."

A waitress came over to take their order, but they hadn't even looked at the menu yet. Sølvi asked her to give them a few more minutes.

Once the woman had left the table, Sølvi turned back to Harvath and said, "There's something else that came up on the footage."

"What did you see?"

"Not a what but a who."

"Okay, *who*?"

"Yevgeny Sarov."

"Never heard of him," said Harvath.

"He's a Russian Consul General to Norway. His consulate is in a tiny Norwegian town, which I am positive you also haven't heard of. In fact, if you have, then I'll buy *you* lunch."

"Try me."

"It's a coastal village, up above the Arctic Circle, called Kirkenes."

Instead of responding, Harvath waved the waitress back over. "I'd like to see the wine list, please." As the waitress walked away to fetch one, he turned to Sølvi and said, "I hope you brought your credit card."

CHAPTER 12

"How do you know about Kirkenes?" Sølvi asked, amazed. "We've never even discussed it."

"No, but Holidae and I have."

"When?"

"This morning, actually."

"What did she tell you?"

"That the Chinese are trying to buy their way into the Arctic. That they have their eyes set on Kirkenes as the European port for their Polar Silk Route. And that Norway doesn't like America trying to get involved."

"Anything else?" she asked, taking the wine list from Harvath and opening it up to the whites.

"Yes," he said, leaning toward her, almost obscuring the list from her view. "She mentioned the deal has been put on hold because the parties are having problems with something called the Arctic corridor. Apparently, they could unload the ships in Kirkenes, but for the project to work, they need high-speed rail lines to be constructed. They can't get those rail lines approved because of staunch resistance from the Sámi."

"Really?" she replied, appearing more interested in the wine list than him.

"Yes. It seems a very cleverly crafted piece of misinformation steeled the entire Sámi population against it. Something about the Chinese allegedly attempting to bioengineer a sickness to kill all the Sámi reindeer."

"Hmmmmm," she said distractedly. "Fascinating."

He knew her too well. Their mentors had been close friends and had been cut from the same cloth.

When her mentor had been killed, she had been tapped to take over for him and run the NIS division he had created. It was a highly creative, outside-the-box department, less bound by rules and regulations than anything else in Norwegian Intelligence. It was very similar to what he was doing with The Carlton Group.

"It's more than fascinating," he said. "It's brilliant."

"I know what you're thinking," she replied, looking up and nodding to the waitress that she was ready to make a selection. "Something that brilliant had to have come from the mind of a really smart, *really* good-looking Norwegian."

"Or someone really sick and twisted who probably doesn't get asked on a lot of dates."

"As the most beautiful woman in Norway, I couldn't possibly know what that's like."

He was about to reply, when the waitress showed up to take their order. Sølvi indicated what wine she wanted as well as what she'd be having for lunch.

Harvath hadn't had much time to peruse the menu, but when he saw the words *Lamb Shank*, he was sold.

Handing his menu back, he waited for the waitress to be out of ear-shot before asking, "Is it common practice for the Norwegian Intelligence Service to interfere with foreign investment in Norway?"

"First," she replied. "I have no idea what you're talking about. Second, Norway is at a crossroads. China's retribution for the Nobel Peace Prize was very painful economically. Now that relations have begun to normalize, there are certain politicians who will say yes to anything China asks, just to avoid a repeat.

"In addition, there are still other politicians who were avowed lovers of China before the prize was awarded. These two groups have begun to knit themselves together. Standing in the breach is a more realistic group of politicians who want to make sure Norway's security is put first."

"And which group do you answer to?"

Sølvi smiled. "As always, I answer to Odin and only Odin."

Harvath smiled back. Odin was the king of the Norse gods. It was also the call sign for Ivar Stang, Director of the Norwegian Intelligence Service. The moniker was highly apropos, considering that the coat of arms for the NIS depicted two ravens: Huginn and Muninn—Thought and Mind—which, according to Norse mythology, were said to bring Odin his information.

Harvath sensed it was about as much of an answer as he was going to get on the subject, so he changed tack. "What can you tell me about Kirkenes and Yevgeny Sarov?"

"He was an interesting choice for a diplomatic position."

"How so?"

"He had only one previous posting. In Kazakhstan. Less than a year."

"What did he do before that?"

"I'll give you one guess," she said.

"Russian Intelligence."

"Smart boy," she replied.

"What branch?" he asked.

"Main Intelligence Directorate."

Known as the GRU, they were Russia's military intelligence unit and considered Russia's largest foreign intelligence agency. They were also its most dangerous, and Harvath hated them with a passion.

They had murdered three people very dear to him: his wife, Lara; his mentor, Reed Carlton; and his close friend and colleague Lydia Ryan, who had been running The Carlton Group.

It was said, "Once a GRU operative, always a GRU operative." If this Sarov character was up to anything nefarious, Harvath would have no problem taking him out, along with Han.

"How big a town is Kirkenes?" he asked.

"It's small. About two square kilometers."

"How many inhabitants?"

"Around three thousand five hundred."

"So why do the Russians have a consulate there?"

"Kirkenes sits on a peninsula at the farthest northeastern part of Norway near the Russian-Norwegian border. Norwegians cross over into

Russia to buy cheaper gas, cigarettes, and alcohol, and Russians cross over into Norway to buy diapers and Apple products that they can sell for a markup back home.

"People also go back and forth to visit friends and relatives. If you live within fifty kilometers of either side of the border, you are entitled to a special border crossing permit. Anyone else needs a specific tourist visa. Officially, that's why the Russian Consulate exists. The Norwegians have their own consulate on the other side, in Murmansk."

"Unofficially, what's the reason the Russian Consulate exists?"

"To provide support for its network of spies in the region."

"How many spies are we talking about?"

"We project, on any given day, that there are up to five hundred Russian citizens in Kirkenes and the surrounding border area. How many of them are spies? That's much harder to ascertain."

"How do you even watch that many people?"

"It's impossible. We don't have the manpower. It's also contrary to Norwegian values. If we followed every single Russian tourist that entered our country, we'd be no better than the old Soviet Union."

"Agreed, but other than border defenses, what's there for anyone to see on your side, much less spy on?"

Sølvi raised her eyebrows. "You don't know?"

"I'm a little rusty on far-flung villages. It took me all summer just to find a good place in Oslo for margaritas. Humor me."

"Vardø, the easternmost town in Norway. It sits on an island called Vardøya, which is connected to the mainland by tunnel. Vardø is home to a joint Norwegian Intelligence Service and American National Security Agency radar system called GLOBUS."

"The one that the Russians have been freaking out over?" he asked, familiar with the system that monitored Russian naval activity, just not its precise geographic location in Norway.

"That's it. In fact, the newest iteration, GLOBUS 3, has just been constructed and brought online. In protest, the Russians moved their SSC-6 coastal missile system to the Sredny Peninsula, just seventy kilometers from Vardø."

"But the SSC-6 is a supersonic anti-ship cruise missile."

"Which can also take out land targets," she clarified, "up to one hundred and fifty kilometers away."

"Putting the GLOBUS facility directly within striking distance."

Sølvi nodded. "Moscow believes the system unfairly upends the balance of power. Their Arctic submarine fleet has always been their insurance policy. If Russia was ever hit with a nuclear attack, they could order the subs to sea and, just off their enemy's shore, retaliate with a nuclear strike of their own. Via Vardø and the GLOBUS system, that capability has now been eroded. They cannot come or go without us knowing what they're up to. Figuring out a way to move their submarines undetected has become a top priority."

"No doubt, but what's the point of repositioning the coastal missile system?" asked Harvath. "If Russia hits GLOBUS, that's immediately an act of war, and the first thing we're going to assume is that they did it to hide submarine movements."

"True, but by then the horse, so to speak, is out of the barn. And once those subs are out of their barns, they're much harder to track and interdict."

"How do you know it's not just posturing by the Russians?"

"It could be," she allowed. "They're bullies. They like to flex their muscles and try to intimidate us. Recently, they launched bombers from the Kola Peninsula and conducted mock runs on Vardø."

Harvath shook his head. These kinds of acts were straight out of the Russian playbook and provocative as hell. They were also an impotent version of chest thumping. The Russians had done similar, dangerously close stunts against American fighters, bombers, and ships in international waters. It said more about Russia's increasing weakness than its strength. But that weakness made them unpredictable and even more dangerous. Some experts felt that a nuclear confrontation was more likely now than at any point during the Cold War.

"Did they cross into Norwegian airspace?" he asked.

"No. They didn't have to. They came right up to the line, which was close enough to launch their weapons had they wanted to while still being over their own territory."

She was right to be concerned. In a war with Russia, it was the prevailing belief that Russia would mount such devastating attacks on America's allies that America would seek to de-escalate before nukes started landing on New York, D.C., Miami, and Chicago.

The Russians, like the Chinese, were devious. Not as smart, but devious nonetheless. An attack on Vardø, early on in a conflict, would buy them some valuable time to get their subs to sea and heighten the fear factor for the United States.

Pivoting back to Han, he asked, "Does the CCTV footage show my guy meeting with Sarov or just in the same area?"

"We're not like London with its ring of steel. There aren't cameras on *every* corner. They were both just seen in the same area. But, to be honest, I don't think it's a coincidence."

"Neither do I," he replied, deciding to read her in. "So why would my guy, who isn't a ghost, by the way—"

"He's not? Who is he?"

"Captain Han Guang. He works for China's Ministry of State Security. Former Special Operations. Looks exactly like the person I was sent after. Apparently, they're cousins."

"He's a spy, then?"

Harvath nodded. "And also, according to our sources, a saboteur."

"So why is he in Norway, hanging around the same neighborhood as the Russian Consul General from Kirkenes?" she wondered aloud.

"That's the exact question I'd like to ask him myself."

"First, you'd have to find him."

"What about his passport? Was it diplomatic or a standard People's Republic of China?"

"Standard People's Republic."

"Do Chinese citizens need a visa to visit Norway?" he asked.

"They do. His was processed by the Norwegian Consulate General in Guangzhou over a month ago. I checked."

"His trip was planned, then. Not spur-of-the-moment. And while there's nothing stopping him from staying at the Chinese Ambassador's residence here in Oslo, if the MSS didn't go to the trouble of providing him with a diplomatic passport, they probably aren't going to risk tying him directly to the Ambassador as a guest."

"Which means," said Sølvi, "he's either in a hotel under the name on his passport, or a safe house."

"Do you have a way of checking hotel registrations?"

"I do, but I'd rather not."

"Why not?"

"Gathering CCTV footage in light of our privacy laws is one thing. It's not easy, but the rules are not as rigorous. The taxi video was more difficult and I had to use a cutout for that, but it was doable. When you call a hotel and ask about a guest, though, the request gets elevated to a manager. The manager then has the responsibility to confirm which law enforcement agency they are speaking with and to confirm the name and department of the officer making the request."

"In other words, it's a real bureaucratic pain in the ass."

"More than that," she said. "It's too easy to get caught. But there is another way."

"What is it?" he asked as he saw the waitress approaching with their bottle of wine.

"Finding a needle in a haystack is all about correctly identifying the haystack. I think I can get you that far, but then you're going to need a specialist, somebody really skilled in IT. I believe you have someone who fits that bill."

Harvath nodded. He did have someone all right. In fact, he had the absolute best.

The only question was whether or not, at 50,000 feet over the Atlantic Ocean, traveling at Mach 0.925 toward Norway, the little man could summon enough computing power.

CHAPTER 13

Harvath didn't want to waste any time. Clinking glasses with Sølvi, he took one sip of wine before stepping outside to make a call.

"How critical is it?" Nicholas asked over the encrypted satellite phone aboard The Carlton Group's new Gulfstream G700.

"Priority one," Harvath replied. "It may prove to be our best chance of getting the jump on Han. Can you do it in-flight?"

A semi-reformed hacker, Nicholas had once made quite a lucrative career for himself in the purchase, sale, and theft of highly sensitive black-market intelligence. He now functioned as the team's IT specialist, and Sølvi had a theory that might help identify their haystack.

There were a handful of hotels in Oslo that went out of their way to cater to Chinese tourists. They made sure to include certain Chinese comfort foods on their menus, understood and were respectful of Chinese culture, always kept at least one staff member on duty around the clock who spoke Chinese, and aggressively marketed to tour companies in China.

If Han was half the spy they believed him to be, he would hide in plain sight. He would rely on weak, undiscerning Western eyes to lump all the Chinese faces they encountered into a single indistinguishable blur. The best place for a single tree not to be seen was in the middle of a forest. Sølvi was certain he would choose one of the hotels on her list.

Nicholas sat his less-than-three-foot-tall frame in one of the jet's plush, leather chairs. His giant dogs, Argos and Draco, lay on the carpeted cabin floor at his feet. "Several of the hotels you've given me are chains, which means they'll have their own essential reservation systems. The boutiques will have contracted it out."

"Can you access them?"

"Given enough time," the little man said, opening his laptop and checking a banking balance. "Though there might be an express route we can take."

"Tell me," said Harvath.

"The first step would be to search for log-ins and passwords for sale on the dark web. If we can find any that would grant us access to the systems, we're golden."

"And if you can't find any?"

"I've got a pretty sophisticated group out of Belarus that can quickly assemble a down-and-dirty phishing campaign. We direct it at each hotel in question. It'll take more money and some extra time, but it can provide more than just reservation info. If we get someone on staff to bite, we can access that hotel's 'bible,' their property management system, which will give us all the guests' personal info as well as what rooms they're in."

"Get started on both."

"Will do," said Nicholas. "And just to be on the safe side, I need you to reach out to Lawlor and have him double the amount in the cryptocurrency account."

"I'll send him a message now," Harvath replied. "Reach out to me when you have something."

After ending the call, he sent a message to Lawlor with Nicholas's request. As soon as he received confirmation that it was in process, he stepped back inside the restaurant and rejoined Sølvi.

"Everything good?" she asked.

"Nicholas liked your idea," he replied, sitting back down. "He's already working on it."

"What idea? I didn't give you anything."

Harvath smiled. "Right. I forgot. My bad."

Touching glasses once more, they enjoyed their lunch before skipping dessert and both heading in opposite directions.

• • •

Back at the apartment, Harvath tucked the bottle of Montrachet in the fridge and set up his laptop on the kitchen island.

On the opposite counter, a digital photo frame cycled through pictures he and Sølvi had taken over the summer. They certainly had made a lot of memories.

As his computer came to life, he poured himself a cup of coffee, plugged in his SD card reader, and inserted the card Sølvi had handed him.

After only a few minutes of watching the footage, it was clear that Han was trying to throw off any surveillance he might have had. Harvath particularly liked the reversible two-color blazer he was wearing, which could also become a vest when the detachable sleeves were removed.

So where the hell was he headed—and why was he so intent on not being followed?

Harvath rolled backward and forward through the footage, paying close attention to what happened after he stepped out of the taxi.

He watched as Han walked and he followed. All of it textbook. Then had come the grand boulevard, the tram, and the moment Han had effectively disappeared. There was no further footage—no indication of where he had gone.

The CCTV streams then switched to a figure identified as Yevgeny Sarov, the Russian Consul General to Kirkenes, walking in the same area. Sølvi had been kind enough to intersperse both streams of footage with map overlays indicating where the videos had been taken.

As he had done with the previous imagery, Harvath slowly moved backward and forward, looking for any sort of clue to tell him what was going on.

Sarov was out of shape and a good fifty pounds overweight. He probably wasn't a fan of walking. The measures he took to check for a tail were perfunctory and appeared to be more out of habit than anything else. He suffered from laziness, an affliction that struck many Russian operatives late in their careers.

Two spies, from two different countries, both within blocks of each other and both running surveillance detection routes. It absolutely wasn't a coincidence. These guys were on their way to a meet. But the questions still remained: Where? And for what? For the life of him, Harvath couldn't figure it out.

He continued to review the footage, hoping to find something that would answer his questions. But after years of doing this, he knew that it was futile.

Even if he could find the location where they had met, it would be a dry hole.

These two were good. Harvath would have to be better.

CHAPTER 14

The very private 116 Club was where the capital's elite came for lunch. Located in a nondescript red town house two blocks from the Hart Senate Office Building, it was referred to as the "political power broker paradise"; a place where neither God nor the media could see you. Its membership roster was one of the most closely guarded secrets in D.C.

The club's specialty was something called "Crab & Crab"—crab served two ways—and it was Spencer Baldwin's favorite.

Despite having gorged himself on seafood on his flight out to California, as well as his midnight flight home, he was hungry for more. "I'll have my usual," he said to the waiter. "And bring us a bottle of the Sancerre. Extra-cold. Lots of ice in the bucket."

As the waiter disappeared to place their orders and fetch the wine, Baldwin turned to his thirty-five-year-old guest, Ethan Russ. Russ was chief of staff to Alaska's senior senator. "How is Senator Dwyer?"

"Doing well," he replied. "We appreciated your help with the last election."

"You ran a good race. And she has done an excellent job for Alaska. I don't think there was ever any doubt."

Russ smiled. "All I can say is that I'm glad we only have to go through it every six years. That primary challenger came out of nowhere and cost us time and money we didn't think we were going to have to spend."

"Nevertheless, you brought it home. Congratulations."

"Thank you. So, of all the people you could be eating lunch with today, how did I draw the golden ticket?"

"I enjoyed working with you and I think you have a bright future ahead. You're smart, aggressive, experienced. Chief of staff for Senator Katie Dwyer isn't your ultimate destination. It's a stop along the way, a springboard to get you to something else. I'm just wondering what that something else might be. A political career of your own? Maybe run for the state legislature back in Juneau?"

Again Russ smiled. "Maybe."

"*Maybe*, my ass," Baldwin replied with a chuckle. "House or Senate?"

"There's a House member retiring in my district. I've been thinking about it."

"Have you talked with the senator?"

He nodded. "She thinks I should go for it."

"What's the competition look like?"

"A local businessman with some pretty serious name ID."

"Sounds like it could shape up to be an expensive race."

"That's the problem," admitted Russ.

Baldwin paused their conversation as the waiter returned with the Sancerre. Once the bottle had been opened, the wine tasted and poured, he said, "What if financing for your campaign wasn't a problem?"

"For a first-time candidate?"

"Humor me."

The younger man thought for a moment. "If I knew the financing was going to be there, it would definitely move me closer to running. What are you suggesting?"

"There's something I need. If you can make it happen, I can get you all the campaign cash you need."

With thoughts of Lindsey Chang playing seductively across his mind, along with visions of how much his bank account was going to swell, he leaned back in his chair and took a self-satisfied sip of wine. *God damn, I'm good at this game. A master, in fact.*

But had his arrogance not been so incandescent, he might have noticed the subtle shift in the chief of staff's expression.

And had he noticed that shift, he might have grasped the dangerous door that had just been opened and through which he had already stepped.

CHAPTER 15

While Nicholas worked on locating Han, Harvath did a deep dive, trying to figure out what the Chinese and Russians might be up to together—beyond their nearly identical voting record on the UN Security Council.

Russia was the world's largest supplier of oil and natural gas. The majority of its reserves were in the Arctic. And while Russia had been blessed with amazing resources, it had simultaneously been cursed with scarce means to deliver those resources.

Instead of flowing south into Central Asia, the rivers of Siberia flowed north into the Arctic Ocean. Everything, up to and including using nuclear weapons to reverse their flow, had been considered and subsequently abandoned.

Enter the Chinese. They had not only funded 20 percent of a massive liquified natural gas plant above the Arctic Circle on Russia's Yamal Peninsula while insisting that 80 percent of the equipment be manufactured in China; they had helped build an 1,100-kilometer pipeline across Siberia, terminating in Shanghai.

The Chinese were said to especially love this pipeline because it provided fuel that could never be interdicted by the U.S. Navy or frozen by the U.S. Treasury.

Writing the high points down on a yellow Post-it Note, Harvath stuck it to the wall of Sølvi's dining room and went back to his research.

In addition to its two diesel-powered polar icebreakers—*Snow*

Dragon 1 and *Snow Dragon 2*, China had recently drawn up plans to build its first nuclear icebreaker. The only other country to have fielded nuclear icebreakers was Russia, which had the largest fleet of icebreakers in the world—forty in total, eight of them nuclear-powered, with three new breakers currently under construction and a dozen more planned over the next ten years.

The United States, though, had zero nuclear icebreakers. In fact, the United States only owned one heavy icebreaker—the USCGC *Polar Star*—notorious for breaking down in the middle of assignments, and one medium icebreaker—the USCGC *Healy*, which had recently caught fire and been taken out of service, creating a severe dilemma.

The *Polar Star*'s area of operations had been in the southern hemisphere and included resupplying the McMurdo research station in Antarctica. The *Healy*'s area of operations had been patrolling the Arctic. The U.S. was way behind the power curve. America needed to scale up—*fast*.

On top of commissioning the construction of six new icebreakers, the National Security Advisor had helped move money from the United States Navy to the Coast Guard in order to lease two privately owned icebreakers. After a coat of Coast Guard orange paint and .50 caliber machine guns, rigid inflatable boats, and a SCIF were installed on each, the vessels were to be immediately placed in service.

While China waited for its nuclear icebreaker to come online, it kept *Snow Dragon 1* and *Snow Dragon 2* in heavy, visible rotation throughout the Arctic.

The fact that the Chinese were pursuing a nuclear icebreaker spooked a lot of people. It would be their first nuclear-powered surface ship and was seen as a bridge to nuclear aircraft carriers. In its territorial waters, China had no need for nuclear aircraft carriers. Those were what you outfitted a navy with that wanted to project force abroad. It was perfectly in keeping with China's desire to position itself as a global power.

Once China had those carriers, it could position them wherever they wanted, including in the Arctic. And if anyone tried to complain, they could say they were just protecting their interests while simultaneously ensuring that sea-lanes remained open and secure. As this was something the United States did, America would have a hard time arguing against China. The polar bear would then be fully in the tent. Harvath added another Post-it Note to the wall.

Ninety percent of all global trade sailed over the world's oceans, and its volume was expected to double over the next fifteen years. With less and less ice, along with the ability to connect almost 75 percent of the world's population, it made sense that much of that trade was going to go through the Arctic.

The fact that Russia had opened up over fifty previously shuttered Soviet military facilities was cause enough for concern. That they were pouring troops and arms into the Arctic only raised the concern higher. Add in the Chinese, and Harvath could see no upside for America and her allies.

In addition to oil and natural gas reserves, there were said to be one trillion dollars' worth of extremely scarce, extremely valuable rare earth minerals in the Arctic. At present, China controlled 80 percent of the global output of these seventeen elements found near the bottom of the periodic table.

Used in everything high-tech from smart phones to F-35 fighter jets, they were considered crucial for modern society and absolutely critical for U.S. national security. Allowing an increasingly belligerent China access to any more of the world's supply was out of the question. America was already too dependent on Chinese manufacturing chains as it was. It needed to wean itself off them as quickly and as fully as possible.

Despite what China might claim its Arctic intentions to be, the next piece Harvath read, detailing its behavior in Antarctica, reinforced that it categorically couldn't be trusted.

In an article in *Forbes*, the United States National Security Advisor—the same man who had arranged for the leasing of icebreakers until new ones could be built—was quoted at length about China's aggressive expansionism on the southernmost continent.

They had been "stress-testing" the Antarctic Treaty for years, their violations growing more and more egregious. Most concerning was that they had been conducting stealth military activities, were assembling a case for a territorial claim, and were engaging in exploration for minerals—all three of which were expressly forbidden in the Antarctic Treaty.

While all treaty members were required to submit to a thorough and often lengthy approval process before beginning any form of construction, the Chinese had just started construction on a fifth "research" station without bothering to notify anyone.

Just as galling as smuggling in soldiers disguised as scientists, the Chinese now wanted a special 20,000-square-kilometer air defense-style identification zone imposed around its tiny seasonal research camp known as Kunlun Station. Kunlun was located on one of the most scientifically and militarily useful sites on the Antarctic ice sheet. The request was outrageous.

Unfortunately, the U.S. was the only treaty member pushing back. The other nations were either too soft or too myopic to recognize and counter the threat.

China wanted Antarctica for itself and was taking the necessary steps to get there. The Chinese were quite savvy when it came to taking advantage of underregulated geopolitical environments. There was no reason not to believe that what they had done in Antarctica they would do all over again up north in the Arctic.

In fact, it had already started. Not only did the Chinese have a research station on the Norwegian archipelago of Svalbard, but they had also managed to finagle "observer" status on the Arctic Council—the intergovernmental forum of the eight Arctic states. There didn't seem to be a tent anywhere without a polar bear.

Harvath looked at his watch. It was just after six p.m. The team was still an hour away from touching down. Picking up his notepad, he went over the list of tasks he needed to complete.

His cottage out on the fjord was too small to accommodate everyone, so Hayes had helped to arrange a different property. It was outside of the city center, with a walled courtyard and a gate. She had given him the alarm code and let him know where a set of keys were hidden. There were towels and linens at the house, but groceries would be his responsibility.

To sneak all of their gear into the country, not to mention Nicholas's dogs, the team would be landing at Værnes Air Station in Stjørdal.

Værnes was the primary airport for the United States Marine Corps Prepositioning Program–Norway, whereby American military equipment rotated in and out of a jointly operated series of secret cave complexes throughout the Trondheim region. Because of the sensitive nature of some of the weapon systems, as well as some of the personnel who transited through Værnes, occasionally customs and passport control formalities could be waived. This evening was one such occasion.

From Værnes, which was in central Norway, it was a short hop to Oslo Airport. There, on the private aviation side, three full-size SUVs would be waiting. As soon as the team had loaded the vehicles, they would drive to the safe house and link up with Harvath.

After shutting down his computer and packing his bag, he left the apartment and headed downstairs to retrieve his car.

He had already told Sølvi what he was up to. She was no fan of the Chinese government and even less enamored of its intelligence services. Her job was to be skeptical of everyone. Loosely translated as "Strategy Section," her division at NIS was all about thinking outside the box. *Way outside* the box.

The Strategy Section was not just mandated to disappear and create a shadow intelligence agency in case of invasion; it was also charged with envisioning attacks and developing defenses before they could take place. Her program reminded him of the Red Cell units back in the United States.

He trusted her as much as he trusted Holidae Hayes. More so, in fact. He and Sølvi had been in the field together and he had seen how she operated under pressure. He'd had no reservations about filling her in on his plans.

No one knew what Han was doing in Norway and why he had linked up with Sarov. The Norwegians should have been very interested in getting to the bottom of it, but—absent some explosive revelation—they weren't going to risk getting on Beijing's bad side again.

That was one of the reasons Sølvi had been slipping him the intelligence he had asked for. No matter how much normalized relations with China meant to Norway, she couldn't let it risk national security.

She also trusted him and knew that he was exceptional at handling something this sensitive. If his involvement became known, he'd take the proverbial bullet. He would never burn her or implicate her government.

Having him on the job provided plausible deniability. He was as tenacious as a pit bull. Once he started, there was no stopping him until he had clamped his jaws down on what he was after and wrestled it to the ground.

Just as valuable as Harvath's tenacity was his intelligence and operational experience. He wasn't merely a blunt instrument. He was highly adept at seeing what might be coming next and improvising on the fly— at adapting and overcoming. It was one of his best attributes.

Arriving at his car, an Audi convertible he had leased for the summer, he tossed his bag and the backpack with his laptop in the trunk and slid into the driver's seat.

Plugging in his phone, he hit the ignition button and dropped the top. There was nothing that said he couldn't enjoy the trip for groceries and then the drive to the safe house. After all, these could very well be the last moments of peace the Fates had in store for him.

CHAPTER 16

Han Guang wasn't feeling well—and it was more than just his unsettling suspicion that he had been followed yesterday.

He had brought medication to help him deal with the increasing pain in his right hip area. The doctor, whom he had paid cash to see, had wanted to send him for more tests, specifically an X-ray, but Han wasn't interested. He didn't have the time. Things were moving too fast and he had needed to be on his way to Norway.

The doctor wrote him a prescription and then, as agreed, turned over all of the notes from his visit. There would be no record.

While it was unpleasant to be in pain, Han had chalked it up to several possibilities: a particularly bad parachute jump he'd had fifteen years ago, a physically demanding career in the Chinese Special Forces, or the rigorous jogging routine he followed. Any one of those things could have been the culprit.

Then there was the inescapable truth that he was growing older. With age, he had been told, comes wisdom *and* pain. They never tell you, though, what form the pain takes.

He had always assumed that it would manifest itself as regret—a feeling of loss over bad decisions and roads not taken. His life had certainly been full of both.

But as he had been leaving the clinic, the doctor put a hand on his shoulder and stopped him. Yes, he explained, his pain could have been the result of a bad parachute jump, a physically demanding career, or overdoing it on his runs. It also could be something much more serious. *Cancer.*

Despite being a hardened person, someone who had seen humanity at its worst and who was unafraid of taking human life, Han had recoiled at the word.

Both of his parents had died from cancer. His older brother and sister too. They had all been smokers. So was he.

He knew he shouldn't be—not with his family's history—but he hadn't been able to stop. He had grown up in a family of smokers. There wasn't a single photograph from his youth where at least one person wasn't smoking. They were Chinese. It was what they did. Not to do so would have been odd, unusual. And once you started, it was incredibly difficult to stop.

Nevertheless, he had tried to trim things back and was only smoking four or five cigarettes a day. He had also increased the intensity of his runs and, as an added precaution, had even begun wearing a mask to protect himself from the polluted Beijing air.

The pain *had* to be injury-related, or perhaps arthritis. It wasn't cancer. He was certain of it. This was an overzealous doctor, and doctors, in his experience, only had two speeds: scold and panic. For the moment, the pills were working, helping to minimize the pain. He'd make room in his schedule for an X-ray once he returned to Beijing. Right now, he needed to be completely focused on his assignment.

His superiors had been adamant that this mission be successful. It had the attention of the people at the very top of the government. He knew better than to disappoint the Politburo. His cousin, a colonel in PLA intelligence, had disappointed them once and had never been seen or heard from again.

Han didn't mind a difficult assignment. What he minded was when a difficult assignment was rushed. And that's what was happening here.

He preferred the luxury of slipping into a country and getting a feel for things before starting. The Russians, though, had moved up the timetable.

The United States Navy's secretive, high-tech submarine the USS *Seawolf* had recently conducted a very unusual and very public port visit to the Norwegian town of Tromsø.

It came amid speculation that the Norwegians had leased Olavsvern, a decommissioned, secret submarine base nearby, to the Americans. Though the base, carved into a mountain along the Balsfjorden, had been closed for more than a decade, Russian Intelligence operatives had uncovered multiple visits by United States Navy personnel over the past year.

The idea that the base might be reopened and that such an advanced submarine might be berthed there, so close to the Russian border, did not sit well with Moscow. Activity in the Arctic was heating up faster than they forecasted, and they intended to maintain superiority. The Chinese would help them do just that.

Han had mixed feelings about the Russians. They fielded some good fighters, but their technology was substandard. In addition, they were a tribe of brutes. As brutes, they lacked a stratum of capable, scientific professionals.

The thing that fascinated him the most was that the Russians couldn't build proper tools. Hammers? Sure. Wrenches? Yes, but not to precision standards. The finer the accuracy required, the better the chance the Russians would screw it up. It was why they had such difficulty putting, and keeping, satellites in space.

From the *Kursk* submarine catastrophe to the detonation of a failed nuclear cruise missile they were trying to retrieve from the bottom of the White Sea, year after year, Russian incompetence had proven to be the rule rather than the exception. How they even maintained their nuclear stockpiles, much less avoided another Chernobyl disaster, was beyond him.

But that incompetence was exactly what had made Beijing's proposition so appealing. China could offer Russia something it needed and that it would never be able to build for itself—a way to cloak its submarines.

The Northern Fleet was about to engage in a substantial naval exercise. Two subs and a group of surface vessels were to leave port on the Kola Peninsula, headed for a choke point in the North Atlantic known as the Greenland–Iceland–United Kingdom Gap.

Moscow wanted proof of concept, certification that the cloaking technology, code-named Black Ice, could do what Beijing claimed. If the test was successful, all Chinese vessels—commercial and, upon proper advance notification, military—would be granted passage through the Northern Sea Route.

It was the ultimate win-win for both nations. All Han had to do was to make sure the test went off without a hitch.

Before that could happen, he had to iron out the logistics, which was why he was in Oslo.

Chinese Special Forces, disguised as research scientists, had already been dispatched to the Svalbard archipelago above the Arctic Circle. Another, smaller contingent, with the help of Consul General Sarov, was in place in Kirkenes.

Details about how the proof of concept would take place was why he and Sarov had met the previous day.

Their governments had agreed that confirmation needed to be via a third party—someone not Russian and not Chinese. Their first choice was to have it be done through an American or, barring that, a Norwegian.

Neither nation's intelligence service, though, wanted to lay all of their cards on the table and reveal what American and Norwegian agencies they had penetrated and to what depth.

Han was a fierce negotiator. The tech being offered to the Russians was of significant military value to them. Norway was their backyard. They had undoubtedly turned more assets here than China. It made sense that Moscow should use someone it had on the inside to confirm the proof of concept.

Sarov couldn't argue. The man's reasoning was sound. He told his Chinese colleague that he would contact his superiors and get back to him. Then they left the meeting, each going his own way.

The next morning, Han received a message. They would be meeting again tonight. Time and place to be determined.

With the day off, Han had wandered near the hotel, taking care not to put too much wear and tear on his hip.

The hotel had a pool and so, late in the afternoon, he had taken a swim. The exercise had been enough to get his heart rate up, but not anything to have caused him pain.

He followed it up with a sauna and shower, after which he stood looking at his reflection in the mirror.

He wasn't a handsome man. The years hadn't been kind to him. Han didn't care. The creases in his face, the lines at the corners of his eyes— these were chapters in the book of his life. The scars peppering his body were testimonials, firsthand accounts of his survival.

They each told a different story, but all had the same ending: No matter what obstacle had been placed in his path, no matter how dangerous, he had always come out on top.

Back in his room, he got dressed, ordered in a light meal, and lay on top of his bed, resting, as he waited for Sarov to contact him.

It wasn't his preferred method of doing business—being at the mercy of another country's intelligence service—but he had been recruited by the MSS because they knew he was the best.

If the proof of concept worked—and Beijing had no reason to believe it wouldn't—it meant a huge leap forward for China. And they would have risked next to nothing.

They were using Russian naval assets and as such were rolling *Russian* dice. There were much worse ways to test a revolutionary piece of military technology.

If it scared the hell out of the Americans in the process—which it should—that would just be icing on the cake.

CHAPTER 17

Harvath had just entered the checkout line, pushing an over-loaded grocery cart while dragging another behind, when his phone chimed. Nicholas had an update for him.

"What did you find?" he asked as he began unloading the carts for the checkout clerk.

"First of all, thanks for making it easy."

"What do you mean, *easy*?"

"I'm being facetious. The name Han Guang is using, Zhang Wei, is the equivalent of John Smith. There are hundreds of thousands of them. It's the most common name in all of China."

"How many in Norway?"

"Right now? Six."

"And in Oslo?"

"Two."

They were narrowing it down. Harvath was encouraged. "And which of those two arrived yesterday?"

"Both of them," Nicholas repeated. "They came in on the same flight."

"What about hotels?"

"We caught a break. They're both at the Radisson Blu Plaza on Sonja Henies Plass."

"I know it," he said, drawing the clerk's attention to the cases of water underneath the cart that needed to be scanned. "Do you have room numbers or passport information?"

"Not yet," the little man replied. "I'm still working on it."

It was great information. They had come a long way in winnowing down the haystack. Now they knew which hotel their needle was in.

"I'm going to drop the groceries off at the house and then position myself in the lobby," he said. "Let me know when you are wheels down in Oslo."

After disconnecting the call, he paid for everything, got it bagged, and loaded it into his car. The supplies took up the trunk as well as a portion of the backseat.

Via GPS, he drove to the safe house. There, locating the keys, he opened the front gate, drove into the courtyard, and parked.

The house was old and somewhat musty, but it would do. It was a five-star palace compared to some of the places he had spent the night in.

It took a few minutes to unload everything, but once the task was complete, he texted Sølvi, hopped into his car, and exited out onto the street.

After locking everything back up and stashing the keys in a new hiding spot, he then headed for the Radisson.

Until Nicholas had ascertained which two rooms their Zhang Weis were in, all they could do was general surveillance.

Even once they had narrowed it down to the exact room, it was hard to foresee anything other than layering in electronic measures. And that would depend upon what kind of equipment Nicholas had brought with him.

Their standard kit was pretty good. Nothing like what the NSA people used, but solid nonetheless. The problem would be translating any communications that weren't in English. Nicholas supposedly had access to a group of interpreters at Langley and they were said to be standing by in case they were needed.

Without evidence of an imminent threat, there wasn't much more Harvath and his team could do beyond watching and listening. Though they had run plenty of snatch operations against bad actors, this hadn't risen to that level. Yet.

Pulling up to the Radisson, he withdrew the biggest banknote he had and asked the valet to keep the car close.

At thirty-seven stories, it was the tallest building in Oslo. Sølvi had brought him here for dinner shortly after he had arrived in Norway. The views from the hotel's signature restaurant on the thirty-fourth floor were incredible.

As he entered the hotel through the automatic revolving door, he was awash in a sea of marble. From the dramatic floating staircase and massive columns to the gleaming floors and tasteful black-and-white-striped walls and front desk, the Radisson Blu was an homage to modern Scandinavian design.

He found a seat in the lobby bar with an unobstructed view and sat down. When the waitress came over, he ordered a coffee.

As she walked away, he studied the stream of tourists, most of whom appeared to be on their way out to dinner or returning from a long day of sightseeing.

The glamorous life of a spy, he mused to himself, wondering if he should have spiked his coffee with a shot of espresso to help keep him awake. Surveillance could be mind-numbing.

On the plus side of the ledger, Harvath's target had no idea who he was, what he looked like, or that he was onto him. That meant Harvath had the advantage.

On the other side of the ledger, Harvath had no idea if Han was even in or near the hotel right now, how he might be disguised, or which doors he used to come and go. If it turned out he had chosen the Radisson because he wanted to blend in with the Chinese guests, using the main entrance made the most sense.

When the waitress came back, she set Harvath's coffee down, along with a glass of water, and told him to let her know if he wanted anything else. That was one of the things he loved about Europe: You could sit all day, or evening, over a cup of coffee and no one would bother you. It made waiting out a surveillance target that much easier. And, as luck would have it, he didn't have to wait that long.

He was just finishing his coffee and about to order a second, when Han appeared.

Rounding the front desk, he crossed the lobby and headed toward the front doors. Harvath took in Han's clothing, especially his shoes and trousers, which likely wouldn't change. Then, paying cash for his coffee, he stood up, made sure to hang far enough back, and followed Han out of the hotel.

Even though the days were still long for this time of year, when Harvath stepped outside, the Oslo sun had already set and the blue-black fingers of evening were threading themselves through the city.

The darkness would make it harder to track Han, but hopefully it would also make Harvath more difficult to detect. Reaching into his pocket, he double-checked and made sure his phone was set to Silent.

It was a busy night, with cars and taxis stacked up in the hotel driveway and a steady stream of traffic out on the street.

Harvath followed his quarry as the Chinese operative skirted the adjacent concert arena and headed northwest. Han continued to practice good tradecraft, using appropriate opportunities to subtly check and see if he had a tail. Harvath's tradecraft, though, was better. Han had no idea he was being followed.

The good news for Harvath was that Han hadn't tried to hail a cab or climb aboard any public transportation. He also hadn't ducked into a shop or a restaurant in order to be out of view to change his appearance.

Harvath had been ready for any and all of those possibilities, but, mercifully, none of them had transpired. It was a straightforward, feet-on-the-street, eyes-on-the-prize situation. Han had given him the slip once before. He wasn't going to let it happen again.

The key to not blowing the surveillance—beyond staying out of the man's field of vision—was keeping what a buddy had once referred to as his *Fuck you* energy in check.

Without saying a word, without even being seen, he had the ability to make the hairs on the back of a man's neck stand up. Right now, though, he was all about remaining invisible and so dialed it as far down as he could.

He followed Han for ten more uneventful minutes. The operative turned corners, crossed streets, twice doubled back, and even came to a full stop to thumb out a text message on his phone—only to return to his northwest heading.

The farther they proceeded, the rougher the neighborhood became. Harvath was seeing lots of graffiti.

On a street named Bernt Ankers gate, they passed a construction site.

It was an old, empty apartment building surrounded by scaffolding. He watched as Han located an unlocked door and vanished inside.

Harvath had a million questions. Chief among them: What the hell was Han up to? Was this his final destination? Or was he merely passing through and planning to exit out a different, unseen door?

There was only one way Harvath was going to get any answers. He was going to have to follow Han inside.

CHAPTER 18

Closing the door silently behind him, Harvath paused to let his eyes get adjusted. There was much less ambient lighting inside than there was out on the street.

The old building had been completely gutted. Cracked plaster, sawdust, and pieces of broken brick and stone lay all over. The tracks of workmen's boots across the floor were so numerous that it was impossible to tell which prints belonged to Han and which way he had gone.

Metal frames, which presumably had held a set of security doors, were all that could be seen still standing in the vestibule area. Up against the far wall were rows of dented apartment mailboxes. A poorly lit stone staircase led up to the next level.

Harvath strained his ears but couldn't hear a sound. Wherever Han was, he was exceedingly quiet. He didn't like it.

He removed the compact tactical flashlight he carried in his pocket and clasped it in his left hand, his thumb poised over the tail cap. It wasn't as good as having a pistol—not even close—but a burst from its strobe was better than nothing, and might even buy him a second to get out of the way or get to his folding knife if he needed it.

He did a quick sweep of the ground floor and then approached the stairs. They curved up and to the right, the landing obscured from view. Once again he stopped and listened but didn't hear anything. There was only one way to go.

The two things he hated most in these kinds of situations were stairs and hallways. They both left you dangerously exposed.

He moved quickly and as soundlessly as possible. The less time he spent on the stairs, the better.

At the landing, there was a cheap wooden door topped with a pneumatic closing mechanism. He reached for the handle, his flashlight at the ready, and slowly pulled it open.

The hallway on the other side was narrow and lined with a handful of doors, one of which was slightly ajar. A faint light could be seen coming from the other side. For a moment, he thought he could hear voices.

He crept toward it, praying he wouldn't kick an errant piece of construction debris or hit a groaning floorboard. The other thing he prayed for was that if Han was on the other side of that door and talking to someone, he was speaking English. Harvath didn't speak any Chinese and his Russian wasn't that hot.

As he arrived at the door, he could hear that the voices were speaking in Norwegian. Then, as a jingle began to play, he realized what he was hearing. One of the construction workers must have left a radio on.

Pausing, he listened one last time for any signs of actual life. There was nothing other than the radio. He pushed the door back just far enough and stepped inside the apartment.

It was in the process of being gutted. A construction light on a tripod in the bedroom was the source of the illumination he had seen. It was also where the radio was. He decided to investigate.

The bedroom, the bathroom, and the closet were all empty. There was no sign anyone other than workers had been inside the apartment.

He needed to get moving. This detour had already cost him too much time. Wherever Han was, his lead was growing, and Harvath was determined not to lose him a second time.

Not wanting to be silhouetted in the doorframe on his way out, he turned off the construction light. He did the same with the radio.

Moving back to the front door, he stopped and listened. The hallway was quiet, but something didn't feel right.

If Han was out there playing peekaboo with him, he was going to be pissed. And when he was pissed, it usually didn't end well for the other guy.

Taking a breath, he steadied himself and snuck a look into the hall. He glanced in both directions. There was no one there. He chided himself for being so on edge.

Quickly and quietly, he made his way down the hall, trying the other doors, all of which were locked. He decided against kicking them in. All that would do was shout a warning that he was in the building. Better to return to the ground floor and see if he could pick up Han's trail somehow.

At the door that led to the stairs, he paused and listened once more. Yet again there was nothing. Readying his flashlight, he turned the handle and pushed the door open with his foot.

The moment he did, he heard the distinct pop of a Taser being deployed by someone on the other side.

Electrified fire raced through his muscles, his body seized up, and he went down hard.

It had been a long time since Harvath had been on the receiving end of a Taser. He hadn't forgotten how unpleasant it was to ride the lightning. It sucked just as much tonight as it had the other times.

No sooner had he hit the ground than there were rough hands all over him. His wrists were cinched behind his back with a pair of flex-cuffs and he was yanked to his feet and half lifted, half dragged down the stairs.

The men on either side of him were big. At least one of them had been drinking. The unmistakable scent of vodka—or "Russian aftershave" as it was known—permeated his nostrils.

As he began to regain his faculties, he noticed a man walking in front of them and it sounded like there was one behind. Four in total.

The man in front had short hair and tattoos up the side of his neck. He wore a gold chain and was dressed in jeans and a sport coat.

The three remaining men looked like rent-a-goons, slabs of beef in cheap dark suits with matching shirts, no ties. Han was nowhere to be seen.

When they got to the lobby, they steered him through the empty security door frames and farther back into the building. There, atop sheets of heavy plastic they had scrounged, an old chair had been placed.

Forcing him down, they secured him to the chair and turned on two sets of construction lights, blinding him.

"*Hvem er du?*" someone asked in choppy Norwegian. *Who are you?* The heavy accent was unmistakably Russian. "*Hva gjør du her?*" they continued. *What are you doing here?*

"Lost my dog," Harvath replied in English, squinting against the glare. The man in the jeans and sport coat appeared to be asking the questions.

Apparently, however, he didn't like the answer, because he sent one of the goons over to drive his fist into Harvath's stomach. The giant hit him so hard, it knocked the wind out of him.

That was another experience he hadn't endured in a long time. It also sucked just as much as he remembered.

Heaving for air, he tried to relax, to take in deep breaths and allow the spasming of his diaphragm to pass.

It took a minute, but once he could breathe again, the questions resumed.

"I will ask again," sport coat stated, switching to English. "Who are you and what are you doing here?"

"I told you," Harvath repeated. "I lost my dog."

"We've been following you since you left the Radisson."

Damn it, he thought to himself. He'd been so intent on not losing sight of Han that he apparently hadn't done enough to make sure he *himself* wasn't being followed. There was no excuse for that. He'd been too focused on his target.

"You don't have a dog," the man declared, "which makes you a liar. You also prefer to speak English, which, judging by your accent, makes you American. I'm thinking CIA. How am I doing so far?"

"You couldn't be further off the mark."

"Let's make it easier. One question at a time. First, your name."

A team of Russians had been camped out at the hotel to make sure Han wasn't followed. That could mean only one thing: He had an important meeting, one that Moscow didn't want him followed to.

But why employ a group of cheap thugs led by a guy in jeans with neck tats? Normally, they'd use more sophisticated operatives out of the local Russian Embassy.

At the moment, the answer wasn't important. Harvath wasn't going to tell them anything, and so he remained silent.

"*Name,*" the man demanded. He was losing his patience.

Harvath refused to answer.

The other goon appeared and pounded him so hard in his right side that he knocked him over, chair and all.

There was no way to brace his fall. Harvath's head hit the concrete floor and he saw stars.

Before he could shake them, the goon grabbed hold of him and righted him in his chair.

"Who are you?" the man repeated. "What is your name?"

Harvath's head felt like it had been split open with an axe. His ribs, if not cracked, were going to be badly bruised. He was good and pissed off. "Fuck you," he replied.

The Russian was nearing the end of his rope. "Why were you following that man from the hotel?"

No matter what he told them, they were never going to let him leave. Not alive, at least. That's why he had been searching for a way to saw through his restraints. If he could get free, he could go for one of the weapons the goons were carrying in their shoulder holsters.

The chair he was tied to, though, was too smooth. There was no spot upon which he could grind or snap off the plastic cuffs.

"I'm not going to ask you again," said his interrogator. "Why were you following him?"

Harvath wanted to make sure the man absolutely understood his response, so he said it slowly, breaking it into two very separate and very distinct words. "Fuck. You."

The man with the jeans, sport coat, and neck tats had had enough and gave an order to goon number three.

But this time, instead of walking up and punching him as the previous two had, this man walked around and stood behind him. He had something in his hand, but Harvath couldn't see it.

He had no idea what it was until the thick plastic bag was placed over his head and pulled back hard around his throat, cutting off all his air.

CHAPTER 19

Harvath threw his weight from side to side, trying to knock the chair over and get the goon to let go. Seconds felt like minutes. Minutes felt like hours. None of it was working. The harder he fought, the faster he was running out of oxygen.

The semitransparent bag over his head allowed him to make out the construction lights and blob-like silhouettes of the Russians standing nearby. But as those started to dim, he knew his brain was going into hypoxia.

With his mouth wide-open, sucking against the plastic, he battled for breath. There was none to be had. His vision began to go black.

Losing consciousness, he thought he heard something. A series of repeated, staccato clacks. They were almost indistinguishable from the noises made by the plastic pulled so tightly around his head and his struggles in the chair. But he heard them nonetheless. *Clack, clack. Clack, clack. Clack, clack.* It was the last thing his mind processed before everything went dark.

• • •

There was no white light. No host of deceased friends and loved ones waiting to welcome him home. Only darkness. *Absolute, permanent, black darkness.*

At the very least, he had expected to see the disembodied spirits of those he had killed, those whose faces had always remained so fresh, so unforgettably permanent in his mind. There was nothing save emptiness.

It was impossible for him to tell how much time had passed before the light made itself apparent.

A pinprick at first, it then exploded in brightness and with it came a rush of delicious, life-affirming air.

Opening his eyes, he saw Sølvi.

"Don't ever do that again," she whispered, trying to compose herself.

He was lying on the floor, surrounded by what looked like dead Russians. The bag had been removed from his head.

Any lingering question as to whether he was still actually alive was answered as his splitting headache came racing back. It was complemented by a searing pain in his ribs as she helped him sit up.

"What happened?" he asked. "How did you get here? How did you know?"

"You told me you were going to stake out the lobby at the Radisson. I wanted to take a break and thought I'd come keep you company. But as I was pulling up, I saw you on your way out. I texted you but didn't get a response. I figured you must have had Han in your sights."

"I did."

"The last thing I wanted was to spoil your surveillance, so I was going to head back to work. That's when I saw two of these guys hop out of their car and start following you on foot. I was worried you might need backup, so I decided to join in—at a distance.

"By the time I arrived, the men I was following were already headed inside. I figured that's where you were. I sent you another text and thought it best to wait. But a few minutes later, when Han exited and you didn't, I decided to see for myself what was going on."

Harvath was very glad she had. "Thank you. How bad was I?"

"*Bad.* If you had a pulse, I couldn't feel it. I gave up and went right to mouth-to-mouth."

"Pretty lousy interrogation technique, if you ask me. Hard to interrogate someone if they're dead."

"I don't know if that was their intent," she replied. "But sometimes stupid people overdo it."

Not only stupid people. He had pushed that line multiple times in his own interrogations. In a couple of cases, he had crossed it and had been unable to bring the subjects back. It wasn't something he was proud of. The circumstances had left him no choice.

"Are they all dead?" he asked, gesturing toward the Russians, pretty sure he knew the answer.

She nodded. "That's the rule. No medical attention until the threat is neutralized."

On the floor next to her was the weapon she had used to kill the men—a suppressed CZ 75 pistol from the Czech Republic.

"We need to scrub the bodies," Harvath said as he got himself up to standing. "Phones, IDs if any, pocket litter, all of it." Picking up the plastic bag that had been used to suffocate him, he added, "Anything you find, dump it in this."

They patted down each of the bodies, removing anything that might be helpful. Harvath found his phone in the pocket of the man wearing the jeans and the sport coat. Sure enough, there were two texts from Sølvi. She was a woman of her word.

She was also a hell of a marksman. The series of clacks he had heard was her double-tapping each of the Russians. She had caught them completely by surprise.

That they hadn't had the foresight to post some sort of a guard was further proof that they were not professionals dispatched by the embassy.

Once they had all they needed, he took photos of them and asked, "What do you want to do with the corpses?"

Picking up a rag, she wiped down the chair Harvath had been secured to, just in case he had left any fingerprints. She then wiped down her suppressed pistol and placed back it on the ground.

"Let's go," she said.

"That's it? We leave everything like this?"

"Just like this."

"What about CCTV footage outside?" he asked.

"There isn't any. Not for several blocks. They knew what they were doing when they picked this spot."

Harvath didn't argue anymore. She obviously knew what she was doing.

Outside, they made a beeline for her car. He tossed the plastic bag into the trunk, right next to the unzipped go bag she carried. Her mentor, just like his, had been a fan of untraceable black market guns that could be easily disposed of and even left at the scene. Down to the shell casings of the subsonic ammunition, there wouldn't be a single thing that could be traced back to her.

"Where to?" she asked as he got into the passenger seat and she started the car. "Maybe we should head back to the apartment. Or out to the cottage. I think we should get you checked out by a doctor. I know one who makes house calls and doesn't ask too many questions."

"I've got a better idea," he replied. Pulling up her GPS, he plugged in the address for the safe house. "My personal physician should be arriving shortly."

CHAPTER 20

Prior to his time in the U.S. Army's elite Delta Force unit, Tyler Staelin had been a Green Beret with the 5th Special Forces Group. There his MOS, or military occupational specialty, had been as a Medical Sergeant known as an 18D. As soon as he had joined The Carlton Group, the team had adopted him as their de facto medical officer.

Switching on his penlight, he checked the dilation of Harvath's pupils and then had him track the beam with his eyes.

Satisfied, he switched it off, put it back in his kit, and addressed his patient. "I've got some bad news for you. It looks like syphilis."

Harvath shook his head and looked at Sølvi. "And people wonder why he stayed a gunfighter and never went to a legitimate medical school."

"I like him," she replied. "He's funny."

Mike Haney, whose background was as a Force Recon Marine and who was passing through the room, carrying gear from one of the SUVs, said, "There isn't anything funny about syphilis. Right, Sloane? How many times have you had it now?"

Behind him was Sloane Ashby, one of the team's youngest operators and the lone female. She was ex-Army and had no trouble holding her own among the boys. "You know what they call an IQ of 160 in the Marines, Mike?" she asked.

"Average?"

"No. A platoon."

Sølvi smiled. "Also funny. I like her too."

"Don't encourage them," Harvath implored her. "It only gets worse."

Staelin popped the lid off a bottle of pills, shook a few out, and handed them to him.

"Penicillin?" Harvath inquired with a wry smile.

"Ranger candy," the man clarified, using the Army slang for ibuprofen. "For your headache."

"What about my ribs?"

"It'll work for those too. I can also give you a couple of cold packs. Twenty minutes on, twenty minutes off. After that, if you think you need it, we'll tape you up."

"You're not suddenly getting too old for this, are you?" asked Chase Palmer as he came through the room hauling a heavy Storm case. Like Staelin, he was also ex–Delta Force.

"How come every time we meet up with Harvath, he needs a cold pack for an owie?" asked Kenneth Johnson, a former Green Beret from the 10th Special Forces Group.

"Because SEALs are damage magnets," said the man bringing up the rear, who loved to jibe Harvath's military career. Peter Preisler had been a MARSOC Marine but had really made his bones in the CIA's paramilitary detachment known as Ground Branch.

Massaging his temples with his middle fingers, Harvath sent a message to his comrades while trying to relieve some of the pain inside his skull.

"They're all exactly the way you described them," said Sølvi, smiling.

These weren't the circumstances under which he had hoped to introduce her to his team. He had figured that at some point she'd come visit the States and he would put together a dinner out or throw a barbecue at his place along the Potomac. He was reminded of the famous line: *Life is what happens to you while you're busy making other plans.*

The only person Sølvi hadn't met yet was Nicholas. And as if on cue, the sound of the dogs could be heard coming from a small room at the back of the house where Nicholas had set up his "office."

The dogs were very happy to see Harvath, as was Nicholas.

"All things considered, you look better than the last time I saw you," the little man said as they embraced. "Even a new haircut. Someone has had a very good influence on you. And I think I know exactly who it is."

Breaking off from Harvath, he padded over and shook Sølvi's hand. "I've heard nothing but good things about you. It is a pleasure to finally meet you in person."

"Likewise," she replied. "What beautiful animals. May I pet them?"

"Of course," said Nicholas. Bringing them to her, he made them sit and then introduced them: Argos, then Draco.

Once the dogs had had enough time to smell Sølvi's hand and get comfortable, he told her it was okay to pet them.

They really were incredible, enormous beasts. She had never seen any dogs like them. As she rubbed their muscular necks and scratched them behind their ears, Nicholas explained how Caucasian Ovcharkas were known for loyalty and fearlessness, as well as how they had been the breed of choice for the Russian military and the East German border patrol.

When he was done, Harvath asked, "How's Nina? Everything on track?"

He smiled. "She's good. The baby's healthy. We just had another ultrasound."

"Boy or girl?"

"We decided that we want it to be a surprise."

Harvath was proud of him. He had come a long way. At first, he was terrified that any child he fathered would, like him, also be born with primordial dwarfism. He knew, though—and Harvath had reminded him—that the gene had to come from both parents and the odds were incredibly, infinitesimally slim.

Nicholas knew this, of course, but becoming a parent had worried him. Because of his size, he counted on the dogs to protect him. How could he protect someone else, much less a child?

Harvath had assured him that he would make an excellent father. Eventually, Nicholas had overcome his fear. His excitement for the baby's arrival was palpable. He would be every inch the proud papa and shower his child with whatever he or she needed, including protection against any harm.

"It'll be a wonderful surprise," Harvath promised. "I'm glad Nina let you come along for this assignment."

"She's drawn her line in the sand," said Nicholas. "It's circled in thick red Sharpie on the calendar. Thankfully, we're still on the right side of it."

"How long until the baby arrives?" asked Sølvi.

"She just entered her third trimester. We've got about twelve more weeks, give or take."

"I wish you both good health and good luck."

"Thank you," Nicholas replied. "And speaking of children, how did your visit with Marco go?"

Marco was the four-year-old son of Harvath's deceased wife. Technically, Marco was his stepson. Sadly, the boy's biological father had drowned before he was born. He was being raised in Boston by his grandparents.

"The visit was absolutely lovely," said Sølvi. And she meant it.

Unable to have children of her own, she doted on her nieces and nephews, but having Marco to themselves for almost two whole weeks was a dream come true.

Harvath had flown Marco and the grandparents over first-class and then he had given them an incredible gift. He put them in the cottage out on the fjord and allowed them to have a proper vacation, devoid of any childcare responsibility whatsoever.

Both of the grandparents had forgotten what it was like to relax. His father-in-law had fished like crazy, while his mother-in-law sat out on the deck drinking wine and reading book after book.

Back in Oslo, Harvath made it a point to get ice cream every day as they took in all the child-friendly attractions the city had to offer—many of them more than once. They visited the TusenFryd Amusement Park, the Oslo reptile park, the Leos Lekeland adventure playground, and their absolute favorite spot, in the nearby suburb of Lørenskog, SNØ—a year-round, indoor winter sports complex where Harvath taught the little guy how to ski.

Whenever she could get away, including via cashing in several sick days, Sølvi joined them. The experience had made their summer, and their relationship, all the sweeter.

For his part, Harvath's greatest fear about the visit had never materialized. He had been worried that the in-laws would be angry with him for finding someone so soon after their daughter's murder. But as a testament to their good taste, they loved Sølvi. And as a testament to their good character, they loved Harvath. He was a part of their family and always would be. The connection he shared with Sølvi was unmistakable. More than anything else, they wanted him to be happy.

When the time came for Marco to leave, it was difficult to say goodbye. Thanks to Sølvi, though, Harvath was able to squeeze out a little extra one-on-one time with him.

The grandparents were not fond of driving in the Audi with the top down, but the little boy *loved* it. Sølvi offered to drive them to the airport in her car while Harvath and Marco took the convertible. It was the perfect final road trip to cap everything off.

Along with all of the photos rotating through the digital frame in Sølvi's kitchen, there were plenty of Marco's visit to remind them of how special it had been for all of them.

Cracking one of the cold packs Staelin handed him, Harvath placed it under his shirt and against his ribs. He then washed down the ibuprofen with a bottle of water Haney had brought him from the kitchen and, looking at his team, said, "Let's put together a plan. Our next SITREP is due in less than eight hours. I want to make sure that we have something substantial to report."

CHAPTER 21

Xing Fen was known as a "short sleeper," someone who needed barely any sleep at all. Four hours a night and she was good. It was a biological gift that provided her with an extra sixty days a year. What did she do with all of that extra time? She had devoted it to the Chinese Communist Party.

No one could outwork her. She stayed later and arrived earlier than anyone else in government. She never slept in and never showed the appearance of being tired. She was a font of boundless, determined energy—a true warrior for China. None of her colleagues, especially the males, could question her work ethic. It played no small part in how she was able to ascend to the level of a Vice Premier.

Each morning she picked up the same breakfast from the same stall—two fertilized duck eggs with partially developed embryos inside known as "feathered" eggs. The unusual delicacy was boiled, served warm, and—based on how long it had been incubated—sometimes included small, soft bones and the beginnings of feathers.

When it came to her morning beverage, unlike many of her colleagues who had been swept up in the coffee craze, she still preferred tea—a pot of which, prepared by an assistant, was always hot and waiting on her desk when she arrived.

She read four newspapers in three different languages before any of her peers were even out of bed. By the time she had eaten her breakfast, she had a better grasp of where the world was and where it was headed than most politicians would all day.

Her second-in-command appeared, as he did every morning, precisely at eight a.m. She already had an agenda prepared with a list of topics she wanted to discuss.

Today she was quite eager for an update on how things were going in both the United States and Norway. They were two of her most active and most important assignments.

"Where would you like me to begin?" the man asked.

"Let's start with the United States."

The second-in-command withdrew a folder and was about to hand it to his boss but hesitated.

"What's the problem?" Xing asked.

"Our asset in the United States, Lindsey Chang."

"What about her?"

"You're aware that she uses some rather coarse methods."

"Isn't that what we pay her for?"

"Technically," said the man, "we pay her for results."

"Has she ever disappointed us?"

"No."

"Then what do we care about her methods as long as she gets the desired results?" asked Xing, motioning her second-in-command for the folder.

The man handed it over and waited as his boss flipped through the pages he had printed out for her. As she did, he explained what she was looking at.

"These are copies of her text messages with Dennis Wo's fixer—the American political fundraiser, Spencer Baldwin."

"She doesn't leave much to the imagination, does she?"

"No, she doesn't. The Americans refer to it as 'sexting.' "

"Isn't Baldwin married?"

"Yes," the man replied. "That is correct."

"Not only does the very attractive Ms. Chang have him eating out of the palm of her hand, but she has also developed some excellent blackmail material. I'm quite pleased."

"Mr. Baldwin is already moving mountains. According to Chang, the first thing he did upon returning to Washington was to have lunch with the chief of staff to Alaska's senior senator, Dwyer, and to make our case."

"And?"

"And Baldwin thought it went very well. He called Chang right after the lunch to give her an update. Apparently, the chief of staff is looking to get into state politics back in Alaska. Baldwin told him that if he could help on the Alaska liquefied natural gas project, campaign funds wouldn't be a problem."

"Very, *very* good," Xing said. "Remind me to thank Dennis Wo for the introduction. What is the next step?"

"The chief of staff wants to refresh himself on all of the data—the potential boost to Alaska's economy, the amount of jobs expected to be created, and so forth. He told Baldwin he would be back in touch with him shortly."

"In the meantime, tell Chang to keep doing what she's doing. Baldwin is obviously very motivated."

"Agreed."

Xing closed the folder and handed it back. "Let's move on to Norway."

Handing her a new folder, the man said, "We have a problem."

"Explain."

"Last night, in Oslo, our asset was followed from his hotel. Han was en route to a second meeting with his Russian contact."

"Who was following him? Norwegian Intelligence?"

"We don't know. As you'll recall, he thought he might have been followed to his first meeting with Sarov."

"What I recall," said Xing, "was that Han had a feeling, a hunch. He never specifically saw anyone."

"Correct. He shared his concern with Sarov, who assigned a counter-surveillance team to watch over him. They're the ones who spotted the tail."

"Then what happened?"

"Han received a phone call. He was told to proceed to a construction site. There, he led his pursuer inside and the Russians apprehended him. Han was then told to leave and continue on to the meeting, which he did."

"It wasn't canceled?"

The man shook his head. "The Russians were confident that they were dealing with just one person and that they had him."

Xing had often found the Russians to be too confident—reckless, even. Had this been up to her, the meeting would have been called off.

"What did Sarov have to say once he got there?" she asked.

"According to Han, the first thing they addressed was his security. Someone knew enough to be following him and knew what hotel he was in. Sarov is going to move him, find him a new place to stay. They took his key card and will have somebody collect his things."

It was the first thing she had heard that made sense. Score one point for the Russians. "What about the man the countersurveillance team captured?"

"By the end of the meeting, Sarov still didn't have an update. He said he'd let Han know as soon as had something."

"I don't like this," she said. "Someone is onto us. Until we have absolute certainty that the operation isn't compromised, I think we need to put everything on hold."

The man understood his boss's apprehension. He also understood that her superiors, not to mention the Russians, would be very unhappy if China backed out now. It would undermine confidence and erode trust. It would also deny Beijing a real-world test—against the Americans—of its new, cutting-edge technology.

He chose his words carefully. "I understand your position. It is wise to be cautious."

"*But* . . . ?" she asked, sensing there was more to what he was thinking.

"If the proof of concept succeeds, which we have every reason to believe it will, you will have achieved an amazing pair of victories. You will have proven that the Black Ice program works and, in exchange for access to that technology, you will have secured from the Russians uninhibited passage through the Northern Sea Route—not just for Chinese commercial shipping but for our naval vessels as well. I imagine that the Order of the Republic would be the least of the honors bestowed upon you."

She knew he was flattering her, but she also knew he wasn't wrong. If she was successful, she'd be a national hero. There would be no end to what she could do within the Chinese Communist Party. But if she failed, there would be hell to pay. Of that, she was absolutely certain.

"You believe we should push forward."

"I believe that we can't afford not to," he said. "Han is our best. That's why you chose him. He understands the importance of his mission. He also understands that no path is ever without stones."

"I don't want *any* stones in his path. Is that understood?"

"Meaning?"

"*Meaning,*" she replied, "I agree with you. We have too much riding on this. Security cannot be left to the Russians. Not at this point. We need to assert control."

"What do you have in mind?"

"I want Han to have backup. *Chinese* backup."

The man thought about it and responded, "I have to move some things around, but I have a team I can get to him."

"Good. Do it. And whoever is following Han, I want them dealt with. No matter what it takes."

CHAPTER 22

A s neither his calls nor his texts were being returned, Yevgeny Sarov decided to check out the construction site for himself.

The lack of communication was troubling to say the least, but it was only compounded by the personnel choice he'd been forced to make.

In a perfect world, he would have selected intelligence operatives from the Russian Embassy. They would have been much better trained. The problem, though, was that Norway took its internal security quite seriously. There was a high likelihood that most, if not all, of the people he wanted were on the radar of Norwegian Intelligence.

And while the country didn't have the manpower to surveil embassy staff on a 24/7 basis, they dipped in and out enough to make him nervous. That's why he had decided to go underground for help.

Unlike in other countries, Russian organized crime kept a somewhat low profile in Norway. The most lucrative of their illicit income streams were drugs and sex trafficking. They used nightclubs and auto repair shops as front companies through which they laundered their money and ran large chunks of their businesses.

Sarov had reached out to an *avtoritet* he knew named Yumatov. An *avtoritet* was the equivalent of a *capo* in the Italian Mafia—a person responsible for a crew of "soldiers." It was Yumatov who had provided the men for the countersurveillance team.

Stepping inside the building, Sarov walked toward the back and instantly recognized the scene for what it was—an ambush.

Clearly, only Yumatov had had time to access his weapon, but it hadn't made a difference. The man hadn't even gotten a shot off; the safety of his pistol was still engaged. He lay on the ground, his jeans and sport coat soaked in blood.

Glancing around, Sarov noted that it had all the hallmarks of a professional, organized hit—one criminal gang set against another.

Perhaps that was what the shooter wanted people to think. After all, last year there had been similar violence between rival factions. In one case, the killer's gun had also been left behind. This, though, felt different.

Crouching down, Sarov examined the suppressed Czech pistol without touching it. The CZ 75 lay on the ground near a chair that had been knocked over. Using his handkerchief so as not to leave any fingerprints, he righted the chair and studied its position.

Based upon the nearby corpses and a set of construction lamps, this was where the interrogation had been taking place. But what had happened? How had it all gone wrong?

Walking over to the lights, Sarov used his handkerchief to turn them on and then tried to piece together what had happened.

The man they had taken captive would have been restrained. He also would have been patted down. There was no way he could have concealed from his captors a pistol of that size, much less one with a suppressor.

Stacking the odds further against him was how bright the construction lamps were. The man's vision would have been seriously diminished.

So, even if he could have broken free, the idea that he then pulled out a weapon and successfully killed everyone in the room was just too much. Someone had assisted the captive.

But who?

Working his way out from the scene, Sarov kept searching for evidence. Then, finally, he found it. *Shell casings*—eight, to be exact, and littered in the same area. The hit was professional. Extremely so.

From what he could tell, the shooter had stepped into the room and fired all eight shots from about the same spot. Each of the deceased had been double-tapped, which spoke to a very talented marksman, probably someone with advanced military training. This wasn't some rival gangster.

If it had been, there would have been a fifth body here—the man they had been interrogating when the shooter walked in. There was no reason to spare him, to leave a witness. It was even more obvious to Sarov that the two had been working together.

That brought him right back to his previous question: *Who were they?* The Norwegians weren't the type to dirty their hands with wet work. *Law and order*, *due process*, and *human rights* were their cris de coeur.

Whatever this was, it was spur-of-the-moment—reactive. The man Yumatov and his crew had grabbed must have had a partner who had gone unnoticed. Focused on the interrogation, they had failed to pick up on the killer until it was too late.

Looking over everything again, Sarov tried to make the pieces fit. Highly skilled gunman. Not afraid to leave the weapon—nor the bodies, for that matter—behind.

In his experience, only two professions operated without fear like that—corrupt police officers and contract killers. And despite what people saw in the movies, cops were not usually precision marksmen.

But the fact that someone was onto Han, had pinpointed his hotel, and was following him strongly suggested the involvement of the Norwegian Police Security Service, known as the Politiets sikkerhetstjeneste, or PST for short. They were responsible for interior security throughout Norway and were akin to Britain's MI5 or the American FBI.

Yet, if it *had* been the PST, that only made the circumstances more confusing. Why not arrest Yumatov and his men? The PST certainly had the authority. Why execute them and leave their bodies and the weapon behind? It made no sense.

That left Sarov to go down the assassin avenue. Did Han have enemies in Norway? If the Chinese operative was to be believed, he had never been to Oslo, nor anywhere else in the country before. He had not personally, nor by proxy, run any prior operations against Norway. This was his inaugural assignment in Scandinavia.

Regardless of who was onto Han and what their reasons might be, the fact was that he had been blown. Sarov had a decision to make. He either had to cut Han loose or make it so that the Norwegians couldn't find him.

Considering how much was at stake, cutting him loose was the least palatable option. Russia not only wanted but badly needed access to

China's Black Ice project. Putting together the proof-of-concept test had been a long and laborious process. That he and Han had to meet in Oslo to hash out final details only went to show how intricate this next phase of the Sino-Russian relationship was. The last thing Sarov needed was to be known as the person who had called it all off. There had to be a better way.

He knew, of course, what that way was. He needed to get Han out of Oslo as soon as possible.

The original plan had been for them to travel the next day to Kirkenes, albeit separately. Han was booked with a group of Chinese tourists leaving the Radisson via bus, which would take them to the Oslo airport, where they would board a charter flight to Høybuktmoen, eight miles west of Kirkenes. That route was now off the table. Commercial airports and train stations had too many eyes and way too much security. They were going to have to drive.

Taking out his phone, Sarov unlocked the app he used to communicate with Han and texted him a quick message: **I'll be there in twenty minutes. Be ready to move.**

Just as he was slipping the phone into his pocket and getting ready to exit the building, Han responded with a request. The moment Sarov read it, he knew that what the man was proposing was a highly dangerous idea.

CHAPTER 23

"The one thing we can all agree on," said Haney as they gathered around the table in the safe house kitchen, "is that Han is not going back to the Radisson."

"Not in a million years," Preisler agreed, pulling a warmed serving dish from the oven, piling it with mountains of spaghetti carbonara, and carrying it over to his hungry teammates.

Sloane and Chase had been assigned the next shift and had already turned in. Everyone else waited until Sølvi had been served, then loaded up their plates.

"He knows he's been burned," replied Johnson, shaking a ton of red pepper flakes onto his pasta. "So he's got to go to ground. But where?"

Staelin smiled. "Any place he thinks he'll be safe from Harvath."

"Which is nowhere."

The team laughed at the joke, but Sølvi felt the need to clarify something. "As far as we know, Han has no idea who was following him. Not exactly."

Harvath nodded. "The Russian with the neck tats asking all the questions—he figured I was American and automatically guessed CIA."

"But unless he was livestreaming your interrogation," said Sølvi, "none of that would have left the building."

She had a good point, and Harvath turned to Nicholas. "What are the chances of us getting into their phones?"

The little man shook his head. "All brand-new iPhones. They could take days to crack. Add on even more time if they were using encrypted apps to communicate."

"Can we back up a second?" asked Haney. "The lead guy was wearing jeans and had neck tats. The other three were dressed like they were headed to some low-rent disco. Not exactly the picture of typical Russian Intelligence operatives."

He was right and it had been bothering Harvath. "If Han is here doing something with the Russians and Yevgeny Sarov is his contact, why not pull a team from the embassy to shadow him? And why wasn't there a team on him yesterday?"

"Maybe you didn't see them," said Preisler.

"Or maybe," Staelin offered, "Han picked up on you and requested protection."

Harvath twirled a piece of spaghetti onto his fork and stabbed a piece of pancetta. "I went back and forth through the CCTV footage a million times. You can check for yourselves. There was no team. There's also nothing to suggest that he knew I was tailing him."

"Up until the point where you lost him," Haney needled him with a smile.

Harvath ignored the jibe and ate his pasta.

Nicholas steered the conversation back in a more productive direction. "If these men aren't from the embassy, which it doesn't sound like they are, they're probably from the criminal realm. The question is: Why go that route?"

"I can think of a couple of reasons," said Harvath. "Han and Sarov are doing something off-book and they don't want the embassy to know. Maybe the embassy has been penetrated and they're worried about a mole. Or, it could be that Han wants to defect or has something to pass to the Russians. If Sarov was put in charge of vetting the opportunity, he might have been told by his superiors, just to be safe, not to involve anyone from the embassy."

"*Or*," Sølvi interjected, "they know that Norwegian police keep Russian Embassy personnel on a revolving surveillance schedule and didn't want to risk that this could have been their night."

Nicholas touched his index finger to his nose and pointed at her. "Occam's razor."

"The simplest answer isn't always the right one," she replied, "especially not in intelligence work, but in this case I think it deserves the most weight."

"So how do we use any of this to pick up Han's trail?" Preisler asked.

"If he makes another reservation with his alias and current credit card," said Nicholas, "we'll have him."

"And if he doesn't?"

"Then we're still at square one."

"What about his room at the Radisson?" asked Harvath, the ibuprofen kicking in and his headache starting to ease. "Whether he comes back or not, we still need to see it, right?"

"Preferably before housekeeping," said Nicholas, agreeing with him. There was no telling what might be in the garbage or Han's personal effects that might provide a lead.

Johnson reached for more red pepper flakes and pointed out, "You're not getting anywhere without a key card, though. The elevator won't operate without one. And even then you'll need to have one coded for the specific floor you're targeting."

"You sound pretty confident," replied Harvath.

At that, Johnson slid his phone over to him. On it, a YouTube video was playing. It showed a tourist riding up and down in one of the hotel's glass elevators. Each time, they had to swipe a key card past a sensor.

Harvath returned the phone and said, "We've also got the issue of the alias Han is using—Zhang Wei. There are two of them registered at that hotel. We don't know which one we want or which room he is in."

"Actually," Nicholas announced as he checked his email, "I just heard from my people in Belarus. They got access to the property management system. Our Zhang Wei, the one whose passport information you sent me, is in room 803."

"Now all we need is a key card. Can you fabricate one?"

"I can do you one better," the little man said. "I can book you into the room right next to his."

CHAPTER 24

Harvath didn't waste a lot of time getting geared up. He selected a Heckler & Koch VP40 pistol, an inside-the-waistband holster, and several extra magazines.

He tucked a flashbang into each coat pocket and helped himself to a set of lockpick tools. Per the floor plan Nicholas had pulled up, Harvath's and Han's were adjoining rooms. That meant they had a common door and, like every other hotel in the world, it was likely secured by a standard lock. Once Harvath was in his room, he'd have it open in no time.

Grabbing communications gear and an empty carry-on bag, he headed outside and tossed his bag in the cargo area of one of the black SUVs. As Preisler got behind the wheel, Harvath took a seat behind him.

Sølvi wanted to come up to the room with him, but he preferred to have her eyes and ears downstairs, so she drove separately with Staelin. Haney and Johnson would follow in a third vehicle, while Nicholas remained at the safe house to coordinate the overall operation.

When they arrived at the Radisson, Harvath gave the lead bellman a large tip, explained that he was headed right back out, and asked if it was okay for his driver to wait. Because of the hour, and more importantly the tip, the bellman was happy to comply.

The great thing about a big, busy hotel was that it was highly unlikely anyone would remember that only a matter of hours ago Harvath had been sitting in the lobby bar, drinking coffee.

Crossing to the front desk, he presented a passport and credit card identifying himself as "Jonathan Taylor" and checked in.

"Mr. Taylor, will you be needing one key card or two?" the attractive young clerk asked.

"Just one," he said with a smile. Though she was all the way over in the lobby bar, he could feel Sølvi's eyes on him.

Once everything, including how and where breakfast was served, had been explained, he headed for the elevators.

Waving his key card over the sensor, he pressed the button for the eighth floor. Then, just as the doors were closing, a voice shouted, "Hold the elevator, please!"

Harvath reached down and hit the Door Open button and Johnson stepped in.

"Hi there, handsome," he said. "Is that a flashbang in your pocket or are you just happy to see me?"

Harvath subtly flipped him the bird as the elevator doors closed and they rode up to their floor.

When the doors opened, a woman with two wheeled bags, one big, one small, stood aside so the men could exit, and then she entered the elevator.

Harvath and Johnson waited for the doors to close and the elevator to head down before checking the emergency stairwells and then approaching their room.

Harvath unlocked the door with his key card and then stepped inside, followed by Johnson, who hung the *Do Not Disturb* sign on the knob.

Inserting their earpieces, they did a quick comms check, swept their room, and got to work.

It turned out that there were two doors separating the adjoining rooms. Harvath quietly opened the first one and then Johnson slipped a tiny fiber-optic camera under the second.

Moments later he reported, "All clear. Nobody's on the other side."

With that, Harvath used his picks, opened the remaining door, and stepped inside.

The TV was on, set to the default hotel welcome channel, but other than that it was quiet.

The bathroom was empty, as was the closet. And not just empty, but *empty* empty. There wasn't a toothbrush, a razor, or a pair of trousers to be seen. Even the garbage cans had been stripped of their plastic trash bags.

As Johnson checked under the bed, Harvath checked the dresser drawers. They were empty as well.

Had Han come back? Had he ever even been here to begin with? The bed, while not fully unmade, was mussed—as if someone had moved the pillows around and had taken a nap without getting under the blankets.

"So much for him never coming back," said Johnson. "It looks like—"

He was interrupted by Nicholas's voice over their radios. "Han just checked out."

"What do you mean Han just checked out?" said Harvath.

"The hotel management system shows he just did an in-room video checkout. Where are you?"

"We're standing in his room," he replied. Then, looking at Johnson, he said, "The woman with the suitcases when we got off the elevator. Let's go!"

As soon as he saw how many floors away the elevator was, he directed Johnson to the stairs. As they ran, he radioed a description of the woman to the rest of the team.

"She just passed us a couple of minutes ago," said Sølvi. "She went out the main entrance."

"I saw her too," Preisler added. "She got into a black Mazda CX-30. Pulled out of the driveway headed southwest."

"Follow her," Harvath ordered.

"Roger that. I'm on it."

"Haney. Be out front in sixty seconds," he then said.

"Roger that," the man replied. "Haney inbound."

"Do you want me to get my car from the valet?" asked Sølvi.

"Negative," Harvath answered. "We'll come back for it later."

When they hit the ground floor, Harvath and Johnson stopped and took a breath. Gently opening the door, they crossed the lobby and exited the hotel. Outside, Haney was idling in his SUV. Sølvi was shotgun. Harvath and Johnson hopped in back with Staelin.

"Go!" Harvath directed, before they had even shut their doors.

Sølvi activated the navigation and communicated over the radio with Preisler, trying to get a fix on his location.

He had his nav engaged as well and had been blowing through red lights, trying to catch up with the woman in the Mazda. He did his best to pronounce the Norwegian street names he was passing.

Eventually, Sølvi had a good idea as to where he was and how they could catch up. She told Haney what she wanted him to do and gave him turn-by-turn instructions.

Minutes later, they caught up with him. Several car lengths ahead, he had his eyes on the Mazda. They followed as it turned onto National Road 4 and proceeded north.

They continued a safe distance behind until they came to a round-about where the Mazda branched off onto National Road 22.

"Where do you think she's headed?" asked Harvath.

"The airport," Sølvi said.

He was no native, but he had been in Oslo all summer and had made more than a few trips out to drop off and pick up friends and family. This wasn't a route he was familiar with.

"It'd be a lot faster if she just got on the main highway. Are you sure she's headed for Gardermoen?" he asked, using the official name for Oslo Airport.

"She's not going all the way out to Gardermoen," Sølvi said, correcting him. "She's going to Kjeller."

"What's Kjeller?"

"A small, one-runway airfield much closer; just northeast of the city."

"Did you hear that, Nicholas?" Harvath asked over his radio.

"Good copy," the little man affirmed.

"I want our bird fueled and standing by. If the target is there and goes wheels up, we need to be right behind him."

"Negative."

"What are you talking about?"

"The crew is timed out."

"Are you serious?"

"It's a seventy-five-million-dollar aircraft. The FAA, not to mention the insurance company, is rather particular about rest periods."

Damn it, Harvath thought. "How much longer will they be down?"

"They're back on the clock at five a.m."

He checked his watch. It was already after midnight. "Any chance we can charter a plane and have it on standby?"

"At this time of night? It would take hours just to find a crew. And even if we could find one, along with an aircraft, where do we tell them we're going?"

Nicholas was right. By the time they pulled together a charter, their jet—along with their crew—would be ready for takeoff. "Forget I asked. We'll keep you in the loop. Be ready to pack up."

"Roger that."

At the light for Kjeller airport, the Mazda turned right onto Storgata street and made its way toward the main entrance.

As it drove into the main parking lot, Preisler and Haney pulled over to the shoulder and killed their lights. The occupants of the two SUVs watched as the Mazda approached a retractable gate. It rolled back, allowing the vehicle to enter, and then closed immediately behind it.

In front of the hangars, the high-pitched whine of jet engines could be heard coming to life.

"Okay," Harvath said over the radio so he could address Preisler and Haney at the same time. "Keep your lights off and let's head for the parking lot."

Putting the SUVs in gear, the men followed Harvath's instructions.

They took parking spaces right up against the perimeter fence and climbed out of their vehicles. They had a perfect view of the airfield.

Less than a hundred yards away the Mazda sat, its headlights extinguished, next to a Cessna Citation CJ3 light business jet.

The air stairs of the jet were down, but no one was visible on the tarmac. It was hard to tell what was happening.

At first, Harvath assumed all of the activity must have been taking place inside the aircraft. Then he saw a faint light come on inside the Mazda—as if someone had just picked up their phone.

Seconds later, the light vanished and the woman from the Radisson stepped out of her vehicle and onto the tarmac.

After pulling the wheeled bags out of the backseat, she walked them over to the base of the air stairs and waited.

No sooner had she arrived than the copilot came down the air stairs, accepted the bags from her, and took them back up into the aircraft. Harvath and his team had yet to set eyes on Han or Sarov.

"Preisler," Harvath said over the radio as the woman returned to the Mazda. "Did you ever get close enough to get her plate number?"

"Negative."

"Johnson, that's now your job. I want you to find a concealed spot near the gate and take down her number when she exits. Preisler, get back in your vehicle and be ready to follow her when she leaves."

"Roger that," the men replied.

"Haney and Staelin," Harvath then commanded, "I want the tail number of that aircraft."

Both men flashed him a thumbs-up.

Once the copilot had raised the air stairs and secured the door, the pilot applied power to the engines. The jet's whine increased, and the aircraft rolled out onto the runway. The Mazda headed for the gate.

Harvath gestured for Sølvi to join him back in their SUV. He needed another favor. A big one.

CHAPTER 25

Harvath's "big favor" was actually a collection of favors. But as much as she loved him, there was only so much Sølvi could do.

First and foremost, she made it clear that, photos or no photos, she wasn't going to run background checks on the dead Russians from the construction site. She'd be signing her own arrest warrant. If she started poking around before the bodies had been discovered, she'd wind up as the prime suspect. It was a nonstarter.

Running the license and registration on the Mazda was another story. *That* she was happy to do.

She was also happy to pull any CCTV footage from the airport. And before Harvath had even asked, she offered to reach out to a contact at the Civil Aviation Authority to see if the jet had filed a flight plan.

Preisler was the first one out of the lot as he followed the Mazda back toward Oslo.

As the rest of the team hopped into the second SUV with Harvath and Sølvi, she was already working the phone. Johnson wrote down the license number and handed it to Harvath. Staelin, now riding shotgun, did the same with the aircraft's tail number while Haney fired up the vehicle and started back to the Radisson. The plan was to get Sølvi back to her car and then head for the safe house.

Despite the late hour, it was amazing how quickly she was able to gather information. Swiss precision and German efficiency had nothing on the Norwegians.

The first thing to come back was the name and address of the Mazda's owner—a Russian woman who lived west of downtown Oslo.

Using her made perfect sense. Both Han and Sarov would have been concerned about being spotted at the hotel. Sending in someone unremarkable, someone no one would have given a second look to, was a smart choice.

It was also good tradecraft. Harvath and Johnson had been so eager to get into Han's room that they had walked right past her.

Harvath was about to ask Sølvi what else she could dig up, when her phone chimed.

"Interesting," she said, reading the text she had just received.

"What is it?"

"Guess where our baggage handler is employed?"

There were only two choices. "The Russian Embassy," he replied.

"Very good. How'd you guess?"

"Her shoes."

"You noticed her shoes?"

"I notice everyone's shoes."

"What about them?" Sølvi asked.

"They were plain, like her. Middle-of-the-road. There was nothing gaudy or over-the-top. Not her hair, not her makeup, not her nails or jewelry. If I had to put a word on it, it would be competent. Professional. Maybe even boring."

"Well, you win the prize. She works in the Joint Norwegian-Russian Fisheries Commission as an assistant to the Attaché. I don't think you can get any more boring than that."

"Good department to hide an intelligence officer in."

"If she's an intel officer, she's amazing. In the seven years she has been in Oslo, there's been nothing to suggest that she's anything other than an office worker."

"Which makes her a good choice to sanitize Han's room and check him out of the hotel," said Harvath. "It doesn't require any special training.

All that's needed is someone halfway intelligent who can properly follow orders."

"Having a diplomatic passport doesn't hurt, either—just in case you get stopped by the police in the process," Sølvi added.

"True."

"We need to assume that Sarov knows about the men at the construction site," said Sølvi. "That's what the airplane was all about. He and Han are on the run."

"I agree," said Harvath as he hailed Preisler and told him to break off his surveillance of the Mazda. The woman was a small fish. They knew where she lived and worked. Following her any further would only risk tipping their hand. If they wanted to catch Han and Sarov, it was better for the two men to believe that they had gotten away scot-free.

"I may have some more good news," she added as she opened her email app and clicked on a message. She then showed her phone to him so he could see it. Four letters were highlighted in bold: **ENKR**.

It was an International Civil Aviation Organization airport code. Harvath recognized that much. Which airport it corresponded to, though, escaped him. He was much more fluent in the three-letter International Air Travel Association codes.

Sølvi could see he didn't know it. "I'll give you three guesses and the first two don't count."

"I'm going to go out on a limb and say it isn't the code for Beijing or Moscow."

"That's correct. It's not."

"Kirkenes?"

"Bravo," she replied.

"How long until they land?"

"It's a two-hour-and-ten-minute flight."

Harvath marked the time on his watch. "Do you have any assets up there who can follow them from the airport?"

"I don't. But I know someone who does."

"Who?"

"Holidae Hayes."

"How do you know that?"

"I've met him," said Sølvi. "American. Ex–CIA. He married a Norwegian woman. Smart guy."

"Smart because he married a Norwegian woman? Or smart as in he's intelligent?"

"Both."

He smiled and shook his head. "What's his name?"

"Phillip Mercer."

Harvath didn't know him, but that wasn't a surprise. There were a lot of former Agency people scattered around the world.

"How are you coming with the CCTV footage?" he asked. "I'd like to confirm that Han was on that plane before I wake up Holidae and ask her to activate Mercer."

"Someone is working on it for me. I don't have an ETA yet."

Call it Harvath's sixth sense, but the closer they got to Oslo, the more his confidence grew that both Han and Sarov were on the jet. And the farther they got away from him, the more difficult his assignment would become.

Finally, he decided to phone Hayes. Two hours wasn't much time to get an operation spun up. Kirkenes was on the doorstep of Russia. When the aircraft touched down, if they didn't have "eyes on," they could end up losing Han for good.

CHAPTER 26

When Sarov and Han arrived, they exited the airport separately. Sarov retrieved his car from the parking lot and headed home, while Han—along with his suitcase—climbed into a waiting taxi and was taken to the Thon Hotel Kirkenes.

A modern, boxy structure, the Thon was the largest hotel in town and sat right at the water's edge. Business had been booming—especially with Asian tourists.

They came to see polar bears and the northern lights. Some even believed that conceiving a child under the lights would bestow prosperity and good luck.

Others came to board cruise ships at the nearby town quay. The opportunities for sightseeing and arctic adventures were boundless, and they had provided Han with the perfect cover.

Kirkenes had long been dependent on the mining of iron ore, its sole industry. Then, as the mine shut down due to poor profits, Kirkenes had discovered China.

Looking to woo Chinese investment and tourism, it exchanged trade delegations with Beijing and launched an all-out charm offensive. The mining town even went so far as to remake itself as the "World's Northernmost Chinatown" for a recent winter festival.

Signs around Kirkenes—normally written in Norwegian and Russian— added Chinese characters. A traditional Chinatown-style archway was constructed, the local newspaper took a Chinese name, and a "Polar Silk Route" market was opened.

While Chinese investment had been mired by Norwegian politics, Chinese tourism had taken off like a rocket. Han fit right in. What's more, the items he transported in his suitcase fit in as well.

In addition to a couple of softcover books on polar bears, he was transporting a digital single-lens reflex (DSLR) camera, a spotting scope, a range finder, and a satellite communicator. To any customs inspector going through his carry-on bag, he would look like a wealthy Chinese tourist on his way to track and photograph polar bears.

The equipment was not what it seemed, though. It was, in fact, a critical part of his assignment. Without it, there would be no proof-of-concept test. That was why he had insisted on returning to the Radisson to retrieve his belongings.

There was also the issue of his medication. While he carried a few pills on his person, along with a passport and currency—just in case he needed to flee—it wasn't going to be enough to see him through the end of the operation.

He had been pleased when Sarov had come up with the idea to send in the woman to retrieve his bags. Now that he had safely arrived in Kirkenes, he could focus on the completion of his assignment.

He removed the satellite communicator, powered it up, and uncoiled a small, magnetized antenna. This corner of the building provided a clear, unobstructed view of the sky, which was why he had requested it. However, satellite communications didn't work very well through glass.

Opening the window, he affixed the magnet to the outside of the frame, plugged the antenna into the communicator, and synced it to his smartphone. The phone's encryption software would make sure his message could be read only by its intended recipient.

Once the communicator had locked onto the Chinese satellite system, the first thing he transmitted was a situation report to his headquarters in Beijing.

The next message was transmitted to a location much closer. Considering the hour, he didn't know if his contact would be awake. Moments later, he received a response: **Transmission received. Everything is in place. Standing by.**

There was nothing else for Han to do but get some rest. He was going to need it. Things were about to get very complicated.

CHAPTER 27

Harvath and Sølvi had stood together under the Radisson's canopy, waiting for her car to be brought around. Neither of them spoke. Even if she had wanted to, she couldn't join him. This was his assignment, and she was expected back at NIS. What little time they had left together was slipping away even faster.

When her car appeared, he wrapped his arms around her and they kissed. Neither had any idea when they would see each other again.

"Be safe," she advised, with her arms around his neck so as not to cause his ribs any additional pain.

"You know me," he replied.

"I do know you. That's why I am telling you to be safe. Head on a swivel. Call me if you need me."

"I'm going to be fine," he said, kissing her again. "I'll bring back some fresh seafood. What is Kirkenes known for?"

"King crab. Big ones. They catch them out in the Barents Sea."

"I'll buy as much as I can haul and we'll throw a huge party."

"Promise?"

"I promise."

After one more kiss, he tipped the valet and helped her into her car. Then he rejoined his teammates in their SUV and they returned to the safe house and packed up their gear.

Once all of the vehicles had been loaded, they made the drive out to

Oslo Airport, transferred everything onto the company jet, and prepared for takeoff.

They had been lucky enough to get catering aboard, and the team grabbed what they wanted from the galley. Fruit, smoked fish, cured meats, bread, cheese, and pastries. Pretty standard. The only thing hot was the coffee. Harvath passed on all of it.

They weren't going to be in the air that long. Their plane was considerably faster and would make much better time than the one Han and Sarov were on. And thanks to a text from Sølvi, he was able to confirm they weren't on a wild-goose chase.

She had come through with CCTV footage from the Kjeller airfield. Both men had been picked up on camera. Harvath and his team were on the right track.

Next, he had called Holidae Hayes. Despite being awakened from a sound sleep, she had jumped right into action. Once she confirmed that she had made contact with Mercer, she began work on the other things that Harvath had requested.

Knowing there was nothing else he could do at the moment, Harvath parked himself near Nicholas and the dogs and made himself comfortable.

"You going to get some sleep?" the little man asked, opening up his laptop.

Harvath nodded. "I'm going to try. What are you up to?"

"Looking at satellite imagery. There's some unusual activity at a couple of Russian naval bases on the Kola Peninsula."

"Which ones?"

"Zaozyorsk and Vidyayevo."

"What kind of activity?"

"Lots of men and material moving around. Ships being supplied. That kind of thing."

"Are the Russians planning a naval exercise?" asked Harvath.

"Not that we know of. That's why we're paying attention."

"What are the odds it's connected to what we're working on?"

"We can't be certain, which is also why we're paying attention," said Nicholas. "It's a quick flight. Get some sleep. I'll wake you if anything pops up."

• • •

It was just before eight a.m. when The Carlton Group's G700 touched down at Kirkenes airport.

Harvath noticed the temperature difference the moment the forward door was opened. While summer was still hanging on down in Oslo, up in Kirkenes it had completely fled.

The air was cold and had a nasty bite to it. Winter was not far off. Having almost frozen to death earlier in the year, he couldn't wait to finish this assignment and get the hell out of here.

As he descended the stairs and stepped onto the tarmac, he could see the vehicles Holidae had organized, waiting for them.

It had already been decided that Sloane and Chase would take over surveillance of Han while Harvath met with Mercer and the rest of the team set up the new safe house.

After transferring the gear to the vehicles, everyone headed out.

With Chase driving and Sloane in back assembling equipment, Harvath jumped into their SUV and rode shotgun for the ride into town.

"Feeling any better?" Chase asked him as they exited the airport and merged onto the main road.

"Headache's gone at least," Harvath replied.

"Is that a good sign?" the younger operative said. "I've never had syphilis."

Harvath was about to respond, when Chase looked in his rearview mirror and asked, "Sloane, is that a good sign?"

Harvath didn't need to look back to know she was giving Chase the finger.

"Your concern for my well-being notwithstanding," Harvath remarked, "let's talk about what we need to focus on. Just over the border, Russia's Northern Fleet is gearing up for something. We don't know what it is. We also don't know if it is connected to the Chinese national we're here to surveil.

"The only thing that matters is that you don't lose sight of him. If he moves, you move—and you move in such a way that he doesn't know he's being shadowed. You also have each other's backs. You don't split up for any reason. Is that clear?"

"Roger that," they responded.

"Good. Do we need to stop and pick up anything?"

"Negative," Sloane replied from the rear seat. "We grabbed some coffee and water, along with a few other things, on our way off the plane. We're more than fine."

Harvath was glad to hear it. He also appreciated her attitude. Sitting in a climate-controlled vehicle was practically a Ritz-Carlton–level experience compared to what all of them had faced at one point or another in their careers. As far as hide sites went, a warm car, replete with coffee, water, and snacks, was hard to beat.

When they pulled into the far end of the Thon Hotel's parking lot, Harvath spotted the vehicle they were looking for and directed Chase to drive toward it. Behind him, Harvath heard Sloane charge her weapon.

"Are you expecting something?" he asked, looking to keep the operational temperature low.

"Have you ever met this guy?"

"Not yet."

"That makes three of us," she replied. "As far as I'm concerned, he's not cool *until* he's cool."

"Good copy," said Harvath, acknowledging her concern. "Stay alert."

In response, she placed a Glock 19, along with two additional magazines, atop the forward armrest.

Chase picked up the pistol, racked its slide, and tucked it between his seat and the center console. The magazines went into a pocket.

Harvath, who was still carrying his H&K VP40, left it where it was in its holster. Just because these two were feeling a little froggy didn't mean he was ready to jump.

They pulled up next to Mercer, who was sitting in a gray Mitsubishi Outlander, watching the main entrance.

After taking another look at the photo Holidae had texted and confirming it was him, Harvath debussed and stepped outside.

The first thing he noticed was the smell of the ocean. There was something different about it this far north. It was more intense than in Oslo. More briny. He liked it.

Mercer popped the locks of his SUV and waved for him to come join him. Harvath obliged. He walked over, opened the door, and climbed in.

The ex–CIA operative was exactly as Holidae had described him. He was a handsome man in his mid-sixties—tall, with a prominent nose and a chin to match. With reddish-brown hair and pale, gray eyes, there was a gritty toughness to him.

Straight out of central casting, he could have strapped on a pair of spurs and walked onto any John Ford or Sergio Leone movie set. Mercer held out his enormous paw and Harvath shook it.

"Welcome to Paradise," Mercer said.

"I wish it was under different circumstances," Harvath replied. "Thanks for doing this."

"Though I earned every penny of my pension—and then some— I still appreciate that Uncle Sugar makes my direct deposits on time each month."

"Understood."

"More importantly," the man continued, "I couldn't pass up the chance to meet Reed Carlton's protégé."

"Did you know him?"

"*Did I know him?* Hell yes, I knew him. I used to work for him. In fact, I was there the day he got his nickname."

CHAPTER 28

"Have you never been told the *full* story?" Mercer asked. "I mean, to be fair, you can't really appreciate a nickname like that unless you know *everything* that took place."

Harvath had never actually heard the full story before. "I'd love to hear it," he replied.

"Perfect. I'll tell you over breakfast." Looking over at Chase and Sloane in the car next to them, he added, "Are those two steely-eyed killers my relief?"

"That's correct," Harvath answered. "They're taking over surveillance. Anything they need to know?"

"If they leave town, they should make sure they're armed. The wolves have been bad this year."

Harvath, who'd had his own brush with wolves just over the Russian border, reassured him, "Don't worry about those two. They're always armed."

"Good. Do you need anything out of their vehicle before we take off?"

"Nope. I'm all set."

"Okay, then," said the ex–CIA man. "Let's hit the road."

The seaside village was small, and it didn't take long to be given the nickel tour, which Mercer admitted was overpriced.

They passed the Soviet Liberation Monument, which had been erected by grateful Norwegians after Stalin's Red Army, in the final months of World War II, liberated Kirkenes and the surrounding area from the Nazis.

Next was the entrance to the Andersgrotta, a World War II–era bunker that could hold up to 2,500 people. Because of its proximity to the Russian border and high concentration of Nazi troops, Kirkenes was the most heavily bombed city in all of Norway, suffering 328 air raids.

Harvath found it ironic that the locals hated the Nazis so much, they erected a monument to the people who had bombed the hell out of their village—even though one such attack had included Soviet high-explosive and phosphorus bombs that burned 170 houses to the ground.

They passed the Kirkenes Church, surrounded with its white picket fence, and then did a drive-by of the Russian Consulate. Mercer made sure to point out the statue of a little bear humping a flagpole just outside.

"Is that for real?" Harvath asked.

"Norwegians," the man replied with a shrug. "There's another one right across the street."

Harvath shook his head. He had no idea if it had been done as a quiet insult to the Russians or not. It reminded him of when he had stepped out of the train station in St. Petersburg years ago to see a dog whizzing on a statue of Lenin. Both sights had made him smile.

Doubling back toward the church, Mercer found a parking spot, shut off his ignition, and said, "We go the rest of the way on foot."

Amundsens was a quaint restaurant and bakery with an outdoor patio, located on a pedestrianized thoroughfare.

"Inside or out?" asked Mercer.

"Up to you."

The man gazed up at the overcast sky. "Let's sit outside. Not many pretty days like this left."

Harvath chuckled and followed him onto the patio.

A waitress greeted them and told them to pick any table they wanted. They chose one in the corner where they could chat undisturbed.

Harvath ordered eggs and coffee. Mercer ordered coffee and French toast.

As soon as the waitress had gone, Harvath asked, "What do you know about the Russian Consul General?"

"Sarov? Not much. According to Holidae, he used to be a spook. In fact, knowing the Russians, he probably still is."

"Anything else?"

Mercer shook his head. "He keeps a pretty low profile."

"The man you followed from the airport this morning has been traveling under the alias of Zhang Wei. His real name is Han Guang. He's a Chinese Intelligence officer working for the Ministry of State Security."

"Another spook."

Harvath nodded. "What do you think they're up to?"

Mercer thought about it for a moment. "The only time the Russians get in bed with the Chinese is when they need something. It could be money. It could be technology. You name it."

"But why not leave that to diplomats? People who can meet unobstructed in Moscow or Beijing. Why risk clandestine, spook-to-spook meetings in Oslo?"

It was a good question. "Maybe," Mercer replied, "Han wants to defect and Sarov is in charge of vetting him. Maybe they have a history together. Maybe they don't. Either way, Norway may have been the only country Han could travel to without raising alarm bells back home.

"And if I'm Sarov, I'm not going to interview him in my own backyard. I've been trained better than that. Oslo would have been the smarter choice."

"Until I showed up and crashed the party," said Harvath.

"In response to which, they hotfooted it up here—just a stone's throw from the Russian border."

"Only after sending an embassy secretary to the hotel to grab his suitcases and drive them to the airfield. Why go to that trouble? If the situation was dangerous enough that you had to flee right away—in the middle of the night—why not just buy the guy new clothes and a toothbrush when you got him to safety?"

"Because he was carrying something of value."

"Such as?"

"Maybe just personal effects, mementos of the life he was leaving back in China."

"I don't buy that," said Harvath. "What intelligence officer would jeopardize his escape by carrying damning evidence? If the Chinese were harboring any suspicions of him and searched his bags before he left the country, it'd be all over. He would have gotten a bullet in the head and the bill sent to his family."

"It could be a million other things. Additional passports hidden in the lining. Cash. Gold coins. A micro drive with schematics for a new stealth fighter. A stolen vial of virus. Who knows? All that matters is that it was important enough to Han, the Russians, or both to risk going back for."

"That I can buy. What about the sudden uptick in activity by Russia's Northern Fleet?"

"At Zaozyorsk and Vidyayevo?" Mercer asked.

Harvath nodded.

"Snap military drills are nothing new for the Russians. It's how they test their readiness."

"What kind of boats are at those bases?"

"Zaozyorsk is home to the 11th Squadron. Typhoon-class submarines as well as Oscars and Yasens."

"Which means ballistic missiles on the Typhoon class and cruise missiles on the Oscar and Yasen classes," Harvath replied.

"Correct."

"And at Vidyayevo?"

"That's the 7th Division. Sierra and Victor classes."

"Attack subs."

Mercer nodded. "Fast and quiet. Meant to protect Russian surface vessels and carry out search-and-destroy operations against American ballistic missile submarines."

Harvath didn't like it. "In the middle of all this, we have the Russians bringing a Chinese Intelligence officer in for a front-row seat."

"You think that's why Han is here? You think it's connected?"

"I don't believe in coincidences."

"Neither do I. So what do you want to do?"

"What I *want* to do and want I *can* do are two very different things. I'd like to put bags over their heads—"

"Han *and* Sarov," Mercer clarified.

"Yes, both of them. I'd like to put them in a very deep, very dark hole and work on them until I get answers. But this isn't that kind of assignment. We've been tasked with conducting surveillance and gathering intel. That's all."

"So your hands are tied."

"To a degree," said Harvath. "But the situation is fluid. Things can change."

"They always do," the ex–CIA man replied as the waitress brought their coffee.

Once she had left the table, he continued. "For the moment, all you can do is keep Han in your sights and report back on what happens."

"Sit and wait," Harvath muttered. "Two of my least favorite activities."

"What about finding a way to smoke them out—to force their hand somehow?"

"My concern is that they'd take off again, just like they did from Oslo. Except this time they'd bolt straight into Russia and that'd be the end of my operation."

"Good point," said Mercer. "So why haven't they?"

"Bolted?"

"Yeah. I could hit the border with a nine iron from here. What are they waiting for? Why smuggle Han out of Oslo, bring him all the way up to Kirkenes, just to stop short of being home free? They're untouchable in Russia. Even if this is a defection, they can keep interviewing him on the other side. If they don't like his answers or whatever item of value he might be offering for his freedom, they can kick him out. Or, better yet, give him the same bullet in the back of the head and shallow-grave treatment he'd get back home. Why bring him this close only to park him in a hotel?"

"I can think of two reasons," Harvath replied, tumbling the possibilities in his brain. "The first one is that this is some kind of subtle torture. The border is within reach—Han's *freedom* is within reach. But unless and until he gives them what they want, he sits here in a quasi–state of purgatory with the ever-present threat of being abandoned or captured by the other side."

"Very possible," said Mercer. "We used that threat all the time at Langley."

"Still do. Because it works."

"Agreed. What's the second reason?"

"The second reason is that whatever the Russians want from Han, it has something to do with Kirkenes. More specifically, it has something to do with Han being *in* Kirkenes."

"Such as?"

"I'm not one hundred percent on it yet," he said, taking a sip of his coffee. "I need to work on it a bit more. It'll come. In the meantime, let's talk about Reed Carlton."

CHAPTER 29

"**O**ur unit," Mercer began, "was called Huracan—after the vengeful, population-destroying, Mayan god of wind, storm, and fire."

"It's where the word *hurricane* comes from, right?"

"Precisely. You didn't come to us when you wanted bad things done; you came to us when you wanted *worse*—worse than what America's enemies were prepared to do. And at that time, America's number one enemy was the Soviet Union and all of the proxy forces it supported.

"Top to bottom, Huracan was Reed Carlton's baby. He had not only come up with the idea but he had also convinced the CIA to let him build it and run it. Our mission was twofold: We both countered threats and worked to destabilize the organizations they emanated from.

"We did that by pissing inside their tents, sowing as much chaos, suspicion, and doubt as possible. We turned members against each other and caused them all to question Moscow. As Reed liked to say, our specialty was putting out fires *with* gasoline.

"He was an amazing field operative, a strategist of the highest order. He was like one of those savants who could handle ten simultaneous chess matches. No matter how many boards he was playing, he dominated all of them."

"He was one-of-a-kind," Harvath concurred. "How did you get hooked up with him?"

"I'd had a good run with the 1st Ranger Battalion, but I was looking for more excitement, a bigger challenge," replied Mercer. "I had heard a lot about Delta Force and decided I'd give it a shot. During selection, I was pulled off an exercise and told to report to the Delta commander. I thought for sure I had screwed something up and was going to be sent packing.

"When I arrived at the CO's office, he told me to sit down, shut up, and do whatever the next person who came into the room told me to do."

"And that next person was Reed?"

"It was. He made me an incredible offer. He wanted me on Huracan. Told me that I'd get to see and do things even the Delta operatives would be envious of. The hitch was that I had to make my decision right there and then. No 'sleeping' on it. No 'Can I get back to you in a couple of days?' Yes or no.

"To say he was persuasive would be an understatement. I was beyond intrigued and took the position on the spot. It was one of the best decisions of my life. I couldn't have asked for a better boss or a more exciting career."

"Yet how is it that I've never met you?" asked Harvath. "I haven't even heard of you. On top of that, I didn't see you at his funeral."

"Things didn't end well between us."

"What happened?"

"Let's just say I had a good reason to get out," Mercer answered. "Actually, a *great* reason."

"Your wife?"

"She was definitely part of it, but I also got offered a different position— one that allowed me to continue working in intelligence and to be based here in Norway. It was a no-brainer—even if Reed didn't approve. That's where we differed. He thought I needed his approval. I didn't.

"Like I said, he was a great boss and I loved my time with Huracan, but it was time for a change. I didn't want to live that life anymore. And as persuasive as Reed was, he was also really fucking manipulative. I could always see it coming a mile away and was subsequently immune to it. Deep down I know he respected me for being my own man. I'm also certain it pissed him off.

"He inferred that my taking another job was a form of betrayal. He'd always seen himself as this father figure and saw me as a sort of son who owed him loyalty and obedience. But I already had a father and was quite comfortable with that relationship.

"When I left Huracan, I never heard from Reed again. I was disappointed, of course, but that's the way the cookie crumbles. If he wanted to act that way, that was his choice. He went on with his life and I did the same with mine. What's the Robert Frost quote? *Two roads diverged in a wood, and I—I took the one less traveled by . . .*"

"*And that has made all the difference,*" said Harvath.

"Amen."

"I'm sorry your relationship with him turned out the way that it did. He was a very proud and often stubborn man. The words *Sorry* or *You were right* didn't exactly roll off his tongue."

"I made my peace with it a long time ago. It's all water under the bridge at this point," Mercer sighed.

"You would have been welcome at the funeral. Had I known all of this, I would have extended you an invitation."

"I'm sure there were a few faces I would have enjoyed seeing, but don't worry about it. I said my own private, personal goodbye from here."

"Nevertheless, you missed out on some great stories."

"No doubt. He was quite the character."

"Speaking of stories," said Harvath. "How he got his nickname would have been a hit at the Irish wake we threw him."

"Depending on who was in the room, I might have had to redact a few details here and there. We broke a lot of rules back then, along with a few laws, but World War Three never happened. I'd like to think it was because of what we did, not despite it."

The waitress came over and set their breakfast orders down. After topping off their coffees, she went to attend to another table. As Harvath began eating his meal, Mercer continued his story.

"Picture Berlin in 1985. It was four years before the wall would come down—something we couldn't even see coming. Not then. Sure, the Soviets weren't doing well. Their occupation of Afghanistan had been a disaster, but they had kept it up because they wanted every Soviet soldier to cycle through that meat grinder and come out having seen combat. That was formidable. No other army in the world had that kind of experience at that time. Not even ours.

"There was, though, another reason they stayed. Quite simply, they had zero idea how to properly extricate themselves and get the hell out. Afghanistan was an anchor tied around their necks. It was dragging them to the bottom of the ocean. We, of course, were putting rocks in their pockets by backing the Mujahideen against them. That, of course, would come back to bite us in the ass big-time, but just like we couldn't foresee the fall of the wall, we couldn't see 9/11 coming either—especially not at that distance.

"Meanwhile, throughout the Soviet Union, the Communist Party was a joke—a mobbed-up bunch of corrupt plutocrats. Sooner or later, the music was going to stop and there weren't enough chairs for everybody. They were all beginning to sense it, and it scared the hell out of them. Most had begun looking for the exits.

"A handful thought that maybe they could reverse the Soviet Union's decline and had begun looking for something that would restore its 'greatness.' Something that would put them back on top.

"One genius at the KGB decided he had a brilliant idea. He wanted to step up to the plate and try to knock one out of the park. Forget for a moment that in the intelligence game your most valuable players hit doubles, maybe the occasional triple. What you do not do is walk up and place everything on hitting a home run. They're just too damn dangerous. Only the Russians could have been desperate enough to try to pull the kind of operation they did.

"So, as I said, it's 1985. September twenty-seventh, to be exact. Wettest day in D.C. history. Almost four inches of rain in twenty-four hours. When we boarded our plane for Berlin, 'Money for Nothing' by Dire Straits was the number one song in the United States. When we landed in Germany, they were all going crazy for some guy named Falco and a song called 'Rock Me Amadeus.' Not exactly my type of music, but at least it wasn't raining.

"The Huracan team had been rushed to Europe because a NATO diplomat and his family had been taken hostage. And not just any NATO diplomat, mind you. We're talking a deputy chief of staff—with lots of top secret information, particularly as it pertained to force strength and nuclear posture. Not the kind of person you wanted falling into enemy hands.

"From all of the available evidence, it looked like the German Red Army Faction was behind the kidnapping. But something didn't feel right to Reed. The entire flight over, he'd been working his sources. Unfortunately, no one knew anything—not even an asset he had within the terrorist organization itself. It was all too clean. Way too clean. Reed smelled a rat. A big Russian one.

"So Reed being Reed, what did he do? He started strategizing. He was looking at pictures of the family, the house, the location where everything went down, the protective detail who were killed, and he began to reverse engineer what had taken place.

"Bit by bit, inch by inch, he began to develop an alternative picture of events. Nobody else could see what he was seeing, of course. At least not yet. The whole thing needed more meat on the bone. So Reed kept pushing.

"As soon as we're wheels down, he reached out to even more contacts. He had CIA station chiefs throughout Europe—including Berlin—push, pull, and cajole their sources. It was perfectly clear to everyone that he was not going to stop until he found a crack of daylight with which to blow the case wide-open.

"And then, two days after we arrive, it happened."

CHAPTER 30

"Word got to Reed about a safe house in East Berlin," said Mercer. "It was allegedly under the control of East Germany's secret police—the Stasi. But as he continued to dig, it turned out the property belonged to the KGB.

"It was considered to be their crown jewel in East Berlin. The site was said to be so secure, they operated from within it with impunity. Absolutely no fear. They believed it was impregnable. The Russians had balls the size of church bells. But Reed Carlton's were bigger.

"From all of the intelligence he had been able to gather, the safe house was where the KGB conducted its most sensitive assignments. Everything pointed to it being the most likely location of the diplomat and his family.

"That wasn't good enough for Reed, though. Not for the kind of operation he was planning. He needed actual eyes on. And to accomplish that, he would need help. Enter the Brits.

"MI6 had a solid operation in East Berlin, particularly that sector. If anyone could get him the confirmation he needed, it was the British.

"The important thing to keep in mind is that, for its day, this was like mounting the bin Laden raid, but with a lot less money and none of the time. We didn't have the ability to mock up an identical structure we could practice on. And our surveillance capabilities back then were nothing compared to what we have today. The best and only thing we had going for us was that the Russians didn't know we were coming.

"Among the team members, we thought that they might also be feeling so untouchable that their guard would be down. But Reed disabused us of that notion right away. 'Always,' he commanded us, 'assume that your adversary is better equipped, better trained, and better prepared for the fight than you are.' It was advice all of us took to heart and never forgot.

"He was completely correct, of course. To hope that we'd make entry and easily dispatch a bunch of half-drunk, sleepy Russians was not only arrogant on our part; it was also stupid and dangerous. He had put the fear of God into us and the operation was better for it.

"While the Brits worked to confirm, or get as close to confirmation as they could, that the diplomat and his family were inside, we got down to the even harder work—crafting a plan to get in and out. And not just of the safe house but of East Berlin itself.

"As was his fashion, Reed preferred to plan backward, starting with the extraction. While there would always be contingencies, he began with the assumption that the mission had been successful and the team had achieved its objective. That meant that we had secured the diplomat, his wife, and two teenage children. All that remained was to get them back safely into West Berlin. And Reed had been very clear about what his expectations were on that front. Because we'd be leaving with four extra people, our escape would have to be via a completely different method.

"Getting into East Berlin was going to be dangerous enough, but when I saw what our means of extraction would be, I'm sure my eyes were bugging out of my head. Nevertheless, it had been decided.

"While we waited to hear from the Brits, we worked up an equipment list and set to tracking down everything we needed and getting people in place. We were fortunate to have the budget we did. It would have been a real pain in the ass stealing some of that stuff.

"By the time the Brits got back to us, we had everything pretty much locked down. The only thing left was to decide if there was enough intel to go on. Based on the Brits' assessment, there was a seventy percent probability that the diplomat and his family were in the safe house. We had reached the go/no go point.

"If we were right and the hostages were inside, then it was 'Screw the

Russians.' They were the bad actors, and any blood would be on their hands. But if we were wrong, and they weren't inside, then we were the ones who would be screwed. Reed made the decision that we would launch the next night.

"I remember that the moon was bright, which was not at all good for us. But we didn't have a choice. It would be at least eight more days before we'd get a moonless night. There was no way we could let the diplomat and his family wait that long.

"Four ultralights were rolled out of a secure hangar at Tempelhof Airport just before midnight. Affixed to the wings of the two-seater aircraft were bright red stars meant to mimic planes from the Soviet air force. The look wasn't perfect, but it didn't necessarily have to be. All we wanted was to give GDR troops a reason *not* to shoot at us if we were spotted.

"Our assault force consisted of four Huracan members—me, Reed, a guy named Davis, and another named Thompson. Because of weight limitations, there was only so much gear we could take with us. Each man carried a pistol, a suppressed MP5 submachine gun, spare magazines, and a handful of other goodies.

"Four pilots with ultralight experience had been flown in from Ramstein Air Base. Like us, we kitted them out with night vision goggles. Their mission was to fly us over the wall to a makeshift airstrip the Brits had set up in the middle of Treptower Park."

"Isn't there a Soviet war memorial there too?" asked Harvath, who had operated in Berlin before as well.

"That's correct. In fact, the best piece of grass for us to put down on was right in front of it, so that's exactly where we landed," Mercer explained. "Unfortunately, it was too risky for the ultralights to sit there in the middle of the park, and wait for us. Therefore, they had only one job—to get us in and then get themselves the hell out.

"It felt like we sat on the tarmac forever, waiting for the all clear to take off. But until the next phase of the operation had been completed, there was nothing we could do.

"A Special Forces team had been sent into the East German state of Saxony. There, they would create the diversion Reed had asked for.

"It had been important that the diversion be big. Massive, even. Anything localized to just the safe house would put the team inside on alert. If the diversion was felt across the city of East Berlin, it was less likely to cause suspicion. And in Reed's estimation, the best way to fool a Russian was to wrap the deception in the cloak of something they were all too accustomed to—state ineptitude.

"At the appointed time, explosives were detonated at the power plants of Vockerode and Thierbach. Seconds later, East Berlin was plunged into a complete and total blackout.

"As soon as spotters confirmed that the lights had gone out, we were given permission to take off."

CHAPTER 31

"The flight was quick. Less than five minutes. The pilots were able to pick out the infrared markers the Brits had laid down and brought the ultralights in for perfect landings. They stopped only long enough for each of us to grab our gear and hop out.

"By the time the third aircraft had touched down, the first one was already at the end of the grass, turning, and powering up to take off.

"Our British contact was keeping watch from the tree line. After we climbed out of the ultralights, he gave us a signal and we made our way over to him. I'll never forget him. He had a ruddy complexion and perpetually bloodshot eyes. The man's name was Ashford," said Mercer.

"*Robert* Ashford?" Harvath asked.

"Yeah. That's the guy. Do you know him?"

Harvath had known him all right. Ashford had been one of the Old Man's most trusted contacts in British Intelligence. But late in his career Ashford had decided to cash in on his position and had succumbed to his lesser angels.

Ashford was working at MI5 at the time, looking to feather his nest and slip into a very luxurious retirement. He made the wrong choice of selling out both his country and his allies.

So egregious was his transgression that Reed Carlton could have had him killed. One word from Carlton and Harvath would have gladly done it. Instead, the Old Man had come up with a different plan for Ashford. In exchange for his cooperation, the Brit's life had been spared, but he had been banished to a small fishing village in Alaska where he worked a backbreaking job on a trawler named *Rawhide*.

When Ashford died, Carlton had sent Harvath to ID the body and confirm it. He was buried in a small church graveyard under the new identity he had been given.

It was Ashford, long before Harvath knew that he was dirty, who had revealed the Old Man's nickname.

"I knew him," Harvath said matter-of-factly. "He died a couple of years ago. Heart attack."

"That's too bad. He and Reed were pals. They conducted a lot of assignments together."

"Did you ever do any ops with him?" Harvath asked, probing for whether Mercer may have been compromised at any point.

"I only encountered him a handful of times. All of which were during my tenure with Huracan."

Harvath was glad to hear that. "So what happened after you were on the ground and had linked up with Ashford?"

"After making sure the ultralights had all safely gotten away, Ashford extinguished the IR beacons and we headed for the KGB safe house. A block away, we met up with a team of ex-SAS operatives who accompanied us for the takedown.

"We had all been through extensive hostage-rescue training. Davis and Thompson, ex–Delta Force, were especially experienced, as were several on the SAS side. According to the intel the Brits had developed, the diplomat and his family were being kept in different rooms on different floors of the house. This made the assault more difficult, but it also meant that the Russians were likely to be more spread out.

"The biggest question of all was whether the KGB officers would kill their captives once they realized an attack was under way.

"Our feeling was that, while normally a terrorist tactic, we couldn't be absolutely sure. We had to operate as if each family member was guarded by an armed antagonist who had explicit orders to kill. That meant that it was of the utmost necessity that the assignment adhere to the maxim: speed, surprise, and overwhelming violence of action.

"In addition to the radios they had brought for us, the SAS guys were carrying ropes and harnesses. They would access the roof from an adjacent building and come down from above. The Huracan team would split in half and hit the front and back doors simultaneously.

"At best guess, there were four, possibly six Russians inside. They were believed to be armed but not heavily. Pistols, maybe shotguns. Not that it made a difference. In a close-quarters hostage situation, any firearm was bad. It was critical that we all excecuted our roles flawlessly.

"As Ashford was the only one among us without deep hostage-rescue training, he was to remain outside as a spotter. If any local military or law enforcement showed up, his job was to slow them down by any means possible—including the use of a pistol and a handful of grenades he had been armed with.

"Once the SAS team was in place on the roof, Davis and I crept up and placed a C-4 charge on the front door while Reed and Thompson did the same in back.

"When everyone was confirmed good to go, Reed gave the order to hit the safe house.

"The charges detonated, throwing open the front and rear doors, and showering the downstairs in wood, steel, and broken plaster. Upstairs, glass shattered as the SAS men exploded through the windows and an old skylight.

"As we made our entry, we tossed out flashbangs and swept from room to room, engaging the Russians.

"Many of the KGB operatives, as hoped, had been asleep—but not all of them. Those who could be shot immediately were. The others returned fire.

"It was a hell of a gunfight. And it wasn't until it was all over that we realized the Brits had underestimated the number of Russians inside the safe house. It was more than double their worst-case scenario. By the time the smoke cleared, we counted thirteen in total, but that wasn't the worst of it.

"The diplomat was found chained to a metal cot upstairs. He had been badly beaten and we would later learn that he had been psychologically tortured via an intensely bright lamp that had remained on, night and day, since his capture. The blackout was the first time the light had been extinguished.

"His son was found in the next room, handcuffed to a radiator. While he had also taken more than a few blows, he was in much better shape than his father. The true horror of the house, however, was what had been taking place downstairs.

"They found the diplomat's wife in the living room and his teenage daughter in the kitchen. Both were bloodied, naked, and appeared to be under the influence of some sort of narcotic.

"On the kitchen floor, near the daughter, one of the Russians lay bleeding from his gunshot wounds but still alive. His trousers were undone. It didn't take a lot of creativity to imagine what they had been doing to the women. That was the breaking point for Reed.

"He spat a question at the guy in Russian, but the man refused to answer. Grabbing the nearest object he could find, he slammed an enormous can of fruit right into the KGB officer's nuts. I'm talking really hard. Then he posed the question again. Still the guy refused to answer. So Reed went to work on him even harder.

"He ended up rupturing both of the Russian's testicles and mangling the hell out of the man's magic wand. None of us had ever seen anything like it.

"We used to joke that Reed only had one soft spot—women, children, and animals. In fact, we used to tease him about it—me included, even though he was my superior. What those Russians had done, however, was absolutely beyond the pale. We all felt it. Reed was not only outraged by it; he was also offended.

"There was a code. Call it a sense of decency. As bad as the Russians were, he expected them to live by it. The Arab terrorists were animals. He expected this kind of savagery from them. But not from the Russians— and especially not KGB operatives.

"He expected a certain degree of Marquess of Queensbury out of them. In a word, he found them ungentlemanly. They had crossed a bright line. Out of a sense of honor, Reed needed to make things right.

"That guy with the busted-up wedding tackle was the only one left alive at the safe house—a message to Moscow.

"The diplomat and his son, as beaten up as they were, were strong enough to walk. The wife and daughter had a much more difficult time. We ended up having to carry them out.

"Ever the strategist, Reed had anticipated that we might be dealing with injuries and had come up with a plan.

"Ashford and his team got us to the extraction point and established a perimeter as we mounted the stairs to the roof of the building.

"We were literally within the shadow of the infamous wall, which was actually two walls. Looking down, we could see the area in between known as the *death strip*. Guard towers, fences capped with barbed wire, dog patrols, anti-vehicle trenches, floodlights, trip wire–activated machine guns, land mines . . . It was a nightmare.

"Reed had selected this spot along the death strip because it was the narrowest. From where we were crouched, we could actually hear people walking down the street and having conversations on the West Berlin side of the wall.

"As Davis, Thompson, and I prepped the diplomat and his family, Reed unpacked and assembled the meanest crossbow I had ever seen. Along with it he had a spool of high-test nylon filament that he slid onto what looked like an improvised reel jack made from a toilet paper stand.

"Affixing one end of the filament to a bolt, he cocked the bowstring and loaded the bolt into the barrel groove. Then, as he shouldered the weapon and activated his night vision scope, he had me burst a quick infrared signal to a car he had waiting on the other side. The driver of the car turned on his own infrared beacon, which was sitting atop a stack of sandbags on the street.

"After taking one last check of the wind, Reed flicked off his safety, exhaled, and let the bolt fly."

"Let me guess," said Harvath. "Nailed it. Dead center."

"Not even close," Mercer replied with a grin. "We didn't know it until after, but not only had he overshot the sandbags but he had almost impaled our driver who had been standing what he thought was a safe distance away, next to his vehicle. The bolt hit the car, went straight through the left rear quarter panel, and came within an inch of puncturing the tire."

Harvath laughed and the pain in his ribs reminded him to pop a couple more ibuprofen. As he reached for his water, Mercer continued.

"Now that the nylon line was all the way across, we attached a steel cable and had the driver pull it over. Once it had reached him, he attached it to the back of his vehicle while I wrapped our end of the cable around a chimney. Then we had him inch the car forward until the line was taut.

"We couldn't send the diplomat or any of his family members out yet. One of us had to go first to make sure it was safe. Davis, Thompson, and I all volunteered. Reed chose Davis.

"Passing on wearing a harness, he clicked the trolley onto the line, made sure it could support his weight, and, with his MP5 slung across his back, swung over the edge of the roof and zip-lined into West Berlin.

"Next, we tried to send the diplomat, but he insisted his family go first. So we explained to his son how the braking system worked, affixed his harness, and sent him across.

"The daughter was to follow, but there was no way that she would be able to sit upright. This is where Reed's preplanning had paid off.

"He had brought along what resembled a canvas body bag. Once she was all set, we attached the bag to the cable, trailed a rope behind it, and slowly lowered her to the other side.

"It was an arduous process that left the daughter exposed for far too long, in my opinion, but it worked. As soon as she was extricated by the driver and her brother, we pulled the bag back and repeated the process for the diplomat's wife.

"After she was safely on the other side, we sent the diplomat over. Then Thompson went. Finally, it was just me and Reed standing on the roof. I told him I'd take the last ride, but he would have nothing of it. I was to go, followed by him. I had my orders and so clicked in and took one of the most exhilarating rides I've ever taken in my life.

"I knew Reed had placed snipers on the West Berlin side, ready to take out any GDR soldiers who might have spotted and shot at us, but no roller coaster before or since has ever gotten my heart beating and my blood pumping like what we did that night. The operation had been a success."

"That's a real hall of fame story. One for the history books," said Harvath.

"Absolutely."

"So what about Reed's nickname?"

"There's always a team debrief," said Mercer, smiling as he remembered it.

"Always," Harvath agreed. "And it's always made better in the presence of alcohol."

"Too true. Which means it won't surprise you to learn that once we got the diplomat and his family safely back to the embassy, we decided to have a drink in order to take the edge off."

"We never did that in the SEAL Teams, but I'll take your word for it that other units like to do that."

Mercer laughed again. "We had agreed to meet Ashford and the Brits, who had their own exfil plan, along with the Special Forces team that had gone into Saxony to hit the power plants. There was a little pub the SF guys had made their spot called the—"

"Leydicke," Harvath interrupted. "Number four, Mansteinstrasse."

"How the hell did you know that?"

"It's a long story. Suffice it to say I was there many years ago and am familiar with the U.S. Army's Special Forces Berlin unit. I know all about how they were a top secret guerrilla force meant to create all sorts of chaos if the Soviets ever overran the wall. The Leydicke was not only where they went to drink; it was an intel hub of sorts. If those walls only had ears . . ."

"Which, thankfully, they didn't," said Mercer.

"Anyway, it's a great bar and played a significant unsung role in the history of the Cold War. There should be a big bronze plaque outside it."

"I agree with you—on everything but the plaque. The place has been in the family for generations and I don't think they'd want the attention."

"Fair enough," said Harvath.

"So we all met up at the Leydicke. The beer was flowing. The crazy SF guys all had their personalized beer steins wrapped at the bottom with pieces of barbed wire they risked their lives to steal from the wall. And we started talking about the op.

"When it gets to the takedown of the safe house, the SAS guys were super-modest and rushed through how it all went down. Textbook. More Russians than anticipated, but nothing that couldn't be handled.

Before you know it, 'Bob's your uncle,' and Reed was administering what the Brits were calling 'cowboy justice.'

"They talked about how merciless he had been and how the Russian had more than deserved it. One of the SAS men had even picked up the can, wanting to bring it out as a trophy, but it had been too big for his pack and so he had left it behind.

"Another proposed that Reed needed a new call sign—something that better reflected his most unique contribution to the operation. At that point, the ideas started flying: *Mad Dog. Crusher. Ball Buster. Pincer. The Nutcracker.*

"Finally, Ashford, who had been sipping on a schnapps, piped up in his effete, proper British accent and said, 'Seeing as how our American colleague so elegantly weaponized that tin of *Prunus persica*, I think it only fitting that he should heretofore be known as *Peaches*.'

"It was, of course, the perfect call sign, and everyone absolutely lost it. I mean falling out of our chairs laughing. *Have Peaches will travel*—as a play on the old TV western—became a regular joke inside, and even outside, Huracan."

Harvath smiled. He had always heard the nickname was a play on how rough the Old Man could be in interrogations. It was good to have a firsthand account of the origin story. He wasn't done asking questions, though.

CHAPTER 32

"How'd you end up in Norway?" he asked as the waitress cleared their dishes away.

"Like I said, I'd had a lot of fun with Huracan. One morning, though, I just woke up and was ready to get out. As a Ranger, my body had taken a pretty good beating. Nothing a couple of surgeries couldn't fix, but the pace and intensity with Reed was creating all new sorts of damage.

"Listen, I'm not complaining. Some guys are rock stars and can keep at it forever. I just wasn't one of them. Did I believe in the mission? Absolutely. Did I mind climbing into the meat grinder day after day after day? Not at all. But then one day it was like a switch had been flipped. I was done. I'd had enough.

"Reed, as I mentioned, was plenty pissed. I tried to make it amicable, but there was no reasoning with him. You would've thought that I was walking out right in the middle of a gunfight. In the end, there was only so much that I could do. He took my departure the way he took it, and that was on him.

"There was this 'ride-or-die' mentality at Huracan. That's all well and good. I understand camaraderie and unit cohesion. But it went beyond that.

"Several of the guys thought Reed was addicted to the job. I think it was a form of penance for him."

"*Penance?*" Harvath asked.

"Did you ever meet his mentor? Thomas Carver Banks?"

"Tommy? Of course. He was a legend. One of the youngest OSS op-eratives in World War II. Killed a lot of Nazis—often by himself and with his own bare hands."

"Back in their CIA days, I think he and Reed got into some serious, height-of-the-Cold-War sort of stuff—things neither of them could blot out simply by closing their eyes at night or saying a few extra Hail Marys."

Though he didn't need to say anything, he felt honor bound to de-fend Carlton. The man had been like a father to him. "Those were tough times," Harvath replied. "Many people will never realize how much was at stake."

"Agreed," said Mercer. "We were very lucky to have them. Believe me, I'm not passing judgment on Reed or Tommy. All I'm saying is that sometimes the job required a certain moral flexibility. It wasn't as cut-and-dried as it was with the Nazis. They had to make tough decisions, far from home, with the weight of the world upon them, and I have no rea-son to believe they didn't make the right decisions. It just seemed like it had taken a toll—at least on Reed.

"It wasn't that he was being chased by some kind of demon but that *he* was chasing after one. And no matter how hard or how fast he ran, he was always one step behind. It's armchair psychology. I could be totally off. In my opinion, he had something to prove, and no matter how brilliant or courageous he was, he felt that he hadn't done enough. I don't know what got him to that spot, but I didn't want to end up that way."

Mercer was describing a side of Reed Carlton that Harvath had never seen. Maybe the Old Man had mellowed with age. Or maybe he had made peace with his past. Regardless, Harvath could understand why it impacted his calculus.

People got into, and out of, their business for lots of reasons. Nearly all of them came on board because they believed in the mission and wanted to defend the country. That was certainly true in Harvath's case.

He had long believed that there could be no American dream with-out those willing to protect it. And while he had loved the summer and everything he and Sølvi were building together down in Oslo, he had been itching to get back to work. It was part of who he was on a cellular level. He had always been about protecting those who could not protect themselves. He could never envision walking away from his career. Not fully.

Yet he understood why many people did. Plenty of them aged out and were forced to take retirement. Others wanted more stability and a job better suited to raising a family. He never faulted anyone for pulling the rip cord. The job was grueling. Not everyone was cut out for it. It had been incredibly tough on him and had exacted a heavy price. But each time he had been knocked back or knocked down, he had come back twice as strong and twice as determined.

That was something he had always felt he had in common with the Old Man. Both he and Reed were like lasers, singularly focused on the mission. At least he had been until he had lost Lara.

To have her killed right in front of him was a shock unlike anything he had ever experienced. Not only had it knocked him down; he had stayed down—for a good long while. He had been forced to reevaluate everything. Especially what he truly wanted out of life and what he was willing to do to get it.

Mercer intrigued him. They were similar in a lot of ways. "Tell me about your wife. You said she was part of your decision to move to Norway. How'd you two meet?"

"We'd just finished a punishing assignment in Marseille. One of the Spanish intel guys had a family home on Mallorca and said anyone who wanted it was welcome to use it. I had some vacation days in the bank, so I took him up on it. While the rest of the Huracan team flew back to the U.S., I headed off for a week of R & R in the Mediterranean sun. I met Hilde my first day there.

"She stepped out of a café in Port de Sóller and I remember never having seen a woman that beautiful before. I stood there gaping, feeling like my feet were set in concrete, as she turned the corner and vanished."

"And you call yourself a Ranger," Harvath said, mocking him good-naturedly.

"Right?" Mercer chuckled. "Once I managed to put my eyes back in my head and shake the tranquilizer dart from my rump, I went looking for her. I tore every inch of that village apart, but I still couldn't find her.

"I felt like an idiot for not having walked up to her the moment I first saw her. I was just kind of stunned by how gorgeous she was. Kicking myself, I headed to the beach and got a few hours of sun before returning to the house for a nice, long siesta. By the time I finally got showered and headed out to eat, the bars and restaurants were packed.

"Before leaving Madrid, I had been given a list of all the best places to try out in Port de Sóller. At a very cool spot called Randemar, I was able to snag a seat on the terrace. This place had everything: super music, a great view over the water, incredible food—ten out of ten. And I had just ordered a gin and tonic, when my fifteen out of ten walked in. She looked even more amazing than she had when I'd seen her leaving the café.

"Needless to say, I didn't make the same mistake I had made earlier in the day. She was traveling alone and I invited her to have dinner with me. And now here I am, living in Kirkenes."

"Obviously, it was meant to be," said Harvath, smiling, "but I think you left out a few chapters of the story."

Mercer nodded. "We started dating. It got pretty serious. And I decided I wanted out of Huracan. After making some quiet calls around D.C., I found out about a NATO liaison position between American and Norwegian forces. It paid well enough, had good benefits, and most importantly was based in Norway.

"Hilde and I got married and spent a lot of time in this area. She grew up here and has lots of family around these parts. When I was ready to retire, this seemed as good as any other place. Being from Chicago, I can almost stomach the winters here, but we still spend as much of them as possible away on vacation."

"Any kids?" Harvath asked.

"Hilde has a son from a previous relationship. He lives up here as well. Works at the joint U.S.-Norwegian radar installation at Vardø."

"Doing what?"

"He's a systems engineer. His job involves things like parametrics, signal processing algorithms, and a bunch of other stuff that makes absolutely no sense to an old knuckle dragger like me."

Harvath smiled and asked him another question. "How do you know Holidae Hayes?"

"I'm kind of the village bicycle. I get handed from one station chief to the next."

"Does that mean you freelance for the Agency from time to time?"

Mercer winked. "Maybe. Just don't tell my wife."

"If I ever meet her, I'll make sure not to mention it."

Standing up, the man said, "Well, get ready not to mention it."

Harvath glanced over his shoulder and saw a stunning woman accompanied by two young men headed down the pedestrian thoroughfare in their direction. She was well above average in height with long dark hair and the bluest eyes he had ever seen.

"What a surprise," Mercer announced, leaning over the patio railing to give his wife a kiss. "I didn't think I'd see you until I got home."

"When a lady gets invited to coffee with two handsome men, how can she say no?"

Mercer shook hands and greeted the two young men in Norwegian before turning to Harvath and making introductions. "Scot Harvath, I'd like you to meet my wife, Hilde, my handsome stepson, Marcus, and his handsome best friend, Arne, who also works at Vardø."

"Nice to meet all of you," said Harvath, who had stood up from the table to greet them. "Would you like to join us?"

"Unfortunately, we can't," Marcus replied. "We've been called in early. All hands on deck today."

"Movement?" Mercer asked, cocking an eyebrow.

"The fucking Russians," his stepson replied, before quickly adding, "Sorry, Mom."

"I'm glad we were still able to meet for coffee," she said, ignoring his bad language. "And it was nice to see you too, Arne."

"You too," the young man said.

"What do you do at Vardø?" Harvath asked.

"He pepper-sprays the protestors," Marcus joked. "And if you show up without your ID, it's his job to strap you to the electric chair."

"Sounds serious."

"It's not," Arne replied. "I'm a security guard at the installation."

"He's the *best* security guard at the installation. Already promoted twice this year."

"Only because my aim with the pepper spray is so good," he joked back.

"Who protests a radar station?" Harvath asked.

"Take your pick," Arne answered. "Animal rights people who say the signals interfere with migratory birds. Supporters of the Sámi people who believe the signals diminish reindeer fertility. Climate change people who believe the signals are causing extreme weather. Anti-American people who want Norway out of all partnerships with the U.S. Civil liberties people who believe the station is being used to spy on Norwegian citizens. Even Vardø locals who complain that the new-generation GLOBUS is bigger than agreed to and *may* cause cancer. We've seen it all."

"And they get violent enough that you have to break out pepper spray?"

"Marcus likes to exaggerate. I've only deployed the spray once. Twice if you count the cannister that ruptured in the trunk of my car. The one time I intentionally deployed it was on a violent, drunk ex-husband who had showed up looking to cause trouble for his ex-wife. Other than that, it is a rather boring place to work."

Marcus feigned outrage, pretending that his friend had just given away a massive state secret. "How dare you? Every day at Vardø is like *Mission Impossible*. Assassins. Car chases. Gunfights. We really have seen it all. And if you say anything different at the bar tonight with Anna and Sigrid, you're no longer my best friend."

"Those poor girls," said Hilde, laughing. "Thank you for the coffee, boys. It was nice seeing you. Let's do it again when you have more time."

The two young men said goodbye and then Hilde came around and joined her husband and Harvath at their table on the patio.

"So, Mr. Scot Harvath," she said, sitting down. "I assume you're the reason my husband slipped out of my bed in the middle of the night and disappeared?"

"I was just sitting here, minding my own business, eating my breakfast. I've never met this man before in my life," Harvath replied with a smile.

"Hmmmmmm," the woman said.

It was one of the most common responses in Norwegian—a place-holder while the speaker decided what to say, or not to say, next.

Harvath could see why Mercer had fallen for her. In addition to her beauty, she was witty and highly intelligent. She reminded him of Sølvi.

"You're never going to believe this," said Mercer. "It turns out that both of us worked for the same person."

"Hmmmmmm," she repeated. "I'll bet that I can spell the name of that person's organization with just three letters."

"Is it CNN?" he asked with a grin.

"No, but you're getting warm," she teased back. "At least warmer than our bed was this morning."

"I'm starting to feel a bit uncomfortable," Harvath interjected.

"You shouldn't," said Hilde. "He likes to think that I don't know that he still works for the CIA from time to time. But once a spy, always a spy. Right, my love?"

Mercer stifled a smile and pulled out his wallet to pay for the breakfast. "It sounds very exciting, but I have absolutely no idea what you're talking about."

"You also have no idea what you're doing," Harvath added, removing cash from his pocket. "I'm paying for breakfast."

"Fair enough," Mercer said as he put away his wallet. "Next one's on me. We'll toast to our old friend."

"Sounds like a plan."

But as Harvath sat with the couple and finished his coffee, he had an uneasy feeling. Something was coming. Something bad.

CHAPTER 33

Wet-work teams were not easy to move from country to country. Much care had to be taken so as not to leave a trail.

In one of the most famous examples of carelessness, the Saudis had sent a team into Turkey to kill a dissident journalist and left clue after clue. It was exceedingly unprofessional. It should have also been humiliating, but Saudi Arabia was a coarse nation not known for introspection or a sense of shame.

China, on the other hand, was quite concerned with how it was perceived by the world. The concept of "face" mattered not just on a personal level but on a national one as well.

The operatives sent to watch Han's back were both experienced and highly regarded. They would make sure he had all the support he needed. His success would be their success. By the same token, his failure would be their failure. And at no point would they embarrass themselves or their nation.

They had been launched from Finland, where Chinese people formed one of the largest immigrant groups. And because Norway and Finland were both part of Europe's twenty-six-nation Schengen Area, they were able to take advantage of an open border.

The crossing at Neiden, just west of Kirkenes, was more a formality than anything else. The guards were so used to seeing Asian visitors that all the Chinese team had to do was hold up their Finnish passports and they were waved right through. There was no search of their vehicle and therefore no risk of the cleverly hidden weapons and equipment they were transporting being discovered.

Per their training, as they drove into town they conducted a slow sweep, familiarizing themselves with landmarks, critical infrastructure, and the locations of first-responder headquarters such as the police and fire departments.

They studied shops and storefronts, looking for CCTV cameras while noting businesses that went out of their way to attract Chinese customers. Based on jammed tour buses alone, it became apparent very quickly that they would have no problem blending in here.

After doing two drive-bys of the hotel, they pulled in at the far end of the parking lot and took their time selecting a spot. They wanted to check out as many of the parked cars as possible. This was the perfect place to watch the front door and all of the comings and goings. If there was a surveillance team outside, they needed to know that.

Convinced that the coast was clear, they chose a parking stall and shut down the engine.

Stepping out into the chilly air, the men stretched their backs and legs. They had been driving for hours, stopping only to refuel. Two of the men lit up cigarettes. Another walked to the water's edge to look out over the fjord. The fourth and final man busied himself for several minutes in the backseat and then in the trunk. Once he was finished, he began unloading their luggage.

As soon as each man had been married up with his bags, the team headed into the hotel.

• • •

Across the street, Chase Palmer lowered his binoculars. The Kirkenes town hall sat on a hill and its parking lot afforded an excellent view of the Thon Hotel. They had relocated there after deciding it wasn't the best of ideas to sit in the hotel lot all day. Eventually, someone was going to notice.

"What do you suppose was taking so long in the backseat and then the trunk?" he asked.

"It looked like he was repacking some of the bags," Sloane replied, scrolling through the photos she had taken. "Are those Finnish license plates?"

Chase raised his binoculars again. "I think so."

"Four Chinese guys from Finland. Interesting."

"Maybe the car's a rental and they just picked it up at the airport."

"Maybe," said Sloane, "but those guys were stretching like it had been a much longer ride."

"So? Maybe they're reindeer spotters. Four nature nerds on the trip of a lifetime. First, they check out the herds in Lapland, then they come over to see what the Norwegians have."

"They didn't look like nerds to me. There was something unsettling about them."

"Like what?"

"I don't know," she considered. "They looked *hard*. Switched on. Like they were taking in everything around them without appearing to look like they were taking everything in. Plus, the way they slowly rolled through the lot? It was like they were checking out all the cars before deciding whether or not they were going to stop and go in. It just felt a little odd. Not how tourists would act."

"If it makes you feel any better, send the plate and photos to Nicholas," Chase suggested. "It'll give him something to do. Let's see if he digs up anything."

Sloane nodded, pulled the SD card out of the camera, reinserted it into her laptop, and sent their colleague all of the information.

"Well, that was fun," she said after setting her camera back up. "Now what?"

"More fun. We continue to wait."

CHAPTER 34

After finishing their coffees and saying goodbye to Hilde, Mercer drove Harvath to the team's safe house. Holidae had found them an excellent spot. In Norwegian, it was called a *småbruk*, or small farm. It was close enough to town but off the beaten path. The less attention they drew, the better.

Spending time with Mercer had been interesting. Harvath wasn't exactly sure what to take from it. Was Mercer who Harvath was going to be twenty years from now? Or was Harvath headed down the path of Reed Carlton, destined to take ever-younger operatives into the field, push the limits, and never let up on America's enemies?

He envied Mercer his time running and gunning with the Old Man. That was something he had never gotten to do. By the time they had met, Carlton had long since retired from fieldwork.

What did give him hope was Mercer's relationship with his wife. It gave him hope that there was a future with Sølvi. He had been concerned about how everything was going to work out. His conscience hadn't been eased by the idea that some publicity-hungry Norwegian MP could get him banned from reentering the country.

He couldn't think about that now. He had to trust that Holidae, as she had assured him, would take care of Astrid Jensen. What he needed to take care of was his mission.

Entering the house, he found Nicholas and the dogs in a downstairs room that had been set up as their tactical operations center.

"What have we got?" he asked, greeting Argos and Draco, then taking a chair and sitting down.

"The phones from the dead Russians back in Oslo have been a zero. So has their pocket litter. Sloane and Chase, though, photographed four possible suspects arriving at Han's hotel a little over an hour ago."

"You've got my attention. What do we know about them?"

Nicholas slowly scrolled through the photos as he narrated. "The Finnish license plate on their car traces back to a fake Internet company in Helsinki."

"Interesting," said Harvath. "What about the suspects themselves?"

"That's where it starts to get good," the little man replied. "We actually have one of them on our radar."

"For what?"

"Between 2010 and 2012, the CIA lost nineteen of its spies in China—some of them deeply placed inside the Chinese government. It was a breach worse than what Aldrich Ames and Robert Hanssen revealed to the Russians. Some of the CIA assets were murdered; others were sent to prison."

"I remember that one was quite publicly executed," said Harvath. "Shot him right in the head in front of his colleagues in the courtyard of a government building."

"*Pour encourager les autres*," Nicholas quoted, using the French expression for an action carried out to discourage dissent or rebellion.

"It certainly didn't make recruitment any easier over there."

"Which was the point. China is already one of the hardest places in the world for us to recruit intelligence assets. The assassinations and jailings were meant to send a very clear message to anyone who might even contemplate working for the CIA. If you do, your life is over."

"What amazes me," said Harvath, "is that the Agency still doesn't know how it happened. They don't know if they had, or still have, a mole, if the covert communications channel used to message the assets was compromised . . . It all remains a massive unsolved mystery."

Nicholas nodded. "They had to burn everything down and rebuild their China operation from scratch. It continues to be some of the most protected and sensitive intelligence gathering they do—maybe even *the* most protected and sensitive."

"So what does that have to do with the man in that picture?"

"The man in that picture, like Han, works for the Ministry of State Security in Beijing. He ran the wet-work team that assassinated the CIA's spies in China. The spy shot in the government courtyard? That man was the shooter. He pulled the trigger. I think it's safe to assume that the other three men with him are in the same line of work."

Harvath was of the same opinion. "Why are they materializing here? Why now?"

"Does it matter?" Nicholas asked. "These guys aren't management. They're labor. They're the brute squad. They do one thing and one thing only—they kill people."

"Okay, then who are they here to kill?"

"Without giving it too much thought, I'm guessing they're here to kill *you*."

"Me?" Harvath blurted.

"They might not specifically know that you're the target, but they know someone is onto Han and their job is to make sure nothing gets in Han's way. That means you."

"What are the rules of engagement here? Has a determination been made on this guy?"

"As in *kill or capture*?" asked Nicholas, who then shook his head. "He's a paid killer. No intelligence value. He goes where they send him. His boss back at the Ministry of State Security is the one the Agency would like to get their hands on. That's the person Langley thinks could help them unravel how so many of their spies got exposed."

"So no one cares what happens to this guy?"

"Nope. Not a soul. But I say that with all the customary caveats about not creating an international incident, not exposing and potentially jeopardizing our operation, and so forth. If you could shove him over a balcony or feed him to a polar bear without anyone being the wiser, I'm sure there's more than a few people back at the Central Intelligence Agency who'd make sure you never paid for a drink again."

"It would be fitting if he met his end in the courtyard of a government building," said Harvath.

"If nothing else but *pour encourager les autres*."

Harvath filed that away. "If they're here to back up Han—which, after what happened in Oslo, makes sense—do we have any better understanding of what Han is up to?"

"Based on his skill set, the powers that be back in D.C. firmly believe this has to do with sabotage. The only strategic target in this part of the country is the GLOBUS 3 radar system at Vardø. The fact that Han is working with Sarov, whose background is with the GRU, bolsters that opinion. This is an operation of military importance.

"Add to it the fact that Russia's Northern Fleet appears set to conduct some sort of naval movement, and the level of certitude back home goes even higher."

"But certitude about what?" asked Harvath. "Are the Chinese and the Russians planning something and Han is just here to do research? Or are they about to push the button and Han is here to carry it out?"

"I think you only need to look to what went down in Oslo, as well as the wet-work team that just showed up," replied Nicholas. "If this was some sort of pre-attack surveillance operation, Moscow and Beijing would have already pulled the plug. The fact that they haven't tells me that they've come too far to turn back. They have invested too much. I think we've got a front-row seat to the main event."

"I don't disagree. How are you coming with getting Han's room number at the Thon?"

"That's proving a little difficult. We pushed another phishing attack at them, but they didn't bite. Our best bet is to wait for the night auditor to come on duty and try again. They're basically glorified accountants and usually so busy, you can sneak things past them."

"What time are we talking about?" asked Harvath.

"Sometime after ten p.m. Even better if we do it after midnight when the auditor is in the thick of his or her duties."

Harvath didn't like having to wait that long. There was no telling if Han would even still be residing in the hotel tonight. They needed to come up with a better plan.

"There's got to be something else we can do," he said.

"If you have any other ideas, I'm all ears," Nicholas said.

That was the problem: Harvath didn't have any other ideas. While he might have free rein to hit the wet-work team if the opportunity presented itself, his primary focus was on surveilling Han and ascertaining what he and the Russians were up to.

He was about to suggest setting up some sort of surveillance on Sarov, when both his phone and Nicholas's lit up. It was a message from Sloane and Chase. Han was on the move.

CHAPTER 35

The best thing Han had going for him was that it was summer and there were plenty of tourists around. However, Kirkenes wasn't Oslo. There were only so many places he could duck into and out of in order to make sure he wasn't being followed.

He did have a serious advantage, though. Two members of the Chinese wet-work team were following him on foot—to make sure his trail was clean—while the other two followed in their car. Sloane and Chase had a hell of a time keeping him in sight.

They switched back and forth every two blocks until reinforcements arrived. Once Johnson and Preisler were on the scene, it made it easier to rotate people in and out.

Not knowing what to expect, Harvath had sent the pair on ahead while he, Haney, and Staelin loaded their vehicle with weapons and equipment. Nicholas remained back at the safe house, ready to facilitate any support they might need.

Harvath had made sure that everyone knew about the presence of the wet-work team and to be on their guard. The last thing he wanted was for them to get the drop on any of his people.

He also didn't want some gunfight erupting in downtown Kirkenes. The political cost of something like that—not to mention the potential loss of civilian lives—was too steep. Unless the Chinese fired first, he wanted to do everything he could to avoid it.

Based upon the report Sloane and Chase had given when Han had first left his hotel, he looked every inch the Chinese tourist—dark trousers, dark Polo shirt, windbreaker, white tennis shoes, and a backpack.

Harvath's assumption had been that the backpack contained additional items of clothing to help alter his appearance as he walked around the village, trying to shake anyone who might be on his tail. Interestingly enough, no one saw him so much as unzip his jacket.

Perhaps having additional manpower running countersurveillance for him put him at ease. Or maybe, in order to draw in any potential pursuers, he wanted to make it look like he had let his guard down. Harvath was all too clear on what the wet-work team was capable of doing if they detected that Han was being followed.

So, if he wasn't using the backpack for disguises, what was it for? Was it the ultimate tourist accessory? Or was he carrying something? Harvath would have given a month's pay to find out.

He also would have given a month's pay to have identified what room Han was registered in back at the Thon Hotel. To have Han out on the street along with the entire wet-work team was a gift from the gods. It was a shame that they couldn't exploit the situation—even if it meant being a man down so that one of the team members could be over there.

Han was taking his own sweet time. He had already visited three souvenir shops as well as a candy store. Harvath was beginning to wonder if he was just killing time until a meeting later in the day or maybe even that evening. That was when he turned a corner and vanished, just as he had done in Oslo.

"Did he walk into another store?" Harvath asked, pressing his earbud deeper into his ear so as not to miss anything that might be said.

"Negative," replied Johnson, who had been tailing Han up to that moment. "It's all houses along this block."

"What about vehicles?"

"I see a white Volkswagen camper van almost at the intersection, preparing to turn left."

Harvath, who was sitting in the front passenger seat of their SUV, looked at Haney and said, "Don't lose them. Go."

Staelin informed them that the two wet-work members had just been picked up by their colleagues, still in the same car from the hotel.

"We'll pick you up at the next corner," said Harvath. "Everyone else, get back to your vehicles and fall in behind us. Let's see where this party is headed."

The fact that Han and his colleagues were no longer on foot gave Harvath hope that something was about to happen—something that would explain what they were up to. The sooner he could get to the bottom of things, the sooner he could get back to Oslo. He had no desire to stay in Kirkenes one second longer than he had to.

At the next corner, Staelin got himself into the backseat and they continued on, with Harvath cautioning Haney not to get too close. Wherever Han was headed, the wet-work team would be going as well. But until Harvath saw their car, he wouldn't be certain they weren't on a wild-goose chase. He alerted the team and told them to be on the lookout as well.

Even in places with mild winters, paved roads could be a pain in the ass to maintain. Above the Arctic Circle, it was a true challenge. Consequently, the number of roads and highways in the region was limited.

At an intersection up ahead, the car carrying the wet-work team swung in behind the camper van and followed as it drove onto the main route out of town. Harvath and his team had caught a nice break. Mingling with other vehicles, they merged their three SUVs onto the E6 Highway, essentially camouflaged and unremarkable.

The challenging E6 was one lane in each direction and considered the northernmost highway in all of Europe.

About four miles outside of Kirkenes, they hit a roundabout and continued following the E6 as it wound its way deeper into the Arctic.

Nicholas fed them updates as they traveled, trying to puzzle together where Han and his colleagues were headed.

It wasn't until they hit a roundabout in Varangerbotn and branched off onto European route E75 that they figured it out. They would be taking this road to its very end—the town of Vardø, home to the GLOBUS radar system.

CHAPTER 36

While the drive from Kirkenes to Vardø was beautiful, with plenty of views of the Barents Sea, Harvath decided to use it to close his eyes and grab some sleep. The only shut-eye he'd gotten was on the short plane ride up from Oslo. Haney would wake him up if he was needed for anything.

He'd been trained to go for days without sleep, but only if absolutely necessary. Even if he could get only ten minutes here or an hour there, it was much better than nothing. He knew his own limitations and how far he could push it. Knocking off for even a little bit now would greatly improve his performance.

He also hadn't realized how tired he was. Settling back in his seat, taking care not to aggravate his ribs, he closed his eyes and fell into a deep, dreamless slumber.

When he awoke, it was because Staelin was leaning forward from the backseat and giving his shoulder a shake. "Rise and shine, princess," the man said.

Harvath straightened up, rubbed his eyes, and tried to get a fix on their position. "Where are we?"

"They exited the highway," Haney replied. "We're on some coastal road now."

Ahead, Harvath could make out the wet-work team's car as well as the camper van in front of it. "Where the hell are they going?"

"We're not sure. That's why we woke you."

Harvath raised Nicholas and asked if he had any idea.

"None," the little man responded. "You just passed the underwater tunnel to Vardø. There's no other way across."

"There's got to be something else out this way."

"Whatever it is, I hope they serve lunch," Haney commented. "I'm getting hungry."

Harvath ignored him and kept his eyes peeled. They were passing through windswept terrain devoid of trees, with rocks that jutted up like broken teeth, punctuated by scrubby vegetation and huddles of ocean grasses.

What structures there were, were either long one-story dwellings with peaked roofs and a chimney pipe at one end or rusting metal storage buildings. It reminded him of towns he'd seen in Alaska.

To their right was a largely empty port surrounded by a long breakwater. But it was what Harvath saw beyond it that captured his attention—the island of Vardøya and the unmistakable white radome of the GLOBUS 3 radar station.

Before he could warn Haney that the location might be significant, Haney said, "Looks like something's happening. They're slowing down."

The team's other two vehicles were far enough behind that it wouldn't be noticed if they pulled over, so Harvath told them to do so.

"And us?" Haney asked.

"We don't have a choice. Keep going. We'll circle back."

"Roger that."

As the camper van, along with the wet-work team, pulled off the road toward the far end of the breakwater, Harvath, Haney, and Staelin kept driving, not even risking a glance in their direction.

Two miles later, near an old snowmobile that had been abandoned by the side of the road, Harvath felt it was safe enough to turn around and double back.

The question now was where they could get the best vantage point to observe what was going on. If they drove down the road to the breakwater, they'd be spotted immediately. They would have the same problem if they tried to come up along the flat, sandy beach on the harbor's interior.

The only possibility Harvath could see were the grassy berms that had been created by blowing sand on the ocean side of the breakwater.

Fifty yards off the coastal road, there was an old barn, its wooden planks bleached silvery-gray by the elements. If they could get to it on foot without being seen, they might be able to make it the rest of the way to the berms. It was a big if. It was also their only option.

With a metal storage building fast approaching, Harvath instructed Haney to pull over and park their SUV behind it. He thought about having Sloane and Chase as well as Johnson and Preisler come join them, but they were better off where they were. The more people they put on the ground, the greater their chance of being spotted. Better to keep them in reserve.

It was much colder here than in Kirkenes. The wind was raw and raked their exposed skin.

"How do you want to kit up?" Staelin asked as he quickly walked around to the back of the vehicle, opened the hatch, and began popping the lids of the hard-sided cases.

The first thing he would have liked to have had were ghillie suits, but they hadn't brought any. The next thing was seriously robust listening equipment, but they hadn't brought that, either—at least, not anything that could compete with the wind and pounding of the ocean. This phase of their operation would be strictly visual. That meant binoculars and a camera with a powerful lens. And guns. Lots of guns.

These guys were about to do something—and Harvath doubted it was going to be good. Even if they pulled a Stinger missile out of the back of that camper van, he wanted to be ready to take them all out.

To that end, he wouldn't have minded having some close air support, but in this line of work it was very seldom an option. They were expected to go in with the weapons and equipment they carried with them.

He had thought about pulling out their small, portable drone—to at least give them an eye in the sky—but as soon as the idea had entered into his head, he had let it go. The wind speeds were too high. Not only would the drone need to draw more power to hover, but its engine would also make a lot more noise. It was a nonstarter.

As he slung his HK416 carbine, he couldn't help but be reminded of Mercer's East Berlin story that morning over breakfast. He hoped that they'd be as successful as the Huracan team had been. He only wished that he had more information about what they were headed into.

Staelin also carried an HK416, while Haney, the best long-distance shooter of the three, opted for the U.S. Navy's new MRGG-S sniper rifle chambered in 6.5 Creedmoor. Built by LaRue Tactical and running LaRue's TranQuilo suppressor, it came outfitted with a state-of-the-art Nightforce ATACR sniper scope and was one of the finest weapons on the planet.

They had decided that if they could make it to the barn, Haney would remain there and set up an overwatch position as Harvath and Staelin worked their way farther down toward the berms. Whether from any wolves that might be about or the wet-work team, Haney would make sure they were well protected.

Once they were all geared up, Harvath peered around the corner of the building, made sure no cars were coming, and then gave the order to move out.

They crossed the coastal road and headed for the barn, moving as quickly as they could.

From this angle, they couldn't see the wet-work team's vehicle or the camper van. It was a double-edged sword. They had no idea what the men were up to, but hopefully it meant that no one could see their approach.

They reached the weather-beaten barn without incident. Taking up positions, Harvath and Staelin covered Haney while he repositioned some old wooden pallets to create a hide.

It wasn't perfect concealment—if someone was looking directly at him, they might spot him—but it was good enough. He had a field of fire that stretched from the parked vehicles all the way across the berms.

"Give me a SITREP," said Harvath. "What do you see?"

"Not much," Haney replied, flipping the bipod down and settling in behind his rifle. "They're all still in their cars. Nobody's moving. It's like they're just sitting there, staring at the ocean."

"They didn't drive all this way just to sit and watch the waves. Keep an eye on them. Let us know when you're ready for us to move."

"Roger that," Haney answered as he adjusted his scope for windage and elevation. "Stand by."

Harvath looked at Staelin and asked, "Good to go?"

Staelin flashed him back a thumbs-up.

He then heard Nicholas over his earpiece. "Heads up," the little man said. "We've got movement from the Northern Fleet. GLOBUS is tracking four Russian submarines that have left their pens. Two from the 11th Squadron at Zaozyorsk and two more from the 7th Division Vidyayevo."

"Good copy," Harvath acknowledged. Then, addressing his team, he said, "Everybody, stay frosty. If it's going happen, it's going to happen soon."

CHAPTER 37

When Haney gave the all clear, Harvath and Staelin kept low and made a beeline for the berms.

They had ID'd one in particular that would provide good cover and still allow them to observe what was happening in and around the vehicles. When they reached it and dropped down behind it, Staelin radioed that they were in place while Harvath pulled out the camera. Powering it up, he began taking pictures.

The wet-work team had cracked their windows and two of them sat puffing on cigarettes. Harvath would have hated to be one of the non-smokers in that car. It reminded him of the "glamour" days of air travel when there used to be smoking and nonsmoking sections. If he had a dollar for every time he had been seated in the first nonsmoking row—right behind the last row of passengers who smoked—he could have purchased his own airline.

He didn't begrudge people their right to smoke. He believed in letting folks make their own decisions. It was when their choices started to impact him that he had a problem with it. Thankfully, smoke being blown in his direction was a problem he was running into less and less, even in Europe. His new pet peeve was people who used their phones' speakerphones in public. Nothing would draw Harvath's "death stare" faster than that.

The first time Sølvi had caught him doing it, it had cracked her up. She had seen him as Mr. Southern California—laid-back and unflappable. The fact that someone being impolite could rankle him like that was endearing. He was a good man, she had said. Things mattered to him—especially when it came to the rules necessary for society to function and for human beings to interact.

"Do we have any clue what we're looking for?" Staelin asked, his weapon at the ready.

"Pornography," Harvath quipped.

"Excuse me?"

"Something that's hard to define, but you absolutely know it when you see it."

"Well, based on what I can see right now," replied Staelin, "unless that camper van is filled with gorgeous flight attendants, I am definitely not interested."

Harvath smiled and kept his camera trained on the vehicles. "Look sharp," he said. "Someone just got a phone call. It looks like they're preparing to get out."

Staelin shouldered his weapon and made ready. Harvath relayed what he was seeing to the rest of the team.

As he did, the sliding door of the camper van slid back and out stepped Han, along with Sarov.

"This is it," said Harvath over the radio. "Whatever's happening, it's going down now. Get ready."

Han slung his backpack over his shoulder as he and the Russian Consul General stepped away from the breakwater and headed down toward the beach.

"Damn it," Harvath cursed. "Another fifty feet and we're going to lose sight of them."

"What do you want to do?"

"We're going to need to find another spot closer to the water."

"Be advised that if you move any further in that direction, you'll be out of *my* sight," cautioned Haney.

Harvath didn't like losing their overwatch, but they didn't have a choice. It was imperative that they keep eyes on Han.

"We're changing location," he said.

"Do you want us to come in and back you up?" Sloane asked over the radio.

"Negative. Maintain your position."

"Roger that," she replied.

Harvath pointed to where he wanted to go. They were going to have to do a little zigzagging to get there, but it was doable. Staelin nodded and they moved out.

Just as important as not being seen was not being heard. Moving through sand, the sound of footfalls was eliminated, but even against the backdrop of wind and waves there was always the threat of pieces of gear banging against each other and giving their presence away.

Every precaution, including wrapping certain items with tape, had been taken to avoid making noise, but the devil was usually in the details. Sometimes, no matter what you did, things happened, which meant that the closer they got to Han, Sarov, and the wet-work team, the slower and more deliberate their movements had to become.

This wasn't anything new for Harvath or Staelin. They were both former Tier One operators who had been on countless covert assignments. Stealth had been woven into their DNA.

They also knew that Murphy's Law always applied: If something can go wrong, it will. Harvath just asked that it not happen now. Not until they got to the bottom of what the hell was going on.

They arrived at the berm he had selected and pressed themselves up against it. It was lower and narrower than it had appeared. Remaining concealed was going to take some doing, especially while trying to photograph what was happening on the beach.

"This is cozy," said Staelin, shoulder to shoulder with Harvath as he set up his camera.

"If you're good," he replied, "when this is all over, I'll let you go in for a swim."

The former Delta Force operative tilted his head up to look at the frigid water and then tilted it right back down. "No, thanks."

Harvath smiled. "That's the difference between SEALs and Delta. You guys got your diver training in the bathwater of Key West. We get ours in the ice bucket off Coronado."

"Which just goes to show you how dumb SEALs are."

Never dropping his smile, Harvath flipped him the middle finger.

"I didn't want to say anything in front of everyone else," said Staelin, "but I need to ask you something. Are you coming back? To the team?"

"Of course I am. Why wouldn't I?"

"For starters, you've been whipsawed worse than anyone else I've ever seen. You lost your wife. You lost the Old Man. You then got a bag over your head and almost didn't make it out of Russia alive—"

"Which," Harvath interrupted, "never would have happened if you hadn't put your .45 against that bush pilot's head and persuaded him to land."

"As Al Capone used to say: *You can get much further with a kind word and a gun than just a kind word alone.*"

"True."

"My point," said Staelin, "is that after everything that happened, you ended up in a dark, dark place. We were more than worried about you. But then you met Sølvi and you bounced. Why the hell come back to the job?"

It was a fair question and one, frankly, he should have expected from his teammates. Yet, while it was a fair question, it didn't come with an easy answer. It required him to open up—something he wasn't fully comfortable doing with other people. A deep dive into his reasoning, whether emotionally or psychologically, wasn't among the cards he was willing to show.

Instead, he responded in terms he felt Staelin would understand. "That's like asking Tom Brady halfway through his career why he doesn't just hang it up and go out on top."

Staelin laughed quietly and shook his head. "One, you're no Tom Brady. Two, you think you're only *halfway* through your career? *Puh-leeze.* Three, the big difference between deciding when to get out of the NFL and when to get out of our business is that in the NFL people aren't shooting at you."

"Fine," said Harvath. "Let's not call it halfway through. Let's say four-sevenths."

"You're nuts. But just to be fair, you and Brady do have one thing in common."

"What's that?"

"An uncanny ability to attract a very good-looking *younger* woman. You definitely outkicked your coverage with Sølvi."

Harvath thought about adding that, like Brady's wife, Sølvi had also been a model, but, peering through the camera, he could see that something was about to take place down on the beach.

Nudging his colleague with his boot, he said, "Game on," as he began recording.

CHAPTER 38

The wet-work team had taken up positions to protect Han and what was about to happen. Sarov, a satellite phone pressed to his ear, stood nearby, watching. Harvath continued to video all of it.

He watched as Han removed a tripod from his backpack, extended the legs, and then mounted what looked like a massive spotting scope on top of it.

Han then pulled out a range finder of some sort and aimed it at the GLOBUS system over in Vardø. Whatever information it gave back, he appeared to use it to make adjustments to the scope.

Once those tasks were accomplished, he withdrew a large-body camera of some sort, mounted it to a secondary head on the tripod, and connected it to the spotting scope with a cable.

Harvath was baffled as to what this guy was doing. Nevertheless, he made sure to relay everything back to Nicholas so that the players in D.C. knew what was happening.

With all of his equipment set up, Han removed a final item. It was too small for Harvath to recognize, but when he saw the Chinese operative typing on it, he realized that it had to be a communications device of some sort.

Han hit Send on his message, and when a response came back, he turned to Sarov and said something. Sarov then spoke into his satellite phone. After a moment, he held up his index finger as if telling Han to wait. Then he swept his hand down as if to say *"Now."*

The Chinese operative sent one more message via his device, depressed two buttons on the camera, one on the spotting scope, and then took a step back—as if the entire setup might be dangerous.

Harvath kept the play-by-play going to Nicholas in Kirkenes. And though the little man asked, Harvath had no idea with whom Han and Sarov were communicating. His guess was as good as Nicholas's and they were both probably thinking the same thing—Beijing and Moscow.

While Han and Sarov glanced back and forth from the equipment stacked on the tripod over across the water to the GLOBUS system, the wet-work team continued to scan up and down the beach.

Harvath couldn't see what they were carrying under their jackets, but he had no doubt that they had come ready to get nasty.

He watched as Han ventured forward and checked his gear. What he was ascertaining, though, was anyone's guess. At least it was until Nicholas hailed him again.

"GLOBUS is down," the little man said.

"Say again?" Harvath requested.

"The system has gone completely black."

"As in a power failure?"

"Negative," Nicholas replied. "They still have power. It's the radar that has failed. They're blind. They've lost all ability to track the Russian subs. I'm being told their screens are totally blank."

"What does Washington want us to do?"

"Stand by."

Harvath didn't like standing by. Whatever was happening with GLOBUS was directly tied to what Han and Sarov were doing down on the beach. There was no telling how many additional subs could be headed out to sea now. Was this simply an exercise, or was it a precursor to something much more serious? Were the Russians getting their submarines into position for war with the United States? This was a full-blown national security issue. Harvath and his team needed to intervene. *Now*.

Finally, Nicholas came back online. "They want you to take Han, Sarov, and the equipment *intact* right now."

"Roger that," replied Harvath. "What about the wet-work team?"

"Expendable."

"Good copy."

They had their orders. Harvath stowed the camera and transitioned to his rifle. As he did, he relayed to the rest of the team what he wanted them to do. He had no idea how many civilians were in the harbor complex, but if they heard gunshots, they were going to call the police. And if they called the police, Harvath wanted to be long gone before they arrived.

Once Haney had successfully moved to his new location and had his weapon dialed in, Harvath gave him permission to fire.

From his elevated position on the berm, his first shot took the wet-work team completely by surprise. The 140-grain Berger Hybrid Precision Match round tore right through the first man's head, killing him instantly.

As the remaining members of the wet-work team scrambled to close ranks and protect Han, pull their weapons, and locate the shooter, Haney fired again and took out another. But in doing so, he revealed his position and drew their fire. He was left with no other option but to take cover. That was when Harvath and Staelin entered the fight. With the sound of gunfire having erupted, they needed to move fast.

Han, his tripod and equipment clutched to his chest, was being rushed to the wet-work team's car. Sarov, out of shape, out of breath, and heaving for air, was already ahead of them. Harvath raised his rifle and took aim at him first.

The round struck the Russian intelligence operative in the back of his left thigh and sent him tumbling to the ground.

As Sarov fell, one of the wet-work team members spun and began firing. Staelin, though, didn't even flinch. He drilled the man with three controlled pairs—all six rounds finding their target.

There was only one wet-work team member left—its leader, the man responsible for the killing of CIA assets in China. He was rushing to get Han to the car.

Harvath lined up his shot, took a deep breath, and exhaled as he applied pressure to his trigger. But before he could let his round fly, there was a suppressed crack as Haney, back up on the berm, beat him to it.

To his credit, Haney hadn't gone for a head shot—much too risky on a rapidly receding target, not to mention the chances that he could have missed and hit Han.

The shot was lower than what's thought of as "center mass" in the shooting arts. Haney hit the guy right in his pelvic girdle, shattering bone and making it impossible for him to stand up, much less keep running. He dropped on the spot.

Han, tossing his equipment aside, went for his own gun, but Harvath was ready for him. He shot him in the shoulder of the arm he was reaching with.

"Let me see your hands!" Harvath yelled as he advanced on him, but Han refused to obey, reaching for his weapon with his opposite hand. So Harvath shot him through his left knee.

Reeling in pain and realizing he was beaten, Han held out his hands where they could both be seen.

Harvath had Staelin go secure Sarov and assigned Haney to watch Han while he bent down to interrogate the wet-work team leader. The man was in a lot of pain.

He had no idea if the man spoke English or not, but if he worked internationally, he had to know at least a little.

"Who do you work for?" Harvath asked.

"Fuck you," the man spat at him.

Having passed his English test, Harvath upped the difficulty level. "Tell me the name of the person you work for, the one who sent you after the CIA's assets, and I'll let you live. I'll even get you to a hospital."

"Fuck you," the man repeated.

Harvath bent down even lower to get right in the guy's face, and that's when the man went for Harvath's throat.

It was a dumb move. Harvath headbutted him, breaking his nose and causing a spray of blood to erupt. He then clenched his fist and hit the guy under his right ear, just behind his jaw.

The pain from both strikes was off the charts, but none of this was getting them anywhere. They had to assume that the police had already been called. It was time to get moving.

Calling in the rest of the team from where they had been blocking the road to prevent an escape, he quickly assigned responsibilities. He wanted to be rolling in three minutes.

As Haney took off to retrieve his vehicle and Staelin's medical bag, they collected weapons and loaded the bodies of the three deceased wet-work members into the trunk of their car.

After patting down the survivors, Harvath took everything they had been carrying, including Han's spotting scope and other related equipment, and placed it all in the back of Sloane's SUV.

Once the scene was clean and Han, Sarov, and the wet-work leader had been bound, gagged, hooded, and loaded into the back of the camper van, Harvath assigned driving duties, and they all got rolling back to Kirkenes.

CHAPTER 39

Spencer Baldwin liked people who moved quickly—people who seized opportunity. Ethan Russ was one of those people.

They had just had lunch the day before. Later that night, Russ had reached out and asked for a breakfast meeting. They were making headway. That was superb. Lindsey Chang would be happy. The sooner he could get this deal cleared for her, the sooner he could get her into bed. Having her underneath him would be almost as pleasurable as all of the money she and her clients were going to be putting into his bank account. The sex was going to be the best bonus he had ever been paid.

Russ had suggested Bistro Bis, which was at the George Hotel and renowned as a D.C. power breakfast spot. Baldwin had thought it a terrific idea. Being seen eating with a senior senator's chief of staff could only further serve to burnish his brand as a plugged-in, mega–power broker. He had said yes instantly.

The young man was already at the table when he arrived.

"I hope you haven't been waiting long," said Baldwin as he sat down, squeezing his girth into the chair.

"Not long," Russ replied, shaking hands. "Besides, I have been putting the time to good use." Closing the folder he had been studying, he slid it across the table.

"What's this?"

"Take a look."

Baldwin opened it and took a few moments flipping through the pages. "You've been doing your homework."

"It's what I get paid to do."

"So why are you sharing this with me?"

"I'm sharing it with you," said Russ as he signaled to the waiter to bring more coffee, "because this Alaska LNG project is worth a lot more than I think you realize."

Baldwin wasn't sure he was following. "A lot more to *Alaska*?"

"Screw Alaska. To *us*."

"What do you mean?"

"I think you were lowballing me."

"Come again?" said Baldwin, his blood pressure beginning to rise.

"Do you think I'm stupid? What was the offer you made me?"

"I told you that if you got Senator Dwyer to remove her objection and to support my clients for the North Slope LNG project, I'd make sure you had all the campaign cash you needed to run for office."

"The money these contracts are going to throw off," said Russ after the waiter had filled their cups and stepped away, "is massive. That's where the real opportunity here lies."

Baldwin smiled. "You want a piece of the ongoing action."

The young man smiled and turned up his palms as if to say *Isn't it obvious?*

"How much are we talking?" Baldwin continued.

"What's it worth to you?" Russ asked.

"You know as well as I do that the senator's backing is invaluable. It doesn't make this a slam dunk, though. My clients still have to win the contract."

"What if they could see the other bids? Before they submit theirs."

Baldwin couldn't believe his ears. "You can make that happen?"

"For the right price."

Lindsey Chang held sway over a lot of discretionary cash and had made it clear her clients were willing to spend money to make money. Even if Baldwin had to kick in a little of his own fee to buy Russ's participation, it would be worth it.

"How about five million dollars placed in an offshore account? Completely untraceable."

"For the billions of dollars this is going to bring in?" the young man said. "You really do think I'm stupid."

"Trust me, I don't think you're stupid. Anything but, actually. How about we double it? Ten million, offshore account, untraceable."

"Fifteen million and I want stock in whatever company they create to house the LNG venture. You can decide what's fair."

"You really have been doing your homework," said Baldwin. "How would the shares be delivered?"

"I know someone outside of politics who can set up a holding company in Panama."

"You may be better at this than I am."

Russ shook his head and smiled. "I don't think that's possible."

"Well, if you ever decide you want to change gears and come over to my world, the perks are pretty damn good."

"Are you hiring?"

"If you pull this off and want to come aboard, I'll make you a partner."

"That's tempting, and I'll definitely think about it," the young man said, "but first things first. Fifteen million. Do we have a deal?"

Spencer Baldwin smiled once more and stuck out his hand. "You, my friend, have got a deal."

CHAPTER 40

Harvath and the team had been on their guard the entire drive back. They were worried that the police would drive up on them at any moment and hit the light bars, and things would go from bad to worse. That would have been the "Murphy" moment. Luckily, it didn't happen.

En route, Nicholas provided Harvath with an update. Apparently, as soon as Han picked up his equipment and started running, the GLOBUS system began to come back online.

The events on the beach had been connected, but to what extent, no one knew. Not yet, at least. Washington wanted to examine the equipment as soon as possible.

Washington also wanted Harvath to begin squeezing whatever information he could out of both Han and Sarov. The U.S. government wanted to know what the Russian Navy was up to and what China's role in all of this was. Harvath had been empowered to employ any means necessary.

Because the prisoners were within earshot, it had been a one-way conversation and he listened in silence. He didn't want to reveal what he did and didn't know. That would be a very bad way to begin their interrogation.

In the back of the camper van, Staelin guarded the prisoners and monitored their injuries. Judging from the amount of noise the wet-work team leader was making from behind his gag, he continued to be in bad shape, especially when they encountered pieces of bad road. Harvath made it his mission to hit every bump and pothole he could find. He was softening the man up. As his injuries were the worst, he planned to interrogate him first.

When they arrived back at the safe house property, Han and Sarov were taken into the main house while the wet-work leader was transferred into the barn. Harvath had the vehicles placed out of sight and then gathered the items he would need to conduct his interrogation.

But when he arrived at the barn, Staelin was waiting for him.

"What are you doing?" Harvath asked. "Why aren't you in there watching him?"

"He has a traumatic pelvic fracture."

"No shit. Courtesy of Mike Haney, USMC."

"I just reexamined him. Based upon his heart rate and systolic blood pressure, his shock index is off the charts."

"Then he better be cooperative."

"His abdomen is distended," said Staelin, "which means he probably has internal bleeding and likely needs surgery and a transfusion. He should have been at a trauma center an hour ago."

Harvath wasn't moved. "Even if there were a hospital across the street, this guy wouldn't be getting any medical attention unless and until he cooperated."

"You're the boss."

"Can I go talk to him now?"

"Be my guest."

Harvath brushed past Staelin and entered the barn. It smelled like kerosene and dried animal dung.

Unable to sit the prisoner in a chair, they had rigged a makeshift cot with a few boards and a couple of old cinder blocks. His plastic restraints had been swapped out in favor of ropes tethered around his wrists and anchored to two different posts. It looked uncomfortable as hell.

Based on the man's earlier antics, Harvath decided to leave the hood over his head. He had no desire to find out if the guy was a biter or a spitter.

He circled the man slowly, like a shark, his boots announcing his presence. Then he spoke, giving the prisoner his standard, pre-interrogation preamble.

"Right now, things can move in one of two directions. They can get better, or they can get worse. You can experience more pain, or we can take your existing pain away. Everything is up to you. Is that clear?"

Harvath waited for an answer, and when one didn't materialize, he said, "When I ask you a question, I expect an answer. If you don't answer me, there will be consequences. Is that clear?"

Yet again there was no answer, so Harvath backhanded the man in the side of his head. He didn't move.

Carefully, Harvath reached down and drew back the hood. The prisoner's eyes were shut. Harvath tapped his face to see if he was conscious. There was no reaction. The man's pulse was thready. He called Staelin back in.

"Like I said," replied Staelin after examining the prisoner again. "He should have been at a trauma center an hour ago. He's not going to make it."

"Can we make him more comfortable?"

Staelin nodded. "I can give him something for the pain."

"Do it," said Harvath. The man was dying. Even though he had been an enemy, there was no reason they couldn't show him a modicum of compassion.

He then called to have Han brought in.

Johnson and Preisler helped walk him into the barn. Sitting him in a chair, they secured him to it and then removed his hood and gag. The first thing he saw was the man lying unconscious on the makeshift cot. Harvath intended to use the situation to his maximum benefit.

"Your colleague isn't doing well," he remarked. "Unless you cooperate, he isn't going to make it."

Han took a breath before responding. "He failed his mission. As far as China is concerned, he's already dead. So am I."

"Then make a deal with me. We can protect you."

"There is no honor in making a deal with you."

"That's okay. We don't have to make a deal. We can just talk," said Harvath. "What were you doing on the beach?"

Han's face was pained but he managed a smile. "I won't be talking. I won't be making any deals. Do what you have to do."

Harvath hated that the man was going to make it difficult. That said, he not only understood but respected his position. That didn't mean he was going to accept it.

"One way or another, you are going to tell me everything I want to know. I take no pleasure in forcing it from you."

With the same pained smile, Han looked at him and said, "We each do what we must do. I'm ready. Let's begin."

CHAPTER 41

Nearly every interrogation subject Harvath had ever been forced to get rough with had asked for it. They had been belligerent, fanatical, or downright evil. Han, however, was none of those. He was merely a professional, like Harvath, doing his job.

Like Harvath, he also adhered to a code—a code that forbade him from willingly handing over what his opponent wanted. For him to save face, it was imperative that he resist.

He had to have known what was in store for him. He also would have known that everyone eventually broke. It was impossible to withstand torture indefinitely. Every human being had his or her limit. It was simply a matter of discovering what that limit was.

Harvath was not going to enjoy discovering Han's. He had a feeling that it was going to be a long and exhausting road.

The Carlton Group had a specialist who was quite adept at chemical interrogation. But he was based in Malta, and there was no telling how long it would take before they could get him on-site. Nevertheless, he had Nicholas send out the request. In the meantime, he began to soften Han up.

Keeping subjects psychologically off balance was key to breaking through their resistance. Instead of proceeding right to some of his preferred enhanced interrogation methods, Harvath had Johnson and Preisler remove Han to a dilapidated outdoor shed.

Leaving his gag and hood in place, they stripped him naked and suspended him from a rafter with his hands over his head. It would be murder on his shoulder wound.

Preisler pulled the rope taut enough so that Han had to stand on the balls of his feet, putting all of the weight on his right because of his wounded left knee.

With the temperature dropping, Johnson purposefully left the shed doors open as he and Preisler returned to the main house to drink coffee and monitor the prisoner via a wireless camera they had left behind.

Sloane and Chase had taken Han's key card as well as the key cards of the wet-work team and gone to the Thon Hotel to search their rooms. Nicholas was conducting a cursory investigation of the equipment Han had been using at the beach and sharing the results with specialized tech departments back at DARPA and the NSA.

With everyone actively engaged, Harvath had Staelin and Haney bring Sarov out to the barn. Once he was there, Harvath had Staelin remove the man's hood and his gag.

The Russian Intelligence officer looked down at the body of the now-deceased wet-work team leader and had only two words to say: "Hermosa Beach."

"Excuse me?" Harvath replied.

"It's a beach community in Southern California."

"I know what Hermosa Beach is," Harvath said, motioning for Haney to sit the Russian down. "Why are you telling me about it?"

"That's where I want to live," he said with a wince. The wound to the back of his thigh sent a bolt of pain through his body as it came in contact with the seat.

"Why?"

"I saw it on television once. It looks very nice. The opposite of Russia. Sunny, warm, people fishing off the pier."

"It's also expensive," Harvath pointed out.

"And I want a new camping van so I can go to the mountains on the weekends."

That was one of the things Harvath liked about Russian spooks. The majority of them didn't live by a code. As soon as they were captured, it was all about looking out for number one. And if they could cut a deal, they would—especially if it meant the ability to start over in a brand-new country.

The last deal Harvath had made with a Russian Intelligence officer had involved moving the man and his entire family to Italy. It had been expensive but completely worth it.

"Do you have a wife?" he asked. "Children?"

Sarov shook his head. "Neither."

"Why would I want to make a deal with you?"

"Presumably," the Russian replied, "you want to know what we were doing on that beach."

"I'm rather confident that I know what you were doing."

"You need the *how*," said Sarov. "Background. Details. Those kinds of things. That information is what I would be willing to trade."

"Your Chinese colleague is going to give me all of that."

"At some point, yes, I am sure he will. But how will you know if he's telling the truth? If his details match mine, then you know they are accurate."

"Or that you two planned your story in advance."

Sarov smiled. "Why would we do that? Neither of us believed we'd be caught."

"Who then ordered the extra manpower?" Harvath asked, nodding toward the dead wet-work leader.

"After Han's superiors learned that he was being followed, they insisted upon bringing in a team from Finland. I assume it was you or one of your people who was following him and killed the men at the construction site in Oslo?"

"You don't get to ask questions. You get to give answers. Based on the quality of the intelligence you provide me, we can discuss *maybe* making a deal."

"How do I know I can trust you?"

"You don't. But I am the best and *only* shot you have. So I suggest you make this worth my time."

CHAPTER 42

Harvath set up a video camera. Some very powerful people back in the United States were going to have to sign off on any deal. He wanted them to see and hear exactly what Sarov had to say. And what he had to say was chilling. The Chinese had figured out how to disrupt America's most sophisticated radar technology.

Not only had they figured it out, but they were also willing to share it with America's enemies. That was a massive problem. After today's stunt at Vardø, alarm bells were already ringing throughout the National Security community. Once they received Sarov's information, the alarms were going to grow much louder.

The Chinese had code-named their program "Black Ice." It wasn't fully space-based—*yet*.

To operate, the system required a form of triangulation—two ground-based, laser-like devices that coordinated with a Chinese low-Earth-orbit satellite.

The ground-based devices were of different sizes and intensities. The device Han carried, which looked like a spotting scope and camera, was the less powerful. It required a direct, line-of-sight view of the target.

The second device was bigger and harder to conceal, and it required a lot more power. The advantage to it, however, was that it could be positioned over the horizon, hundreds of miles away.

When asked where device number two was currently located, Sarov refused to answer. Only when his deal was approved would he reveal its whereabouts.

That was a pretty big fucking question mark to leave hanging out there. Was it in Norway? Russia? Sweden? Finland? Back in China? No matter how strenuously Harvath cajoled him, the man wouldn't say a word.

For an instant, he had considered getting rough with him, but that wasn't the right thing to do. They had come this far. Harvath needed to live up to his end of the bargain and present the request to his superiors back home.

More important, it was imperative they be made aware of the other device. Once they knew where it was, he had no doubt they would want to launch an operation to retrieve it. Reverse engineering the Black Ice system and figuring out how to defend against it were going to be a top priority.

He had Haney and Staelin keep an eye on Sarov while he returned to the house to contact his boss back at The Carlton Group.

As he entered, he saw that Sloane and Chase had returned from searching the rooms at the Thon Hotel.

"Find anything?" he asked.

"Not much," said Chase as he pulled a pill bottle from his pocket and tossed it to him.

Harvath looked at it. "What's this?"

"We found it in Han's room. Nicholas had somebody at Langley translate the label for us. Pain medication."

"Do we know why Han would have pain meds?"

"Nope," Chase replied. "Why don't you ask him?"

Harvath had a lot of questions he wanted to ask the man. Hopefully, when he got around to it, Han would be much more cooperative. Right now, however, he needed to update Gary Lawlor.

Walking into the room Nicholas was using as his ops center, he saw that the little man already had a video call going with their boss. Harvath sat down next to him and filled Lawlor in on everything Sarov had said while Nicholas uploaded the interrogation footage and fed it back to the United States.

"Give me twenty minutes," said Lawlor, who then disconnected the call.

"What do you want to do about *him*?" Nicholas asked, tapping on a screen that showed the live feed of Han suspended from the rafter in the shed.

Harvath looked at the bottle of pills and decided he'd try to talk with him again. Walking into the kitchen, he poured himself a cup of coffee and told Johnson and Preisler to follow him outside.

"Lower him," he instructed when they arrived at the shed.

Preisler untied the rope and fed it out slowly while Johnson helped ease Han into a chair. He was unable to stand—even on his good leg—and was shivering.

"I think these belong to you," said Harvath as he held up the pill bottle and gave it a shake. "Tell me what I need to know and I'm happy to let you have them."

Cold, weak, and in intense pain, Han looked at Harvath and simply replied, "No."

"Take him back up," Harvath said to Preisler as he set his coffee down and walked out of the shed.

He returned a few minutes later with a bucket full of ice-cold water. Once Johnson and Preisler were out of the way, he tossed it at Han, soaking the Chinese Intelligence officer.

Then, picking up his steaming mug of coffee, he turned and strode back to the house.

He knew all too well what being wet and cold—on top of being in serious physical pain—could do to the human mind. Han was going to tell him what he wanted to know. Harvath just needed to speed up the process.

While he waited for Lawlor to get back to him, he reached out to Mercer. He had four dead Chinese and a car from Finland that he wanted to have magically disappear. The ex–CIA man told him he'd be there shortly.

Entering the kitchen, he helped himself to one of the traditional Scandinavian open-faced sandwiches Sloane had picked up in town and popped a couple more ibuprofen. His ribs were still bothering him. What he needed was a long, hot shower.

He was halfway done with his lunch when Nicholas summoned him. Lawlor was on the line. Topping off his coffee, he stepped across the hall to the room that the little man was using as their tactical operations center.

"We've been given an okay on the deal with Sarov," Lawlor said as Harvath sat down in front of the computer. "Can't guarantee it'll be Hermosa Beach. It could be Redondo, or they might stick him in Torrance, but don't tell him that. As long as his information leads to the recovery of the other device, he gets a golden ticket."

"Good copy," Harvath replied.

"Call me back as soon as you have something."

"Will do."

Disconnecting the video call with Lawlor, Harvath picked up his mug and headed back out to the barn to speak with Sarov.

CHAPTER 43

Harvath checked in on Han as he passed the shed. Nothing had changed. The man was in terrible shape but still had no desire to cooperate.

That was fine by Harvath. Hopefully, he wouldn't need him. He moved on to Sarov and the barn.

The Russian eyed him warily for several moments, sizing him up as he tried to ascertain whether or not he was telling the truth about the deal. Finally, Sarov spoke.

"The second device is on Svalbard. It's an archipelago halfway between here and the North Pole."

Though Harvath knew about as much about Svalbard as he did Kirkenes, he had heard of it. "*Where* on Svalbard?"

"I assume on the main island."

"You don't know?"

"That part of the operation doesn't involve me."

"Who *does* it involve?"

"My colleague, Anatoly Nemstov. He's the Russian Consul General in the town of Barentsburg."

"Why him?"

Sarov shrugged. "Moscow wanted to protect the different phases of the operation. Compartmentalization."

"Why does Russia have a consulate so high in the Arctic?"

"It's a matter of national pride. We have the northernmost diplomatic outpost in the world."

"How is Nemstov supposed to take possession of the second device?"

"Once I had confirmed that the Black Ice technology worked as promised, I was to contact Anatoly and give him a password, activating his phase of the operation. There was someone—I assume another Chinese Intelligence officer—he was to contact and arrange for the handoff of the other device."

"Do you know who this person is or how they were to make contact?"

Sarov shook his head.

"How exactly were you going to confirm that the technology worked *as promised*?"

"I have an intelligence asset inside the GLOBUS station."

Harvath absolutely didn't like the sound of that. "I am going to need that person's name as well as all of the information you have on them."

"I assumed you would," the Russian replied. "In the meantime, I would like something to eat and drink."

Harvath nodded to Haney, who left the barn to go round up some food.

Continuing his questioning, he asked the Russian, "Do you believe the device is in Barentsburg?"

"It could be anywhere. Maybe even on one of the other islands."

"What was your colleague supposed to do with it?"

"My understanding was that he would bring it back to Russia. Just as I was supposed to with the other device. But only if the test was a success. Of which, I must ask: Was it?"

"You're forgetting the rules. I'm the only one who gets to ask questions," said Harvath.

Sarov smiled. "It worked. Amazing."

"Just to be clear," Harvath pressed on, "the handoff of the second device, the second phase of the operation—it wouldn't begin until you had notified your colleague in Barentsburg, correct?"

"That is correct."

"How soon would he be expecting to hear from you?"

"Within twenty-four hours."

"Why that kind of a window?"

"My asset would have to finish their shift at Vardø," said the Russian, "return home, and reach out to me to set up a physical meeting."

• • •

Harvath questioned Sarov for several more minutes until Haney returned with a tray. Confident that he and Staelin had everything under control, he left the barn and headed back to the house. Once again he stopped at the shed to speak to Han.

"You never want to be the last one to make a deal," he said to him. "Always better to be the first one."

Han was shivering and didn't respond.

"Sarov told us everything," Harvath continued.

"He knows," the Chinese Intelligence operative replied, his voice barely above a whisper.

"Excuse me?" Harvath said.

"He told you everything *he* knows—not everything *I* know."

"Well, he knows a lot. Enough, in fact, that I'm not even sure what value you could provide at this point. He made a very good deal for himself. You can too—*if* you have something I can use. That said, this is the last time I am going to offer you one. From this point forward, things will only get much worse. It is up to you. The pain and discomfort you're feeling right now is going to seem like heaven compared to what's coming."

Han was quiet for a full minute. "Cut me down," he requested.

"Not until I see some cooperation from you."

"What kind of deal can you make me?"

"First, you answer one of my questions," said Harvath, removing the bottle of pills from his pocket. "What are these for?"

"Pain."

"What kind of pain?"

"My right hip—the one you have been forcing me to stand on. The doctor thinks it may be cancer. I have a family history. Cut me down. Please."

Looking into the camera, Harvath told Johnson and Preisler to come out to the shed. Once they arrived, they gently lowered Han and placed him in the chair.

"May I have my pills, please?" the man asked, suffering etched across his face.

"Before I do, tell me something that the Russians *don't* know."

"There's a fail-safe built into the equipment. A kind of kill switch. If the Russians tried to take the equipment apart and reverse engineer it, it would be triggered. If our operation became compromised, we could trigger it ourselves. Beijing can also trigger it remotely."

"If you don't report in," said Harvath.

Han nodded.

"Is there a way to circumvent the kill switch? To disable it?"

"First, my pills. Then we talk about a deal."

CHAPTER 44

By the time Mercer showed up at the safe house, Harvath had already sketched out the rough parameters of a deal with Han and had transmitted it back to Lawlor for approval: full Mayo Clinic treatment if he, in fact, did have cancer; residency in the U.S.; and an apartment in San Francisco with a view of the bay.

Unfortunately, like Sarov, the Chinese Intelligence officer had been kept in the dark as to where on Svalbard the other device was and who, on behalf of the Ministry of State Security, was handling the transfer to the Russians.

He agreed to explain how to neutralize the kill switch and to make contact with his superiors in Beijing so that nothing appeared amiss. Harvath was wary of him making contact with Beijing but left that decision up to Langley. The last thing they needed was for Han to transmit a distress code and for the second device to have its kill switch engaged before they could get their hands on it.

If Han wanted to screw them over, he absolutely could—and Harvath hated that the U.S. was in the weaker position. There was no way of knowing if Han would be transmitting a distress code or if his instructions for disabling the kill switches wouldn't actually activate them. "You don't have a choice," he had said, echoing Harvath's words to Sarov. "You'll have to trust me."

He instructed Johnson and Preisler to get Han relatively warm and relatively comfortable. If word came back to go at him with a hammer and tongs, he didn't want to have to start from square one.

While he waited for Lawlor to get authorization for the deal, he joined Mercer and gave him a rundown on what had transpired. Then he popped the trunk on the wet-work team's car and gave him a look at the bodies inside.

"Where's the fourth guy?" Mercer asked, all business.

"In the barn."

"So, do you want all of this *gone* gone? As in never a trace? Or do we just not need the Norwegian police spinning up an investigation till we're safely out of the country?"

Mercer was a thinker. Harvath liked that about him. And he was willing to bet that the Old Man had too.

"*Gone* gone," Harvath replied. "As in never a trace."

"Okay, then I'm going to need a cow call, a case of peanut butter, and someone to drive my vehicle for me."

Harvath looked at him, hesitant to ask. "I understand needing another driver. What are the peanut butter and cow call for?"

"Wolves are like dogs. They love peanut butter. They also love female moose. We're going to coat the bodies with peanut butter and use the cow call to draw them in, maybe even bleat a little bit like a calf. But we'll have to get moving soon. I want to be in position by sunset.

"Send one of your people with cash to get the peanut butter. There's a couple of stores in town, so have them spread the purchases around. Just in case. If some lucky farmer bags a wolf and opens it up to find human remains and they can still detect peanut butter on the animal, we could have a problem."

"Understood," replied Harvath. "And the cow call?"

"There's a sporting goods store I know of. I can take care of that."

"Anything else?"

"Yeah. Have someone dig around in those corpses and pull out any bullets. The wolves are doing us a favor. The least we can do is clean up their meal."

"I'll put our medic on it," Harvath said. "What are you going to do with the car?"

"In the forest I have in mind, there's a deep, scum-covered pond. Nobody fishes in it. Nobody swims in it. We'll sink the car there. I'll be wearing gloves, so make sure your people have wiped it down for prints before we leave.

"Finally, it should go without saying, but I'm going to ask anyway. Have you scrubbed them?"

Harvath nodded. "No phones. No ID. No pocket litter. No jewelry. I'll have someone take the tags out of their clothes."

"Don't bother," Mercer said. "We're going to strip them naked and I'm going to burn the clothes at another site on our way out of the forest."

"I'm beginning to think you have done this before."

Mercer smiled. "While I'm having all of this fun, what are you going to be up to?"

"Awaiting instructions."

"The old *Hurry up and wait*. I don't miss that."

"I think in this case the emphasis is going to be on *hurry*," said Harvath. "What do you know about Svalbard?"

"Cold and very dangerous. You wouldn't need a case of peanut butter up there. The polar bears would practically pay you for the pleasure of munching on those corpses. Those fricking things actually stalk humans. Give me wolves any day."

"Trust me, wolves are no bargain."

"We'll agree to disagree." Mercer smiled. "What's the assignment?"

"I'm waiting for orders, but I expect I'm going to have a little sit-down with the Russian Consul General in Barentsburg."

"A nice sit-down or a not-so-nice sit-down?"

"I don't think he's going to be happy to see me. And I think he's going to be even less happy about answering my questions."

"I hope you brought more rugged clothes than what you have on now. How are you planning on getting there?"

"We've got our jet."

"You'll need the governor's permission to land. They've got a ton of restrictions. Could take days, depending on what his staff have on their desks. Even if you got a quick turnaround, if anything goes sideways with your op, you're going to be a prime suspect and the tail number on your plane is going to get flagged on every Interpol-connected computer around the world."

Harvath looked at him. "How do people normally get there?"

"SAS flies there direct from Tromsø," said Mercer, looking at his watch, "but you've already missed today's flight. Your best bet is to grab the flight from here to Tromsø tomorrow morning and connect—*if*, that is, you can get a seat. Those flights are often booked well in advance."

"What about by boat?"

"It's five hundred nautical miles from here. Basically, halfway between Norway and the North Pole. We might be able to find one of the local fishing trawlers to take you, but with the weather that's coming, all of them are returning to port. I don't know that we could find somebody crazy enough to take you. If you can hold till morning, that's probably going to be the most prudent option."

"I haven't been tasked yet," Harvath said. "Nevertheless, it'd probably be a good idea to start asking around about a trawler."

"I can make some calls."

"Thank you. I should also see if there are any seats on that flight tomorrow."

"I'd do that right away," said Mercer. "Then at least you've got a backup plan."

"And the sporting goods store you're headed to—can I pick up more Svalbard-appropriate gear there?"

The ex–CIA man nodded. "They're an excellent outfitter."

"Let me hand out assignments to the team and get the airline ticket process going," Harvath said, turning to walk inside. "And then we can head out."

"Sounds good," Mercer concurred. "I'll be in my truck, getting the boat search started. And by the way," he added, "bring your credit card. This place ain't cheap."

CHAPTER 45

Kirkenes, Mercer explained as they drove, was the jumping-off point for the High Arctic. The last slice of real civilization before entering an almost dystopian, alien land.

"Have you ever been to Svalbard?" Harvath asked.

"Three times," the man answered. "All for operations."

"How'd they go?"

"Badly. If I never see that place again, it'll be too soon."

Harvath smiled. "Glad I asked."

"The weather is going to be terrible up there. I already told you it'll be cold, but you'll probably get sleet or freezing rain. No matter how bad it gets, always remember the local motto: *Svalbard. It can always get worse.*"

"The tourism office ought to put you on retainer. I can't wait to see the place."

"Plenty of people love it. They come back every year. I'm not one of them."

"Is the weather that bad?" asked Harvath.

"*Everything* is that bad. Svalbard is this weird place where, when things are going well, they're going well. But when things go bad, they keep getting worse. Whether it's the weather, the Russians, whatever. Our joke was that it wasn't the snowstorms you had to worry about on Svalbard; it was the shit storms. The place, in my opinion, is cursed."

"I know next to nothing about it. Apart from the fact that you're not a fan, what can you tell me?"

"The main island has three towns," Mercer replied. "None of them are connected by roads. There are roads once you get to a town, but to get there you have to either go by boat or wait until winter and use a snowmobile."

"That's nuts. You can't 4x4?"

"Nope. You'll destroy the ecosystem."

"Wait a second," Harvath said, remembering something he had read. "Svalbard is where the doomsday seed bunker is, right? If the world ever suffers some sort of apocalypse, seeds for almost every fruit, vegetable, flower, tree, what-have-you, are stored there."

"Correct. The Svalbard Global Seed Vault is about three klicks outside of the main town of Longyearbyen. The Norwegians spent nearly ten million U.S. dollars to build it, and anyone who wants to store seeds there can do so for free."

"Why build it there?"

"The main island has no tectonic activity and the location of the vault is over a hundred and thirty meters above sea level, so if the ice caps ever melt, the idea is that the seeds will be safe."

"Interesting."

"The whole history of the place is full of weird facts and fascinating stories. It was discovered by a Dutch explorer, Barentsz, in the sixteenth century, but it wasn't settled until the seventeenth century when whalers set up communities there to operate out of when pushing further north in search of their quarry. There were also a lot of hunters—many of them Russians—going after walrus, polar bear, and fox.

"By the late nineteenth century, it had become a hot Arctic tourism destination and a base for Arctic exploration. Coal was also discovered.

"In 1910, lots of talk started picking up about who Svalbard really belonged to, but the talks were tabled with the outbreak of World War One. It wasn't until after the war and the Paris Peace Accords that the Svalbard Treaty was signed, granting sovereignty over the archipelago to Norway. The interesting twist, though, was that all the nations party to the signing were granted equal fishing, hunting, and mineral exploration rights.

"It belongs to Norway, but other nations are allowed to exploit its resources?" Harvath asked, a bit surprised.

Mercer nodded. "You had countries as far away as Japan, India, and New Zealand sign on. No one can say the Norwegians aren't some of the most generous people on the planet.

"Anyway, part of the deal is that Svalbard has to remain demilitarized. That largely went out the window in World War Two when the Nazis occupied Norway. With the help of the Brits, the Norwegian government-in-exile agreed that Svalbard's settlements should be leveled so as not to leave anything behind that could be of value to Hitler.

"The Nazis intermittently built weather stations on Svalbard, only to be chased off. The Norwegian government-in-exile established a garrison there, only to have it destroyed by the Nazis. Then the Norwegians reestablished it. It was this whole cycle.

"In fact, the soldiers based at the final Nazi weather station on Svalbard were the last German troops to surrender in World War Two."

"How do the Russians and Barentsburg tie in?" asked Harvath.

"After the war, the Norwegians reestablished the settlements at Longyearbyen and Ny-Ålesund, while the Soviet Union focused on Barentsburg, which they had purchased from the Dutch in the 1930s—the main focus of which is mining coal.

"The Russians built a lot of ugly, Soviet-style buildings there. One of the wildest is a space-age–looking sports complex with an old gym and an enormous rusting swimming pool, which, when the boilers aren't broken, is filled with heated seawater.

"The village itself is comprised of about four hundred inhabitants, most of whom are coal miners from eastern Ukraine. Because of the terrible Arctic conditions, they get paid more than they would back home, but none of them stay more than a couple of years.

"The Russian mining company Trust Arktikugol pretty much owns and runs the place. Compared to the Ukrainian laborers, the Russians in Barentsburg consider themselves white-collar. The only thing more omnipresent than vodka in that place is coal dust."

"What's security like?"

"Because of the polar bears, almost everyone carries a rifle. Maybe not always in town, but definitely if you're going to set foot outside the city limits. It's an absolute must."

"Police?"

"Practically nonexistent. There's no crime. You're not even allowed to live on Svalbard if you don't have a full-time job. If you're retired and crazy enough to want to live there, you have to have proof of income. If you can't take care of yourself, they won't have you."

"That sounds rather un-Norwegian."

"It's generous social services and cradle-to-grave care in Norway proper, but in the brutal High Arctic, it's survival of the fittest. Speaking of which, if I'm the Chinese, I'm going to do as much on my turf as possible."

"Meaning?" asked Harvath.

"*Meaning* I'd make the Russians come to me on Svalbard," said Mercer. "I'd make them come to Ny-Ålesund, where their scientific research station is."

"They sit on the Arctic Council *and* they have a research station on Svalbard?"

"They're one of ten nations, including the Norwegians, who have research facilities there. It's considered the northernmost town in the world. Like Barentsburg, it was also a mining town at one point, but smaller."

"How small?"

"Currently? Year-round? Thirty to thirty-five residents. But in summer the population explodes to about one hundred and twenty, the bulk of which are engaged in research."

"Sounds like an easy place to hide scientific equipment," said Harvath.

"Are you kidding me?" Mercer laughed. "There's all sorts of stuff up there. You could hide almost anything right in plain sight and nobody would give it a second thought."

"Good to know, but for right now, I have my sights set on Barentsburg and the Consul General."

"Totally understood. That's where the intel points. I'd do the same. If you get tasked with going, have you thought about how you'll handle it?"

Harvath's phone vibrated. He looked down and read the message. "For starters," he said, "it looks like I'll be going it alone. I got the last and only seat on tomorrow's flight. My guy is now working on getting me from the airport in Longyearbyen to Barentsburg."

"I can tell you from experience that the consulate is practically Fort Knox. It sits higher up the mountain than anything else, surrounded by a truckload of cameras and a wrought-iron fence. Whatever you're looking to do, it should be in town. Tomorrow's Friday. All of them take a long, boozy lunch. The Consul General won't be hard to find.

"Aside from the company canteen, there are only a handful of restaurants in Barentsburg. My guess is he'll be at the Red Bear Pub & Brewery, or about a block up at the Rijpsburg Fish Restaurant in the Barentsburg Hotel. Just look for the vehicle parked outside with plates marked *CD* for *Corps Diplomatique*. They'll be followed by four or five numbers—all in yellow—on a reflective blue plate."

"Then all I have to do is figure out how to convince his security detail to take the rest of the day off," Harvath said.

Mercer smiled again. "I may be able to help on that."

CHAPTER 46

T he sporting goods shop reminded Harvath of what a dry goods store on the edge of the Yukon might have looked like in the 1800s. They stocked every conceivable item someone could need for an expedition into the High Arctic.

This time of year, average temperatures in Barentsburg ranged from 45 degrees Fahrenheit to 38. But, true to the inhospitable picture Mercer had painted of Svalbard, the archipelago was expecting a storm system to move in. Temperatures in the next twenty-four hours were forecast to drop to below freezing.

Harvath started his shopping by selecting a mountaineering jacket—something windproof and waterproof that he could layer clothes underneath to stay warm. Just as important, he wanted a muted color—nothing neon. He wanted a hue that would blend in rather than stand out against the landscape. At this time of year, before the snows had set in, that meant greens and browns. He found a weatherproof jacket from a Norwegian company called Norrøna in dark olive and tried it on. Satisfied with the fit, he picked up a pair of their trekking trousers in the same color, a wool cap, neck gaiter, heavier socks, a fleece, and a pair of gloves. The boots he was already wearing would be fine.

Mercer met him at the counter, where he had already stacked up a few items of his own: stormproof matches, a headlamp, a small weapons cleaning kit, cold weather lubricant, batteries, camping snacks, a space blanket, a first aid kit, and a cow call.

"He's paying," the ex–CIA man said as Harvath walked up and handed his items over to the clerk. Then, looking down at Harvath's boots, he added, "We'll also need a can of waterproofing spray."

Once everything was placed in bags and paid for, they left the shop, returned to Mercer's SUV, and headed back to the safe house.

Harvath took stock of where everything stood. Chase had picked up the peanut butter. Staelin had fished the bullets out of the dead bodies, and Haney had helped him remove the fourth corpse from the barn and load it into the trunk. Nicholas had an update from Lawlor.

Arrangements had been made for Han and Sarov to get medical treatment for their gunshot wounds at Landstuhl—the overseas medical hospital run by the U.S. Army—before bringing them to the United States.

Lawlor wanted a four-person security contingent, including Staelin as medic, to fly with them down to Germany. Harvath could choose which team members would go, but Lawlor wanted them wheels up before dark. Nicholas had already informed the flight crew to begin prepping the jet.

Harvath decided to send Haney, along with Preisler and Johnson. Chase would help Mercer dispose of the bodies and the wet-work team's car, while Sloane would remain at the safe house to help Nicholas or Harvath with anything they might need.

It wasn't the perfect setup, but it rarely was. Harvath understood the need to get Han and Sarov to a proper medical facility. Bullet wounds were a magnet for infection, and sometimes much worse. There was only so much Staelin could do in the field. Better get them into a top-notch hospital setting.

Besides, it wasn't like any of them would be coming along to Svalbard with him. Harvath was going to have to handle that job on his own.

"We should be back around seven," said Mercer. "Still up for dinner with me and Hilde? We could do it around eight o'clock and make it an early night, seeing as how you're on the first flight out in the morning."

Harvath looked at his watch. "Sure. Just let me know where to be."

"I'll have Hilde make a reservation and we'll text it to you."

"Sounds good. Be careful out there. Make sure not to get any peanut butter on you."

"Not a chance," Mercer replied, putting on a pair of gloves and sliding into the wet-work team's car. "See you tonight."

Harvath watched as the ex–CIA man drove off, with Chase following in the man's Outlander.

Next, Johnson and Preisler climbed into one of the other SUVs with Han, now clothed, and Sarov. Once all of their gear was loaded, Haney slid behind the wheel and started the vehicle.

"Remember," said Staelin, walking over to say goodbye, "if you need us, we're just a phone call away."

"*Of course* he's going to need us," added Haney, leaning out his window. "He *always* ends up needing us. Can we go now, please? I want to stop and pick up something to eat on the plane."

"No stops," Harvath replied. "That's an order."

"Whatever you say, boss," said Haney, appearing to flip Harvath the bird in his side-view mirror.

"If he attempts a stop," Staelin said as the pair shook hands, "I promise to shoot him."

"I can always count on you," said Harvath, who then watched as his colleague got into the vehicle and the team left for the airport.

Heading inside, he walked up to his room and started a hot shower. When he climbed in, he let the water pound on his neck and shoulders for several minutes. Then he did his back for a moment before raising his arm and turning to the side so the water could work its magic on his ribs.

Unfortunately, it didn't feel as good as he thought it would. He stood there anyway, hoping that the heat might yet soothe his aches and pains.

When he'd had enough, he skipped the cold blast of water he normally exposed himself to, turned off the shower, and stepped out. Wiping the steam from the mirror, he stared at the connected islands of black and blue along his right side. The Russian at the construction site back in Oslo had really done a number on him.

He shaved, brushed his teeth, and dried his hair before returning to his bedroom. Picking up his phone, he set the alarm. He wanted to see if he could close his eyes for a little bit.

He lay down on the bed, shut his eyes, and—just as in the car—quickly fell asleep.

When the alarm woke him, he had been out for several hours. Reaching for his phone, he checked his messages. Mercer and Chase had successfully completed their operation and were on the way back. The name and address of the restaurant Hilde had selected for dinner was also included.

Sitting up, Harvath thought about heading downstairs to make an espresso but decided instead to phone Sølvi. It would be nice to chat with her before he had to take off for Svalbard the next day.

Unfortunately, both her cell phone and office phone went to voicemail, which meant she was probably in a meeting. He sent her a text to let her know he was having dinner with the Mercers and asked her to give him a call later if she could. If not, he promised to call her in the morning.

He pulled on a pair of jeans and a fresh white shirt. Not exactly black-tie, but Kirkenes wasn't that kind of town. Things here were pretty casual.

Downstairs, he stuck his head into Nicholas's room. "Anything new to report?"

"Nothing at the moment. You off to meet Mercer for dinner?"

"Shortly. Do you want to come along?"

The little man shook his head. "Thank you for asking, but I have a bunch of things to work on here."

Harvath wrote down the name of the restaurant on a Post-it Note and handed it to him. "Look up their menu online and let me know what you'd like me to bring back."

"Are you sure?"

"Happy to do it."

"Thank you," Nicholas replied. "I'll do that."

"In the meantime, I'm going to make an espresso. Want one?"

The little man nodded and pulled up the restaurant on the computer while Harvath walked into the kitchen to begin making the coffees.

Harvath had always enjoyed coffee but had become a real aficionado this summer. Sølvi had really helped him up his game.

Per capita, the Norwegians were some of the biggest coffee consumers in the world. He'd had a lot to learn and she had helped him.

Pods were good in a pinch, but they weren't as good as the real thing. So addicted had he become to the espresso machine at Sølvi's apartment that he had bought another one for the cottage out on the fjord. He didn't afford himself a lot of luxuries in life, but that one—along with renting the convertible and buying the best meats he could find—were worth it.

The safe house, unfortunately, didn't have an espresso machine, only one that took pods. Nevertheless, he was glad to have it. It was better than no espresso at all.

As the machine buzzed and whirred, he grabbed a bottle of water and popped some ibuprofen. Then, when the drinks were ready, he walked back over and sat down with Nicholas.

"Here's my order," Nicholas said, handing over the Post-it Note in exchange for the coffee.

Harvath read it over to make sure he could decipher the little man's terrible handwriting. He had teased him about it once and Nicholas had been quite good-natured about it. He had said that he wished he could blame it on having small hands, but the truth was that he used to have excellent penmanship. However, since he now did everything via phone and keyboard, he seldom used a pen these days except to sign his name. Even filling out a check was a struggle. He had to put forth a lot of effort in order to make his letters and numbers legible.

It was an affliction that Harvath also suffered from in part—a consequence of our modern, Internet-enabled lives in which we don't write letters or even postcards anymore.

"How is my ride from Longyearbyen to Barentsburg looking?" Harvath asked as they drank their coffees.

"The mining company in Barentsburg charters out their helicopter to make extra money on the side. Provided the weather holds, it'll be standing by for you."

"And if the weather doesn't hold?"

"Then the boat to Barentsburg is probably not going, either, and you'll have to wait for the storms to pass. For now, let's keep our fingers crossed that the weather cooperates, the helo is operational, and our old friend Murphy is off vacationing in some other country far, far away."

CHAPTER 47

T he restaurant—or rather the *resort*—that Hilde had selected for dinner was less than a fifteen-minute drive from Kirkenes.

A huge tourist attraction in winter, its hotel carved from snow and ice was famous worldwide. Its enterprising owners had even figured out how to refrigerate the "Snow Hotel" so that guests could stay there and enjoy the experience year-round.

Harvath had to hand it to Hilde. With the day that he'd had, this was a nice distraction. What's more, he was always impressed with people who took pride in their hometowns and wanted to show them off.

The resort had a smattering of charming wooden cabins that could have been right out of *The Hobbit*. But at the end of the long driveway was the showstopper. It looked like a cross between a glitzy, high-end ski lodge and a massive Viking longhouse. Crafted of glass and timber, the building served as the resort's stunning main restaurant with unbelievable views over the Langfjorden. Hilde had booked them a table right up against the window.

When Harvath parked and entered, and the hostess showed him to the Mercers' table, he found Hilde with a glass of wine, enjoying the vistas by herself.

"Hello, Hilde," he said, thanking the hostess.

"Hello, Scot," she greeted him.

"Where's your handsome husband?"

She rolled her eyes. "I'm not sure where he *was*, but he smelled terrible when he got home—like campfire smoke mixed with I don't know what. He thought he'd just change his shirt and we'd jump in the car and come over here. I told him that wasn't happening. He needed to take a shower first and then he could join us once he was all cleaned up."

Harvath smiled. She really did remind him of Sølvi. Scandinavian women, Norwegians in particular, had zero problem speaking their minds and laying down the law. It wasn't weird or bossy; it just *was*. They didn't BS you. They simply spoke their minds and told the truth as they saw it.

"How about a drink?" she asked, waving the waiter over.

"Sure," Harvath replied as he sat down.

When the waiter arrived, Hilde spoke to him in rapid-fire Norwegian, apparently making a couple of jokes, because she got him laughing.

Looking at Harvath, she asked, "What do you like to drink? Do you like shots? *Akevitt*?"

"Tonight isn't a good night for shots," he replied, fully schooled in the Scandinavian liquor also known as aquavit. "I have an early flight."

Hilde smiled at the waiter. "It's okay if I take him down to see the other bar?"

"Of course," the man replied. "I think he will enjoy it."

"What other bar?"

"It's amazing," Hilde said, standing up. "Trust me, you're going to love it."

Gesturing at the gorgeous view, Harvath asked, "More amazing than this?"

"It's different," she replied, "but very cool. Come on."

He knew better than to argue. Standing up again, he followed her through the restaurant, to the main door, and outside.

"Where are we going?" he asked.

"This way," she answered, pointing to an offshoot of the road Harvath had driven in on.

The night was cold. The crisp air was full of the scent of pine—lush and fresh.

Despite the cloud cover, it was still very light.

"The land of the midnight sun," said Harvath, looking up. "It must be interesting living with the sun in the sky twenty-four hours a day."

"It's actually quite nice," Hilde remarked.

"How long does it last?"

"In this part of Norway, it begins around the middle of May and ends toward the last week of July."

"So it will be ending soon."

Hilde nodded. "Yes. It lasts even longer up on Svalbard. There it begins in mid-April and doesn't end until the third week of August."

"What about the polar night season?"

"November to January," she said with a shudder. "No sunlight at all. That's when we like to take our vacations."

Harvath smiled. "I don't blame you."

"Tell me about your girlfriend. The one in Oslo. Phillip says she is very beautiful. And smart."

"She is."

"Is it serious?"

"Why do you ask?"

"Just curious. Phillip sees a lot of himself in you."

"We've definitely got a few things in common."

"Including falling for a lovely Norwegian," she said with a smile.

Harvath laughed. "Sølvi told me that she thought Phillip was very smart. When I asked her if she was referring to his level of intelligence or the fact that he had married a woman from Norway, she said, *Both*."

It was now Hilde's turn to laugh. "I like her. A lot."

They walked in silence for a few moments before Hilde posed her question once more. "So, *is* it serious?"

"We're figuring things out," Harvath replied. "I have to go back to the United States. It may be complicated for a bit."

"I will tell you something that someone told us many years ago when we were trying to figure things out. If you have the determination, the distance doesn't matter."

It was good, simple advice. It also fit what Harvath had always held as three key ingredients to happiness: something to do, someone to love, and something to look forward to.

He already knew that his career was his *something to do*. He was just hoping that Sølvi could be both his *someone to love* and his *something to look forward to*.

He was about to thank her, when up ahead he saw the resort's other big attraction.

"Is that our destination?" he asked, looking at the entrance for the Snowhotel Kirkenes.

"You can't come all the way to the Arctic and not visit Scandinavia's best snow hotel."

"I thought Sweden had the best," he replied, teasing her.

"Sweden's is made out of ice. That's nothing. Ours is made out of snow. Everyone knows that snow is much more difficult to work with."

"Of course. Everyone knows that."

She appreciated his sense of humor and smiled yet again as she led him inside. He was instantly awed by what he saw.

From the intricate Viking longboat, carved completely from an enormous block of crystal-clear ice, to the enormous carvings of figures from Norse mythology that seemed to leap right off the walls, the level of artistry was amazing. And adding to it all was absolutely perfect blue lighting, which seemed to make the snow appear whiter and the ice more brilliant. If Harvath had a bucket list, spending a night here would have gone on it.

As it was, his teammates had always joked that, with his intense devotion to work, the only thing he had was a *Fuck it* list. *That terrorist won't come out with his hands up?* Fuck it, we'll go in through the roof. *There's how many guys guarding that compound?* Fuck it, how big a bomb can we drop?

Perhaps a bucket list wasn't a bad thing to have. And maybe he and Sølvi could not only look forward to being together but to doing some very cool, out-of-the-ordinary things.

"Okay, mister," said Hilde as she walked Harvath up to a long, curved bar made of ice, "if you are going to date a Viking woman, you have to learn how to drink like a Viking man."

One of the last things Harvath needed to be taught was how to drink like a Viking. He had cross-trained with more Finns, Swedes, and Norwegians than he could remember—and that training had always ended with evenings soaked in alcohol. What's more, because his call sign was *Norseman*, the peer pressure to prove he was worthy of the *Viking* moniker had been off the charts. He not only knew how to drink like a Viking; he knew how to battle through the next day's hangover like one as well.

Nevertheless, he enjoyed Hilde's spirit and went along with her playful taunt. "What do I have to do?"

She spoke to the barman, who smiled and removed two perfectly round shot glasses shaped from ice. He also pulled out a special bottle of *akevitt*. It had been frozen in a block of ice, and the ice had been intricately carved with Viking knots and Norse runes.

"This is the real Viking *akevitt*?" Hilde asked the large, bearded barman, who looked like he could have been a Viking himself.

The man joked as he poured, "Under Norwegian law, we're not supposed to serve it to Americans. But if you promise not to say anything, tonight we'll make an exception."

Harvath shook his head and smiled. "You have my word."

"You have a good face," said the barman, sliding their drinks to them. "I think I can trust you."

Hilde asked the man a question in Norwegian and he nodded, saying, "Yes, you drink it all at once and then you must crush the glass, Viking-style, on top of the bar."

Raising his glass, Harvath clinked his with Hilde's and said, "*Skål!*"

"*Skål!*" she replied.

They both tossed back their shots in one go and then smashed their glasses onto the bar.

It was much stronger than the *akevitt* he was used to and it burned like fire going down.

She looked at him and laughed. "Now," she said, "you're a *real* Viking."

"Finally," he replied.

Hilde checked the time on her phone. "We should get going back to the restaurant. Phillip will be here soon."

Harvath insisted on paying for the shots and gave the bartender a nice tip, thanking the man for initiating him.

As they walked back, Hilde told him of all the winter activities at the resort, including pickup at the airport and transfer via dogsled. They were happy to provide hot drinks or champagne to make the ride even more enjoyable.

Harvath was definitely starting a list of things to do with Sølvi, and the Snowhotel Kirkenes was going on it. Astrid Jensen notwithstanding, if their jobs were going to require them to spend the majority of their time seeing each other in Norway, why not make it exciting?

• • •

When they arrived back at the restaurant, Phillip Mercer was already at the table, waiting for them.

"Did you take Scot down to the snow hotel," he asked, standing to kiss his wife, "and make an official Viking out of him?"

"I certainly did," she replied.

"Wait a second," Harvath said to Hilde as he shook hands with her husband. "You've done this before? I thought I was your first."

Hilde winked at him. "You're not my first, but you were very special."

"That's the same thing you say to me," Mercer laughed.

"But with you, Phillip, I always mean it," she said, allowing him to pull out her chair for her.

When they were all seated, the waiter came over and took their drink orders. Hilde still had her glass of wine from earlier. Harvath shifted to water. Mercer ordered a scotch and soda.

"You clean up well," Harvath said once the waiter had left the table.

"So do you," the ex–CIA man replied.

"How was the rest of your day?"

"Same old, same old. You know. Nothing much interesting ever happens around here."

"Why do I get the feeling that I don't want to know what's been going on between you two?" Hilde asked.

"I'm just trying to change Scot's mind. He thinks he wants to move up here and set up house with Sølvi."

She looked over at Harvath. "Is that true?"

"Not a word of it," he replied. "The winters are just a little too cold and a little too dark for me."

"But if she's the one . . . ," said Mercer, his voice trailing off.

Harvath ignored him and focused on Hilde. "Sølvi's family is all from south of Oslo. It was bad enough that I kept her largely to myself this summer. If I ever tried to move her anywhere other than closer to them, I don't think the police would ever find my body."

"They sound like good Norwegian people," she replied.

"They are. I like them."

"And if you make her happy, I'm sure they like you too."

"Actually," Harvath joked, "they're quite shallow. They only like me because I'm so good-looking. It's demeaning, but it's a start."

"Well, now that you're a Viking, they have no choice," Mercer observed. "If they don't love you, Norwegian law says you're free to burn down their house."

Hilde shook her head and handed the specials card to Harvath. "That's not true. Technically, you're supposed to carry away their women first, then you can burn down their house."

Mercer held up his index finger in warning to Harvath. "Think very carefully about carrying away *all* their women."

Mrs. Mercer turned to her husband. "Is that a mother-in-law joke?" she asked. "Are you referring to *my* mother?"

"Never, my love," he replied. "Your mother is an absolute angel. I often feel we don't spend enough time with her."

"We *don't* spend enough time with her," said Hilde.

"Maybe we can see her this weekend."

"That would be nice. Maybe after I do the grocery shopping on Saturday?"

Mercer shot a quick conspiratorial glance at Harvath before responding, "That sounds perfect. In fact, please make sure to pick up some extra peanut butter. Just to have around. I hear there's been a run on it lately."

Had Harvath had a mouthful of water at that moment, he might have done a full-on spit take.

There was no question, though, that Hilde was onto him. She might not have known completely what he was talking about—thank God— but she knew her husband well enough to know when he was playing with her. They obviously enjoyed joking about his relationship with her mom.

Moments later, the waiter arrived with their drinks and took their dinner orders. It was evident that Mercer and Hilde dined here a lot. They knew right away what they were going to eat. He opted for the reindeer filet. She chose the salmon.

Harvath had thought about going for the lamb chops, but Mercer talked him out of them and into the reindeer. It was shades of the butcher shop in Oslo all over again, except this time he was being talked into something truly exceptional.

They spent the meal laughing and trading stories about Reed Carlton, toasting the Old Man as they went along.

It was a fitting tribute—an additional wake for the Old Man to make up for the one Mercer, the former protégé, hadn't been able to attend. Harvath understood how important this was. Hilde, to her credit, was riveted throughout.

At the end of the evening, Harvath faked needing to go to the men's room, found the waiter, and gave him his credit card.

When he came back to the table and was provided the receipt to sign, Mercer wasn't pleased. "What the hell is this?"

Harvath smiled. "I never would have thought of burning my maybe future mother-in-law's house to the ground with her in it, but that's a million-dollar idea. The least I can do is pay for dinner."

"That's terrible," Mercer replied, feigning shock.

"So it really *is* serious between you and Sølvi," Hilde exclaimed, smiling.

• • •

As they left the restaurant, Mercer put his arm around Harvath. "You're a sneaky bastard," he said. "Dinner was supposed to be on me."

"There were a few deutsche marks left in the going-away fund. I think the Old Man would have appreciated them being spent like this."

"I'd like to think so too. He was the greatest of all time, even if he was a bit mercurial. Nevertheless, Hilde and I had a wonderful evening. Thank you."

"It was my pleasure," said Harvath as Mrs. Mercer walked ahead, giving them a chance to converse privately.

"Huracan is a part of my life that she doesn't know much about. Worse, there's only so much I can say. It's almost completely classified. Having her meet you and like you adds a little nobility to a shadowed part of my past. So thank you for that too."

"You're welcome," Harvath replied, understanding where the man was coming from.

"Before we say good night," Mercer said, changing gears, "let's talk real quick about your trip to Svalbard."

"It doesn't have to be quick. Take as much time as you want. You head the Svalbard chamber of commerce, after all."

The ex–CIA man chuckled. "The next time I see you, you also won't be a fan, believe me. Until then, I told you that I had something that might help you with the Russian Consul General's security detail. Take this."

Mercer handed Harvath a folded piece of paper and Harvath opened it. "What is it?"

"A building in Barentsburg, just off the port," the man replied. "Everything is built on stilts there because of the permafrost, so it's easy to crawl underneath. In the southwest corner, if you follow my directions, you'll find a fake beam with a railroad spike. Inside, there's a capabilities kit with a firearm and a few other items—things that were a pain in the ass to smuggle onto Svalbard but that may prove helpful."

"I don't know what to say," said Harvath, "except that I'm very glad I paid for dinner."

"Let's be clear," Mercer clarified. "If you get caught with anything from that kit, you don't know me. And if you don't return everything, we're going to have words."

Harvath smiled, folded the paper back up, and tucked it into his pocket. "Can I ask you a question?"

"Shoot," said Mercer, watching the lights of Hilde's car pulse as she engaged her key fob.

"At the sporting goods store, you had me pick up a lot of maintenance items—a cleaning kit, lube, batteries, et cetera. How old is this capabilities kit? When was the last time you operated on Svalbard?"

"Three years ago."

"Okay," said Harvath, thinking it through. "Batteries, especially in cold conditions, degrade over time, but they're easy enough to swap out. What about the weapon? Did you winterize it?"

"No. I didn't have time."

"What else is in the kit?"

Mercer tried to recall everything he had put in there. "Suppressor, knife, handheld GPS unit, a trauma kit, two clean thumb drives, additional magazines and ammo for the pistol, and a bottle of premium Russian vodka."

"That's quite the stash," said Harvath. "Hopefully, I won't need much of it."

"Barentsburg is like fucking Tombstone. My advice to you is to get in, get the gun, and get your business done as quickly as possible. And once it is, get the hell out of there."

"I'm starting to really think you don't like that place. There has to be something good about it."

"The only thing good about that whole godforsaken archipelago is putting it in your rearview mirror."

"So you're a *maybe* for the Svalbard chili cook-off next month?"

Mercer smiled and offered his hand. "Stay safe. If there's anything else you need, you know how to get ahold of me."

"I will," Harvath replied, shaking the man's hand. "Thanks again—for everything."

At Hilde's car he stopped to say goodbye.

"Determination beats distance every time. Don't forget it," she said, giving him a hug.

"I won't," he said, hugging her back, even though it hurt like hell.

Then he watched as they got in their cars, backed out of their parking spaces, and drove down the road.

He stood there until they disappeared from view. They were good people, solid people, and they made an excellent couple. It had been a pleasure spending time with them.

Climbing into his own vehicle, many things were playing out across his mind. Not only what tomorrow was going to bring but also what was on the other side of that tomorrow. What was his future really going to look like? And was determination actually stronger than distance?

As if on cue, his phone chimed. Glancing down, he saw a message from Sølvi. She was sorry to have missed his call earlier, was on her way home, and wanted to know if he would like to chat.

Smiling, he activated her number. It would be good to hear her voice. Once he got on that plane the next day, there was no telling when he'd be able to speak with her again.

CHAPTER 48

Xing Fen arrived at her office, breakfast in hand, earlier than usual. Her assistant apologized for not having her tea ready and rushed to prepare it.

Sitting down at her desk, the Vice Premier powered up her computer and logged on to the Ministry for State Security's encrypted system. She was eager for news of the Black Ice test.

Opening the file, she went to the most recent entry. Han had not reported in yet. That wasn't unusual with field operations. There were many reasons why an intelligence officer might miss a communications window. It was only when they missed two in a row that you began to get nervous.

The good news was that their operative on Svalbard had filed his report. According to him, he had been in touch with Han and everything had gone off as planned. Whether or not they had successfully incapacitated the GLOBUS system, though, was still unknown.

The Svalbard operative was waiting to hear from his Russian counterpart, as it was the Russians who had a source in Vardø. Only the source could confirm whether the test had worked. As planned, they had everything ready to go once the Russians secured confirmation.

While not an emotional person by nature, Xing was experiencing a surge of exhilaration. So many big things were about to happen for China—and, by extension, for her as well.

She had an exquisite bottle of Armagnac at home. It would be the perfect liquor to celebrate with. Maybe she would even treat herself to some caviar.

Clicking out of the file, she surfed over to a new report from their operative in America, Ms. Chang.

She was continuing to have good luck with Dennis Wo's American fixer, Spencer Baldwin. There was a request for a large payment to the chief of staff for Alaska's senior senator.

According to what he had told Chang, Baldwin felt the financial arrangement was more than fair and would help secure the Alaska LNG Project.

There was also a request to allocate funds to send Mr. Baldwin a bottle of his favorite bourbon.

Xing scrawled a note for her second-in-command authorizing all of it and had her assistant place it on the man's desk.

Finally, speaking of Dennis Wo, the young Singaporean had renewed his request to be allowed to travel to Hong Kong.

In her buoyant mood, Xing was tempted to grant the request—even though she knew it would mean him sneaking off to gamble and chase expensive whores in Macau.

There was also still the chance of his government launching a snatch operation to bring him back home to face the consequences of his actions.

The risk simply wasn't worth it. She had too many good things going. Nothing was going to mar her good fortune.

Scribbling another note to her second-in-command, Xing told him to deny the request. With that work done, she set her sights on the rest of the day.

But as she tried to focus on reading her newspapers, she found her mind drifting to Norway. Something was bothering her.

Returning to the file, she searched for the latest report from the protective team sent to watch over Han. They hadn't posted an update, either.

Anxiety began to push away her feelings of exhilaration. *What if someone had gotten to Han and to the protective team?*

She started to write another note but then set down her pen, choosing instead to use her mobile device. Quickly, she typed a message to her second-in-command. She wanted him in her office ASAP.

Something wasn't right with the operation. She was sure of it.

CHAPTER 49

When Harvath landed from Kirkenes and turned on his phone, there was a text waiting from Holidae Hayes. All it said was **SAS Lounge**.

Stepping off the plane, he found a map of the terminal and located the lounge, which was near the security checkpoint.

It was fronted by a long glass wall, allowing Harvath to do a walk-by and assess the situation before entering. He had no problem spotting her.

He was traveling on an SAS Plus ticket, which he scanned at the entrance, and was granted access.

The space was what Scandinavian Airlines referred to as a "café" lounge, smaller than a true airport lounge but better than nothing for a regional airport. It was German minimalism meets Nordic design—hard stools, hard benches, and tiny round tabletops.

They offered snacks, coffee, and Wi-Fi. Nothing to cartwheel over, but it got you out of the public area and afforded a little more privacy.

"What's up?" he asked as he removed his coat and sat down next to her, placing his backpack on the floor between his feet. "Everything okay?"

"Everything is fine," Hayes assured him.

"What are you doing here? Are you coming to Svalbard with me?"

She shook her head. "I had a talk with Mercer last night. After you had dinner. He mentioned the Chinese research station at Ny-Ålesund. The Agency thinks he might be right."

"What about it?"

Hayes unlocked her phone and handed it to Harvath so he could scroll through the pictures. "We were able to pull some satellite imagery. It's not great, but there definitely was some interesting activity leading up to what happened yesterday."

"All I see is a bunch of people coming and going. How do we know this is anything other than a normal day for them?"

"That's the problem. We don't."

"You flew all the way up here from Oslo to tell me that?"

"Not just that. Barentsburg used to be famous for offering cell service only via a Russian carrier. Then, several years ago, the Norwegians came in and customers were able to select which service they wanted. We've developed new intelligence that, regardless of which carrier you choose, the Russians are still hoovering up your data. So, when you get to Barentsburg, make sure your phone is turned off."

"Okay," said Harvath. "But also something you didn't need to fly up here to tell me. Why are we having a face-to-face?"

"Because I have something to give you," she replied, removing an envelope from her briefcase and setting it between them. "Don't open it now."

"What is it?"

"Two decades ago, when the Chinese were building their Arctic Yellow River Station, we were able to get to one of the contractors. He wouldn't risk planting any surveillance equipment for us, but he did get us a key."

Harvath looked again at the envelope. "Whatever's in there looks a lot bigger than a key."

"They don't use regular keys. It gets too cold. They snap right off in the locks. What's more, drop a regular key in the snow and good luck finding it until next summer. These special keys are also easier to manipulate with the heavy Arctic gloves the teams use."

"This you did need to see me in person for," he admitted. "Although you could have sent a courier."

She shook her head. "Something this sensitive, it needed to be me."

"Understood. If Barentsburg turns out to be a dry hole, I now know what my next stop will be. Anything else?"

"Yes. The Russian Consul General you'll be seeing, Anatoly Nemstov. You should know that he was in Afghanistan for a while."

"Their war or ours?"

"Both. But it's ours that we're most interested in."

Harvath looked at her. "What did Nemstov do?"

"He ran a program that brought Chechens into Afghanistan to train the Taliban in guerrilla warfare tactics. The emphasis was on vehicular ambush and roadside bombs. Though he didn't plant any devices or pull any triggers himself, he's got a lot of blood on his hands. He's dangerous. So be very careful with him. His security as well. He will have picked the best people he could get his hands on."

"I'll keep that in mind. Thank you."

"You're welcome," she replied. "That's it from me. My flight back to Oslo doesn't leave for an hour, but you don't have to babysit me. If there's something else in the airport you want to do before your flight, feel free."

"Actually, I have a couple of questions," he said.

"Sure. Go ahead."

"Why didn't you tell me that Mercer worked for the Old Man?"

"When I put people together for a job, all that matters is that I was the one who put them together. I don't pass résumés around getting everyone up to speed. What you all decide to discuss in the field is your business."

"Fair enough," said Harvath. And he meant it. It was a good, professional answer.

"I heard you got along great, though."

"We did. I like both of them."

"For what it's worth, they liked you too. You've got friends for life in Kirkenes. Any time you come visit, I'm guessing the spare bedroom is all yours."

"Which brings me to my next question," he replied. "How are you doing getting Astrid Jensen off my case?"

"I'm working a couple of different avenues. Don't worry."

"No offense, Holidae, but when people tell me not to worry, that's precisely the moment where I start worrying."

She smiled and gave him a wink. "Those people, though, aren't me. I've got this. I'm serious. You get done what needs doing on Svalbard and leave everything else up to me. Okay?"

"Okay. I'm trusting you."

"Good. Because not only am I going to get rid of her, I may have a little cherry on top at the end for you."

"Like what?" he asked.

"Like never you mind. I'm working on something."

As career CIA, and a station chief no less, the woman knew how to lie. Harvath, however, was an expert at spotting lies. It looked and sounded to him as though she was telling the truth. What she was up to, though, he hadn't a clue.

"How are you set for cash?" she asked, changing the subject. "Walking-around money."

"I'm good. The team flew in with funds, so I'm all set."

"As long as you're sure, because I got authorized to supplement you if you need it."

Harvath smiled. "Langley's not worried I'll blow it all on my assignment?"

"It's Svalbard. They're not worried."

"Out of curiosity, how much did they sign off on?"

She patted her briefcase and said, "Ten thousand. Half in U.S. dollars. Half in Norwegian kroner. A veritable king's ransom up there. How much are you carrying?"

"Enough for one of the queen's ugly stepsisters. I'll take whatever you've got. Just in case."

Removing a folded newspaper with an envelope in the middle, she set it upon the table and stood up. "I'm going to get a coffee. Can I bring you one?"

"Yes, please," he replied. "Black."

Once she had walked away and he had scanned the room to make sure no one was watching them, he placed the newspaper in his backpack and tucked the envelope with the key into one of the pockets of his mountaineering jacket.

When she returned, they made small talk. Much of it about how the summer had been for them and what life would be like for Harvath back in D.C.

At the appointed time for boarding, Holidae stood and went to give Harvath a hug.

"Gentle," he said, warning her about his ribs.

"One word I never thought was in your vocabulary," she laughed, being careful.

"Very funny. I'll see you back in Oslo."

"I'll hold you to that. We need one more great party at your place."

"Tell Sølvi to start putting together the guest list."

"Will do."

Harvath watched as she left the lounge and then got himself another coffee, this time an espresso. Letting the envelope full of cash slide farther into his pack, he removed the newspaper, settled back in his seat, and made himself comfortable.

Before an operation, he had learned to appreciate slowing down. Reading the paper, which was thankfully in English, was the perfect way to just take a breath and relax. He had no idea how fast he'd be moving once he touched down in Svalbard.

For a moment, drinking his espresso and digesting the articles, his life felt sane, almost normal.

Then they called his flight and the beast inside him opened one of its deep, black eyes. It was time to reenter the game. Time to go to work. Time to hunt.

CHAPTER 50

"**I** want to see you," said Baldwin. "The jet is already paid for. Why not? We would have an amazing time."

"What about your wife?" Chang replied.

"What about her? She has been begging for a trip to Bermuda with her girlfriends. And would you believe it?" he chuckled. "Suddenly, I'm more than happy to give that to her."

"Are you sure?"

"More sure than I've ever been about anything. I'll put you up at the best hotel. We'll eat in the best restaurants. It'll be wonderful."

"Before I say yes," she replied in the breathy voice that made him crazy, "where do we stand on everything?"

"It's all on track. The paperwork is being drawn up. The corporation is being created down in Panama. I could even arrange for you to meet Senator Dwyer's chief of staff and discuss the Alaska LNG Project while you're here."

"I don't think that would be a good idea. You're our representative. You should remain the face of the venture in Washington."

"Of course," he said. "You're right. I'm just so excited about the prospect of having you here that I would do anything."

"Anything?"

"Yes. *Anything*. All you have to do is name it."

Chang had been empowered by Beijing, if the situation presented itself, to press on another matter critical to China's interests. "Do you know a man at the State Department named Adam Benson?"

"The U.S. Special Representative for the Arctic? I have met him a couple of times. We have close friends in common. Why? I don't think he's going to be a problem in Alaska with the LNG project."

"I'm not worried about Alaska. I know you have it *well* in hand. My clients have a position in another venture, in Norway. A town called Kirkenes. They have been trying to make some headway there, in an infrastructure project at the port, but the United States keeps whispering in Oslo's ear, telling them not to do the deal.

"If Mr. Benson could be persuaded to change his mind, my clients would be very grateful. *I* would be very grateful."

"And how, exactly, would you be willing to show your gratitude?" he cooed.

"Imagine the deal you're now putting together via Panama and double it."

"That's impressive."

"Shhhhh," she scolded him. "I'm not done yet."

"Sorry."

"You make Alaska and Kirkenes happen, and not only will you see your money double, you'll be able to see me whenever you want. I will be at your beck and call."

"I like the sound of that," he replied. "I like it a lot."

"I thought you would. Start making some phone calls. Show me you're willing to do what it takes for me to come spend the weekend with you in D.C."

Baldwin could feel his face flushing. No woman had ever spoken to him this way. Lindsey Chang was driving him absolutely crazy with desire.

"I'll reach out," he said. "In the meantime, let's get the jet catered and file a flight plan. I'll fly out to pick you up. We can enjoy the whole ride back, just the two of us. In complete privacy."

"Focus on Benson," she whispered. "Call me back soon with good news."

And with that, the line went dead.

CHAPTER 51

The last seat available on the Tromsø-to-Svalbard flight was also its worst seat—on the aisle, all the way in the back, next to the lavatory. It was like sitting behind the last row of nonsmoking, only worse.

When the man next to him got up to use the lav, Harvath removed the envelopes Holidae had given him and examined the contents.

He did a quick flip through the currency, eyeballing the denominations and double-checking the amounts. Both stacks were as advertised.

Next, he opened the other envelope and looked at the odd-shaped key. There were no markings on it, nothing to indicate who or what it belonged to, only a small pencil-width hole at the other end. Through it, a piece of paracord had been looped and tied off.

It reminded Harvath of using "dummy cords" in the SEAL teams, especially in cold-weather operations. There, critical pieces of equipment, like a pistol, could be tied to operators so the item wouldn't go astray, even if it was dropped or the SEAL lost his footing and tumbled down a mountain.

Tucking everything away, he heard a chime, followed by an announcement from the leader of the cabin crew.

Because of inclement weather on their route to Svalbard, drink service was being suspended and all passengers were being asked to return to their seats and check the security of their seat belts.

Harvath could only imagine the *I told you so* look he would have gotten from Mercer at that moment had the ex–CIA man been sitting next to him on this flight to Svalbard. *A sign of more to come,* he would have said, shaking his head.

Not long after the announcement, the air began to get choppy. Harvath had no idea what his seatmate had been doing in the bathroom, but by the time he finally came out and sat back down, he looked like he had gotten knocked around pretty good.

As the man fastened his seat belt, Harvath cinched his a little tighter. He'd been on some horrific flights in his life but had walked away from all of them. He didn't expect anything different from this one.

In fact, the absolute best thing they had going for them was that it was an SAS plane with a Norwegian crew. They knew what they were doing. Sitting back, all he could think was *Thank God, no Russians are at the controls.*

· · ·

The nearer they got to Svalbard, the rougher the weather became. On the occasions that the clouds parted and Harvath could peer out his seatmate's window and see the ocean, it was remarkable how angry it looked. The waves appeared tall enough to swallow a supertanker. It wasn't surprising that Mercer hadn't been able to find a boat willing to make the journey.

As the captain announced their final descent into Svalbard Airport, Longyearbyen, he warned passengers that he expected it to be rough. In fact, the air was currently so unstable that he ordered the crew to remain seated. Rather than do their final cabin check, they relied on the passengers to do as they were asked. Using the PA system, they instructed everyone to stow their tray tables, bring their seats to the full upright position, and make sure that seat belts were fastened low and tightly across waists.

They even went so far as to remind passengers that there was an air sickness bag in the seat pocket in front of them. *Everything but a communal recitation of the Lord's Prayer,* thought Harvath.

Nearing the airport, they entered the boundary layer and the turbulence spiked, shaking the plane like a giant pissed-off baby with a tiny plastic rattle.

Because of the crosswind, the pilot brought the plane in at an angle—a procedure known as "crabbing," whereby the nose of the plane is pointed into the wind to help the aircraft maintain a straight line.

As the plane was about to touch down, the expert pilot flared and "decrabbed," applying a little rudder to align the aircraft with the runway centerline.

The rubber tires bit into the asphalt, the plane was safely on the ground, and the passengers burst into spontaneous applause.

Harvath glanced at his seatmate and watched as the man unclenched his hands from the armrests and the color slowly began to return to his face. If he hadn't been a drinker before this flight, something told Harvath the guy had just found his reason to start.

The plane came to a stop, the ground crew came out, and a set of airstairs were driven up to allow the passengers to deplane.

Moving into the aisle, Harvath took a step back so that his seatmate could exit first. The sooner the man got some fresh air, the better. Harvath also figured that it was safer being behind him rather in front of him, just in case he got sick before he was outside.

Harvath slung his pack and walked to the forward door, making sure to thank the crew and compliment everyone on such a great landing as he left.

Exiting, he immediately noticed how much colder it was on Svalbard than it had been in Kirkenes—dramatically so.

At the bottom of the airstairs, a man in blue coveralls with wild, unkempt hair and about a week's growth of beard sat on a Club Car, holding a cracked chalkboard. On it was written the name of the alias Harvath was traveling under: John Ramsey.

Harvath gave him a nod and the man tossed the chalkboard on the backseat.

"Baggages?" he asked in a thick Russian accent.

"Only this," said Harvath as he got into the passenger seat and set his pack on his lap.

"Okay, we go."

"Okay," Harvath replied, mimicking the man's accent and eliciting a small grin.

While Harvath was no fan of the Russian government, the Russian people were a different story. He was willing to judge them one at a time and come to a decision based on their character and how they comported themselves. The best ones he met tended to be the hardest working—blue-collar Russians. And if there was one thing he had learned over his career in dealing with people from different cultures, the shortest distance between two people was a good laugh.

It was the flip side of an interesting personal coin Harvath carried within him. On the other side was inscribed: *Have a smile for everyone you meet—and a plan to kill them.*

At first glance, the two maxims would have appeared contradictory, but in fact they were quite complementary. People who liked to laugh were rarely people you needed to worry about killing.

Harvath spoke some Russian, but he rarely showed those cards when he was in the field. He preferred to play the "dumb American" and force them to speak English. It put them at ease and then, when they spoke to each other, he could listen in and get a much better feel for what they were thinking.

Harvath engaged the driver of the Club Car in small talk as they drove toward the other end of the tarmac. The man's name was Oleg. He came from a coal-mining town in Novosibirsk Oblast in Siberia. He had been on Svalbard for three years.

In return, Harvath shared his cover story with the man. He was a high school history teacher from Ottawa, Canada, on summer vacation, writing a book about mining towns.

Oleg either found it so boring, or he didn't speak enough English to understand what Harvath had said, that he didn't ask any follow-up questions. He simply kept driving.

Soon enough, Harvath could see their destination—an aging blue, white, and red twin-turbine Mil Mi-8 Russian helicopter.

Because of the availability of better and cheaper coal, revenues in Barentsburg had taken a nosedive. In order to shore up the town's finances, they had done a hard pivot to tourism. Like Russia after the collapse of the Soviet Union, anything and everything in Barentsburg was for sale, or at least for rent—including the mining company's helicopter.

Pulling up next to the big bird, Oleg introduced "John Ramsey" to the pilot, a tough, squinty-eyed Russian named Pavel, who was conducting his preflight safety check.

Harvath shook hands with the pilot and then Oleg helped him into the cabin and gave him his choice of fold-down seats. Harvath chose to be right behind the cockpit.

Oleg plugged in a headset and handed it to him.

"How long until we depart?" Harvath asked.

The Russian looked out the nearest oval-shaped window, gauged how far along the pilot was, and said, "Five minutes."

"Excellent."

"Beverage services?" Oleg asked, removing a mercifully unopened bottle of water from his coveralls and offering it to him.

It was an interesting quirk of many Russians he had met over the years that, when speaking English, they added an *s* to words that didn't require it.

"*Spaseeba,*" Harvath replied, unconcerned about revealing his modicum of fluency by employing one of the best-known words in the Russian language.

Oleg touched his other pockets and said, "I forget snacks. I come right back."

Harvath held up his hand. "It's okay," he replied, nudging his backpack with the toe of his boot. "I brought my own snacks. Thank you."

"I can go get," the Russian assured him, pointing to the nearby hangar.

"It's okay. Really. I'm good."

"Five stars good?" Oleg asked.

Harvath didn't know what he was referring to until the man took out his phone and showed him their Internet rating. The app Yelp really was everywhere. It had made it all the way to Svalbard.

"Absolutely. Five stars good."

The Russian flashed him the thumbs-up and Harvath returned the gesture.

A few minutes later, Pavel climbed into the cockpit, took the right seat, and began to turn dials, flip switches, and press buttons, bringing the helo online.

Outside, as the massive rotors started to turn, Oleg removed the chocks from the tires.

Slipping on his headset, Harvath asked, "How's the weather?"

"Is Svalbard weather," Pavel replied. "No problem."

"Then we're only waiting on the copilot and flight engineer?"

"No copilot. No flight engineer. Only Pavel and Oleg."

Russians, Harvath thought to himself, though he had to admit, he liked both of these guys. They were a bit cocksure, but true flyboys.

Oleg hopped into the left seat, closed the door, and, placing his headset on, buckled up and said, "Houston, we are ready for liftoff."

"Roger that," Pavel replied. Glancing over his shoulder at Harvath, he said, "Sit back, relax, and enjoy the flight."

As power was increased to the engines and the rotors began to roar, the helicopter lifted off—one of Harvath's favorite sensations. With it, he started to hear music.

It took him a moment to recognize the song, but as Oleg increased the volume from the cockpit, it was unmistakable: "Sweet Emotion" by Aerosmith—one of Harvath's favorite songs by one of his favorite bands.

Flying toward Barentsburg, he wondered if maybe Mercer had just gotten off on the wrong foot with Svalbard. Maybe it wasn't as bad a place as he made it out to be.

Then the first burst of wind hit the helicopter.

CHAPTER 52

The second gust was even stronger. The helo was rocked hard, but Pavel quickly regained control. He was one hell of a pilot.

"Everything okay?" Harvath asked, over his headset.

"All good. All good," Oleg replied, turning to smile and flash a thumbs-up.

Shortly thereafter, Pavel noticed something on the ground and pointed it out to everyone. "Polar bear," he said over their headsets.

Even from above, it was an enormous, majestic animal. It was something to be admired and feared. Carrying a rifle, while also doing all you could to steer clear of such a creature, was the smart way to handle things.

A few minutes later, they came into sight of Barentsburg.

Gazing out the window, all Harvath could think of was how grim the mining community appeared. The town, with its coal-fired power plant, reminded him of something out of *Mad Max*.

Flaring the big helo, Pavel brought it in to the heliport for a perfect landing. Oleg hopped out, grabbed the chocks, and stabilized the tires.

Stepping down from the helicopter, Harvath reached into his pocket and pulled out a one-hundred-dollar bill for each of them.

The looks on their faces said it all. The men were extremely grateful for his generosity and thanked him profusely. It also reinforced what Holidae had told him. The amount of money he was carrying in his backpack was indeed a king's ransom on Svalbard.

Harvath then asked if they had a "courtesy" car to get him into town. The men smiled and pointed him right to it—the Barentsburg bus.

With a laugh, Harvath thanked them, slung his pack, and headed over to it. As he walked up the road, he noticed coal dust beginning to accumulate on his boots.

While waiting for the bus, he reached for his phone out of habit, wanting to check his messages to pass the time. Thankfully, he had turned it off when leaving Tromsø and hadn't turned it back on. The Russians had no electronic record of his presence in Barentsburg, and if he played his cards right, they never would.

Eventually the bus arrived and he stepped aboard, paying his fare in Norwegian kroner—one of the four major currencies accepted on the archipelago.

It was a short ride to the port, where he disembarked and, walking a circuitous route, even stopped to pick up a coffee and a sandwich.

Once he was confident that he wasn't being followed, he headed for the building in the photo—the place where Mercer had secreted his capabilities kit.

He walked around the block twice, looking for cameras as well as babushkas sweeping stoops or lurking in doorways.

Seeing nothing, he moved to the quietest side of the property, dropped down, and crept underneath the building.

It took him several minutes of navigating around the pylons until he found what he was looking for—the fake beam with the railroad spike. Opening it up, he carefully withdrew a thick canvas bag containing Mercer's capabilities kit.

The pistol was the first thing he pulled out. He had figured Mercer as a 1911 guy like the Old Man. Instead, what he found was a Beretta 92FS.

The weapon wasn't in great shape, but it could have been much worse. Getting out his cleaning kit, he quietly went to work, bringing it back to life.

Twenty minutes later, after he had wiped off any excess oil, he reassembled the Beretta and racked the slide multiple times. Content that everything was in working order, he set it aside and examined the suppressor.

It was a SureFire Ryder 9-Ti. Harvath had used many of these in the past. They were wickedly quiet. And, with indexed and numbered baffles, they were a breeze to disassemble, clean, and reassemble. It took less than five minutes to prep.

Then, putting on a pair of latex gloves from the trauma kit, he ejected all of the rounds from the magazines, wiped them down, and reloaded them. He had no idea if Mercer's prints were on the shell casings, but, just in case, he wanted to make sure they were clean.

He checked the screen and housing of the GPS device for cracks or other damage. Everything looked good—until he opened the battery compartment.

Mercer hadn't been kidding when he said he'd left in a hurry. Both batteries had been left inside the unit and had corroded.

Prying them out, he looked inside. He had fresh ones, but the battery compartment would need to be cleaned with some sort of household acid like vinegar. Right now, he had neither the time nor the inclination to hunt down a grocery store.

So he tucked the pistol, suppressor, and extra magazines into his front coat pockets and placed everything else, including the latex gloves, in his backpack. Then he crawled out from under the building the same way he'd come in.

He brushed the coal dust off his clothes as best he could and continued into town.

As it was almost the lunch hour, his plan was to reconnoiter the two restaurants and formulate plans of action.

The Red Bear Pub & Brewery was the first establishment along his route, and he hoped it wasn't the one the Consul General Nemstov was going to pick.

Its only parking was along the street. Fine for a drive-by shooting. Not so good for snatching a Russian diplomat in the middle of the day.

Complicating matters was the fact that there wasn't a good spot from which to observe the brewpub without being seen. He hoped that the restaurant up the street at the Barentsburg Hotel would offer more options.

To Harvath's chagrin, it was even worse. While the hotel had a nice little side parking lot, it sat alone, with even fewer places he could conceal himself.

And as if things weren't bad enough, a cold rain had begun to fall. In the back of his mind, Harvath could hear Mercer laughing.

Putting up his hood, he continued on.

Moments later, he watched as a silver Toyota Land Cruiser with *Corps Diplomatique* plates drove past and turned into the hotel parking lot.

When the vehicle came to a stop, a man in the front passenger seat stepped out, unfurled an umbrella, and then opened the rear passenger door for another man. The pair walked together inside as the driver turned the vehicle around, parked, and followed his colleagues into the hotel.

Even though Nicholas had shown him a picture of Anatoly Nemstov, he didn't need to see the Consul General's face from this distance to know it was him. According to Holidae, there were no other diplomats in town, nor were any scheduled to be there, much less with vehicles bearing diplomatic plates.

Nevertheless, Harvath wanted to make a positive identification. He also wanted to get the hell out of this rain.

He decided to follow them inside.

CHAPTER 53

Before going inside, Harvath did a quick sweep of the vehicles in the lot. Not only had Mercer explained that there was almost no crime on Svalbard, but the residents were very trusting, leaving their homes unlocked and the keys in their cars and snowmobiles. That appeared to be the case here as well.

Every vehicle was unlocked, and all of the drivers had left their keys or fobs behind. Every driver except for the man piloting the silver Land Cruiser. The Consul General's security agent had locked it up tight.

There was a ton of junk in the cargo area—maybe even enough that he could have hidden himself beneath the partially folded tarp and ridden back to the consulate with them undetected. Had he been willing to use his phone, he could have photographed the VIN, texted it to Nicholas, and asked him to hack Toyota roadside assistance to pop the locks remotely. But he wasn't supposed to be using his phone and there was no telling how long that would take. He was going to have to try something else.

Entering the hotel, the first thing he noticed was the shoe cubby, along with a sign explaining the local custom of visitors removing their shoes so as not to track coal dust inside. A wicker chest with complimentary slippers stood nearby.

Harvath untied his boots and, following protocol, placed them in one of the cubbies. More than half the patrons had ignored the complimentary slippers and so he did too.

Shaking the rain from his jacket, he walked deeper into the hotel toward the restaurant. Stopping at the hostess stand, he pretended to look at the menu as he did a quick sweep of the room. In the corner, along with his two security agents, Harvath positively identified Anatoly Nemstov.

As he did, the hostess returned from seating another party and asked if she could help him.

"Is it required that I sit in here?" he asked. "Or is it okay to sit in the bar?"

"The Icebreaker bar is completely fine. You can order any of our food in there," she replied, offering him a menu.

Harvath thanked her, accepted the menu, and crossed over to the bar. It had been designed to look like the interior of an old icebreaker and provided a terrific view—of the Russian Consul General and his men.

Taking a seat, he hung his jacket off the back of his chair rather than on one of the hooks near the entrance. He preferred to keep the gun as close as possible. There was still no telling how things would go down.

When a young man came over to take his order, Harvath glanced at the menu and decided on the fish of the day—locally caught haddock—along with hot tea and extra lemon.

The server thanked him, accepted his menu back, and went to place his order. Next to an old diving helmet behind him was a row of books, none of which were in English. He picked the closest one, set it on the table, and opened it up. If he couldn't be on his phone scrolling like the rest of the customers, he had to find to something else to do so as not to appear out of place.

Once the server returned with his hot tea and lemon, Harvath reached down into his backpack and removed the GPS device. He had already removed the bad batteries, so all that was left to do now was to clean out the alkaline discharge. And the next best thing for the job after vinegar was lemon juice.

Squeezing a drop into each battery well, he waited a minute and then employed a small unused brush from the weapons cleaning kit to wipe away the white crystalline residue.

He turned the GPS device upside down and gave it a few good taps beneath the table to make sure all the fouling was purged before twisting his napkin in each well so that it was dry. He then inserted new batteries and turned it on. Even though he couldn't receive a signal indoors, the unit had no problem powering up.

Satisfied, he shut the device down, returned everything to his pack, and went back to leafing through his book.

As he did, he tried to figure out how he was going to handle the Consul General and his team. Taking him inside the hotel was out of the question—way too many witnesses.

That meant it would have to happen outside. He could get ahead of them, fake an accident, and hope they stopped, or he could come up from behind, cause an accident, and force them to.

The problem was that there was no way of knowing if there were any more security agents back at the consulate. Any security detail worth their salt would communicate a stop back to base.

If Harvath was going to get to them, it was going to have to be outside and before they got rolling. That meant the parking lot, which didn't leave him with a lot of options.

The only thing it had going for it was that he hadn't seen any cameras out there. That was a definite plus.

The downside was that it was a very public space. If anyone was out there, he was going to have to make a very serious call. One he prayed he would not have to make.

Eating his lunch, he tried to develop clever alternative scenarios, but none of them held water. There was only going to be one way to do this.

From his table in the Icebreaker bar, Harvath watched as the Consul General not only ate but continued to drink with his security detail. As Mercer had predicted, it was quite the boozy Friday lunch.

By the time the party rose to leave, they were a bit too loud and unsteady on their feet.

After finishing what was left of his third espresso, Harvath paid his bill in cash, then walked out to the cubby, put his boots on, and exited the hotel.

Standing in the service area off the parking lot, he removed the suppressor from his coat pocket, spun it onto the threaded barrel of his Beretta, and waited for the Russians to appear. Minutes later, they did.

He watched as they stumbled to their Land Cruiser. The fact that security agents would get drunk with their protectee was both thoroughly unprofessional and thoroughly on-brand for Russia.

Perhaps it had something to do with the camaraderie of being in a shit posting in a remote, bitterly harsh location, but that shouldn't have mattered. They had made a major mistake and now they were going to pay.

When security agent number two tilted his umbrella backward onto his shoulder, blocking any view of what was behind him, Harvath struck.

He came out hard and fast, double-tapping both agents in the head. Follow-ups weren't necessary, as they both collapsed to the ground. The Consul General, though, took Harvath by surprise.

Spinning with an agility that belied his age and sobriety, he drew a small pistol and swung it toward him.

Harvath reacted quickly and stepped off the line of attack, but in doing so, the uppercut he had launched missed its intended target—Anatoly Nemstov's jaw.

Instead, there was a *crack* as the edge of Harvath's watch caught the Russian's mouth, knocking two of his front teeth loose in a spray of blood.

Before the Consul General could regroup, Harvath swung back around with his pistol, slamming the man in the side of the head, knocking him out cold.

Popping the tailgate of the Land Cruiser, he yanked back the tarp. Then he dragged security agent number one over, followed by security agent number two.

Even though he had been working out the entire time he'd been in Norway, getting two dead bodies, especially men of this size, up and into the cargo area was a serious struggle.

One at a time, he pushed and heaved until he had them in and then he went for Nemstov.

Using the belts and neckties from the dead security men, he hog-tied the Consul General like his life depended on it—because it did.

Every rule in the book said you removed all threats before you transported a prisoner, but Harvath was more concerned about getting out of there before anyone saw them.

Lifting Nemstov up, he dropped him onto the corpses of his body-guards, covered them all with the tarp, and closed the tailgate. Then he walked around to the driver's door, picked up the Consul General's gun as well as the umbrella, and tossed them into the passenger-side footwell as he got behind the wheel.

When Harvath hit the start button, he had to love the advancement in technology. Rather than looking through the pockets of the dead driver for his keys, he only needed to have him close enough for the sensor to pick up his fob.

Before putting the big SUV in gear, he looked over his left shoulder. Despite the weather, both his window and the window behind him were still splattered with bits of blood and brain. It was going to take a lot of rain to wash them away. So, rather than draw attention to it as he drove through town, he simply lowered the windows and left them down.

He exited the lot, heading back the way he had arrived, toward the heliport and the very edge of Barentsburg. But somewhere along the way he was going to have to find someplace private, someplace quiet and off the beaten path where he could interrogate his Russian prisoner.

Then, remembering his flight in, he got an idea.

CHAPTER 54

The bouncing and jostling of the Land Cruiser must have eventually awakened the Consul General, because ten minutes after they went off-road he began yelling for help.

Harvath let him scream. There was no one around to hear. The Russian could yell until his throat was raw. It wouldn't do any good.

When Harvath got to his destination, he killed the engine and walked around back.

Popping the tailgate, he pulled back the tarp and found that the Consul General had flipped over onto his back. He looked like a snapping turtle, cursing so hard in Russian that his teeth were clacking.

Harvath waited for his moment and, when the man opened his mouth wide enough, shoved his suppressor in as far as it would go.

As Nemstov gagged, Harvath rolled him sideways and made sure he hadn't palmed anything dangerous. Then, pulling his weapon out of the man's mouth, he stood back and gave him another good tug, rolling him out of the truck and letting him drop onto the ground.

The hog-tied Russian fell with a good thud. In fact, Harvath could have sworn that he heard a *whoosh* as the wind was knocked out of his lungs. But the weather and the wind being what they were, it was hard to tell.

He looked out over the bleak landscape as Nemstov heaved for air and said, "This is not a safe area. Did you know a polar bear was spotted nearby a little while ago?"

"Who are you?" the Consul General wheezed, looking up at him. "What do you want?"

"Who I am doesn't matter. What I want is to negotiate. So maybe we're getting off on a bad foot. I want the Black Ice equipment."

"I don't know what you are talking about."

Harvath shook his head. "I was worried you might say that. We really are getting off on the wrong foot. The only question is, right or left?"

"What?" the Russian replied.

Before he could say anything else, Harvath grabbed his right leg, aimed his suppressed pistol against his ankle, and pressed the trigger.

Nemstov let out a bloodcurdling scream that could be heard above the wind and echoed back off the mountains like thunder.

"Let's try this again," said Harvath. "I want the Black Ice equipment."

"I don't have it. You son of a bitch," the Russian moaned through his gritted teeth.

Harvath moved to the man's other ankle and replied, "With one foot out of commission, you're on crutches. With both out, you're in a wheelchair. What's it going to be? Where is the equipment?"

"You're too late. It's as good as gone."

"What are you talking about?"

"The handoff is already happening."

"How? You were supposed to wait for confirmation."

"From whom?" The Consul General groaned. "Sarov? You think his source was the only one we had at Vardø?"

That was something Harvath hadn't considered—that Russians would have a backup, someone in addition to Sarov's source who could confirm whether or not the Chinese test had been a success.

"Tell me where the equipment is."

"I already told you," Nemstov insisted, "you're too late."

"Wrong answer."

Pressing the trigger, Harvath sent a round through the man's other ankle.

The Consul General howled even louder this time, and it echoed even longer.

"I will keep you alive and we can do this for hours," said Harvath. "I promise you it only gets more painful. Or you can talk to me, tell me what I want to know, and I will drop you at the hospital and disappear forever. The choice is up to you."

The Russian clamped his jaw shut and refused to answer.

"Tell me about your portion of the test. Where did it take place? Who were you with?"

He gave the man a second to answer, and when he didn't, he shoved the suppressor right in his ass.

"Give me an answer right now, Anatoly, or you'll be shitting via a colostomy bag for the rest of your life. I don't think Mother Russia gives out medals for that."

"Wait! Wait!" Nemstov implored. "Ny-Ålesund. It happened in Ny-Ålesund."

"And who were you with?"

"The Chinese have a military operative working out of their research station. A man named Wen Ying. He is posing as a scientist."

"Describe him to me," Harvath demanded.

"He's different than the other scientists. He's very tall. Almost six feet, which is unusual for the Chinese. He's lean and very fit."

"Where exactly did the test take place? At their research station?"

Nemstov shook his head. "Nearby. An old satellite ground station . . . once used by the European Space Agency's tracking network to provide radio tracking and telemetry for its original, low-Earth-orbit satellites."

"What did the Black Ice equipment look like?"

"It was housed in a gray, hard-sided, weatherized case about the size of a military footlocker. It had handles on the sides for carrying and had multiple rubber-covered ports for cables."

"How was it operated?"

"With a ruggedized laptop. The software on it told the box what to relay to the Chinese satellite. That's all I know," the Consul General insisted. "I'm not a scientist."

"You were supposed to bring the equipment back to Moscow," said Harvath. "It was your responsibility. What happened?"

"Yes, I *was* supposed to bring the equipment back, but the Kremlin changed its mind. It was deemed too sensitive. They decided to send a team in to pick it up."

"What kind of team?"

"Spetsnaz—Russian Special Forces."

"By what means?"

"They were going to come in via water, launched from one of our submarines."

"When?"

"With the tide," said Nemstov. "Like I said, you're already too late."

"Where are they landing?" Harvath demanded. "Where are they picking up the equipment?"

"I don't know. As soon as it was decided it wouldn't be transferred to me, I was cut off. My contact with Ying was handed over to the Spetsnaz commander. That's all I know. *Everything.*"

Harvath believed him.

Unscrewing the suppressor from his Beretta, he slipped it into his left coat pocket and then slipped the pistol into his right.

"You have to untie me and get me to the hospital," the Consul General begged.

Harvath ignored him as he patted down the corpses and stripped them of their weapons.

"Help me!" the Russian wailed, lying on his belly in the rain. "I told you what you wanted to know."

With both of the dead security agents denuded of weapons, Harvath dragged each one of them out of the Land Cruiser and let them drop almost on top of Nemstov. Then he bent to untie him.

"What are you doing?" the man asked.

"I'm letting you go," said Harvath.

"No, no, no. Our deal is that you take me to the hospital."

"That's going to be a problem."

"What are you talking about? Why?"

"Considering how many American and allied troops you helped kill, I can't do that."

The Consul General glared at him. "You're going to leave me here? To freeze to death?"

Harvath looked up at the looming shape of a polar bear on the horizon—drawn by their scent and the noise. "I think freezing to death is the least of your worries."

The Russian seemed to be able to read his mind and frantically dragged himself around the rear wheel of the truck to see what was coming.

"You can't do this!"

"Watch me," said Harvath.

"But I cooperated. Isn't that worth something?"

Harvath thought about it for a moment. "You did cooperate. And that *is* worth something."

"Thank you," Nemstov replied, lying on the ground, relieved.

Picking up one of the dead security agent's sidearms, Harvath ejected the magazine and said, "The tactics your Chechen fighters introduced in Afghanistan increased Taliban lethality by sixty percent."

The Consul General didn't know how to respond, much less if he even should.

He watched as his captor removed three rounds from the magazine and then ejected the lone round from the chamber and dropped the un-loaded pistol in front of him.

"That means that, statistically, you reduced Coalition troops to a four-in-ten chance of survival when encountering those Taliban forces," Harvath continued.

"You are mistaken. I never—"

Harvath held up his hand. "Let's not do that. You know what you did. And *I* know what you did."

"What do you mean?"

Harvath opened his hand and showed the man the four rounds of ammunition he was holding. Then he pulled his arm back and threw the ammunition as far as he could.

"Those troops never knew when the attack was coming, but they always knew the danger was out there. You now also know the danger is out there," Harvath said. "So is your ammo. If you can find all of it, I give you about a forty percent chance of survival—just like those troops. Good luck."

Closing the tailgate, Harvath stepped around the Russian, who grabbed for Harvath's pant legs as he got back into the driver's seat.

He sat there for a moment, watching as the polar bear moved closer. The beast was even more majestic than it had looked from the air.

Harvath hit the start button, put the Land Cruiser in gear, and did a wide U-turn around Nemstov. The last he saw of him in his rearview mirror, the Russian was crawling wildly into the brush, dragging his mangled feet behind him, in a desperate search for the ammunition. Coming down the hill was the polar bear.

While part of him would have liked to have stayed to watch the entire thing, the rain was turning to sleet and Harvath needed to get to the heliport.

Hitting the gas, he sped back toward the main road, haunted by the feeling that even Pavel and Oleg might have their limits when it came to Svalbard weather.

If he couldn't convince them to fly him to Ny-Ålesund, everything would be over.

CHAPTER 55

Harvath stopped only once—to remove the vehicle's diplomatic plates and throw them, along with all of the Russians' guns, into the sea.

When he arrived at the heliport and left the Land Cruiser behind one of its outbuildings, the rain, mixed with sleet, was still coming down.

"What do you think?" he asked.

"Not good," Pavel replied. "But still Svalbard weather."

"Can you do the flight?"

"Maybe."

"I'd be willing to pay," Harvath offered.

"Why so important? Tomorrow better weather. We go then."

"There's someone in Ny-Ålesund I need to see. They'll be gone by the time we get there tomorrow."

"Someone for your book?" Oleg asked.

Harvath smiled at the man. "Yes, someone for my book. Someone important."

"Flight is 110 kilometers, but weather will get worse as we fly north," Pavel pointed out.

"But we could make it."

"Would be pushing, but I think we make it. Problem is might not make it back. Have to stay overnight."

"Would that be a problem?" Harvath asked. "I will pay you for your time."

"How much moneys?" said Oleg.

"Five thousand dollars for each of you. Half in U.S. dollars and half in Norwegian kroner."

Pavel turned to Oleg and had a heated discussion with him in Russian. From what Harvath could understand, they were arguing over the price.

Finally, Pavel turned back to him and said, "Your offer is too much," said Pavel. "Two thousand each is fair price."

"And you pay for drinks at Ny-Ålesund," Oleg added.

"I can do better than that," Harvath replied, removing the bottle of premium Russian vodka from his pack and showing it to them. "Do we have a deal?"

"We have deal," Pavel agreed, shaking hands and looking at the sky, "only if we go now. Ten more minutes, we not able to get off ground."

• • •

As Pavel and Oleg did their preflight check, Harvath sat inside the helicopter, listening to the rain-sleet mix coming down and feeling gusts of wind rock the enormous bird from side to side on its fat tires.

He had made it to the heliport by the skin of his teeth. A few minutes later and he might not have been able to convince the Russian pilot and his assistant to take off at all.

Harvath was flying by the seat of his pants, and it wasn't lost on him that this was exactly the way the Old Man *didn't* like doing operations. Mercer had been right on the money when he had described Carlton's habit of designing missions from the exfiltration backward. It was a solid, proven means of planning for successful ops.

But the kind of assignments Harvath often took weren't as cut-and-dried. The deck always had fifty-two cards, but any number of them could be wild. He was paid to achieve successful outcomes, however. Getting to success—surmounting all of the unforeseen circumstances that popped up along the way—was why he had the reputation that he did.

Even so, at this moment, he had no idea how he was going to get out of Ny-Ålesund, much less off Svalbard, with the second Black Ice device.

He could see himself trying to explain to Lawlor, the CIA Director, and the President that he had checked the equipment in at the SAS desk in Longyearbyen but it never showed up on the baggage carousel when he arrived at his final destination in Kirkenes. That was never going to fly. Nor would he ever attempt to do something like that. When he got his hands on that device, he wasn't going to let it out of his sight until he personally handed it over to the right people.

Back at the safe house, he knew Nicholas was working on his exfiltration, trying to come up with the perfect plan to get him off the archipelago and back to Norway proper. He only hoped the little man figured out something soon. He didn't want to remain on Svalbard one second longer than was necessary.

• • •

When the preflight check was complete, Pavel, dressed in foul weather gear and an offshore inflatable life jacket, climbed into the cockpit and began bringing the old helo to life.

As he did, a similarly kitted-out Oleg opened the main hatch and handed Harvath a bunch of gear, including a rifle in a blaze-orange, waterproof, dry-bag scabbard, along with an additional life jacket.

"Put on," the Russian instructed.

Harvath understood why. In addition to large swaths of rough, inhospitable terrain, they would also be flying over miles of ocean. He flashed him a thumbs-up.

Once the rotors were hot, Pavel gave Oleg the signal to remove the chocks from the tires. After stowing them, Oleg hopped into the cockpit, put on his headset, and booted up his playlist.

Pavel applied power to the engines and the helicopter began to lift off. After affixing his offshore life jacket, Harvath removed the key Holidae had given him and hung it around his neck. As he did, he began to hear music through his headset.

Though he was a die-hard funk fan, Harvath loved classic rock, and Oleg had picked the perfect Norse mythology–inspired song to launch them on their way up to Ny-Ålesund: "Immigrant Song" by Led Zeppelin.

A hard-core, propulsive jam about ice, midnight sun, war making, and Valhalla. Harvath couldn't think of a better way to go into battle.

CHAPTER 56

Helicopters, it was said, didn't fly—they merely beat the air into submission. But halfway between continental Norway and the North Pole, it felt as if the air were winning.

As sleet slammed against the exterior, another sixty-plus-mile-per-hour gust rocked the airframe. The rotors groaned in protest. There was only so much the helo could handle. They were pushing it beyond its limits.

Scot Harvath didn't need to see the water to know the slate-gray ocean was roiling with whitecaps. This far above the Arctic Circle, where moisture from the south collided with icy polar winds, massive depressions formed, unleashing nightmare weather.

If anything went wrong, there would be no rescue. No one back at the U.S. Embassy in Oslo, much less anyone at the White House, would acknowledge him or the mission he was on.

He glanced at the cracked face of his watch, Nemstov's blood crusted atop its bezel. *Just a little further,* he thought to himself. *We're almost there.*

Ignoring the pain in his ribs, he reached for his pack and double-checked everything. It was all still in place. *Take care of your gear and your gear will take care of you.* It was a mantra that had saved his life again and again.

Under his mountaineering jacket, he felt the cold press of metal against his skin. No one knew if the odd-shaped key hanging from a piece of paracord would even work—not after all this time.

If it didn't, all of the danger, all of the risk, would be for nothing and the consequences would be deadly. Failure, however, wasn't an option.

That was the world he lived in. He wasn't interested in easy tasks. In fact, he had always chosen the most difficult, the most perilous assignments.

It was how he was wired. No matter how bleak the scenario, he would never give up. Success was the only outcome he would entertain.

But as yet another gale-force blast of frigid air convulsed the helicopter, causing it to swing violently from side to side, he began to have his doubts.

Moments later, an alarm began shrieking from the cockpit, and Harvath knew they were in trouble.

Pavel and Oleg, thankfully, were able to regain control. The bird was still swaying, but nowhere near as badly as before. It looked like everything was going to be okay.

Then there was an earsplitting crack. It sounded as if the helo had been hit by lightning. It was followed by the tail rotor completely shearing off. And as it did, the helicopter began to spiral.

They were going down.

CHAPTER 57

As the helicopter lost altitude, it began to corkscrew even faster. Pavel fought to regain control while Oleg sent out a distress call. Fighting against the ever-increasing G's pinning him to his seat, Harvath craned his neck to try to snatch a look out the window. They appeared to be over land, which was bad. With each spin, however, he saw that they were getting closer and closer to the ocean, which could potentially be even worse.

"MAYDAY. MAYDAY. MAYDAY," Oleg continued, repeating the full call—identifying the aircraft and giving their GPS location and situation. But every time he said, "OVER," and waited for a response, none came.

They were spinning faster and faster, drifting farther and farther off course.

"BRACE FOR IMPACT," Pavel ordered.

"BRACE! BRACE! BRACE!" Oleg instructed, saying the word over and over again.

As Harvath assumed the best crash position he could, he made himself a promise. If they survived, he was never, ever coming back to Svalbard.

When they finally ran out of air to fall through, they hit and hit *hard*. It was like crashing into concrete. The rotors as well as the landing gear snapped like twigs.

As the helicopter rolled to one side, Harvath realized that not only had he survived but they had crashed into the ocean.

"Pavel?" Harvath called as he unbuckled his harness, threw off his headset, and climbed out of his seat. "Are you okay? Oleg?"

With the engines dead, it was eerily quiet. Outside, however, the waves and the sleet were pounding the helicopter. And soon enough his ears could detect another sound. Looking down, he saw water flooding in. They were sinking. Fast.

This was no longer Pavel's helo. This was Harvath's ship and he was going to make sure his crew got out and back to shore alive.

"Pavel!" he barked in his command voice. "Oleg! Time to move! Right now!"

The cockpit door had slammed shut at some point and was jammed. Bracing his boot against the wall, Harvath pulled with all his strength and popped it open.

Both Pavel and Oleg were still strapped in. Oleg was conscious but disoriented, bleeding from a gash in his head. Pavel was completely out and one of his legs appeared pinned. There was a rupture in the helo's nose and the freezing cold water was entering faster in the cockpit than back in the cabin.

"Oleg, look at me," said Harvath, grabbing the man under his chin and forcing him to focus. "We need to help Pavel."

Oleg looked around, trying to orient himself. Harvath took a second to do the same.

They weren't as far out to sea as he had worried that they would be. The coast was reachable. The swim, though, would be bone-chillingly ferocious. Unless . . .

"Oleg," he said. "Is there a life raft?"

The Russian nodded.

"Where is it?"

"Canister. Starboard side. Main cabin."

"Excellent," Harvath replied. "You will help me get Pavel out of his seat and then we will go to shore together. Understood?"

Again, still somewhat in a fog, the Russian nodded.

"Good. Stand up."

Harvath explained what he wanted him to do. Then, counting to three, he released Pavel's harness. With a little work, they were able to free his leg, lower him from his chair, and carry him into the cabin.

While Oleg gathered up what supplies he could, Harvath raced for the canister containing the life raft. His boots were soaked and his feet were already going numb from the cold water.

Pulling out the canister, he removed the lashing and climbed up toward the hatch. The moment he opened the door, sleet and seawater began pouring inside. It didn't take long for the rest of him to get soaked as well. Holding the painter, as the rope was called, he pushed the container out, and gave the line a strong tug.

Nothing happened. He tried again. Still nothing. Harvath pulled again, harder this time. Then again. And again once more. Finally, something happened. The rope broke and the storm carried the container away.

Dropping back down into the cabin with a splash, Harvath looked at Oleg. "The raft was defective."

"*Defective?*" the man replied, seemingly unaware of the word's meaning.

"*Slomannyy,*" said Harvath, using the Russian word for *broken*, and then followed up with another Russian word. "Can you swim? *Plavat?*"

Oleg nodded.

"Good. I will swim with Pavel. I need you to carry anything you can, but especially the rifle. There are many seals onshore, which means there may be polar bears close by. Do you understand?"

"I must bring rifle," the man announced.

"Yes," said Harvath. "We need to move quickly. Go."

They had only minutes left, if that, before the enormous helicopter slipped beneath the waves and sank to the seafloor.

Harvath found his backpack and, using the garbage can liner in the cabin, waterproofed it as best he could.

Once Oleg said he was ready, they prepared to exit and make the excruciatingly painful, bone-chilling swim to shore.

Harvath was glad to have had training in cold water, but the worst the temperature ever got in the San Diego Bay was in the 50s. Just based on what he knew about the Arctic and how quickly his feet had gone numb, the water they were in right now had to be in the 30s. If they didn't move straight and fast like torpedoes, they were going to die before they ever reached the coast.

Harvath had Oleg climb out first and stand on the sleet-lashed helicopter. Throwing up a rope, he looped the other end around Pavel. Together, with Harvath pushing and Oleg pulling, they managed to get the unconscious Russian out of the aircraft. Then, once Harvath had retrieved their essential gear, he had Oleg jump.

As soon as the man hit the water, his life jacket automatically inflated. Leaning over the side of the helo, Harvath handed him the rifle.

Then he carefully lowered Pavel, whose vest also automatically inflated and kept him faceup as the waves threatened to bash him against the side of the helicopter.

Putting on his pack, Harvath then followed, jumping into the absolutely frigid water and joining the men.

Once his life jacket inflated, he wrapped the other end of Pavel's rope around Oleg. This way, he wouldn't lose either of them.

"It's closer than it looks," he lied, grabbing Pavel by the collar as he began to swim. "The sooner we get to shore, the sooner we get warm."

Harvath looked back only once. Just long enough to watch the helicopter slip beneath the surface of the storm-tossed sea and disappear.

From that moment forward, he never looked back. All he focused on was keeping Oleg motivated and getting to shore.

It was the most agonizing, most brutal swim of his life.

CHAPTER 58

As Harvath dragged Pavel up onto the beach, the Russian was still unconscious. Oleg was so exhausted and riddled with cold, he could barely stand. Crawling out of the water, he collapsed on the ground, shivering violently. It was imperative that Harvath get them out of the storm and figure out a way to get all of them warm.

Through the curtains of wind-driven sleet, he spotted a small cavern. It wasn't much, but it would provide some shelter, which was a start.

Helping Oleg to his feet, he pointed to it and said, "Go. Don't stop until you get there."

While the man stumbled down the beach, Harvath took off his life vest, grabbed Pavel under the arms, and began pulling him to safety.

The swim had taken almost every ounce of strength he had. Battling the waves had required a herculean effort. But they had made it. And if they could make it this far, they could make it the rest of the way. No one was dying on his watch.

The seals, unaccustomed to human beings, barked and moved off as the men approached.

Just getting inside the shelter of the cavern, out of the storm, made a huge difference.

Oleg's hands and fingers were so numb, he couldn't remove his life jacket. Harvath helped him and then did the same for Pavel.

He propped the two life jackets against the wall and had Oleg sit with his back to them, like cushions. He then maneuvered Pavel over and told the Russian to draw his colleague in tight, wrapping his arms and legs around him.

Now it was time to make a fire.

Harvath knew the signs well enough to see that hypothermia had set in. What he did in the next several minutes would be the difference between life and death for all three of them.

Ignoring his own shivering and pushing through his exhaustion, he patted his pockets. He was trying to remember in which one he had placed the lighter Mercer had picked out for him at the sporting goods store in Kirkenes.

No matter how many times he felt each pocket, he couldn't find it. Then he remembered. He hadn't purchased a lighter—he had purchased a set of stormproof matches. They were in his backpack, along with all of his other supplies, which he had set down when he took off his life jacket. Confusion was another dangerous hallmark of hypothermia.

He hated going back into the storm, but he had no choice. Without the matches, they wouldn't be able to start a fire.

Even with them, they might still have a problem. Not only were his hands and fingers almost completely numb, but Svalbard was devoid of trees. Birds here nested on the ground, using moss and grasses. Harvath didn't know what, if anything, he would be able to find to burn.

Then, ten yards farther up the beach, beyond his backpack, he saw it—a seal carcass.

It had been mauled pretty good, likely by a polar bear, but was only partially eaten. Something must have frightened the predator off. A meal like this wasn't something a bear walked away from. He wondered if their out-of-control helicopter, roaring through the sky overhead, might have spooked it.

Whatever the reason, the kill was fresh, which meant the bear might still be close. And if it was close, that meant that it could come back. Harvath made a mental note to unsheathe the rifle and have it ready.

Dragging the seal down the beach proved to be too much. He was just too cold and too wiped out.

Returning to the cavern, he removed the space blanket from his pack and covered the Russians with it, taking care to tuck it in around them.

Next, he pulled the rifle from the dry bag. After inspecting it and making sure a round was chambered, he leaned it against the wall where Oleg could get to it if he needed to.

Then, retrieving the knife from Mercer's capabilities kit, he went back out to do a fast and ugly field dressing of the seal.

As he did, even in the driving storm, his body shaking from the cold, he said a silent prayer of thanks.

It took him two trips to finally get everything back to the cavern. Moving along the beach, he kept his eyes peeled for anything he could use for tinder. Without it, there wasn't going to be a fire. Unfortunately, he hadn't seen any—no moss, no grasses, nothing.

He knew there had to be something. The cold was messing with his brain. He wasn't thinking straight. Taking a deep breath, he closed his eyes for a moment. That's when it came to him.

Opening his eyes, he reached for his pack. He had plenty of tinder. Ten thousand dollars' worth, to be exact.

Removing the currency, he set it aside along with the case of storm-proof matches and used the rocks to quickly build a fire pit.

When everything was ready, he removed a small plastic spoon that came with one of the snacks he had bought in Kirkenes, struck a match, and lit it on fire.

It was one of the survival tricks he had learned a long time ago. A normal-size plastic spoon would burn for about ten minutes. From this little one, he figured he could get three or four minutes at best, but that was all he needed.

Placing the burning spoon into the fire pit, he carefully placed crinkled dollars and kroner, building up the flame.

When he got it where he wanted it, he used the bones he had removed from the seal as a grate and placed pieces of fat on top of it.

Seal blubber, he had learned years ago in his winter survival training, spoiled rapidly but made excellent fuel.

With the fire going and beginning to give off respectable heat, he needed to focus on getting warmth *into* their bodies. Everything he had been taught called for hot liquids. But what did he have that they could warm up?

A voice in the back of his mind encouraged him to look in his pack, and there it was—the bottle of water Oleg had given him during the "beverage services" portion of their inaugural flight.

Setting it close enough to the fire to get the temperature they needed, however, was a no-go. There was too great a chance the bottle would rupture or melt, and then they'd lose all of their water. But that wasn't their only option. He also had a bottle of vodka.

Despite the warming sensation it gave, alcohol consumption was considered the mother of all no-no's at the height of a survival situation.

Using the empty rifle scabbard as a bladder, Harvath opened the bottle and poured it all in. The vodka had plenty of other uses and there was no point in wasting it. Now, thanks to the glass bottle, he had a melt-proof reservoir in which to heat their water.

Filling the bottle with the water, he placed it near the fire. While he waited for it to warm, he dug into Mercer's trauma kit and found another mylar space blanket, which he removed from its pouch and wrapped around himself as he placed more seal blubber on the fire. If they could successfully rewarm themselves, everything else was possible.

He didn't like the fact that Pavel was still unconscious. That was very bad. Despite his frozen hands and fingers, Harvath had given him a cursory examination but had failed to ascertain what was wrong with him. The longer the pilot remained out of it, the more Harvath's concern grew.

When the water had been sufficiently heated, Harvath poured in a couple of oral rehydration packets from the trauma kit, swirled the bottle around, and sipped at it for a moment before moving over and helping Oleg take a few drinks.

Slowly, they shared the bottle back and forth. As Pavel was unconscious, giving him anything to eat or drink was out of the question.

Lemon-flavored water Harvath never would have given much thought to tasted like liquid gold. As wonderful as the fire was, it didn't feel nearly as good as that hot beverage, the warmth suffusing his core and radiating outward through his body.

Laying even more blubber on the fire, he was grateful for the heat. The sky hadn't killed them. The ocean hadn't killed them. The cold wasn't going to kill them. There was no question in his mind. They were going to make it. Now, he needed to think about what came next.

Unzipping his coat, he pulled out his cell phone and fumbled with the power button. He had no idea where they were or if he could even get service.

Nothing happened. The phone was dead, killed by seawater. There was, however, something else worth trying.

Reaching into his pack, he removed the GPS device that he had resuscitated at lunch. Powering it up, he placed it at the edge of the cavern and waited.

There were a bunch of reasons GPS units ran into problems in the Arctic. From ionospheric interference to the limits of orbital inclinations, getting a decent reading this far north could be a real roll of the dice.

With the storm raging, Harvath was fully prepared for the device to fail to link up with enough satellites to produce a result, but that wasn't the case. It did. And it did so almost immediately.

They were about five miles south of Ny-Ålesund, along the eastern coast of the Bøgger Peninsula. If he followed the beach, he could be there in less than an hour.

That meant, of course, that he would have to leave Oleg and Pavel behind. But if he didn't go, there was no way that any help was going to come.

Stacking the blubber where Oleg could reach it and place it on the fire, Harvath said, "We're not far from Ny-Ålesund. It's very close."

Oleg smiled. "That's what you said about swim to beach. You were lying then, or now?"

Harvath smiled back. "Now I'm telling you the truth."

"Truth is good."

"Truth is good," Harvath agreed, putting his hand on the man's shoulder. "I will go get help. You need to stay here, keep getting warm, and protect Pavel. Can you do that?"

"Yes," the Russian replied. "I can do that."

CHAPTER 59

Harvath took off his mountaineering jacket, wrapped his core with the mylar blanket, and then put the coat back on.

Saying goodbye to Oleg, he shouldered his pack and headed out into the storm.

Hood up, head down, Harvath was resolute. Despite the lashing sleet and the clawing wind, he would not be beaten. *Determination over distance,* he told himself, adopting Hilde's phrase to suit his current circumstances.

But as he trudged on, he felt a chill rolling down his spine. It wasn't the weather, however. Something else was happening. Something wasn't right.

He stopped and looked behind. Visibility was poor. What little he could see was nothing but empty beach. The hypothermia continued to play tricks with his mind. He was becoming paranoid.

Nevertheless, the Beretta pistol, which had stayed miraculously dry in his pack, now sat in his outer coat pocket. He was taking nothing for granted.

He kept moving. So much time had been lost. It was critical that he get to the Black Ice device before the Spetsnaz team did.

To shake the frozen fog from his brain, he tried to anticipate where, and how, the Russian Special Forces soldiers would make landfall. Would they come in via a minisub? Or would it be via a rigid inflatable boat?

The storm would provide only a certain amount of cover. The best thing about it was that it would keep most people indoors.

Other than that, there was no full cover of darkness coming. Not this time of year and not this far north. It was, after all, the "land of the mid-night sun."

Spetsnaz soldiers were very well trained. The only limits imposed on them were financial. Often their missions were cut short or curtailed because of budget constraints. The cheapest way for them to land was by boat—and it posed the greatest risk of them being detected. A minisub posed the least amount of risk of exposure, but minisubs didn't grow on trees. They were very expensive, both to operate and maintain.

That said, with the Northern Fleet headquartered so close, Harvath figured they could lay their hands on one. In fact, they probably already had, attaching it to one of the submarines they had launched during the Black Ice test and the blinding of the GLOBUS system.

If the Spetsnaz team did intend to come in via minisub, the only remaining question was where they would land. To figure that out, he was going to need more information—information he intended to extract from Wen Ying the moment he got his hands on him.

He was just beginning to formulate his plan for hitting the Chinese research station when he felt another chill race down his spine.

Spinning, he pulled the pistol, expecting someone or something to be right behind him. There was nothing there but the storm. At least, that's what his eyes and ears told him. His instincts, however, told him something completely different. He was being stalked.

He stood there straining his ears above the roar of the wind and the crash of the surf. The sleet raking his hood was all but deafening and he pulled it back so he could listen even more intently. It was useless.

Keeping his hand gripped tightly around the butt of the Beretta, he returned the pistol to his pocket and continued walking—looking over his shoulder every few moments.

Adding to his problems, the storm was becoming more intense. The wind, sleet, and cold were all getting worse. With each step, the numbness and pain in his body was mounting.

He couldn't stop. He had to keep going. He needed to get help for Pavel and Oleg. He also needed to get help for himself. That was becoming more apparent with each passing second. Without dry clothes and more warm liquids, he wouldn't be able to help anyone, much less successfully complete his mission.

He made it a good thirty yards before he felt the chill race down his spine once more. This time it was accompanied by a noise—and the noise wasn't human.

It was guttural, a grunt of some sort, and came from what sounded like an enormous creature.

Harvath spun to see a massive polar bear—twice the size of the one outside Barentsburg—barreling toward him. Its snout was covered in blood, which Harvath prayed was seal and not human.

He went for his pistol, knowing full well that even under perfect conditions it would be extremely difficult to bring down an animal this big with a nine-millimeter. Suffering the effects of hypothermia wasn't going to do much to help his marksmanship.

The bear let out a throaty roar as it closed the gap and Harvath began to draw his weapon. But before he could get it all the way out of his pocket, there was a blinding flash of light.

The polar bear skidded to a halt, sending rocks and sand in all directions. It flared its nostrils in the storm as if trying to decide what to do.

Then, just as suddenly as it had appeared, it turned and receded up the beach, disappearing from view.

Harvath looked at the woman who had fired the flare.

"Are you okay?" she shouted over the wind.

Next to her, a man held a rifle at the ready, just in case the monster of a bear should return.

The patches on their jackets identified them as members of the joint German-French research project AWIPEV.

"There was a helicopter crash," Harvath replied. "The pilots are in a cavern up the beach. They're suffering from hypothermia. One is unconscious."

"Do they have a rifle?" the man asked.

"Yes."

"Good. I will go to town and organize a rescue party. You need to get dry and warm. Our station is close. Emele can accompany you."

The woman nodded and, putting away her flare pistol, unslung her rifle, and motioned for Harvath to follow.

CHAPTER 60

A quick walk from the beach, there was a collection of huts that formed the Jean Corbel research station.

As soon as they stepped inside the residence structure, Emele helped Harvath begin peeling off his wet clothes.

He made sure not to allow her to see the key hanging from his neck or feel the weight of his coat with the pistol in its pocket.

Wrapping him in blankets, she brought him a large mug of tea and asked him a series of questions about his condition.

She was quiet and professional. She found a container of broth, poured it into a pan, and placed it on the stove to warm.

"Thank you," Harvath replied to each kindness.

"You are very lucky that we found you when we did," she said. "All of us who operate outside of town must have polar bear training. You have no idea what that creature could have done. I am glad that the flare worked. We are always supposed to use the flare first. It would be a pity to shoot such a beautiful animal."

Harvath had also had polar bear training and was well aware of what that animal could have done. He agreed with her—it would have been a pity to shoot the bear; but he would have done it anyway.

Although the soup was a simple consommé, it was one of the most delicious things he had ever eaten. The warmth from it, coupled with the heating inside the hut, spread throughout his body. Soon enough, he could begin to feel his fingers and toes again.

While he worked on a second cup of soup, Emele found him something to wear—weatherproof, insulated coveralls like those she and her colleague were wearing, complete with AWIPEV markings.

There was a name tag on his, which read *Badeaux*. He ran his finger along it.

"Georges is in Paris, delivering a paper," she said. "I don't think he would mind you borrowing some of his clothes. His boots will probably fit you as well."

Once again Harvath thanked her, then posed a question, "How far is it to town?"

"It's not far. About five kilometers."

He did the math. It was roughly three miles. "I need to get going."

"Now?" she asked as he began to get dressed. "You want to go back out into that storm? The only reason Pascal and I were out there was because a piece of our equipment, a sensor, down at the beach was malfunctioning. At least wait until it passes."

Harvath shook his head. "I need to be there when they bring the pilots back."

"Are you sure you are up to it physically?"

"Yes. I'll be fine."

The Frenchwoman looked at her watch. "Well, you can't go alone, especially not without a rifle. I'll go with you. I have a couple of things I need to do in Ny-Ålesund anyway."

He nodded and looked at his own watch, which, because of the cracked crystal and having been submerged in water, was no longer working.

There was a clock on the stove.

"Is that the correct time?"

Emele checked it and then nodded. "Yes. I have to go to the other hut to gather some things and leave a note for my colleagues. I'll be back in five minutes and we can get going. Does that work for you?"

"It does. Thank you."

"You are welcome," she replied. "And please stop thanking me. This is what we do in the Arctic. We help each other. If we didn't, none of us would survive."

• • •

Once she had left for the other structure, Harvath transferred the pistol from his jacket, hung the key back around his neck, and loaded up his pack.

Wearing warm dry clothes and having consumed hot liquids, he thought he would be ready to greet the wet, icy cold outside. He was wrong. It felt even more bitter than it had before.

As they walked into town, Emele asked if he had a cell phone. Because of all of the sensitive experiments carried out at the various research stations Ny-Ålesund was considered a radio silent area. No Wi-Fi, Bluetooth, or cell phone signals were allowed. Everything that transmitted or received had to be hardwired. That meant that computers had to be plugged into Ethernet cables and all cell phones had to remain in airplane mode.

Harvath told her that wouldn't be a problem, as his phone was in "ocean" mode and wouldn't be receiving or transmitting any kind of signal ever again.

When they arrived in town, she gave Harvath two options. He could make himself comfortable at the "Blue House," as AWIPEV's headquarters were known, or rest and get something to eat at the service building mess hall where meals, snacks, and coffee were available. They also had two computers with free internet access.

He opted for the mess hall. And though she had told him not to, he thanked her once again.

As the Frenchwoman went to make contact with a Norwegian colleague, he watched until she was out of sight and then changed his course. He needed to get to the Chinese research station as quickly as possible.

He also was going to have to be very careful how he handled himself once he got there. Ny-Ålesund wasn't completely devoid of security. They had a unit known as the "Watchmen," whose priority it was to keep polar bears from wandering in but who could be called upon for other circumstances requiring trained men with guns. Harvath preferred not to have to deal with them if he could avoid it. With the Chinese and the Russians, his dance card was almost full up.

In addition to giving him info on the town, Emele had also pointed out the buildings and which research organization each one belonged to. When she indicated the Yellow River Station, he paid particular attention.

Now that he was alone, he wanted to give it an even closer look. Then he would decide upon his best course of action.

Making his way over to the building, he noticed an uptick in traffic, both on foot and by vehicle. Dinner service at the mess hall was beginning and, despite the storm, people were starting to stream in.

It was Friday, which meant the official beginning of the weekend and access to alcohol—which, during the week, was off-limits. The scientists had worked hard all week and now they could let their hair down.

But as the dinner hour struck, he knew the chiming clock signified something else—high tide. And with that high tide would come the Russians.

Harvath was running out of time.

CHAPTER 61

A t Ny-Ålesund, China really did have its nose deep inside the Arctic tent. Their Yellow River Station was one of the biggest and most impressive facilities in town.

Clad in red metal siding, the two-level building comprised over 5,500 square feet of space. Connecting its two floors was a pair of exterior metal staircases—one on the north side of the building and one on the south.

On the roof was an observatory. On the ground floor, flanking the main entrance, were a pair of large ornamental lions carved from white marble.

Inside the building were laboratories, offices, storerooms, and dormitories capable of housing up to twenty-five people.

As far as the interior was concerned, Harvath was most interested in the storerooms. If the Black Ice equipment was on-site, he had a feeling that was where he would find it.

But where would he find Wen Ying?

Not that he needed to find the military operative. In fact, he would have been perfectly happy recovering the device and leaving town without the Chinese or the Russians knowing he had been there. However, he put the chances of that happening about even with surviving a charge by a polar bear.

Watching the facility from behind a smaller structure nearby, he noticed a gray Toyota minivan pull up. The driver tapped his horn twice and a group of scientists in foul-weather gear exited the second floor, hurried down the stairs, and got into the van. As soon as the door was shut, the driver rolled toward the mess hall.

It made the most sense that the living space would be upstairs and all of the research and official duties of the research station would be carried out on the ground level. Much more efficient that way. No lugging samples and equipment up and down the stairs.

Except for some sort of 4x4 utility truck parked behind the structure, Harvath didn't see any other vehicles. And once the van had left, he didn't notice any further activity. It was time to get himself inside the facility.

Grabbing what he needed from his pack, he tucked it where no one would find it, affixed the suppressor to his pistol, and, after secreting it inside his coveralls, headed toward the building.

There was no way of telling who, if anyone, was inside. But just to be safe, he avoided the main entrance in the center of the station and opted for the door on the south side.

When he got there, he held his ear near it and listened for any sign of life, but hearing anything above the sleet and wind was practically impossible.

Because of the threat of polar bear attacks, all doors in town were mandated to remain unlocked—just in case someone needed to seek shelter. Reaching out with his gloved hand, he tried the handle. It was unlocked. He opened it and quietly stepped inside.

The room he entered resembled an airlock, a space where scientists could slip into or out of their gear without letting the frigid polar wind blow all the way into the station.

There were coat hooks, shelves, lockers, and benches, as well as a weapons cabinet stocked with scoped rifles, shotguns, flare pistols, and ammo.

Harvath approached the next door, which had been fabricated out of thick steel. It had a small porthole, which he carefully peered through. He couldn't see anyone on the other side. He took a moment to listen but still didn't hear anything.

He tried the handle, but, unlike the outer door, this one was locked. Now came the moment of truth.

He removed the key from around his neck and inserted it into the oversized lock. *A perfect fit.*

Turning the key, he felt all of the tumblers fall, then came the satisfying click of the lock releasing. The door swung open noiselessly on its chunky but well-oiled hinges and Harvath crossed into the station proper.

There were rows of worktables covered with equipment. Counters, just as cluttered, ran along the perimeter of the room. Blackboards and whiteboards lined the walls. The air held the faint smell of chemicals. No scientists were visible.

Harvath headed down a short hallway with a wide wooden door. The door was unlocked. He hung his key around his neck again.

Flipping on the lights, he saw that he had discovered one of the storerooms. This one, however, was filled mostly with supplies. The equipment had to be in another room, perhaps closer to the other entrance. Turning out the lights, he continued moving.

Passing through a cluster of offices, he entered a second lab with another hallway and a wide wooden door. This door was unlocked as well.

Harvath opened the door, turned on the lights, then realized he had discovered the equipment storeroom. There were shelves crammed with all manner of scientific gear. Along the floor and stacked at the far end, were crates, soft-sided containers, and various hard-sided containers. Harvath searched for one around the size of a footlocker.

It took him a few minutes of moving things around, but then he found something. Crouching down, he flipped up the hasps, lifted the lid, and was about to peer inside, when a long shadow fell over him from behind.

He moved to his right just as piece of pipe meant for his head came slicing through the air. There was no time to draw his weapon.

Launching from his crouched position, he exploded like a rocket, landing a devastating punch against his attacker's jaw.

Wen Ying stumbled backward, dazed, but quickly regrouped and came at Harvath with the pipe.

He was astoundingly fast, striking at him again and again and again. It was all Harvath could do to pull equipment off the shelves and parry the blows.

He had no idea where the Chinese operative had come from or how he had found him. The only thing he knew for certain was that the man was relentless—that and the fact that he had beaten Harvath practically to the back corner of the storeroom.

If Harvath didn't do something to change the trajectory of this altercation, it wouldn't take much for Ying to land a blow that would lay him out.

Out of the corner of his eye, Harvath spotted an aluminum briefcase and lunged for it.

The move exposed the left side of his back and his attacker landed an amazingly vicious blow. The pain felt like he had been hit by a bat wrapped with red-hot barbwire. This guy had officially pissed him off.

Using his rage as fuel and the briefcase as a shield, Harvath spun and advanced on his attacker, blocking blow after blow, forcing the man backward. But then the man got lucky.

He swung with an incredible amount of force, connecting with the case alongside Harvath's left hand, smashing his index finger.

The pain was like having his finger sliced off. Not since Harvath was a little boy and accidentally got his finger caught in his parents' car door had he felt anything like it. But instead of dropping the case, he fought harder, with more fury and more intensity.

When the man cocked his arm to let the pipe fly yet again, Harvath drove the briefcase forward into his attacker's face—and didn't stop there.

Stepping into the assault and closing the distance, he went for a match-ending blow, kicking the operative as hard as he could in the nuts.

As the man's knees buckled and he crumpled to the ground, Harvath swung the briefcase and caught him once more under the jaw, this time knocking him unconscious.

CHAPTER 62

Harvath's hand hurt like hell. Looking down at it, he saw that his index finger was bleeding, the nail was hanging off, and it was already turning black-and-blue.

But, true to his training, he adhered to one of the most important rules in combat, which was that medical attention—even to oneself—couldn't be rendered until the threat was neutralized.

The metal shelving in the storeroom was bolted to the concrete floor, but Harvath gave them multiple very strong pulls to make sure. Convinced that they were reliable anchor points, he began yanking the cords out of all the electronic items within reach.

Rolling Wen Ying onto his back, Harvath centered him in the middle of the floor and spread his limbs like a starfish. He tied off his wrists and ankles and made sure the knots were slip-proof and tight as hell. Then shredding a stuff sack, he gagged him and headed back to the supply room.

In the office area, he pulled a first aid kit from the wall and treated his finger with alcohol wipes, antiseptic cream, and a bandage as he walked. Then, when he arrived at the supply storeroom, he grabbed a roll of duct tape and wrapped a length of Alabama chrome around his index finger.

From that point forward, he knew exactly what he needed. Removing the items from the shelf, he helped himself to a gown, gloves, two masks, and safety goggles. He didn't have time to work on the Chinese operative. His cooperation needed to be total and absolutely immediate.

While Harvath had double-majored in political science and military history in college, in his general education requirements he had really enjoyed chemistry. His basic understanding of the subject had made him a standout in his explosives training as a SEAL.

He was no chemistry expert—not by a long shot. But he knew enough to be dangerous. And in Wen Ying's case, his knowledge could very well prove deadly.

Arriving back at the equipment storeroom, he closed the door behind him. Normally, that would be a really bad idea, but that's why he had brought the masks—both for himself.

Harvath moved quickly and put on all the protective gear. Once he was ready, he poured a tiny bit of ammonia on a rag he had found on a worktable and held it under his attacker's nose. Instantly, the man's eyes snapped open. *Wide.*

"Welcome back," said Harvath. "Beijing wouldn't have sent you here if you didn't speak English, so don't pretend you can't understand me. Is that clear?"

The man struggled against his bonds, trying to free a hand or a leg.

"I'm in a bit of a hurry," Harvath continued, "so I want to show you something."

Ying stopped struggling and looked at what he was being shown.

"Do you know what hydrofluoric acid is?"

The operative shook his head.

"It's one of the most dangerous and corrosive chemicals you can find in a lab. I'm not really sure what your scientists use it for, but I was thrilled to find it in the supply room. Now let's skip to the good part.

"Here's why you're not going to be as thrilled as I am that I found it. Exposure to hydrofluoric acid causes horrific tissue burns, and if you're splashed with enough of it—just two and a half percent of your skin— you can look forward to a very painful and very rapid death.

"So, like I said, I'm in a hurry. Therefore, I'll give you one chance to answer my question. If you don't, I'm going to soak your hand in the acid. It'll be terrible, I promise you. But the upside is that I'll ask the question again. If you tell me the truth, everything will be over. If you don't, I'll douse your forearm. And just so you know, this is where the chances of cardiac arrest start going through the roof. Of course, I'll do everything to keep you alive so we can keep going, but I have to be honest: In the keeping people alive arena, I have a *very* bad track record. What do you think?"

The Chinese operative glared at him.

"I'm going to take that as a good sign," said Harvath, loosening the man's gag. "Let's start. You're responsible for transferring the Black Ice technology to the Russians. Where is it?"

"You're too late."

Behind his mask, Harvath smiled as he unscrewed the bottle of acid and carefully picked it up. "Right hand or left hand? Any preference?"

"The Russians will make landfall within the hour and the equipment will be gone."

"Tell you what," said Harvath, "Relax your left hand and I'll limit the damage to just a couple of fingers."

"Fuck you," the operative said.

"Funny, I just heard that from one of your colleagues. It must be the first thing they teach you guys in spy school."

Tipping the bottle slightly forward, he splashed the acid onto the man's hand, and Ying screamed in pain.

The smell from the operative's burning flesh was so terrible that Harvath wished that he had been wearing three masks.

Setting the bottle of acid down, he replaced the man's gag and waited until he had stopped screaming before loosening it again.

"I gave your contact, Nemstov, a choice about his feet," Harvath said. "Crutches or a wheelchair—one foot or two. He foolishly chose the wheelchair. And do you know what happened?"

Ying shook his head, his chest heaving and his eyes watering in pain.

"Before he could even pick out a wheelchair, a polar bear ate him. Isn't that terrible?"

The operative didn't respond.

"You can still wipe your ass with your other hand," Harvath said. "But if you don't cooperate with me, that's the part of the garden I'm going to water next. It's up to you. Where's the Black Ice equipment?"

As the man formulated his response, Harvath picked up the bottle of acid and made ready to splash Ying's other hand.

"Out past the runway Ny-Ålesund uses for supply planes," Ying moaned, his blackened hand burned like fire. "Near the old Kongsfjord Telemetry Station. The glacier comes down underground, ending in an ice cave by the beach. The equipment is there."

Harvath, still threatening the man with the acid, compelled the operative to explain exactly how to find it and what the equipment looked like.

While he couldn't verify that what Ying was telling him about the location was true, the description of the box matched up with what Nemstov had relayed.

"Okay," said Harvath.

"Okay what?" Ying replied, consumed with pain.

"Now we're going to find out if you're telling the truth," Harvath answered, pulling his weapon.

CHAPTER 63

The two-man Russian naval Spetsnaz team landed their swimmer delivery vehicle in a rocky inlet, just beneath the telemetry station, and crept up the beach.

The entrance to the ice cave was difficult to find. It was a hole in the ground about the size of a village well. The only way down was via a long aluminum extension ladder. A piece of climbing rope, presumably for moving supplies up and down, was secured to a boulder nearby.

According to the briefing they had been given, the Chinese were conducting ongoing research in the cave as a cover. The equipment that the operatives were there to retrieve—a laptop and a hard-sided case—had been placed about thirty feet from the base of the ladder. It was stacked with other scientific gear so as not to attract any undue attention should anyone stumble upon the cave.

The men had been provided with photographs indicating exactly which items to remove. All they had to do was pinpoint them, extract them, and transport them back to the submarine that was waiting for them just out to sea.

In their minds, and in the mind of their commander, it was a relatively simple operation. It was why only two of them had been dispatched. The joke, as they had planned their mission on board the submarine, was that the U.S. Navy SEALs would have sent two or three times as many men.

The Spetsnaz had huge egos. It was a wonder they could squeeze their swelled heads through the opening and climb down the ladder at all.

Both men were carrying short-barreled AKS-74U carbines, also known as a "Krinks," and 9mm GSh-18 pistols with rounds designed to pierce body armor. If push came to shoot, they'd be fierce opponents in a gunfight—especially one that happened in close quarters, such as in an ice cave.

• • •

Harvath had parked the Yellow River Station's utility truck behind one of the buildings that serviced the airfield and dragged Wen Ying out of the backseat.

He had replaced the gag and tied the man's hands behind his back. But because he needed him to walk in order to lead him to the entrance of the cave, he hadn't bound his legs.

Getting Ying's six-foot frame down the ladder had been a pain in the ass—matched only by the danger of Harvath following, gun in hand, then making sure the man remained facedown on the cave floor and didn't try anything stupid. Luckily, he hadn't.

Just before they had dropped into the cave, Harvath had seen the Russians arrive. He wasn't surprised to see they had sent only two men. That was entirely in keeping with the Spetsnaz ethos. He was simply grateful that he and Ying had arrived before them.

That said, it wasn't as if they had tons of time on their hands. In fact, they had barely enough to get down the hole and hide themselves before the Russians made entry.

Harvath had brought a small jar of hydrofluoric acid with him—enough to push the Chinese operative over the two-and-a-half-percent exposure limit—and with the few moments they had, he made it very clear what would happen to Ying if he didn't cooperate.

Then they hid themselves and waited for the Spetsnaz soldiers to climb down the ladder and into the cave.

Harvath had hoped that they'd beat the Russians by enough time to grab the equipment and be gone before they arrived. Now he was going to have to go to Plan B. What plan B was, however, he hadn't completely decided.

Carrying a laptop straight up a twenty-foot ladder was no problem. Hauling out a box the size of an extra-large beer cooler—weighing God only knew how much—was something else entirely.

The smart play was to make that the Russians' problem. Let them waste their sweat and muscle bringing it to the surface and then take everything from them. Smoke them both and drop them down the cave entrance.

His only problem was Ying. He either had to knock him out again or hog-tie him and hope he didn't get free during the time it took to kill the Russians. He couldn't keep an eye on the Chinese operative and take out the Spetsnaz operatives at the same time.

The best option was to hog-tie Ying. If Harvath knocked him out, there was no telling how long it would be until the man regained consciousness. He hadn't brought any ammonia to revive him, and there was no way he was carrying him straight up twenty feet of ladder.

Just behind where the equipment was stacked, the cavern took a dog-leg to the right. That was where Harvath decided to take cover.

He had Ying lie facedown again on his stomach. Next, he placed the jar of acid under his chin and up against his throat. Then he placed his boot at the base of the man's skull. If the operative tried anything at all, it would take only a quick downward stomp to break the glass and end the man's life.

As the Russians came down the ladder, Harvath placed his injured duct-taped index finger against his lips and softly warned, "Shhhh."

Ying didn't move.

The soldiers approached the equipment and slung their Krinks. They might as well have been at the liquor store, picking up cases of beer for the weekend.

After IDing the case with the laptop as well as the weatherized box with the rest of the equipment, they began moving it all down the cavern toward the entrance.

Then Ying lashed out with his foot, kicking the wall, and both men froze.

Harvath hesitated, not wanting to kill the Chinese operative if he didn't have to, but then the man did it again. And again. And again. He was *warning* the Russians.

This time Harvath didn't hesitate. He stepped hard on the back of the man's head, causing the glass jar under his chin to break, splashing him with acid.

As he screamed from behind his gag and the Spetsnaz soldiers went for their weapons, Harvath stepped out from where he was hiding, raised the twelve-gauge shotgun he had taken from the Yellow River Station, and began firing.

With each blast of 00 buckshot meant to take down a polar bear, he racked the weapon and fired again.

He kept going, cutting the Russians to ribbons, peppering bloody bits and pieces of them across the ice cave's walls.

All told, it was one of the most disturbing scenes he had ever left behind. A "Picasso," as it was known in the business.

The message to Beijing and Moscow would be unmistakable. You fuck with the United States at your peril.

CHAPTER 64

T he key was to keep the utility truck out of sight, at least until morning. Not a hard thing to do during a storm.

Only the Chinese scientists would miss it—and they were all enjoying Friday night at the mess hall. What's more, as long as Wen Ying was unaccounted for, they would figure the 4x4 was with him.

Getting the laptop out of the ice cavern had, as predicted, been a piece of cake. The other piece of equipment, however, had been a ton of work. By the time Harvath arrived at the mess hall, he had more than earned a celebratory beer.

Wearing AWIPEV coveralls, he wasn't paid any undue attention, although a couple of scientists asked him if he was new, to which he replied, "Just filling in for a few days."

After Harvath paid for his beer, he went to the quiet area where the computers were and attempted to make contact with Nicholas. They were on an unsecure system and spoke in shared codes and roundabout language.

The little man was overjoyed to hear that Harvath was all right and that his mission had been a success. He also had a bit of good news of his own. Mercer had found a captain of a fishing trawler who couldn't make it back to Kirkenes and had been forced to wait out the storm in Longyearbyen. The vessel could be at Ny-Ålesund harbor at five a.m. Was Harvath interested?

He absolutely was interested. With everything that had gone down, that was the last piece of the puzzle he needed to solve—how to get home. Now that it was figured out, he could tick off the next thing on his list.

Finishing his beer, he left the mess hall, reclaimed his backpack from its hiding place, and walked over to the infirmary.

He was delighted to see that not only was Oleg doing well and hadn't been eaten by the polar bear, but that Pavel had regained consciousness and, other than a bump to the head and a bad fracture of his leg, was expected to make a full recovery.

Grabbing two paper towels from the dispenser near their sink, he divided up the remaining cash in his pack, wrapped up each portion, and handed them over.

"It's too much," Pavel insisted yet again. "More than we agreed on."

"Take it," said Harvath. "I'm sorry about the helicopter."

"The company has insurance," Oleg replied. "It was very *old* helicopter."

Pavel nodded. "They want to take our official statements in Longyearbyen. A plane will be here tomorrow afternoon. Two p.m. Will you be coming with us?"

"Of course I will," Harvath lied, taking no pleasure in it. "I will see you then."

For all the obvious reasons, he couldn't be connected to Svalbard or anything that had happened there. Once Sølvi had a full readout on everything that had transpired, his hope was that the Norwegian Intelligence Service, along with a little help from Holidae at the CIA's Oslo station, could smooth things out.

He said goodbye to the men and walked over to AWIPEV's little blue house, where he was offered a pullout couch. He couldn't remember the last time he had slept so well. In fact, had it not been for the small alarm clock they had provided, he might have slept for days.

After brewing a cup of drip coffee, he made it down to the dock with the Black Ice equipment just as the Kirkenes-based *Senja* motored into the harbor.

The boat's weathered captain, with his stubby pipe, navy blue peacoat, and wool hat, was a true pro. He glided effortlessly up to the pier and didn't even bother tying off. He waited just long enough for Harvath to load his gear and hop aboard. The man had a hold full of fresh catch and he was anxious to get back home.

Harvath was looking forward to the cruise. The storm had cleared, the skies were bright, and he had five hundred nautical miles to do nothing but watch the water slip past and let his mind wander.

• • •

When they finally arrived in Kirkenes, Philip Mercer was standing on the dock. Behind him were Sloane and Chase.

As the young operatives unloaded the Black Ice equipment and carried everything up to their SUV, Harvath thanked the captain and spent a few minutes walking and talking with his friend, the ex–CIA man.

"The names from Sarov and Nemstov—the Russian Intelligence assets at Vardø—were a huge get," said Mercer. "In fact, you'll love this. When the Norwegians moved in to arrest them, one of them ran. My stepson's best friend, Arne—"

"The security guard?" Harvath interrupted.

"The very same. Well, when the one suspect bolted, Arne pepper-sprayed him in the parking lot, knocked him down, and took him into custody. He's being promoted to deputy chief of security."

Harvath chuckled. "Good for him."

"I heard you had it rough up there."

"Let's just say you're not wrong about Svalbard. If I never see it again, it will be too soon."

"Did the capabilities kit come in handy?"

"Very," said Harvath, handing over his backpack.

"What's this?" asked Mercer.

"It's what's left of the kit."

"I told you that you had to put it back."

Harvath smiled. "Technically, you told me I had to 'return' it. That's what I'm doing—*returning* it to you."

"You have no idea what a pain in the ass it's going to be to figure out how to sneak all this stuff back up there."

"I have every faith in you. By the way, I'm not charging you for bringing your Beretta back from the dead, as well as that GPS unit."

Mercer shook his head and grinned. "So what now?"

Harvath watched as the captain came toward him with a large Styrofoam box stuffed with ice and king crab. "Now I head back to Oslo."

"And Sølvi."

He nodded, and a smile swept across his face. "And Sølvi."

CHAPTER 65

THREE DAYS LATER

"You're not going to do something crazy like propose, are you?" asked Harvath.

"Don't flatter yourself," Sølvi replied, smiling.

"Then why am I wearing a suit and tie? And why are you not telling me where we're going?"

"Because it's a top secret operation."

"Which starts at the rooftop restaurant of The Thief hotel?"

"Just shut up and do as you're told," she ordered.

Harvath grinned. She was *totally* going to propose to him. He didn't know how he felt about it, however. Things had moved pretty fast between them. But if this was what she wanted, he wanted it too. He was comfortable with it. His answer would be yes.

As far as locations went, The Thief made sense. It was where he had turned up out of nowhere a couple of months ago to surprise her and to tell her that he wanted them to spend the summer together. If they were going to seal an even deeper commitment to one another, The Thief was the place to do it.

When they stepped out of the elevator and onto the outdoor terrace, the weather was perfect. Blue skies and bright sunshine. Summer in Oslo appeared to be making a valiant last stand.

Walking back to their usual table, Harvath was surprised to see someone already sitting there—Holidae Hayes.

Like Sølvi, she was also dressed to the nines. She had a big smile on her face and an even bigger glass of champagne in her hand. *What the hell was going on?*

The women greeted each other with kisses. Harvath gave Holidae a hug as he sat down.

"Congratulations," the CIA station chief said as she handed him a shirt-size box with a ribbon around it.

"Isn't this a little premature?" he asked. "Sølvi hasn't even popped the question yet."

"You're an idiot," Holidae asserted. "Open it."

Harvath did. Separating the tissue paper, he pulled out a copy of *Aften-posten*, one of the Norwegian daily newspapers.

He glanced up at her. "Isn't a toaster or a blender a more traditional gift?"

Hayes shook her head. "Just beneath the fold, genius."

Harvath scanned down until he found it. His Norwegian being what it was, all he could make out was the name Astrid Jensen and what looked like the words *sex trafficking*.

"You're welcome," the CIA woman replied.

"You got her busted for sex trafficking? That's awesome. Illegal as hell and kind of hard to believe, but awesome."

"Always making jokes," said Sølvi, taking the newspaper from him and reading the article.

"I did exactly what I told you I was going to do," Holidae explained. "I gave her a bigger headline. In exchange for forgetting about you, she is able to take credit for helping take down one of the biggest sex trafficking rings in Norwegian history."

"Is this true?" Sølvi asked, pointing to the paper. "The young girls were taken from refugee camps and tricked into believing they were being resettled?"

Holidae nodded. "There were some very bad people behind this. The CIA had information, as well as a witness who was seeking asylum in Norway, that it thought could be helpful to the Norwegian Police. My boss agreed to allow everything to flow through Jensen's office."

Harvath looked at her and smiled. "Thank you."

"You're welcome."

"So we're celebrating, then. You've already got champagne. Why don't I order us a bottle?"

"We can each have a glass. For now," Sølvi replied.

"Why?" he asked. "What's going on?"

"He doesn't know?" Holidae asked.

Sølvi shook her head. "Sometimes secrets are a good thing. They make life a little more exciting."

"This secret definitely will," the CIA woman agreed.

"This isn't a proposal," Harvath said, studying them both. "And it isn't a going-away party, because I don't think we could throw a better one than we did two nights ago out at the cottage."

"It was an amazing party," said Sølvi. "The best of the summer. And how incredible was it that everyone could be there?"

"What was incredible," Holidae added, "was that king crab. We need to make sure that *all* of your assignments end in a great food or wine region."

Harvath brought the topic of conversation back around to his question. "So, we all get one glass of champagne. And then what?"

"And then you'll see." Sølvi smiled as she beckoned the waitress over.

• • •

As they sat enjoying champagne and the best views in town over the Oslo fjord, Harvath regaled the two ladies with stories of his assignment. From polar bears to sailing home on a fishing trawler, it was like something out of a movie or an old adventure novel.

When the appointed time came, Sølvi led the party downstairs to the lobby, where a six-door, twenty-foot-long Audi A8 L extended limousine was waiting for them.

Once they were ensconced in the supple leather interior, and the driver had returned to his position behind the wheel, they pulled gently away from the hotel.

Harvath knew better than to ask any more questions about where they were going. Instead, he looked at Sølvi and remarked quietly to himself about how beautiful she was. Seeing her all dressed up, regardless of what they were about to do, took his breath away.

She was still every inch the stunning fashion model and could still be gracing magazine covers today if she wanted to. The fact that she didn't want to, that she preferred serving her country—especially from within the cutthroat world of intelligence and espionage—made him love her all the more. She was one in a million, and he, more than anyone else, appreciated how rare that was. The fact that she wanted to be with him, proposal or no proposal, made everything else in his life worth it. *Determination over distance.* No matter what happened, no matter what the world threw at them, he was going to make this work.

The drive through the center of town provided no clues as to what their ultimate destination was. They could be headed anywhere.

But then the limo turned onto a private paved drive. It was blocked by tall iron gates and machine-gun-toting police officers.

As the vehicle neared, the guards stood back, opened the gates, and waved them through. They were now on the grounds of the Norwegian Royal Palace, and Harvath was beginning to grow even more suspicious.

"Sølvi?" he asked. "Do you want to tell me what we're doing here?"

"Nope," the woman responded.

He then looked at Holidae, who shrugged her shoulders and feigned not having a clue in the world. For one of the CIA's best, she was a terrible liar.

A footman met them at a discreet side entrance, well out of view of photographers who liked to capture the comings and goings of royal visitors.

Inside, a member of the palace staff took over and led them to an ornate study and asked them to wait before stepping back into the hallway, closing the door behind him.

"Do we sit?" asked Harvath, pointing at the seating area near the grand fireplace.

"We most definitely don't sit," said Sølvi. "Not unless we are invited to and not until the King himself sits down."

"The King? That's who we're here to see?"

"Among others," she replied. "You'll be fine. You worked at the White House. I know this isn't the first time you've been around royalty."

He smiled. She had no idea. He had been around plenty of royalty, including the King of Jordan, who once backed him up in a helicopter gunship. But that was a story for another day.

He barely had time to admire the paneled walls with their beautiful rows of colorful leather-bound books before a small door on the other side of the room opened and the King of Norway stepped in.

And as if that weren't a sight in and of itself, it was the woman walking behind him who caught Harvath's attention.

Suddenly he had a feeling that he knew what all this was about. There was just one detail missing.

The King was a handsome, impeccably dressed man who radiated charm and intelligence. As this was an informal audience, he took charge, introducing himself to his guests.

Harvath knew not to initiate a handshake but to wait for the King to do so, which he did. He then turned and introduced the woman who had entered behind him.

"Mr. Harvath," the man said. "I know you both met, but I would like to make a formal introduction. This is Mrs. Bente Gundersen."

The woman extended her hand and Harvath gently shook it. He had not seen the older woman since foiling the robbery at the ATM. With all that had happened, it seemed like a lifetime ago.

"Bente," the King continued, "was a longtime resident of our household before she retired. She was our children's most beloved governess. What you did in protecting her was an act of courage and chivalry. On behalf of Mrs. Gundersen and all of the citizens of Norway, I would like to thank you. Your example is one to be extremely proud of."

"Thank you, your Majesty," Harvath replied, knowing that the less said—especially in a situation like this—was always the best way to handle oneself.

Pressing a button at his desk, the King gestured for his guests to join him for tea near the fireplace.

They all thanked him and followed him over. Once he had sat down, they followed suit.

He was an exceptional conversationalist and had done his homework on Harvath, asking about his upbringing in Southern California, his time as a competitive skier, and nonsensitive questions about his military background.

Throughout tea, Harvath politely engaged with the King, answering all of his questions, eventually drifting into a detailed discussion about sailing.

To his credit, the King made sure to engage his other guests by asking them specific questions and listening intently to their responses.

Learning that Mrs. Gundersen had been a governess for the royal family answered Harvath's question about why the King had taken an interest in what had happened at the ATM. As Sølvi was his significant other, he could even understand why she had been invited for tea.

What he couldn't understand, however, was what Holidae was doing here. Why invite the CIA's Oslo station chief? There was still a piece to this puzzle that was missing.

It wasn't until Mrs. Gundersen said her goodbyes and a staff member arrived to accompany her out that things began to come into sharper focus.

"So," said the King, "shall we proceed?"

Proceed with what? Harvath hadn't a clue. But he knew the only answer to a question in this kind of situation was *Yes* and he responded politely and accordingly.

As they followed the King out of his study, he glanced at Sølvi, who winked at him in return. Looking over his shoulder at Holidae, she gave him the same fake *I have no idea what's going on* expression she had in the limo. Neither of these two were any help whatsoever.

After a short walk down a carpeted hall lined with oil paintings, they arrived at a gilded reception room where three very select additional visitors were waiting.

The first was the American Ambassador to Norway, Michael Mc-Court. Standing next to him was Sølvi's boss "Odin," better known as Ivar Stang, Director of the Norwegian Intelligence Service. And next to him stood Ellen Jagland, head of the Norwegian Police Security Service.

The King made formal introductions, everyone shook hands, and then the other reason Harvath had been invited to the palace was finally made known.

Odin approached the King and opened a velvet box.

"Your courage extends far beyond what you did for Mrs. Gundersen," said the King. "Your heroism in relation to the GLOBUS 3 system in Vardø, and your pursuit of our shared national security interests on Svalbard, are deeply appreciated."

The King removed a golden Cross of St. Olav inlaid with a red cross and a large V and topped with a crown. He hung it around Harvath's neck, declaring, "For outstanding service in the interest of Norway, I present you with the Royal Norwegian Order of Merit."

• • •

Champagne was served, and as the King had other duties to attend to, he said goodbye to his guests before his glass was even half-empty.

Odin and Ellen Jagland left shortly thereafter, followed by Holidae Hayes and Ambassador McCourt, who rode back to the embassy together. Finally, only Harvath and Sølvi remained.

Not wanting to overstay their welcome, they availed themselves of the royal limousine and had the driver return them to The Thief, where, per Sølvi's request, their table had been kept waiting.

As they sipped a final glass of champagne and ordered oysters, Harvath gazed at her yet again. It was going to be really tough being away from her.

They both had something to do and someone to love. What they really needed was that something to look forward to. Something beyond just seeing each other when they could grab vacation time.

"So you're not going to propose to me, are you?" he asked, smiling at her.

She smiled back with the thousand-megawatt smile he adored and said, "Norwegian women can be very forward. We can also be somewhat old-fashioned. It's nice to be asked."

"In that case," Harvath replied, removing a velvet box of his own and getting down on one knee, "will you marry me?"

The ring, which he had purchased the day before, was amazing. He hadn't known how or when he would pop the question. He only knew it was something he wanted to do before he left for the States.

Here, atop The Thief, where their relationship had officially started, seemed the perfect place to take it to the next level.

Throwing her arms around him, she kissed him. "Yes," she said. "Yes, I will."

CHAPTER 66

Spencer Baldwin had booked Lindsey Chang into the best room of the elegant Hay-Adams hotel. Her French balcony directly overlooked the White House. It was one hell of an aphrodisiac.

The only thing sexier, in his mind, was watching him work—which was what he allowed her to do next.

After she had refreshed herself from the flight in, he set her up in the hotel's fabled Off The Record bar. A power broker's playground, it was considered the best place in D.C. to be seen and not heard.

She ordered a cosmo and Baldwin told the bartender to put it on his tab. Then, seeing his guest arrive, he stood up and told her to enjoy the show.

"Mr. Adam Benson," said Baldwin as he greeted the U.S. Special Representative for the Arctic and guided him to the table he had reserved. "Thank you for meeting me."

"My pleasure," said Benson, a distinguished-looking man with a chiseled jaw and a runner's build. "You've got powerful friends in all the right places."

"I'm all about relationships. I hope you and I can be friends too."

"That's what fuels the Washington engine. Let's talk."

"What should I call you?" asked Baldwin as they sat down. "Special Representative? U.S. Envoy? Arctic czar?"

Benson smiled. "You can call me Adam."

"Perfect. What do you like to drink, Adam?"

"A Gold Rush."

"I'm not familiar with it. What's in it?"

"Bourbon over one huge rock of ice with honey syrup and lemon juice."

"Sounds delicious," said Baldwin, who waved the waiter over, ordered two of them, and then got down to business. "Where do you see yourself in ten years, Adam?"

"Is this a job interview?"

"Maybe."

"Ten years is a long time in this town," said Benson.

"You'd be surprised how quickly time flies," Baldwin replied. "If you don't set your goals early, you're going to have a hell of a time getting to where you want to be."

Benson nodded. "Excellent point. I really enjoy the Foreign Service. I guess an ambassadorship would be nice."

Baldwin leaned in. "It'd be nice? Or is that what you want?"

"I've never had it put that directly. An ambassadorship is what I want."

"Good. Now you've got the beginnings of a goal. The next question is: *Where* do you want to be ambassador?"

"Specifically?" asked Benson. "I don't know that I've given it that much thought."

"Come on, Adam. I can tell by looking at you that you're an ambitious man. If you could wave a magic wand, which U.S. Embassy do you see yourself in?"

"Paris," Benson said. "No question."

"That's a hell of a good choice. Right off the Place de la Concorde. The five-star Hôtel de Crillon across the street. You've got excellent taste. There's just one problem."

"What's that?"

"That ambassadorship is a plum posting—one of the absolute best the American President can dole out," Baldwin explained. "It doesn't go to career Foreign Service officers. It goes to mega–campaign donors or people who can bundle tons of money for a candidate."

"You're right," said Benson, a realist. "But you did ask me what I would do if I could wave a magic wand."

"Do you know what business I'm in?"

"You're a political fundraiser."

Baldwin leaned forward even farther. "I also hand out magic wands. Not to everybody. Just my friends."

"I'm listening," Benson replied.

"I can't promise you Paris—that's up to POTUS—but what if I could move enough money through you in the next election that you'd be one of the top contenders for that ambassadorship."

"I'd say I'm still listening. What would you expect in return?"

"I need the U.S. to drop its resistance to Chinese investment in the Norwegian port of Kirkenes."

Benson fell silent as the waiter came back and set their drinks down.

"Changing American foreign policy?" he said after the server had walked away. "That's a major ask."

"What if I could sweeten the deal?" replied Baldwin, sensing he had him and just needed to set the hook.

"Are we talking money?"

"Even better—stock in the company created to helm the port project. The certificates would be placed in an account of your choosing in Panama."

Benson took a sip of his drink and said, "Walk me all the way through it."

• • •

Forty-five minutes and two more cocktails later, the details of Baldwin's plan fully sketched out, the men stood up and shook hands.

"Did you drive?" Baldwin asked. "I can ask them to validate your parking."

"No, thank you," said Benson. "I took a cab. But it's so gorgeous outside, I think I'm going to walk. How about you?"

Stealing a glance at Lindsey, the man replied, "I've got something else planned."

• • •

The pair shook hands once more and Benson exited the hotel and headed north on Sixteenth Street. As he had been instructed, he acted naturally and didn't look back.

At K Street, he turned left and two blocks later climbed into the white windowless panel van and unbuttoned his shirt.

"Did you get everything?" he asked.

The FBI agent in charge of the investigation helped remove the microphone and replied, "All of it."

CHAPTER 67

Ethan Russ loved jogging outside. The D.C. weather, however, didn't always love him back, especially in the summer. They didn't refer to Washington as the swamp for nothing. The heat and humidity could be killers.

Today, though, was extraordinary. This was exactly the kind of day he loved. And there was no place he loved more to run than surrounded by history on the National Mall. The Washington Monument, the U.S. Capitol Building, the Lincoln Memorial . . .

It truly was extraordinary.

With his earbuds in and his favorite playlist on repeat, it felt as if he could run forever. During that time, nothing else mattered. His mind would hit Pause and he would enter an almost Zen-like state. The only thing better was the rush of endorphins that flooded his system after it was all over.

Crossing Seventh Street, he could see the roof of the Smithsonian Castle up ahead. He was remembering the first time he had ever visited there, when his thoughts were interrupted by a flashing light and the blaring of a police klaxon.

He turned to see an unmarked four-door sedan, the kind of vehicle favored by police detectives, or in this case members of the FBI. Someone wanted his attention. Removing his earbuds, he walked toward the car.

The man in the passenger seat, wearing a navy suit and wire-rim glasses, rolled down his window.

"Great day for a run," said William Lamb, head of the FBI's Counter-intelligence Division.

"Not many like this left," Russ replied. "To what do I owe the honor?"

"On behalf of the Bureau, I wanted to say thank you. If you hadn't reported Spencer Baldwin to us, I don't know if he ever would have hit our radar."

"How'd the meeting go with Benson?"

"It just wrapped up," said Lamb. "With all of the audio you both helped us get, he'll be going away for a long time."

"Good. I hope the Chinese get the message."

"They're going to get it all right. Trust me. At the very least, Baldwin is going down for bribery of public officials and failing to register as a foreign lobbyist. His Chinese handler-cum-honey-pot is going down for espionage."

Russ rolled his earbuds in his hand. "I suppose you'll be in touch?"

"If we need any further statements. Going forward, it'll be the prosecutors at DOJ who will be handling everything."

"You all know how to get ahold of me."

Lamb nodded and was about to roll up his window, when he added, "You're a good man, Ethan. You could have taken the money, but you didn't. A lot of people—unfortunately, a lot of them in politics—probably would have gone the other way. I hope you do run for office. We need more good people in those jobs."

Smiling, the young man returned his earbuds to his ears, tapped the roof of the car, and resumed his run.

• • •

Baldwin, excited and nervous all at the same time, knocked on Lindsey's door. She opened it, already in a state of undress, wearing nothing but lingerie.

Stepping into the room, he hung the *Do Not Disturb* sign on the knob and closed the door.

"You look good enough to eat," he told her.

She smiled the practiced smile she had been taught. She was anything but excited. His forehead was already damp with perspiration. The thought of his sweaty body on top of hers was enough to make her blood run cold.

"I'm so glad you like it," she cooed, doing a pirouette so that he could take in the total magnificence of her young, firm body.

"What did you think of my performance in the bar? An entire hour with the U.S. Special Representative for the Arctic. Are you pleased?"

"Is he going to work with us?"

Baldwin grinned. "He's definitely going to be on board."

Lindsey smiled back. "Let's celebrate."

"Oh, we're going to celebrate, all right," he said, reaching out and running his fat fingers across her skin.

"I brought you a present."

"You're the only present I need."

She broke away just as he was trying to wrap her in his embrace.

From her suitcase, she pulled out a bottle of bourbon and held it up. "Pappy Van Winkle. If I recall, you're a fan."

"Huge fan," said Baldwin. "I take it—"

"Neat," she replied. "I remember."

Kicking off his shoes, Baldwin untucked his shirt and lay on the bed.

Lindsey poured a drink and handed it to him. She also poured one for herself.

Taking a sip, he savored the amazing liquor. Then, resting the glass on his ample midsection, he looked at the White House through the open windows. Smiling as the young woman climbed atop the bed next to him, he said, "It doesn't get any better than this."

But no sooner had the words left his mouth than someone was pounding on their door.

"FBI!" a voice yelled from out in the hallway. "We have a warrant for your arrest. Open up!"

EPILOGUE

T rue to his word, upon landing at Landstuhl Regional Medical Center, Han had revealed how to disarm the fail-safe measures on the Black Ice equipment.

Once all of it had arrived back in the United States, NSA and DARPA began taking it apart and studying it. The technology was quite ingenious, exploiting a previously undetected flaw in air defense systems that had spilled over into some of the West's most sophisticated radar technology. It was going to take time, but they were on track for developing a way to fix it.

In the meantime, Han had received a diagnosis and it wasn't good. He had a form of bone cancer. His prognosis, however, was excellent. He had been moved to the Mayo Clinic in Minnesota and was receiving the best care in the world.

When Harvath was given his next assignment, he asked for permission to go visit the Chinese operative and solicit his help.

No one knew if the man would cooperate. He had already fulfilled his end of the bargain. Harvath suggested they sweeten the pot. After reviewing his proposal, his request was granted.

Hopping on the Carlton Group jet, he had flown to Rochester, picked up a car, and had driven to the clinic to visit Han.

"What's that?" the man had asked after they had caught up and Harvath had been read in on his treatment.

Handing over the padded envelope, Harvath said, "Open it."

Inside was a U.S. passport with Han's new identity, a driver's license, a credit card, and a checkbook for the bank account that had been established for him.

"Want to see your new apartment?" Harvath asked.

Remaining stoic although he was somewhat overwhelmed, Han nodded.

Harvath handed the man his phone and let him flip through the online photos.

"That's mine?"

"It's all yours," said Harvath, removing a set of keys from his pocket and presenting them.

"Thank you," said Han.

"You don't have to thank me," Harvath replied. "That was our deal. You need to just focus on getting better."

"I was worried about what might happen. But this gives me hope."

Harvath smiled. "I'm glad," he said. "By the way, you can't live in an empty apartment, so I requested money for furniture and the request was granted. Fifty thousand dollars. It has already been deposited in your account."

Han's eyes widened. "Really?"

"Of course. That's a very nice apartment. You can't decorate it with garbage."

"In Chinese culture, we revere our uncles, especially the generous ones. I guess now I get to revere my Uncle Sam."

Harvath nodded. "Your Uncle Sam has been quite generous."

Suddenly, Han began to sense that something else was going on. Straightening up in his hospital bed, he asked, "What's the catch?"

"No catch," said Harvath. "I just have a question."

"Which is?"

"If I wanted to kill your boss, how would I do it?"

• • •

In Beijing, nestled next to the Forbidden City, were the former imperial gardens known as Zhongnanhai, current home to the Chinese Communist Party.

Each morning, after she had purchased her feathered eggs, Vice Premier Xing Fen liked her driver to drop her off at the entrance, rather than in the secure parking lot nearby, so that she could walk the grounds and commune with her ancestors. She was not only a staunch party member but a devout traditionalist who understood that reverence for the past could gain her an even more prominent position in the future.

Because she was a short sleeper and arrived so early, rarely were her morning constitutionals noticed. But enough eyes had seen her that word had spread.

She had developed a reputation as a bit of an ascetic. It was an image that bolstered her political persona, and so she had continued the behavior.

Her favorite places were the quiet, isolated courtyards. In the predawn darkness, it was easy to imagine oneself in a different time, a different dynasty. If you ignored the workstations and file cabinets behind the windows, you could almost forget you were in the courtyard of a government building.

Breakfast in hand, as it was every morning, her mind was a million miles away. Though careful to alternate her daily routine, she was now on hallowed ground, and, as such, she was thinking about everything the day held in store.

Six of her operatives had gone missing. Only one of whom, who had been terribly burned by acid, had been identified. What's more, there had been a spike in chatter about the CIA assets in China who had been killed or imprisoned. As the person responsible, the uptick bothered her. Not enough, however, to add security beyond her driver.

Walking was her answer. No matter what the problem, it had always helped lead her to a solution.

This morning, as the first pink rays of dawn began to break over Zhongnanhai and the Forbidden City, she hoped that walking would help her again.

Moving into another courtyard, deep in thought, she failed to notice the figure that stepped out of the shadows behind her.

A second later, Scot Harvath fired the silenced round that completed his assignment and then headed to his extraction point.

He couldn't wait to get home. He had an engagement party to plan and a fiancée to introduce to his friends and family.

ACKNOWLEDGMENTS

After the crazy year we just spent, I am more grateful than ever for you, my wonderful **readers**. Being able to communicate over social media and keeping our conversations about books and love of reading alive has been fantastic. Thank you for all your support.

I am also grateful for all the amazing **booksellers** out there. They are the lifeblood of our communities and serve as on-ramps to escape and adventure. They will always have my deepest gratitude.

Books are collaborative efforts. Bringing the twentieth Scot Harvath thriller to life involved some of the smartest, coolest, and most enjoyable people inside and outside of publishing. I want to thank the following for all of their generous assistance:

A TON of Russian expertise was called upon for the research of this novel. The marvelous **James Carafano** of the Heritage Foundation and **Tom Nichols** of the U.S. Naval War College are not only brilliant in their respective fields (and great follows on Twitter), but they're plugged in everywhere on all things Russia. Because of them, I was able to lean on two very distinguished scholars who were patient with me and a lot of fun to work with: **Luke Coffey** of the Heritage Foundation (who has actually been to Svalbard) and **Michael Petersen** of the U.S. Naval War College (who knew things about Russia's Northern Fleet I could not have found anywhere else). My thanks to you all.

A big push for a stronger American presence in the Arctic has come from the highly astute former National Security Adviser **Robert C. O'Brien**. Robert has been a dear friend of mine for years. I am exceedingly grateful for all the time he spent discussing foreign policy and national security with me for this novel. Thank you, Robert.

My other terrific friends **Sean Fontaine**, **Michael Ralsky**, **Mark La Rue**, **Pete Scobell**, **Sidney Blair**, **Rebecca Merrett**, and **Knut Grini** contributed invaluable background materials and technical expertise that I would have been lost without. Thank you all very much for everything.

I read so much in preparing to write my thrillers that it is impossible to list all the excellent **journalists** whose articles I have found fascinating and informative. If you would like to know more about the real-life foreign policy and geopolitical issues covered in *Black Ice*, I highly recommend the work of **David Chrisinger**, **Craig Hooper**, **Ben Kesling**, **Sherri Goodman**, **Marisol Maddox**, **Elisabeth Freese**, **Isabella Borshoff**, **John Grady**, **Marc Lanteigne**, **David Axe**, **Michael T. Klare**, and **Jackie Northam**.

The daring infiltration and exfiltration methods described in the East Berlin section of the novel were inspired by the real-life exploits of the **Bethke brothers**. The lengths that people will go to in order to be free are boundless.

As many of you know, last year I lost my friend and publisher **Carolyn Reidy**. I cannot tell you how much I miss that amazing woman. I dedicated *Black Ice* to her but want to say one more thank-you. You were the best. Thank you for everything, Carolyn.

One of the greatest things about being a part of the fabulous Simon & Schuster family is how many talented people work there. The marvelous **Jon Karp** stepped up to take over the ship upon Carolyn's untimely passing and has done an amazing job. We couldn't be in better hands. Thank you, Jon, for your grace, your professionalism, and your sense of humor. I value you and our partnership and appreciate all the support you have given me.

In my two decades with Simon & Schuster, I have been blessed to work with my sensational editor and publisher, **Emily Bestler**, the entire time. You know you have a terrific working relationship when there are more jokes being cracked than whips. Thank you for all the insight, advice, friendship, and great ideas. It continues to be an absolute pleasure being one of your authors, and I look forward to many more years to come.

Nothing gets done without the outstanding **Lara Jones** (who took a curveball of a grammar question and knocked it out of the park this year) and the rest of the top-notch **Emily Bestler Books team**. My thanks to you all.

My exceptional Atria publisher, **Libby McGuire**, and associate publisher, **Dana Trocker**, are absolute titans. The best feeling is knowing that around the clock, your team is coming up with new ways to get your books into the hands of more people. I really appreciate you both. Thank you.

Speaking of people who are always coming up with new ideas, nobody beats my stupendous publicist, **David Brown**. The man is the Terminator of PR. Nothing stops him! He's also a terrific human being. Surround yourself with smart people who love to laugh, and everything will figure itself out. Thank you, David.

Working remotely, I did not get to visit with the magnificent **Gary Urda** this year. He's not only one of the sharpest people on my team, but he's also a hell of a lot of fun. A bourbon over FaceTime isn't the same as one in person. We'll get there, though! Thank you for everything you continue to do for me, my friend.

The awesome **Jen Long** and her amazing crew at **Pocket Books** continue to bring the heat! You all are such pros, and I want you to know how much I continue to value you. If you are holding a Brad Thor paperback in your hands, it is because of Team Jen. Thank you, all, for everything.

There is only one word you can use to describe **Al Madocs** of the Atria/Emily Bestler Books production department, and that word is *astounding*. Al is not only a great guy to sit and chat with, but he's also a genius at his job. He is the one person who has pulled my bacon out of the fire more than anyone else. Al, I cannot say thank you enough (for everything). I remain eternally grateful for all the effort you put in on my behalf.

Not being able to pop into people's offices to say hello and catch up is something many of us are missing. That goes double for me, because I love the people I work with and really like to let them know how much they mean to me. This year, I'm missing some truly extraordinary people, including **John Hardy**, **Colin Shields**, **Paula Amendolara**, **Janice Fryer**, **Liz Perl**, **Nicole Bond**, **Suzanne Donahue**, **Milena Brown**, **Gregory Hruska**, **Lexi Dumas**, and **Stuart Smith**. The reason everything works so well is because you all work so hard. Thank you!

And while we're talking about working hard, the world-class **Atria/ Emily Bestler Books** and **Pocket Books sales teams** are at it around-the-clock. I am so grateful for each and every one of you. Thank you for every single sale. Nothing we do is possible without you. You all are superstars.

The cover art is one of the most exciting parts of the process, and nobody beats the incredible **Jimmy Iacobelli** of the Atria/Emily Bestler Books art department. His art is breathtaking. When it comes to Jimmy, you *can* judge a book by its cover. Thank you! You nailed it yet again.

The exceptional **Simon & Schuster audio division** continues to produce the best audio books on the planet. Their dedication to every step in the process is awe-inspiring. I am deeply indebted to everyone at S&S audio and want to say a special thank-you to **Chris Lynch**, **Tom Spain**, **Sarah Lieberman**, **Desiree Vecchio**, and **Armand Schultz**. Thank you.

My remarkable copyeditor, **David Chesanow**, helped me to look better than I deserve. Thank you for your diligence and commitment to getting things right.

My spectacular agent and dear friend, **Heide Lange** at **Sanford J. Greenburger Associates**, could not have been more helpful during the writing of this novel. She is not only a gifted negotiator and dispenser of sage counsel, she is also a witty, charming, and wonderful friend. Thank you, Heide, for everything.

Heide is also one of the best judges of talent you'll ever meet. Her phenomenal team excels at everything. They are also wonderful people. My deepest thanks to everyone at **Sanford J. Greenburger Associates**, including **Iwalani Kim** (congrats on your promotion), **Madeline Wallace** (welcome to the team), and **Charles Loffredo** (thank you for keeping the trains running on time).

Here at Thor Entertainment Group, I want to give a very special thank-you to the absolutely fabulous **Yvonne Ralsky**. You were an incredible help throughout this process, as you are every single day. The only thing I value above your professionalism is your friendship. Thank you for all things great and small you have done for me.

My tireless, solid-gold entertainment attorney and dear friend, **Scott**

Schwimer, has been part of my life for more than twenty years. I can't imagine a single moment without him. He is so good at what he does and never misses an opportunity to help others be better. He is truly one of a kind. Thank you for all that you do for me every day, Scottie.

I always save the very best for last. I want to thank my beautiful, loving **family**. My remarkable wife and fantastic children provide me with the fuel to write my thrillers. They inspire me to do my absolute best and to never settle for anything less. I couldn't ask to be surrounded by more wondrous people. I love each of you, and thank you for everything.